Jaclyn the Ripper

BOOKS BY KARL ALEXANDER

Time After Time*

A Private Investigation

The Curse of the Vampire

Papa and Fidel*

Jaclyn the Ripper*

*A Tom Doherty Associates Book

KARL ALEXANDER

Jaclyn the Ripper

A TOM DOHERTY ASSOCIATES BOOK

NEW YORK

JACLYN THE RIPPER

Copyright © 2009 by Karl Alexander

Edited by James Frenkel

A Forge Book
Published by Tom Doherty Associates, LLC
175 Fifth Avenue
New York, NY 10010

www.tor-forge.com

Forge® is a registered trademark of Tom Doherty Associates, LLC.

Library of Congress Cataloging-in-Publication Data

Alexander, Karl.
    Jaclyn the Ripper / Karl Alexander. — 1st ed.
        p.   cm.
    Sequel to: Time after time.
    "A Tom Doherty Associates book."
    ISBN 978-0-7653-1894-7
    1. Wells, H. G. (Herbert George), 1866–1946—Fiction.   2. Jack, the Ripper—Fiction.   3. Wives—Fiction.   4. Time travel—Fiction.   I. Title.
    PS3551.L3569J33   2009
    813'.54—dc22

                                                                2009034611

First Edition: November 2009

Printed in the United States of America

0 9 8 7 6 5 4 3 2 1

For all my good girls: Kateri, Damien, Laura,
Dennette, Maggie, Annabelle, Ruby, Ava Rose
and Rainy May

Acknowledgments

Jaclyn was conceived over lunch and conversation with my good friend Hammad Zaidi. Thanks, dude. . . . The prime mover behind the novel was my manager, John Bennett. Without his insistence and determination, *Jaclyn* never would have been written or published. Thank you, John. . . .

My oldest friend in this universe is Dr. Appletree Rodden, Ph.D., M.D., a scientific genius in his own right, who happily answered medical and scientific queries. Thanks, Tree. . . .

Thanks also to my editor, Jim Frenkel, for his insight and patience. . . . But thanks most of all to Kateri for being there . . . and here.

Jaclyn the Ripper

Before

In 1893—on the run from Scotland Yard—Jack the Ripper stole H. G. Wells's time machine and journeyed to 1979 San Francisco. Outraged, Wells followed, determined to bring the Ripper back to justice in Victorian England. Along the way, he met Amy Catherine Robbins, a modern American woman, and they became time-crossed lovers. In a showdown, Wells used his scientific genius to send the Ripper to infinity without the machine, leaving him stuck out of time. Then Wells and Amy journeyed back to 1893. Two years later, they were married, convinced that they would live happily ever after. Thirteen years passed, and in another universe. . . .

After

4:53 A.M., *Sunday, June 20, 2010*

Flash.

The West Pavilion of the J. Paul Getty Museum exploded silently from within, obliterating the darkness, rendering the night instantly translucent like an overexposed negative. A millisecond later, the flash receded, and everything looked as it had before. But it wasn't.

Teresa Cruz, temporarily blinded, jumped up from the small desk in the lobby, and was blinking for her vision to come back when her walkie-talkie crackled.

"What's happening over there?" said Peterson in the security room. "I lost all my monitors!"

She jerked her radio up from her belt. "I dunno. . . . Lightning, maybe?"

"Check it out, will you?"

"Copy."

If it had been lightning, it would have been lightning with no meteorological disturbances, lightning with clear skies. Lightning with no thunder. It wasn't lightning. *What was it, then?* Teresa did a three-sixty, taking in the exhibition posters, the signs, the literature racks, the H. G. WELLS—A MAN BEFORE HIS TIME banner spanning the back wall of the lobby. She swallowed hard. The flash had come from one of the galleries, from inside, yet even the night outside had lit up. She tried to convince herself that it had been an electrical short, but knew in her heart it wasn't. There was no burning smell, no smoke, and the night-lights were still on. She straightened her blue blazer and charcoal-gray slacks, was aware of her heart pounding.

"I'm jonesin' for a gun, Peterson," she said into her walkie. "They ought to let us carry guns."

"You need backup, sweetie?" he said sarcastically.

"Forget it."

Angry, she snapped off her radio. Peterson had always been on her case, saying she was "too gutless" to be a security officer and that management had only hired her because she was a female Hispanic. *I don't need him or his abuse.* Yet she paused, looked outside and was afraid. Her eyes lingered over the fountains and pools, the rectangular museum courtyard that stretched to the rotunda splashed yellow by recessed lights, then the other pavilions framing the courtyard, their travertine stone faces ghostly white under the soft moon. Then she frowned, shook off her fear, squared her diminutive shoulders and strode to the galleries: those large, tasteful rooms delineated by archways so that one gallery framed another as if they themselves were works of art. In the first room, she stepped around display cases of memorabilia, faded manuscripts and original editions of books, then moved past stark black-and-white photographs that documented the turbulent life of H. G. Wells. None of it registered, so drawn was she to a strange light emanating from the center gallery where they had installed his time machine.

Roped off, the time machine sat alone in the room. An intense bluish glow was fading from the engine compartment, leaving it silhouetted against the gray gallery walls. The tapered, steel-plated cabin rose eight feet above the engine and resembled a primitive space capsule. When she'd first seen the machine, Teresa had found it squat, ugly and askew, reminding her of those monolithic stone sculptures carved by her Mayan ancestors. Of course, *The Utopia* had never been known to work, the brochures all said. Regardless, she was frozen in the archway like a lower mammal caught in the headlights of an onrushing car, held spellbound by the time machine's inexplicable glow of energy.

And then—behind its small windows oxidized from age—something moved. The cabin door opened. A figure stepped out, ignored the ladder and sprang lightly to the gallery floor, landing in a crouch and looking around warily, its chest heaving.

Disbelieving, Teresa shook her head slowly. She couldn't stop staring, couldn't deny what she was seeing. Not only had something alive emerged from the time machine, but in the darkness, that something glowed a toxic reddish green. Distracted, the figure turned back, reached up on tiptoes and took a prism-shaped device from inside the cabin, shoved it into a slot beneath the door.

Suddenly, the figure noticed itself and saw what Teresa had seen. Emitting shocked little cries, it held its arms away from its body and tried to back away from itself—its aura—then desperately tried to rub the colors off, but the glow came from within as if an X-ray.

Teresa had seen enough for a lifetime and backpedaled out of the gallery. The figure spun around, saw her moving, came for her at a fast trot. Cowering in the archway, Teresa brought her radio up to her mouth. As she keyed it to call Peterson, the figure ripped it from her hands and hurled it across the room. Teresa ducked instinctively. The walkie hit the wall and shattered. Astonished, frozen, she watched the figure detour around her and disappear in the lobby, heard the door close behind it.

Suddenly angry—more with herself than with this creature—Teresa balled her fists, reminded herself that she was a security officer, and a damned good one at that. She sprinted after the figure, pushed against the glass doors of the entranceway, burst outside.

Running up the courtyard, little feet whisking on stone, the figure saw that under the moonlight the toxic glow had faded from its skin—its normal flesh color returned. *Perhaps the glow was merely a harmless fourth-dimensional residue,* it thought. Then it realized that it was wearing

rags and needed clothes or whatever the human condition cloaked itself with these days. Except that was the least of its problems. Something was wrong—terribly wrong. The figure couldn't run as fast as it
remembered from the streets of London and then San Francisco. Its
stride was shorter, its breath not as quick and easy, its hair too long and
falling in its face. And these things kept slapping up and down—what
were these *things*? Distressed, the figure was about to stop and examine
itself when it heard footfalls and turned. The security guard—that pathetic little bitch with TERESA CRUZ on her nameplate—was in hot
pursuit. Normally, it would confront this Teresa Cruz, but in this here-
and-now nothing was normal, nothing at all. Fearing the worst, not
knowing where or even what it was, the figure ran faster, ran gasping for
breath, finally veered toward the rotunda. It went inside, looked around
wildly, didn't appreciate the graceful sweep of glass and stone. It gravi-
tated to the darkness, where it huddled, a wounded beast, under the
curved staircase. As it worked to catch its breath, it wondered if it had
eluded the security guard or if others were on the way. Then, in the absence of light, it saw that glow creeping back in its skin. It recoiled,
tried to brush the glow off again, but then Teresa Cruz was coming into
the rotunda. The figure bolted from under the stairs, not so much running from Teresa as from itself. It raced for an alcove, read MEN'S REST-
ROOM, rushed inside the well-lit space and went to the mirror.

The figure shrieked with horror, had to hold on to the sink to remain upright. It wasn't the glow it saw, for that had disappeared with
the light—it was something else entirely. "Good God, no," the figure
moaned. "Please, God, no!" The figure shut its eyes tightly, willed itself
to see a different reflection—the familiar dark, forbidding countenance
with thin lips, long nose and beady, hooded eyes that it loved and
remembered—but when it looked again, the image was inevitably the
same.

The figure saw a dark-haired woman with wide-set almond eyes, full
lips, cute upturned nose, and smooth ivory skin—a woman comfortable with a worldly, bemused smile no matter where or when—a
woman in the shredded remains of a late-seventies leisure suit. Even

with the agonized expression she was wearing at this moment, even in rags, the woman was undeniably and classically beautiful.

Instinctively, she felt between her legs.

Nothing was there.

"Nooo!"

Sobbing, she covered her face, turned away from the mirror, sagged against the sink, numb with questions. She had been a man before, a formidable, dark shadow of a man. *This is a joke, a cosmic mistake of some kind, this is unacceptable. I hate women, I unequivocally hate them, I—* She straightened up and noticed her body reflected in the brushed aluminum wall adjacent to the stalls. Like her image in the mirror, it was perfect—so perfect, in fact, that she was reminded of her sister, Penelope, teasing and posing before their first indelible moment of passion behind the caretaker's house. Hyperventilating, the woman clutched the sink for support again, then turned back to the mirror, recalling that she had forgotten the special key—she had left the damned key in the time machine. She was about to scream at her exquisite reflection that she had to get the key and go back to a time where she would recognize herself when Teresa Cruz banged into the restroom.

"What in the hell do you think—"

Growling, a blur of movement, the woman grabbed and propelled Teresa forward, slammed her headfirst into the mirror.

"Don't you know who I am?!"

Stunned, Teresa staggered back, but the woman jerked her forward. Windmilling her arms and kicking, Teresa tried to free herself from the iron grip, but was no match for the woman's strength.

"Don't you know who I am?"

The woman slammed Teresa into the mirror again, then grabbed her by the hair, forced Teresa to look into her eyes.

"Don't you recognize me?!"

Teresa tried to say something to save herself, but the woman rammed her into the glass twice more in quick succession, splitting her lip and breaking her nose. Blood sprayed on the mirror, the sink, the floor.

"Don't you know who I am?!"

Again, she slammed Teresa into the mirror, this time with such force the glass cracked. Teresa went limp.

"An eternity ago that bloody little fool your museum is celebrating sent me to the end of time!" the woman shouted. She pile-drove an unconscious Teresa into the mirror until it finally shattered and shards of glass rained on the metal sinks and tile floor. "For an eternity, yours truly has been—has been—"

Has been what? Where? Her chest heaving, she stopped, let go of Teresa, watched her crumple to the floor. Her last conscious memory was of that fateful day in 1979 when H. G. Wells pulled the declinometer from the time machine and everything exploded into an oblivion echoing with one last agonized scream. *Mine.* She had no clue how many years had—or hadn't—passed since then.

Has been what? Where?

She hadn't known that on the event horizon of the black hole once called Earth were trillions of entities: other-universe forms that resembled protozoa in a variety of shapes, colors and designs. She hadn't known that one in particular possessed the seed of her resurrection—at least in part—and that this one elongated entity was thin enough to move easily in the dense yet vast gravitational field. It looked like a scaled pennate diatom, was both unspeakably ugly and beautiful in its symmetry, and possessed X and Y chromosomes that spiraled within its frustules, those indicators some three billion years old in the universes. More important, the entity had instincts, and when the time machine materialized in the endless sea of forms, this thing slipped eel-like between the door and the cabin and festooned itself to the chair, at long last insulated from the silent, profound blackness that stank of burnt plastic.

Had it been three hours ago or four?

She hadn't known that there was no time in that cesspool of nothingness, that residue of life squandered, so the question mattered not. Then the entity had sensed movement. Consciousness. Life. Even purpose.

Inexplicably, a mind had been reborn in the time machine's chair, then senses. Instinct had given way to reason and, alas, feelings.

Except she had been a "he" then.

And then the machine had tumbled end-over-end in an endless, colossal limbo. He had no clue that in this black hole once called Earth he and the machine had already been crushed by gravitational force to specks floating in a molecule-sized solar system. He had no clue how that had changed him from an unspeakably ugly and beautiful entity— or if it had at all. That he and the machine remained whole at all was due to the indifference, the dark energy that ruled the universes.

The Current Year Indicator had read 2353. If that were the end of time, then in the year of our Lord 2353, the human race had finally blown itself up. Moreover, the fact that the machine had traveled on its own to infinity meant that somewhere in time Wells had made a grave error.

The "he" was aware of the chair in the cabin, the crumbling switches and cracked dials, was aware of his existence again and wondered what sublime Omnipotence was behind his rebirth. Then his form had brushed something. He had assumed it was one of those sludge-crabs Wells wrote about that supposedly existed at the end of time. If true, he was famished and would eat it, but no, instead of a crab it was the prism-shaped device sparkling from within—that nasty, elongated de-clinometer. Some fool had pulled it and not put it back in its proper place, so indeed, there it was, resting on something dark like a pillow. Had he smiled then? Of course. Instead of sustenance, the mistake had been his salvation, for if the declinometer had been in place, the time machine would not have traveled to infinity.

Entities outside the craft had fallen away, dissolved, and the black-ness became a temporal gray mist. His memory had come back, and he vaguely recalled the diagrams in Wells's laboratory from that fateful night in 1893—that unless one overrode the Rotation Reversal Lock, the time machine automatically returned to its home hour after a ninety-second delay. But *only* if the declinometer was in place. With-out that "rudder," the machine could only travel to when it had come from, and the Time-Sphere Destination Indicator read: year, 2010; month, June; day, 20; time 12:01 A.M.

The machine gathered speed, spun into a sea of quantum foam, was vaporized and hurtled along the fourth dimension. Years later, as traveler and machine took on substance and form, as their mass expanded, the "he" had savored the ride, confident of a smooth transmogrification.

Trucido ergo sum had been his first coherent thought. He imagined Wells as a bloody, eviscerated corpse, and—though he was no devotee of Shakespeare—he mused: *All's well that ends badly.*

Then something had gone horribly, horribly wrong.

She stole a glimpse of her lovely face in the mirror, turned her back on herself again, still numb with unanswered questions. She didn't know about reformulation errors. She didn't know that no one had ever come back from infinity before, and that given the length of real time traveled, the quantum foam had altered *his* chromosomes. In genetic terms, a pitifully weak Y chromosome from his foppish father had been mysteriously trampled by a full-blown X chromosome from an yet-to-be-identified source. A classic Turner syndrome. No, she hadn't known that on Sunday, June 20, 2010, shaped by the mysteries of dark energy and emerging from the temporal mist of the fourth dimension, Jack the Ripper would be reconstituted as a woman.

Teresa moaned. The woman who had attacked her stepped back and observed critically, as if taking in an unfinished canvas. Teresa moaned again. Moved by an instinct not lost in her metamorphosis, the woman straddled the little security guard and started strangling her. Teresa twisted, bucked. Surprised her victim still had the will to resist—angry her hands weren't big and strong enough to end it quickly—the woman picked up a shard from the broken mirror and slashed Teresa's throat.

Sighing, the woman straightened up, appreciating the blood pooling around Teresa like spilled paint. She closed her eyes, and in her mind's eye saw a red rose opening in the sun. Then she frowned. This Teresa was no East End alley slut. Money had not changed hands, there had been no penetration, no thrusting, no sweet slime—where was the pleasure in this? The woman smiled a pretty, disarming little-girl smile as the answer came. *Necessity has always been the mother of invention, so as long as we find ourselves in this dubious year of 2010—as long as we must kill—why not take pleasure in the pure simplicity of the act not fouled by an ejaculatory release?*

Somewhere a thermostat clicked, interrupting her thoughts, and a breeze wafted in through the restroom vents. Chilled, the woman hugged herself, reminded of her rags, her gooseflesh, her nipples embarrassingly hard. She took Teresa's keys and cautiously ventured out the door.

She hurried across the alcove, rode the elevator down to the service floor, pleased that pushing buttons had replaced the accordion gates and straps of nineteenth-century lifts. *We must be in a new, modern art museum, not one of those decrepit salons or cathedrals of Europe. True, the place was featuring the dubious accomplishments of H. G. Wells, but surely they must have paintings by Goya, works like David's* "The Death of Marat."

In the employee women's lounge, the woman located Teresa Cruz's locker, looked askance at her wardrobe. *Where on God's earth are we that people wear clothes like this?* Having no choice, she dressed, then regarded herself in the mirror.

The faded blue jeans were tight, yet strangely comfortable, but what drew the woman's eyes was her midriff showing, then her ample breasts, provocative in a gray T-shirt two sizes too small. She wondered if other women looked like this or if Teresa Cruz was a prostitute in her leisure hours. Preoccupied with her image, the woman didn't focus on the yellow happy face on her T-shirt, and the inane "Have a nice day" printed below. Instead, she tucked her glossy black hair up inside Teresa's cap, blue with a silly red heart on it, figuring that would give her a shred of respectability. She slipped her feet in Teresa's sandals, then rode the elevator back up to the courtyard level intending to get the special key from the time machine. When she reached the men's restroom, she hesitated, vaguely dissatisfied.

Jack would've never left a woman murdered so anonymous, so mundane. We would've sung to the world that we'd been out and about, we'd have left something for the boys of Scotland Yard. After all, are we not in a museum? Do not artists sign their work?

In the restroom, she locked the door, then pulled Teresa's corpse to the stalls and propped it up on one side. With a shard from the mirror, she meticulously cut away the little guard's uniform shirt, then began a surgical procedure first learned in anatomy class and later practiced on Penny, her sister. The woman longed for the gold pocket watch with Penny's likeness inside the lid, lost in 1979. She missed its music box playing an innocent French lullaby. Nevertheless, she hadn't lost her touch, and with a few quick, practiced incisions, excised Teresa's kidney. Smiling, she rinsed it off in the sink and put it in the pocket of her jeans, then washed her hands as if finishing up in a surgery. Her smile grew larger when she saw that as before she had avoided getting bloodstains on her clothes. If nothing else, being a comely lass hadn't affected her expertise. And all with a shard of glass, too.

She unlocked the door, looked both ways and headed across the rotunda toward the courtyard and West Pavilion, formulating a plan. She would stay in 2010 long enough to track down and cut up Wells. Then—with the special key—she'd have carte blanche to choose her victims regardless of history. Perchance she'd travel back to mid-nineteenth-century Turkey and, say, disembowel that do-gooder Florence Nightingale, who was tending to the flotsam and jetsam of the Crimean War. She smiled. *Perhaps a trip into the past will make me a man again, and I can rape her as well.*

Halfway across the rotunda, she heard footsteps and glanced up. A security guard was coming down the circular staircase. The woman tensed, ducked in the shadows, walked faster.

"Hey!"

The woman spun around, started running back the way she had come.

"Hey!"

Panicked, the woman looked for escape, finally saw an emergency exit beyond the men's restroom. Without breaking stride, she hit the bar on the door and burst out on an expanse of stone.

The alarms went off.

The awful noise reverberated off the buildings, the stone, resounded in her ears. She vaulted over a wall, fell into a hedgerow, rolled, fell again and landed on a manicured lawn. Unmindful of her scratched and bleeding arms, she got up and ran for the safety of an arid hillside ragged with smog-dusted scrub.

11:42 A.M., *Sunday, June 24, 1906*

H. G. Wells and a soft-spoken constable from Sandgate talked at the front door, the constable raising his voice over the muffled roar of the surf from below the cliffs. The police had been looking, had made inquiries, yet had turned up nothing, and there was no evidence of foul play. The constable promised they'd go on searching, then said good day and Godspeed, his words lost in the wind. Upset and worried, H.G. watched him avoid a hodgepodge of croquet wickets on the lawn, mount his bicycle and start back to town.

"What did he say, sir?" asked the housekeeper, wringing her hands in the foyer, though she had heard every word.

"Nothing we didn't already know, Mrs. Vickers."

His wife was missing.

No one had seen her since dinner the night before. They'd been having another festive weekend at Spade House. Joseph Conrad, George Bernard and Charlotte Shaw, the Henry Jameses, the Webbs, the Blands, and a host of others were down from London to welcome H.G. home from his first tour of America. They'd had the usual literary banter during the croquet games, the usual political arguments at tea, the usual speculative theories at dinner. The only cause for raised eyebrows had been W. K. Chichester arriving late from a pub and demanding to know if Wells had witnessed the earthquake in San Francisco. No, H.G. had replied, he had been in Chicago. After Chichester's recitation of a ruined city on fire, H.G. had tuned out the seismologist's grandiose claims of having predicted the quake, turned a deaf ear to his prattle about using revolutionary scientific methods to predict even bigger earthquakes in the future. H.G. was tired of science. He was more interested in charades; he was more interested in seconds of bread pudding and cognac. He was *most* interested in finding his lover-shadow—that other consciousness, that perfect woman who mirrored everything he held good and true, who matched him sexually and intellectually, that soul mate he thought he had found in Amy. Alas, no. His lover-shadow had vanished shortly after they were married.

Ironically, Amy's charade had been the highlight of the evening. Full of fun, a picture of loveliness, she had taken center stage in the parlor, was urging clues from the guests, making them laugh and grumble, holding them spellbound as they attempted to guess the name of a modern novel. At that moment, H.G. had felt a surge of pride and love for her—like years ago when they'd been unabashed lovers.

After the guests had run the gamut of obvious titles, Amy had folded her hands over her chest and affected a swoon. "Heart!" cried Charlotte Shaw. Amy had nodded encouragement, then in a moment of inspiration had run to the switch and turned off the light. A puzzled silence. Then an inebriated Joseph Conrad had boomed, "Heart of Darkness!," and the room exploded with laughter and applause. By the time H.G. felt his way through the literal darkness to the switch and turned the light back on, Amy had disappeared, but no one thought anything of it. In fact, Conrad was still hee-hawing with laughter, prompting George Bernard Shaw to say that if Joseph were any more potted, he'd be a parlor palm.

Soon after they'd all said good night, H.G. had started worrying seriously about his wife. It wasn't like her to miss saying good night to her guests; she was such a gracious hostess. Thinking she'd gone for a moonlit stroll as they used to when they were lovers, he went looking for her, but she wasn't in the gardens or on the beach. Then when he didn't find her in the nursery putting the boys to bed he figured that she'd gone to the city with Dorothy—yet why wouldn't she have said something? When it was such a late hour?

The telephone rang. H.G. rushed to the alcove between the kitchen and parlor, but Mrs. Vickers got there first and lifted the receiver off its cradle on the wall. "061 Sandgate," she said. He eavesdropped while she exchanged pleasantries with Mrs. Ford Madox Ford. As soon as he heard the drift of the conversation—that none of the Fords had seen Amy since last night either—he went to his study like a child to his room, sat backward in his desk chair and gazed out at the channel, the distant coastline of Picardy and Normandy lost in the haze. Combing his luxuriant mustache with his fingers, he didn't know what to think. Or do. He felt trapped in this, their treasure house by the seashore. Six years ago, he'd had it built for her, making sure the carpenters built it pleasant and spacious, and installed all the modern conveniences.

"Perhaps she went to Mass, Mr. Wells."

He turned and scowled at Mrs. Vickers, who had come into the room behind him, a specter of false morality. "She left last night."

"St. Matthew's has services at eleven," she replied, as if she hadn't heard.

"The day my wife goes to church," H.G. declared in his thin, reedy voice, "is the day Queen Victoria resurrects herself as a giant paperweight to sit upon men's minds for another half century!"

"Is that so?" Mrs. Vickers replied. "Well, maybe you don't know your wife as well as you might think, Mr. Wells."

"Balderdash!"

He left his own study to get away from her stultifying presence, went outside for the fresh sea air that always restored his spirits. He knew Amy better than he knew himself. They'd been time-crossed lovers, hadn't they? She'd come back to the nineteenth century with him, and two years later they had married, vowing that there would never be any falsehood between them. As long as they were staying in Victorian England, they pledged to turn conventional morality upside down and expose its hypocrisy. Together they would be an explosion of moral light. H.G. and his fragile girl from the future who adored boating in

Regent's Park, cycling through smoky London for story ideas, wine and cookies before making love in front of the fire. His Venus Urania. Most definitely his lover-shadow.

And then on a rather ordinary day, after overhearing him tell the children for the umpteenth time to ask their mummy, she decided that he should call her "Jane." He was shocked, yet didn't refuse, except my God, why on earth would she want to be "Jane"? He supposed his success had something to do with it, then shook his head, unwilling to blame himself. No one had told her to put her own life on hold for him. No one had insisted that she become secretary, typist, house mistress, exchequer, shopper, gardener, not to mention "Mummy." He had always been willing to settle for her love and nothing more. She knew that, yet somewhere in their eleven-year marriage, she had changed regardless. True, she'd been ill on occasion, but so had he, and after settling in at Spade House, they'd both been disgustingly healthy. It hadn't mattered. She had withdrawn from him, never giving him a reason except to say they must "get on" with life and work.

She'd never said why, so he could only guess that it was his wanderlust, his need for trysts. The French called them "passades"—sex without love or guilt—which in lighter moments he likened to having a pint in a strange pub after a trying day. Except he had never been able to *not* feel guilty, for he truly loved and respected his Amy, and refused to lie to her. Ultimately, to save their marriage and her own self-respect, she had proposed a modus vivendi: In all matters they would remain steadfast partners. Except for sex. Should either of them have the urge to stray, they were free to do so and free to talk about it. So liberated, he had agreed enthusiastically.

He hadn't seen his lover-shadow since.

H.G. picked a daffodil from Amy's lush, abundant garden, absently put it in his lapel and started back to the house. Obviously, the modus vivendi hadn't worked. Obviously, Amy was fed up with a husband who attracted women like moths to a flame. Obviously, she was unhappy with a marriage that had unwittingly become a social experiment. Moreover, she probably wasn't thrilled to have a house with brand-new nineteenth-century appliances—antiques by her standards—though she never let on. Sighing unhappily, he thrust his hands in his pockets. The conclusion was inescapable. Amy had left him.

I hereby swear never to call or even think of her as Jane again. She was Amy when we met; she was Amy when we were lovers; she will be Amy when I see her again or I will insist that she call me Herb, and we will go raise sheep in Suffolk.

Mrs. Vickers was in the kitchen helping the cook prepare lunch for the remaining weekend guests, who had bicycled off to Sandgate on a lark and would be back soon. Exasperated with H.G.'s presence, she told him that since he had driven his wife away, he'd better see to the boys in the nursery before they did something unspeakable as well.

"I've become a nanny now, have I?" He left the kitchen without waiting for her retort. Suddenly angry, he wondered why Amy would leave him when they had guests and, above all, without warning. Why now in these, their halcyon days of fame, fortune and notoriety? How many wives could boast of a husband who had published ten best-selling books and was becoming a prodigious thinker? And what about the boys?

They were playing quietly in the nursery upstairs, angelic in matching sailor suits, dividing the floor into countries without borders so their wooden trains didn't have to stop. He loved them intensely and was fiercely proud of their instincts. Almost five, Gip was dark and ebullient with limpid blue eyes, like him; at two, Frank was blond and more absorbed, like his mother. They looked up and grinned when they saw him, then went back to their trains and didn't speak until he sat down between them and began pushing a car and making "choo-choo" sounds.

"Where's Mummy?" asked Gip.

"She had some errands to run," H.G. lied smoothly.

"On a Sunday?"

Surprised, H.G. couldn't think of what to say.

"She's not having a passade, too, is she, Daddy?"

Shaken, H.G. dressed in his pure-wool tweed suit—the mark of a true progressive, so they said—and he, too, left without saying good-bye to his guests. He opened the doors to the new shed he insisted was a garage, though everyone else, especially Mrs. Vickers, called it a car-riage house. He paused, looked fondly at the Humber tandem he'd had made specially for them. They had crisscrossed the countryside on that bike, pedaling hard, stopping for tea or a pint, then pedaling easy, Amy laughing and saying downhill was better—it was like making love after a quarrel. He frowned sadly at the memories, the thought of Amy being the first to flee Spade House, the first to run from their domestic claus-trophobia when she had always been the moral stockade to which he always returned. No, he wouldn't be taking the Humber today—no bob-bing up and down on the bike like a boy, the seat behind him empty and forlorn.

Instead, he pulled a tarpaulin off the 1905 Triumph motorbike he had purchased just before his trip to America in April. He dutifully checked the oil and petrol, donned goggles and leather helmet, then pushed the bike out to the road and started it, the engine popping, making a tiny, turn-of-the-century roar. He took off for the Sandgate station and the one o'clock train, helping the single-cylinder engine ac-celerate to forty by pedaling hard, then relaxed, loving the wind that pulled at his suit and whistled past his ears.

He bought a ticket for London, sat alone in the parlor car and gazed out at the countryside, realizing the futility of his trip. He had no idea where to find her, especially if she'd gone to the city to be with a man. Suddenly, he raised his eyebrows, realizing that she didn't necessarily have to be engaged in a passade. Maybe she'd fled merely to be by her-self. She had always spoken wistfully of having her own place, of being free to explore "Catherine," her secret persona, that part of her which de-sired to write poetry and contemplate beauty. Maybe—at long last—she'd taken a flat and decided to *become* Catherine. *If so, it's a damned sight better than Amy*, he thought. Still, he wouldn't have any idea where to look for her. She handled their finances now. She could lease a flat or a villa and he'd never know if it was in London or France. Passade or no, his only chance of finding her was to start with her friends.

He got off the train at Charing Cross, zigzagged through quiet Sunday-afternoon streets to the faded, peeling lodging house off Harley Street where Dorothy Richardson lived in attic rooms. A would-be novelist still working as a secretary, Dorothy had befriended Amy in the Mornington Crescent days, had nurtured the friendship through the years, but was always looking over Amy's shoulder. At him. Though she was quite sensual, he was put off by predatory females and so far had avoided her. Despite his chronic promiscuity, he drew the line at Amy's friends. He recalled last night when Amy had been alone with W. K. Chichester. Dorothy pointed it out to him and suggested that they go for the proverbial walk on the beach, to which he replied, "She's merely practicing charades, Dorothy. Let's not become one."

He stopped abruptly on the lodging house steps. Had Dorothy said something to Amy after that? Had she, thinking it might get her somewhere, concocted some desperate, imaginary tale about going to bed with her best friend's husband? He strode through the door, ignored the lodgers in the drawing room and ran up the four flights of stairs to her door. Out of breath, he knocked, waited, knocked insistently, waited, was about to knock a third time when the landlady called up the stairs.

"She's gone out, sir."

"I don't suppose you'd know when she'll be back," he said, coming down the stairs.

"No, sir."

"Was there another lady with her by chance?"

"No, sir."

"A rather petite gentlewoman with hazel eyes and blond hair arranged in a bun?"

"No, sir."

H.G. left the lodging house without a clue. Going back to Sandgate wasn't the answer, but he had to keep moving or he'd go mad. He flagged down a hansom and told the cabby to take him to 7 Mornington Place—the house in Mornington Crescent near Regent's Park where it had all started. He'd built his time machine there and had been telling old friends from the university days of its existence when Dr. Leslie John Stephenson aka Jack the Ripper had stolen it and gone to the future. H.G., full of piss, vinegar and indignation, had followed, landing in San Francisco because by 1979 *The Utopia* had been discovered in his bricked-up basement laboratory and was on a world tour.

He'd chased Jack the Ripper through that fair city and had almost been killed out of his own time. Needless to say, he failed to bring Leslie John Stephenson back for a nineteenth-century reckoning, but did succeed in sending the monster to infinity, a retribution all its own. Ultimately, his sojourn had been worth it. He had met Amy Catherine Robbins in 1979; she—and true love—had come home with him. A few years later, Queen Victoria was dead, and it was the dawn of the Edwardian Age. Long live La Belle Époque, Art Nouveau and the notion that anything was possible. So blessed, H.G. and Amy played hard at love, not to mention literature and new ideas. He smiled nostalgically. Those had been their true halcyon days.

At 7 Mornington Place, he got out of the hansom, paid the cabbie and stood at the iron gate. He gazed fondly at the tall, narrow brick house, its trim freshly painted forest green. Here, Amy had helped him write *The Time Machine*, insisting that he make it credible so the reader would become mesmerized. Along the way, he had immersed her in his time-travel theories, and she had proven a quick study. Ultimately, the book they sent to W. E. Henley was detailed and accurate enough to sell extremely well. Thereby—thanks in part to Amy— "scientific romances" had been born. His gaze rose to the bedroom window upstairs. They used to kiss in that window and then he'd hold her from behind so they could look out at the night and see the stars as one. How perfect, how magical she had felt in his arms. Alas, she had been Amy then.

They'd moved to Woking when Mrs. Nelson, the housekeeper, passed on, but H.G. kept the lease on the house. In 1900 after he had Spade House built for Amy, in a fit of nostalgia he purchased 7 Mornington Place outright, though he didn't need the space and hadn't used his basement lab in years. He blushed guiltily: Amy had assumed that he kept the old house as a shrine to their marriage, but as the years passed and their love cooled, it had become a rendezvous for his passades, he realized ruefully.

He unlocked the front door and let himself inside. He stood in the hall by the cupboard inhaling the old smells, letting the silence settle over him, then stepped into the drawing room he'd always insisted was a library and swept his eyes over the worn, eclectic furniture, the books he'd left behind. Nothing had changed. The room reminded him of a museum, yet he knew someone had been here recently. He sensed it.

"Amy?" he called. "Are you here, Amy?"

He listened. Nothing. Not even a sound from the pendulum clock on the fireplace mantel. He automatically wound and set it—already a quarter past three, his pocket watch read—then took comfort in the rhythm of its ticking, his fingers drumming counterpoint on the mantel. His brow furrowed. The more he dwelled on the silence, the more certain he became that she'd been here. He went into the kitchen hoping to see a lukewarm teapot and marmalade on crusts of toast. Amy always left the crusts, but, no, the counters were spotless and the dishes in their cupboard. He turned.

The door to the back stairs yawned open. Had he left it that way his last time here? Never. An open door was like an unfinished thought, especially the door to his laboratory. He crossed the room in three giant strides and looked down the stairs, his jaw working furiously. The basement door was also ajar, an incandescent yellow glow shining through, but that wasn't what he saw first. Like a rose dropped for remembrance sake, a paisley-pink envelope lay faceup on the third step down. Heart pounding, he picked it up, tore it open.

Dearest Bertie——

This is the hardest thing I've ever done, for I dearly love you and Gip and Frank, and I always will. But you know those nights when I wake up sobbing and don't know why? Well, I finally figured out it's because I never said good-bye to my mother or Daddy. (I never said a world of things to Daddy.) I never told them how much I love them, and I can't stand them thinking I'm dead somewhere and not knowing how I feel about them! Yes, I know it's been thirteen years, but you understand, don't you? You see, I never got to tell them about you, Bertie. They never had a chance to say that we were okay, to give us their blessings. That might sound rather absurd and traditional to you, but love and respect and kindness for all people is important to me.

And all those insufferable times there's been a wall between us, and we can't get the magic back, and you are at a loss because life is going so swimmingly well for us? I figured that out, too. I think that for sake of our marriage, we need to separate for a while . . . let the warm and tender memories gather themselves so that we will desire more of them. As you would say, we need to escape our "domestic claustrophobia." I know that I will miss you terribly, but if I don't go home, I won't miss you at all, and that is worse. I'm sorry, I cannot allow our love to die without doing something. I hope you're not too terribly angry, Bertie, but I refuse to grow old in a marriage that has gone cold.

Furthermore, what about the earthquakes? I could never live with myself if I didn't try to save my family. Honestly, I don't think we can rationalize or ignore that seismologist after he predicted the San Francisco earthquake last April. You probably don't believe that an even bigger one is going to hit San Francisco in 2010, but I can't take that chance. My family lives there!

Yes, my dear, I am coming back to you, the boys and Spade House, but just in case something happens, I'll never forget you, my 'Bits and Bins.'

> *All My Love,*
> *Amy*

p.s. Be good to the boys.

He felt weak, sagged against the wall, slid down until he was half-sitting on a stair. *Great Scott, she's nipped my time machine!*

3:21 P.M., *Sunday, June 24, 1906*

H.G. read the letter again, deliberately ignoring her comments on their marriage because the truth was too painful, and he was in no mood for self-criticism. Rather, he focused on her last paragraph, then looked off, furious. "An even bigger earthquake in 2010?" Rubbish. That blasted drunken fool of a seismologist had filled her head with such unconscionable drivel—some heretofore unknown scientific discovery about earthquakes, no doubt—that she had bolted from her life.

Once again, he recalled Amy in the library with Chichester, hanging on his every word, a pale and wan Amy counting years on her fingers, no doubt from 1979 to 2010. And he had told Dorothy Richardson they were practicing a new charade. He was about to crumple up her letter when he remembered that seminal night thirteen years ago when he'd told his friends about his *own* heretofore unknown scientific discovery. They laughed derisively at his theory: time is not absolute; time functions according to the laws of the Gaussian coordinates; therefore, time is flexible in boundless universes of parallel realities stacked like cordwood along the fourth dimension. They had jeered at his vision, his logic: because the universes are in constant states of flux, one can hopscotch through the years if the mechanics exist. If time is like space or a dimension, he supposed, why can't we go forward or backward like we can in the other three? When they demanded proof, he asked them if they could recall specific moments from their own past lives. They could, of course, so—*quod erat demonstrandum*—their memories proved that they themselves had traveled through time.

"Preposterous!" they hooted at his claim to have built a working time machine. Someone asked how it was possible to travel to a time before his so-called machine existed, and he replied that the rules of causality did not necessarily apply to the fourth dimension or translate from one universe to another. They shouted him down, and ironically, as their uproar went on, Leslie John Stephenson aka Jack the Ripper stole that very same time machine to escape Scotland Yard, upstaging them all.

Suddenly, he wondered if he was reacting to Chichester the same way his friends had responded to him. In truth, he had been away from his lab—not to mention Amy—writing "realism" for so long that he could've become closed-minded. Though he wasn't yet forty, maybe he was already suffering from the dawn of middle age. Perhaps there was a shred of truth in Chichester's prediction. More importantly, what about Amy?

She couldn't have taken the time machine, he told himself, suddenly recalling the day they came back in 1893. *I didn't tell her about the bicycle lock. I didn't tell her that I put it on the central gearing system so that no one would ever use my time machine again.* He rushed downstairs into his laboratory, automatically slowing when he saw his monolithic creation in the center of the room and smiling with relief that apparently Amy hadn't gone anywhere. He mistakenly touched the cover to the engine compartment.

"Ouch!"

He jerked his hand away, put his fingers in his mouth. *Good bloody Christ, the machine's hot.* Then he saw his diagrams messed about on the workbench, and—speaking of paperweights—his simple bicycle lock on top with a pink rose poked through its hasp. He was wrong. Damnably wrong. Amy had taken his machine—except she must have forgotten about the special key. If the key were left in the control panel, the machine automatically returned to its home hour after a ninety-second delay. What's more, she'd left the lights on in the lab. Scowling, he circled *The Utopia*, examined its steel plates, bolts and rivets, the glass windowpanes he would replace if there were a more durable, flexible alternative, all of it. He saw nothing glaringly wrong and assumed that she'd made it back to her future in one piece—as long there hadn't been any reformulation errors.

He climbed up and peered in the windows as if a child looking in an old classroom. Indeed, the special key in the control panel confirmed his suspicions, meaning Amy was stuck in 2010, and if he ever wanted to see her again, he'd have to go and get her. He opened the cabin door, reached in for the key and pulled, but couldn't get it loose. He lifted his eyebrows in surprise—*Good Lord, did she bend it trying to get it out?*—then got his pliers from the workbench, clambered back up inside the cabin and tugged on the damned thing till it popped loose and he sprawled back in the chair.

"Where on earth have we been?" he whispered to the key, for it was badly corroded a sinister black-green.

Back at the workbench, he delicately filed the burrs off the key, then buffed it with a wire brush. He sighed and looked off, wondering if she'd actually planned her journey or had gone off impetuously. No, this was no spur-of-the-moment trip, he fumed, this wasn't merely because of Chichester's predictions. Just weeks ago on a cold, rainy night he'd come to bed expecting only the warmth of the covers, but she had scooted close to him and started talking about time travel. He was pleased with her waxing nostalgic about their one great adventure together, her words in his ear lulling him to sleep. Now he realized she hadn't been sharing memories so much as she had been sharing dreams. Dreams without him. He bit his lip to keep himself from crying. *For her sake, I hope she had sense enough to take the greenbacks she'd brought back from 1979.*

When the key was shiny brass again, he glanced at the diagrams Amy had pulled out, was pleased she'd at least looked at them. He read, "By its peculiar rotation, the time machine must reduce the time traveler to a *spirit* or body with no intrinsic mass and move it through endless universes of flux to a date predetermined by speed and real time traveled." He remembered writing those words in 1893, twelve years before Einstein published his theory of relativity, and was proud of Amy for having the courage to use the machine despite knowing that she would be vaporized. *Yes, but where the devil is the diagram of the declinometer and my cautionary note? Had she read it? Had she read it before she took the machine . . . ?*

He found diagram and note lost at the bottom of the stack. Obviously, Amy hadn't looked at them. Yet his time machine had come home by mistake, meaning that she could have panicked and pulled the declinometer. He sincerely hoped she hadn't, for if she had, then his machine would've gone to infinity before coming home. *And that would explain the badly corroded key*, he thought ominously.

He looked to the machine for answers, carefully removed the prism-shaped declinometer and wiped it clean of an extratemporal residue that never failed to remind him of a pointillist watercolor glowing from within. He inspected it for telltale scratches and found none, so there was no way of knowing whether *The Utopia* had gone to yesterday or infinity.

He replaced the declinometer, then went in the engine compartment with his tools, rags and a liter of grease. He checked the Rotation Reversal Lock circuitry, made sure the insulation wasn't cracked, then inspected the Interstices Vaporizing Regulator. Like a space-time weather vane, if it detected danger, it kept the machine from stopping until the nearest safe landing date. *Jolly good. It hadn't overheated.* He lubricated the engine proper, going from the buffers of industrial diamonds to the pulse generator to the stainless-steel gears, adjusting every part so like a fine Swiss watch, the engine would have a precise symphony of movement. Not that it needed tuning—it didn't need tuning at all—he was merely avoiding the inevitable.

"Blasted dust everywhere," he muttered, wiping off the components, shaking more extratemporal residue from his rag. He worked his way to the heart of the engine: those twisted crystalline bars that juxtaposed and concentrated electromagnetic fields which in turn created high-energy rotation enabling the machine to rocket along the fourth dimension.

When he had first come back from 1979, awash and glorious in time-travel afterglow, he'd hypercharged the engine, thanks to his brief immersion in late-twentieth-century technology, so it could go three years a minute instead of two. Not satisfied, he had also added an autoclock to the Time-Sphere Destination Indicator which self-adjusted for changes in time zones, should *The Utopia* still be on a world tour. Like a fat man in a circus, he mused sardonically.

He eased back out of the engine compartment. Despite his stubborn conviction that someday a world-state would reign supreme, he wasn't anxious to time-travel again. It wasn't merely the journey itself, a headlong rush that reduced one to quantum foam; rather, it was the fear of a reformulation error—that he wouldn't be reconstituted correctly at the destination hour. And even if the trip went smoothly, what would 2010 be like? 1979 had been a dismal potpourri of hurried, alienated men creating more and more advanced technology as if they, themselves, were machines. Ironically, those men depended on that very same technology, so one wasn't certain who was serving whom. Since coming home, he had lived with the new hope and idealism of the Edwardian Age, and had regained confidence in science and technology and the inherent goodness of man. Still, it was one thing to write speculative essays and books and quite another to go witness the reality. Conceivably by 2010 some genius would have synthesized a collective mind. Or the United Nations he so eagerly read about in 1979 would have moved closer to his dream of a world-state and a lasting peace for all mankind, and he would prove himself wrong about an egocentric mankind with a sinister technology.

Will you quit your infernal procrastination? For better or worse, Amy is the love of your life. He took the bicycle lock off the workbench, though he didn't need it. He'd bring Amy back before they left, and the lock would still be on the central gearing wheel keeping *The Utopia* safe from "the tomb robbers of the future," for lack of a better term. However, if *The Utopia* was on a world tour in 2010 and he *forgot* to lock the central gearing wheel while searching for Amy, there was a slim chance some errant child could slip past the barriers and accidentally propel himself through time, but that was a risk he would take. If Malthusian predictions held true in the twenty-first century and the world had a serious population problem, the loss of a thoughtless child was not necessarily a bad thing. He sighed and did not recall his own childhood. He slipped Amy's pink rose in his lapel and took a stack of hundred-pound notes sterling from the safe, then went to the basement door and switched off the lights.

A dim ambience from the casement windows lit his way back to the machine. He climbed up, stood in the cabin door. The control panel, its switches and dials appeared as new as when first installed; the brass fixtures gleamed as if polished yesterday; the stainless-steel Rotator Control—the eastward position sent one to the future, the westward to the past—would move easily. In 2010, the brass would be green with age, and the Rotator Control quite possibly rusted and stuck. Coming back through time, however, *The Utopia* rejuvenated itself, a phenomenon that still baffled him. No matter. As a motorcar mechanic might say, the old girl still had some years left on her. He glanced down, chuckled with surprise.

"Silly girl."

Amy had left her purse by the cabin chair.

He swung inside and settled himself in the chair. It wasn't as big as he remembered it. He smiled ruefully. *The chair is exactly the same as it was thirteen years ago. It's the pilot's backside that has gotten larger.* Sheepish, he read the Destination Indicator: year, 2010; month, June; day, 20; time, 12:01 A.M. Usually, Amy was in bed long before midnight, so he had no clue what had possessed her to go to that wee hour. Maybe fear. Theoretically, he would arrive with reassurances while she was still in the vicinity wondering what in the world she had done. Yet he made no move. Though not one to trust intuition, he felt that something was seriously wrong and looked for a sign. He gasped.

Blood was on the floor.

Barely discernible in the dim light, it looked like a trail of shiny black paint. *Amy. My God, what have you done to yourself?* Hurriedly, he pulled the medical kit from under the chair. Other than himself, Amy was the only one who knew it was there, and, yes, she had opened it. The blood must be hers. A sterile bandage and roll of gauze were gone; the tincture of iodine had been opened. She had probably cut herself in a rush to get out of the machine. Muttering, he cleaned up the blood with a piece of gauze, then realized he was procrastinating again. *Good Lord, man, go get her!*

He strapped himself in the chair, turned the key and engaged the switches, listened gloomily to the engine's characteristic hum as it warmed—familiar like a Mozart melody once heard, never forgotten. He shoved the Accelerator Helm Lever forward until it locked in the flank position. As the engine whined and the machine began spinning, he suddenly recalled why he had put the lock on the central gearing wheel in the first place. It was so that man could not play God—as he had done in 1979. Yet here he was on his way again, his beloved wife already a casualty of an unfamiliar future.

A crystalline flash.

He felt himself melting, merging with the flux, lifted out of 1906 and sent rocketing along the fourth dimension. He realized a split second too late why man—at least this one—shouldn't play at the supernatural.

He didn't believe in God.

7:36 A.M., *Sunday, June 20, 2010*

Now West LAPD crime scene technicians were in the men's room off the Getty's rotunda, working in that electric atmosphere that comes with an unusual murder destined for headlines. They moved in concert, their movements stiff and robotic, a ballet typical of their century and the megacity they served. Yet in their midst, one stood out, her hair glossy black under fluorescents, her tailored blue lab coat a cut above the dirty white worn by her colleagues.

Amber Reeves was speaking softly into a tiny HD video camera as she panned down the body of Teresa Cruz and tried to avoid the lead forensic photographer. Behind her, fingerprint technicians methodically dusted and lifted latent prints from the bathroom stalls while lower-level criminalists bagged broken glass from the mirror. The photographer had powdered the traffic area between the corpse and the door, then side-lit the dozens of footprints that had emerged and flagged off the ambient top light so the impressions would photographically separate from the floor. He had mounted his old Nikon F2 on a tripod—digital cameras didn't work for footprints—and was moving back for a wide angle just as Amber bent down for a tight shot of the jagged hole in Teresa's side. The photographer backed into her, knocking them both off-balance.

"Jesus." He turned and frowned at her, then went back to his camera and lined up a shot almost parallel to the floor.

"Amber."

She glanced away. Lieutenant Casey Holland was in the doorway—thick, stolid and definitely not handsome in Sunday-morning sweats. She liked him better in suits, crisp shirts and ties. He motioned her out of the room.

"Morning." She gave him her patented warm smile.

"What's up with this?" He gestured at her video camera.

She shrugged, thought of a bunch of excuses, but offered none—she hated to sound lame. Besides, they'd always been honest with each other. "I picked it up at Samy's."

"Yeah?" Casey nodded at the photographer, lifted his eyebrows. "Well, Rogers there thinks you're going for his job."

"Oookay. And I'd want to spend my time shooting footprints because . . . ?"

"It's a stop along the way."

She blushed and looked down. The lieutenant was uncanny. He could sense ambition almost as fast as he could solve crimes and invariably used it to his advantage.

"Shouldn't you be in there taking DNA samples?"

"I really don't think the killer left trace evidence behind."

"You're a psychic now?"

"C'mon, Lieutenant, the blood is all hers."

"A splatter expert, as well."

She blushed again. "Besides—"

"I know, Amber. She wasn't raped, and we're getting two weeks worth of fingerprints."

She was already going for her backpack and the field kit inside. As she came back to the doorway, he added, "Try for epidermal traces from where he strangled her."

"Okay, okay."

"And stay out of my face." He patted her on the ass, a friendly gesture in that no sexual tension existed between them. Yes, he appreciated her curvaceous body, her panache and joie de vivre, but he was happily married with two kids and had made a point of telling her that when she'd taken the job a year ago so that they *could* work together. He also insulated her from the others. They knew she was a superior technician and resented her for it. They knew that while they were doomed to crime scenes and corpses, she would quickly rise above their ghoulish toil to a better life.

She had no such confidence in herself.

Lieutenant Holland frowned at her, gestured curtly with his head. She nodded back, eased into the bathroom, gave Rogers a wide berth, kneeled by the corpse and went to work.

Dutifully, Amber took DNA samples from Teresa Cruz's bruised neck, under her fingernails, from some of the curiously bare footprints Rogers had already photographed, and just to satisfy the lieutenant, added samples of blood as well. She frowned petulantly, not convinced that she had anything more than biochemical trash for the circular file back at the lab, and moved on. She followed the killer's escape route—now luminous with powder—from the bathroom to the emergency exit and the stone path that ended at a six-foot wall, the expanse fenced with phosphorescent homicide tape. She went up the ladder marked "LAPD," observed the technicians combing the lawn and bushes beyond, then studied the dent in the hedgerow where the killer had fallen. At first, she saw only leaves and broken branches—nothing out of the ordinary— then pushed down on the hedgerow as if a body had landed on it. A dark-red speck caught her eye—dried blood on a broken twig that the techs fanning out down the hill had obviously missed. Grinning triumphantly, she bagged it and hurried back to her field kit.

On an LAPD field table, she hooked up her laptop to the portable lab's TMC-2000a which tested for DNA, arranged the samples and began the tedious process. While waiting, she overheard Lieutenant Holland interviewing the security guard, Peterson, on a concrete bench next to the water fountain.

". . . we couldn't find her," said Peterson, "and I was having problems in the room. One monitor went down and then they all went down. Like dominoes."

"I'll want the disks," said Holland.

Peterson nodded. "Anyway, Cedric called me on the walkie—he's all shook—and I'm going down to take a look, and I saw this guy, and I yelled, but he was like *gone*, you know?"

"What did he look like?"

"I dunno. Like anybody. But he was in the shadows, so, you know." Peterson shrugged.

"What was he wearing?"

"Baseball cap, T-shirt and jeans, I think. I'm not sure."

"You aware that he had on the deceased's street clothes?"

"Huh?" Peterson was flabbergasted. "You gotta be kidding. I mean, why would he do that? What happened to his clothes?"

"We're still looking." The lieutenant made a note. "Any paintings missing? Museum pieces? Stuff like that?"

"No, sir, not so far." Peterson looked down thoughtfully, then back at Holland. "Did he really cut out her kidney?"

"Yes."

"Jesus."

"You from here, Peterson?"

"No, sir."

"Well, that's what wackos do in this town. They wanna make the six o'clock news. Everybody in L.A. wants to be a fucking star. . . ." He handed Peterson his card, gave him a long, blank look. "Call me before you go anywhere, okay?"

Forty minutes after the lieutenant was done with Peterson, Amber was checking her results for the third time, not fathoming what the DNA program was telling her about the blood sample she had taken from the hedgerow. Determining the karyotypes had been a piece of cake, but then she had seen something abnormal with the sex-determining chromosomes 46. They were neither clearly XX nor XY, but looked more like those of a botched Klinefelter's syndrome: Most cells appeared to be XXY; but a few seemed to be XYY and a few even appeared to be an impossible

XXYY. The only thing for certain was that none of the cells was clearly XX or XY, and that the Y chromosomes were so weak that they might as well have not been there at all. She wasn't sure what to do next, and was starting to be annoyed with herself for feeling helpless, when Holland's shadow loomed over the laptop screen from behind her.

"You milking it, or what?"

"No, I'm not milking it."

"That machine's supposed to be fast."

"It is fast."

"So then what've you got?" he said. "A Hispanic male suspect roughly the same size as the victim. Maybe a relative, right?"

"I don't know."

He frowned impatiently and muttered unintelligibly. Blushing, she worked the keyboard and brought up all three inconclusive test results on a split screen.

"All the other tests were normal," she added.

"What other tests?"

"The victim's blood."

"Why would you test her blood?"

"For comparison," she said, her face growing hot.

"Then you corrupted the perp's sample," he said bluntly, "the only one we had."

"I did not!"

"You corrupted the damn sample!"

"I most certainly did—"

"Amber," he interrupted. "Go count to ten."

She got up from the chair and backed away, angry and surprised. He had never talked to her like that before.

"Take a break," he said, then sat down and began running the procedures himself. "Go soak up some grace and beauty."

She started off.

"Put on some lipstick, too."

"Screw you," she said under her breath.

———

The farther away Amber got from the crime scene—sans lab coat and latex gloves—the more relaxed she became, and by the time she'd wandered through quiet rooms of Renaissance, then Restoration art, she was in a gentle, reflective mood, musing ironically about this, her first trip to the Getty, thanks to a brutal murder. *I've forgotten. My God, I've forgotten grace and beauty.* She wiped away sudden tears. Before the police, she had been an innocent soul, a bright-eyed summa cum laude graduate from UCLA with a degree in English literature. But rather than go on for her Ph.D., she opted to support her mother, who had just lost her job as a salesclerk, couldn't get another one and was too young for Social Security—not that she could have lived on Social Security. So Amber had taken a down-and-dirty master's program in criminalistics because she could make fifty grand a year right out of the gate working for the LAPD. Once financially stable, she'd figured, she could go back to the history and literature she loved, yet she hadn't counted on the hard, cynical edge to her personality that a year with the police had given her—or her desire to escape it. Then—from a page out of Dickens—her mother had gotten lung cancer. Four months later she was dead, leaving Amber a legacy of unpaid medical bills: a dismal, unavoidable reason to go on working.

She sat down on a bench amid dreamy pastels by French impressionists and went on crying, thankful that the murder had closed the museum, and she was alone right now. She hadn't realized how much she'd missed her books, the poetry and art, the blossoming creativity of the Edwardian Age, that genteel, lingering romance from another century, wistful in her mind. She wiped her eyes, thought it colossally unfair that she'd become a user-friendly tech who had to analyze acts of violence and their desecrated victims to make a living.

Her cell jangled.

Lieutenant Holland was on the phone telling her to come back and pick up her stuff. He'd scheduled a strategy meeting at the office after lunch and wanted "everybody's theories about the crime," the subtext being that he'd already run fingerprints, footprints and trace evidence through the NCIS database and had come up with nothing.

"Was I wrong about the chromosomes?"

"No." He hung up.

She smiled, vindicated.

When she got back to the crime scene, her colleagues had already left, replaced by coroner's deputies, their sardonic humor echoing in the rotunda. She tuned them out, packed up and wheeled her kit down the steps of the arrival plaza to her car. She paused thoughtfully. The car annoyed her. It was a used bone-white Mercury Milan with the usual stuff including iPod and GPS, but the longer she drove it, the more indifferent she became. It was just another modern appliance, and right now, she hated it for that. She wanted a world with personality, a world with sensibilities.

So—desiring one more taste of what must have been a glorious past—she put her stuff in the trunk, then went back through the rotunda and along the long, empty courtyard, appreciating the sound from the fountains, melodies that blocked the ugly roar from the 405 less than a mile away. She went inside the West Pavilion, gathered herself, stood in silence before the H. G. WELLS—A MAN BEFORE HIS TIME banner, half-wishing she'd been born in the nineteenth century. A sigh, and then she strolled inside. Ignoring the rope barriers, she touched red-leather original editions atop display cases that held manuscripts and "picshuas." Aside from his books, articles and inventions, Wells habitually drew crude cartoons that were droll, witty commentaries on little moments in life deserving of some sort of recognition before becoming history obscura.

As she passed *The Utopia* in the center gallery, she gave it a patronizing smile, yet didn't go inside, not interested in failed inventions, though she gave Wells credit for trying. She paused before a giant photograph over the archway to the gallery and studied the man. In a six-by-six-foot heavy metal frame, Wells appeared larger than life; he was quite the handsome author at twenty-nine, smiling and looking off at some "significance," his dark eyes twinkling mischievously above a bushy mustache. Yet he seemed filled with self-importance, and she liked him better in a smaller display of photographs. At forty-five, he still had the dark hair and mustache, the same disarming smile, but his face was thicker and not so angular. Above all, he seemed both wise and accessible. He had a father's face and was actually looking at the photographer as if sharing an intimate moment.

Suddenly, the world went white.

Amber gasped and staggered back, threw her hands out to protect herself. Blinded, she lurched into a display case, felt its glass top, then its side as she eased herself down to the floor and wondered what had happened. Had a bomb hit the Getty? There hadn't been an explosion—it was more like everything had been erased. She grabbed her cell phone and was trying to find the right keys for 911 when her vision returned. Relieved, she glanced in all directions. Nothing had changed. Everything was as— No. everything was not the same.

A blue glow from the center gallery flickered on the arches in the pavilion, then quickly faded. Astonished, she was slowly getting up when she heard someone running across the lobby. She saw a man in a dark, Edwardian-style suit who looked like he'd stepped out of a period-piece English movie. The man hit the door at full speed, disappeared outside.

No. It's not possible. That didn't just happen.

Did it?

9:47 A.M., Sunday, June 20, 2010

H. G. Wells stopped short on the museum courtyard, struck by its simple, clean beauty, its fountains and celebration of water as an art form, its graceful Mexican cypress trees. Then he sagged against the travertine stone of the West Pavilion, realizing with horror that he was in broad daylight. He pulled out his pocket watch; it read 9:48 A.M., confirming that something had gone terribly wrong. He had set the Destination Indicator for 12:01 A.M.—the same time that Amy had arrived—and here it was morning instead of night and over nine hours later. Granted, there was no absolute time in a universe without boundaries, but to arrive that far beyond one's destination was preposterous, especially after a journey of a mere 104 years. *Perhaps leap years confused the autoclock. No matter. I'll have to fix the blasted thing. Yes, but what about Amy?* He hadn't seen a blood trail leading away from the machine, which meant she must have bandaged her wound properly and was all right. He squared his shoulders and started back inside to check the calibration on the Destination Indicator, then heard voices and turned. Security guards were at the other end of the courtyard. He flattened himself against the building, looked behind him, saw stairs. He went down two at a time, not certain if the guards had seen him or how he would explain himself. On the second landing, he paused to catch his breath and automatically felt his pockets, making sure he hadn't forgotten Amy's purse or the special key. He had no desire to be lost in a year he knew nothing about, that before had existed only in his imagination.

His hands were greasy from putting the bicycle lock back on the central gearing wheel. He wiped them off on his trousers, glanced up at slate-gray skies. Aside from the stone and glass complex, the immense sculptured space that surrounded him, he could have been in London, but for a strange, persistent roar that came from beyond the museum. It could have been a river, but wasn't; it was so loud it drowned out a soft breeze through the trees. He vaguely recognized the sound from 1979, envisioned a stampede of motor cars nearby, hoped he was wrong.

Where am I? More important, where is Amy . . . ? Hopefully, she has found a modern doctor who has waved some enlightened machine over her wound and instantly sealed it.

He glanced warily behind him, then descended the stairs to a lawn, took a path through trees to a giant, circular garden that resembled an amphitheater featuring concentric circles of flowers in its center. He wondered if he were in some symmetrical Stonehenge, was soon lost on another path through exotic bushes, flowers and trees, bridges over brooks that played melodies with water, and nothing was sharp or angular. Like the stone-and-glass creation behind him, the garden was an homage to the curve, and he continued on, filled with joy to find himself amid such futuristic beauty and solitude. It settled over his ragged psyche and soothed him, and despite the absence of Amy, his spirits soared. *No Philistines, no twenty-first-century technowizards of war and alienation could have created this remarkable environment. Only enlightened artists and architects have held sway here. New men, citizens of the world who have discovered a way to harness the technology that mocked and almost killed yours truly thirty-one years ago. How marvelous. An enormous, sprawling museum that stands as a shrine to the possibilities of the human condition.*

A nasty, mechanical growl shattered his reverie.

He turned and stepped back under a giant tree fern. A squat brown figure in dirty clothes topped by goggles and a sweat-stained cap with "L.A." on it worn backward came down the walkway blowing leaves, the greasy engine on his back making him resemble a creature from Jules Verne. Only when the figure stopped and idled the blower to let him pass did Wells realize that he was actually human and not some worker-android. He stepped forward and shouted over the popping of the engine.

"My good man, do you have the time?"

The man shook his head, shrugged and grinned.

"Do you know what day it is?"

The man lifted his goggles. "*No hablo.*"

Exasperated, H.G. spoke louder still—as if volume somehow increased comprehension. "DO—YOU—KNOW—WHERE—I—AM—?"

"*No hablo.*"

The man detoured around Wells, continued down the walkway, his blower once again at flank speed.

H.G. frowned. He considered himself cosmopolitan in that he was fluent in French, could speak Italian and hold his own in a German or Russian restaurant, but he'd never had the time or inclination to learn Spanish. Perhaps it was the Moorish influence on the Iberians? He stopped abruptly; his eyebrows rose.

"My God, am I in Mexico?"

Concerned, he started uphill, hurried to get away from the annoying sound of the blower, asked himself why this worker—if indeed he was Mexican—needed to waste his time with mindless tasks. *If they can design such a wonderful space, why not engineer Mother Nature so that she need not shed leaves at all?* He looked behind him. The man was zigzagging across the lawn now, wielding his blower as if it were a broadsword and he were fighting some invisible foe.

Bewildered, H.G. left the garden, climbed yet another flight of stairs, and emerged before the museum restaurant. He was relieved its signs were in English, noticed a row of newspaper racks similar to those he had seen in 1979 and squinted through the plastic: "*The Los Angeles Times.* June 20, 2010. Sunday edition. Westside." He didn't bother with the headlines.

So I'm in Los Angeles, am I?

His breath whooshed out in a distinctive rush, a habit begun when he was a student at the Normal School of Science, an expression of wonder at knowledge or discovery. At first his classmates had thought it funny, then came to rely on H.G.'s "whooshes" for their own discoveries.

He skirted the restaurant and descended to the arrival plaza, staying close to the walls, in the shadows. TV news vans were double-parked in front of police cars, and camera crews straggled in and out of the rotunda. Wells had seen this in 1979 as well, and figured a special event must be going on inside which would explain why this spectacular monument to twenty-first-century man was closed. The ribbons of yellow tape waving in the breeze didn't register. In fact, after his haphazard tour of this wonderful museum and garden, Wells was so enthused about the future, so glad he'd come, so proud that perhaps he hadn't been wrong about mankind, it never occurred to him that this "special event" was the scene of a particularly vicious crime, committed by a psychopath from his own time.

He considered Amy. Her parents lived in San Francisco—if they were still alive—so more than likely that was where he would find her. Since she was from the twentieth century, he wasn't worried about her ability to function in this world. She'd been gone for only thirty-one years. He was more concerned about himself and how he would in fact get to San Francisco.

For lack of an alternative, he started walking, but paused on the other side of the arrival plaza at an empty information booth and learned that the space-age complex before him was the J. Paul Getty Museum. He was about to take a brochure when he saw the tram. Enthralled, he half-ran to the Upper Station, boarded the lead car and hunted for an ignition switch—as in the motorcars he'd admired in 1979—thinking that one quick turn would engage the tram's engine and move him down the hill. He hadn't realized that the tram was pilotless, like a "people mover" from one of his "scientific romances." Nor had he seen the operator behind the tinted glass windows of the station wondering what in hell he was doing.

Amber had.

As the operator came out the station door intent on removing Wells from the tram, Amber stopped him with her police ID.

"We're part of the investigation."

"Oh."

"Start the tram."

"Okay."

Amber swung onto the last car, perched on a seat and watched an alert and eager Wells through the glass windows. The tram clicked twice, then glided silently downhill as if on air, and she clutched the seat bars, jittery with excitement, enthralled with this *gentleman* who had stepped out of a time machine, of all impossible things. She was going to go wherever he was going, and was strangely liberated. If nothing else, she felt alive and schoolgirl-happy again, that hard edge from police work packed away with her field kit. Lieutenant Holland's strategy meeting was the farthest thing from her mind.

They approached the Lower Station. Amber's face hurt from smiling, but she couldn't stop even if she wanted to. This was her first ride on the Getty tram, and she would always remember it as her portal to the universe. This ride was taking her away from the mundane, the ugly and mean of her everyday life. This ride was lifting her into a world of impossible possibilities. For her, the first time on the Getty tram was pure magic.

10:32 A.M., *Sunday, June 20, 2010*

Uncomfortable in an overstuffed chair, the woman ate the first of two scones between sips of tea, unaware of lingering masculine stares, not yet realizing that one man had taken a table nearby so he could undress her with his eyes while pretending to read a newspaper. She was famished, and if Teresa Cruz's money hadn't bought her the scones, she would have eaten the little security guard's kidney.

The woman was at a place called Starbucks, two blocks away from a highway that serviced streams of motor cars resembling miniature trains without track or sensibility. She loved the wide, flat road of the red-and-blue 405 signs, the concrete slicing through that old whore Mother Nature. In fact, she had rested in one of its underpasses until the sun came up and, if need be, would go back again tonight.

Two cyclists came in, the door stirring the air, and the woman caught a whiff from her own body. It wasn't that nasty, harsh odor she recalled from when she was a man on the hunt for whores. Rather, it was a sweet musk, that same perfume her sister gave off before they'd go hand-in-hand behind the caretaker's house. *Yes, but I am not Penny—I must find a bath or a shower.*

She finished her scone and dabbed at her mouth, put off by the paper napkin. *Whatever happened to linen?* She sighed stoically and sipped tea—a passable Earl Grey—then leaned back in the chair, annoyed by Teresa's shirt stretching taut, annoyed by her own breasts. She must find respectable attire—something Jack would deem suitable—something masculine, except the way these men of 2010 dressed was questionable at best. Their trousers stopped at the calves, a perversion of knickers. They all wore pullover shirts with inane quotations, billed caps and sandals that flopped. True, she had loved the disco shirts and bell-bottoms in 1979, but they were flamboyant and elegant compared with these outfits. She assumed the wires hanging from the ears of these men had something to do with the small, strangely bright screens on their tables. Portable television, perhaps? If not, then it must be the small devices they were talking into, obviously the telephones of the day. She felt a pair of eyes and frowned. *Why does that man keep staring at me? Has he figured out that I am a misincarnation from out of time or does he want to take me behind this coffee store and have at me?* She gave the man a murderous scowl, not realizing that her expression came off as an innocent yet sensual pout.

She bit into the second scone, but her hunger had deserted her. She seethed with rage at whatever force in the cosmos was responsible for her becoming a woman. *Wells—that brilliant little fool—must have done something indecent before his machine got away from him. Yet he has to be here somewhere in this world of concrete and motor cars, stupid clothes and dirty-brown skies, and I will find him and make him wish that the most he knew about the vagaries of time was how to set his pocket watch.*

Then it suddenly occurred to her that maybe she was wrong. Maybe Wells wasn't here at all. When she had arrived in 2010, she had panicked because of her toxic glow, yet still had the wherewithal to replace the declinometer and prevent the time machine from going back to infinity. Now—in her mind's eye—she saw that the dark, pillowlike thing underneath it had been a purse. *God knows Jack saw enough of them on the cobblestones of Whitechapel, and I'm quite certain that H. G. Wells wouldn't be caught dead carrying a purse.*

Which means the girl must be here.

Bemused, the woman chuckled. *Perhaps the girl grew tired of his clever diatribes and his philandering ways and took his machine to get away. That would explain the declinometer, loose on the floor. And given the special key stuck in the dash, no doubt Wells will be coming here, too—not just for the girl, but to rescue his beloved machine. What to do, what to do.*

Start with the girl. Amy Catherine Robbins.

The woman's logic whisked away her anger, and she became aware of music floating from small speakers, a soft, sweet female voice lending a pleasant, relaxed atmosphere to the place. It filled her with a sense of well-being. She smiled unconsciously and nodded along with the music, then noticed her reflection in the window behind her chair. Once again, she was surprised by her image, yet this time didn't mind her lovely face. *I'm really quite beautiful, and if that gives people in 2010 the wrong impression, that's actually quite marvelous. It will make deception and betrayal mere child's play.* Then she saw her breasts, her voluptuous curves and below. She gripped the chair and looked away, loathing her body, for it made her like her sister, like whores everywhere.

"She's great, isn't she?"

Startled, the woman turned. It was the man at the nearby table, leaning over his newspaper, his hand twitching nervously, a brittle grin on his puffy face. He had yellow-brown eyes and a scraggly red beard and he wore his cap backward, concealing his thinning, frizzy hair. The rest of him seemed ordinary, what with a roll of flesh over his belt and trousers.

"I beg your pardon?"

"Norah."

"Who?"

"Norah Jones. You were smiling, so I figured you liked her stuff."

"Actually, I prefer Grieg," said the woman, unaccustomed to her own voice and its musical lilt. "Edvard Grieg."

Red beard responded with a blank look.

"Wagner, perhaps?" she said blithely. "Have you heard of him?"

"Oh, I get it. You're into opera?"

"Certain operas, yes," she replied, thinking of *Medea*. She started to get up, already bored with the conversation and wanting to get away from this wine grape of a man.

"Hey, wait a sec," he said. "So . . . what are you up to?"

She paused, not sure what he meant.

"I mean, like right now." He grinned stupidly, revealing straight teeth that were unnaturally white.

She appraised red beard and the insinuations in his eyes, wondering where it would lead with him and what he could do for her. True, he wasn't a woman, a whore, but he was part of that sexual dynamic, and that might be enough. Besides, she needed to practice for her eventual encounter with Wells, and if nothing else, this red beard probably had a shower at his flat.

"Your cap's on backwards," she said impulsively.

"You're *so* wrong."

He reached over and turned her cap around so that it matched his, then leaned back and laughed, and soon she found herself laughing with him, her voice high and sweet like a little girl's.

They were in a cream-colored Porsche Boxster on the other side of the 405, turning off Sunset and heading into the hills. As they wound past well-kept homes with manicured landscaping, she lounged in the passenger seat and chuckled at the irony. One of her fondest memories from 1979 had come in a brand-new Porsche 944—black like Dolores Clark, the beautiful rich girl Leslie John Stephenson had met at a disco. They'd danced for hours under flashing, colored lights. They'd done drinks and a tête-à-tête, and then she'd driven them to San Francisco's John McLaren Park, intending to christen her car with their hot breath fogging the windows, their ecstasy, their juices mingling on black-leather seats. Dolores couldn't have known that most of the bodily fluids spilled in her car would be her own blood.

The woman smiled nostalgically. "What's your name?" she asked.

"Mike." Red beard gave her a mock salute and tapped the car's accelerator. "Mike Trattner. How about you?"

The question startled her. She couldn't very well say John or Leslie or even Jack. Indeed, what sobriquet would she choose? She took off her cap—her hair cascaded down—then smiled as it came to her. She turned her radiance on him and said low:

"Jaclyn."

"Jaclyn? That's it?"

"That's it."

He chortled nervously. "Well, that's okay with me. . . . Hey, you're not a cop, are you?"

He pulled off the road on a grass-covered slope, backed the Boxster up to a grove of eucalyptus, killed the engine. Jaclyn liked the sudden quiet, the view of Brentwood below. Without the overcast, she could've seen the Pacific though she didn't know it was there. Nevertheless, she appreciated the irony of the beautiful vista in that they were a mere 343 years away from mankind annihilating its own planet. Then the irritating tap of his nervous fingers on the steering wheel broke the solitude.

"Okay." He gripped her thigh as if it were a life raft. "How much?"

She swept her hair back and stared off, her anger barely under control. It was one thing to be trapped in a woman's body, yet quite another to be taken for a common harlot. "For what?"

"How much does a hundred get me?"

She swung around and gave him a coy smile, yet her fingernails were digging hard into the armrest lest she lose it and start clawing his face. She whispered, "More than you could possibly imagine."

He handed her the bill. She stuffed it in the pocket with the kidney and was wondering how far she was going to take this charade, but he gave her no chance for thought. He grabbed her head and mashed his lips against hers, his jaws working, forcing her mouth open. He stuck his tongue deep inside.

Repulsed and infuriated, Jaclyn bit down hard on his tongue, ignored his muffled scream. She gripped him tight so he couldn't escape, worked her teeth like serrated blades and finally severed it.

She let go.

Howling in pain, he leapt from the car, hopped up and down, coughed and retched, his voice fading to a hoarse scream.

She spit tongue and blood on the dash, swung from the car and went after him, her rage unfulfilled.

Wide-eyed with fear, his hands up, he backed away, but she was coming on fast. Before he could escape, she kicked him hard in the groin. He screamed again, went down, rolled into a ball and writhed in the grass.

Jaclyn watched him for a moment, then went back to the Porsche, her own groin stirring with excitement. She started the engine and revved the accelerator, but nothing happened. Then she remembered that as he drove, he was constantly moving this stick-thing back and forth. She jerked on it. The Porsche lurched backwards and hit a eucalyptus tree. She frowned. *Ah, yes. The "R" must be for reverse.* Letting the engine idle, she carefully moved the shift to "D," felt the little sports car lean forward like a thoroughbred at the gate. She glanced up. Trattner was on his knees now, blood streaming down his front. He had one of those tiny telephones to his ear, was trying to talk, but instead, brayed like a wounded donkey.

She hit the gas and lurched forward.

He made one futile attempt to get out of the way, but the Porsche hit him in the back, and he pitched forward on his face. She drove over his legs, then stopped and looked back. He was still trying to save himself, crawling through the grass with his arms, his useless legs dragging behind. She shifted into "R" and backed over him on a diagonal, crushing his head and torso.

She stopped again, saw his flattened body, vaulted from the Porsche and suddenly was convulsed with laughter. Bent over, slapping her legs, tears streaming down her face, she giggled helplessly and pointed at him. Finally, she managed a breath, a deep sigh, and got hold of herself. She looked off thoughtfully, realizing that her laughter was the closest she'd come to a sexual climax since 1979.

She heard a small, tinny sound, cocked her head, picked up Trattner's phone and put it to her ear.

"This is the emergency operator. Is someone there . . . ? Hello . . . ? Hello, is someone there . . . ?"

She tossed it away, having no need for a telephone, then had second thoughts and retrieved it. The voice was still coming from it. Panic seized her—as if this voice had somehow witnessed what she had just done—and she pressed every button on the tiny device until it went black and silent. She almost threw it away again, then hesitated, slid it in her pocket.

She gazed at red beard's corpse as if it were a sundry store. *What else might one need in this questionable time and place?* She had observed the way people conducted business at Starbucks, so she rooted through his pockets. Not much had changed in thirty-one years, except these days customers slid plastic cards through an electronic device for goods and presumably services. Michael Trattner's wallet had several of these magical little things plus two hundred dollars cash, a driver's license and a picture of his wife.

Sign him and be done with it.

She ransacked the Porsche for a knife or something sharp so that she might take another organ, yet found nothing. Then she discovered the car keys, examined them, and, no, they really wouldn't do for a surgery. She put them in her pocket, anyway, not knowing why, but trusting her instincts. She went back to her search. Still nothing. Frustrated, she was about to give up when she spied the piece of his tongue she'd bitten off, limp on the dash. She recalled when she was Jack; she would send Scotland Yard letters deliberately written in Cockney with crude sketches designed to taunt them. If she couldn't butcher this Michael Trattner, she could paint on him, she could leave the coppers a contemporary work of art. But what? She noticed the stupid happy face on Teresa Cruz's T-shirt, went back to the body, turned it over and ripped off Trattner's shirt, exposing a generous expanse of belly. Using his head as a well, she dipped the tongue in his blood, drew a happy face on his belly, the words "REMEMBER ME?" underneath. She placed the tongue in the middle of the face like a flaccid nose, brushed off her hands in the grass, hurried to the road and started down the hill.

Minutes later she heard a helicopter, but thought nothing of it,

blissfully unaware of GPS technology and that the West LAPD had ze-
roed in on Michael Trattner's cell when he didn't respond to the emergency operator before she had turned the phone off. It didn't matter.
When the helicopter was circling the scene, she was a half-mile away,
still hidden by the trees.

Near the bottom of the hill, the road widened, and around a curve she
came upon homes much smaller and closer together than the ones
farther up, and she recalled walking from, say, her childhood home at
Aesculapius across the countryside to a village replete with sounds and
smells. So here, she expected motor cars, people, movement of some
kind, even dogs barking, but was greeted with a profound quiet, a
silence that washed away the afterglow of murder and made her flesh
crawl. She frowned nervously and reminded herself, *I am the harbinger
of bad tidings. Of all people, I should not be apprehensive or afraid. Yet
I am.*

The helicopters again, circling, nosing into canyons—their alien
noise, not comforting. Jaclyn walked faster, tried to fill her mind with a
leitmotif from *Götterdämmerung*, but Wagner was far away from the
Brentwood foothills and could not soothe her.

Up ahead, a motorcar shot out of a side street, tires squealing, engine growling, and came straight toward her. She hesitated, then froze;
she knew better than to run. POLICE was emblazoned on its side. She
might have escaped in Whitechapel in 1888 or 1893, but no midnight
London fog, no honeycomb of narrow alleyways could help her here.
She was caught in the open on a wide street in broad daylight, and
these two patrolmen were not mere bobbies with whistles and night-
sticks. They had a motor car and pistols. Yet much to her astonishment,
they seemed concerned for her. The one on the passenger side leaned
over the door so his arm appeared huge—a masculine gesture she
hadn't seen before—but she did recognize his grin, his eyes that mem-
orized her body.

"Excuse me, ma'am, but this area has been cordoned off."

"I'm just out for a walk, sir."

"I'm sorry, but you're not supposed to be on the street. There's been a murder, and we have units in the area looking for a suspect."

"Really?" She feigned surprise, looked up and down the street, hugged herself. "That's awful."

Inside the car, the driver leaned forward so she could see him. "You live around here, ma'am?"

"Why, yes, of course."

"Well, why don't you let us give you a ride home?"

"That would be lovely."

She got in the car without hesitation, knowing that one false move, one wrong word or gesture, and their demeanor would change. True, she had cunning and guile, yet she wasn't sure it was enough to overcome these muscle-bound coppers in military-pressed blues. *Jack could've taken them, what with his knives and the strength of Satan, but I am him only in spirit.*

The driver eyed her quizzically in his rearview mirror. "Where we going, ma'am?"

The idea came to her as soon as he'd asked, proving that she was not necessarily marooned in an alien year and that Satan did indeed "ride the horses of dark energy," his influence touching every corner of every universe and beyond. She glanced at Michael Trattner's driver's license, then looked back at the patrolman and smiled.

"1407 Bowling Green Way."

The patrolman nodded and made a left turn.

Jaclyn studied the picture of Trattner's wife, released a ragged sigh. The longer she looked, the more the wife reminded her of Penny, the only one Jack ever loved, the one who betrayed him. Her mouth overflowed with saliva, and she swallowed hard.

"Here you go, ma'am."

The car stopped. Twins in lust, both patrolmen flexed and grinned stupidly at her, invitations on their square faces.

As she got out and turned to thank them, the copper in the passenger seat handed her his card.

"You need anything, you *see* anything, you give us a call, okay?"

"Thank you."

She gave him a little flutter wave—startling herself, for the gesture was totally feminine, hence alien to her soul. Yet she continued on across the street, then up the flagstone walkway over the lawn toward a white Spanish-style bungalow. She had planned to skirt the house and keep on going, but heard the patrol car idling in the street and knew that they wouldn't leave until she was safely inside. No cars were in the driveway, a good sign, but no guarantee that the house was empty. Her heart thudded, but she minced up the steps, went straight to the front door. She turned, smiled and waved at them again, then pulled out Michael Trattner's keys, found the one for the house and shoved it in the lock.

11:53 A.M., *Sunday, June 20, 2010*

Brakes squeaking, the shuttle bus pulled into a turnout at LAX and stopped, the driver calling out, "America West, Southwest, US Airways."

H.G. gazed at this new world framed by a dirty window, taking in the dubious wonder of snarled traffic on World Way North, cars, vans and buses fighting for position, the bold anarchy of pedestrians crossing the street despite red lights, then cars coming straight for them, an ugly ballet of mindless machines and indifferent people accompanied by blaring horns and the flatulent noise of buses. He winced at the shadow of a low-flying commuter jet, its echoing roar, then tried to catch a glimpse of it, but failed.

"Southwest."

H.G. turned. The driver made eye contact in his rearview mirror and nodded curtly.

"Thank you—you're extremely kind, sir," he said. At the museum's lower tram station, a worker in a bright-orange vest had told him that Southwest Airlines was the fastest way to San Francisco on short notice.

When H.G. stepped on the curb, the bus pulled away, enveloping him in a cloud of moist emissions. He waved away the stench, but stayed where he was, bewildered by the crush of humanity—lines everywhere, a sense of desperation, and noise. It made Charing Cross station and downtown London seem like oases of solitude. *It is Sunday, for God's sake. Shouldn't they all be in church?*

He thought of the Getty Museum's futuristic beauty, its celebration of art and design that had lifted his spirits and made him feel positively good about man and technology in the twenty-first century. That did not jibe with this grubby center for aeroplanes, claustrophobic with people, reverberating with noise. *One can only hope the museum is not a mere enclave in a Philistine world.*

An unusually loud roar made him look up. Resembling an enormous pterodactyl, an aircraft nosed skyward, wisps of the overcast diffusing its blue and silver skin. Given his trip to 1979, he had already seen what had become of the Wright Brothers and their infernal flying machine. Now, he was surprised that the aeroplane looked much the same as it had some thirty years ago. He wasn't sanguine about its future then, having learned about World War I and its progeny. In fact, after returning home, he had decided that it was time to warn the public with a serialized novel he would call *The War in the Air*. His publisher, Frederick Macmillan, expected dueling hot-air balloons or "flying sausages"—those hydrogen blimps that sometimes floated above Berlin and the Black Forest—but Wells had said no, I am going to write about the world's deteriorating political situation and the subsequent horrors of airships bombing cities and creating mass death and destruction. The blank look from Macmillan told him that he might as well have said—as he had before— time machines.

He watched the metallic pterodactyl until it disappeared above the overcast and hoped that such a magnificent airship was a sign that in the last three decades mankind had abandoned war as a commonplace excuse for failed diplomacy. He then looked back at the frantic people of 2010 and couldn't help but wonder if diplomacy hadn't been abandoned instead. He scowled in frustration. None of this was helping him get to San Francisco or a wife who might or might not be badly injured.

Thinking of Amy, he made his way inside the terminal, read the signs—electronic and otherwise—was stopped by one in particular.

What in God's name does "terrorist threat, yellow" mean? Are there cowards among us or does the notice refer to some collective emotional instability caused by overcrowding? Or perhaps a modern disease? He hadn't a clue. Nor did he notice the security guards, hungry for incidents. They watched the crowds relentlessly, yet saw nothing unusual, and settled for a restless boredom.

H.G. got in the queue for ticket purchases. It barely moved, giving him time for a closer look at the humans around him. Almost all were physically much larger than people from his world, and he assumed that advances in medicine and nutrition must be the reason. He didn't notice that many had fat rolling over their belts, so fascinated was he by their attachments. Half of them had wires hanging from their heads, tiny electronic devices in their hands that lit up when touched, and even more had those ubiquitous boxes at their ears which he'd first gawked at when his shuttle bus had collected passengers. Obviously, these people were using the grandchildren of their telephones.

Who the devil are they all talking to?

A woman in front of him bent over to fish a candy bar from her overnight bag—*Luggage with wheels, how marvelous!* Her sleeveless shirt rode up from her denim trousers—in 1979 they'd called them jeans—revealing a butterfly tattoo. Embarrassed, he glanced away, but couldn't stop searching for more tattoos. He saw them all around him— on arms, legs, bellies, necks, even faces—different sizes and designs, some so hideous he had to turn away, others, not so absurd, not so ugly. *Something tribal must be going on in this century, when tribal ceremony shouldn't be necessary in a civilized world. It must be an aberration, a ritual left over from a useless tradition or a mindless throwback to the Aurignacian period.*

He heard small, tinny voices behind him and turned curiously. A man wearing tinted glasses and a cap ridiculously askew was riveted to something electronic in his hand. H.G. peered over his shoulder. The man was absorbed with a drama on a miniature screen, oblivious of the wait and frustration all around him. H.G. couldn't hold back a huge grin, a warm feeling that validated the "what if" in his soul. In 1899, he had imagined "a moving picture player" in his novel *When the Sleeper Wakes*, a leisure-time device for when one was not near a theater or concert hall or, say, a discreet hotel room with a pretty girl.

The man noticed him and removed the bud from his ear. He winked. "If you go to an Apple store, they got 'em on sale."

"Ah, yes," said H.G. as if sharing a joke, "between the peaches and plums, right . . . ?"

The man gave him a weird look and turned away, but now H.G. was staring at a girl, wondering if the spot on her nose was a diamond or a pimple. Rather than seem unduly strange, he asked, "Excuse me, miss, is there an exchequer who changes currency at the counter?"

"You gotta go to an ATM."

Helpless, he was about to ask what on earth did she mean when a cheerful, musical voice spared him the humiliation.

"I know where they are."

He found himself staring up at a woman with cobalt eyes, Medusa-like black hair and perfect breasts behind a pale-blue, V-neck blouse above tight, faded jeans.

She led him toward double doors. "I'm Amber Reeves."

"Herbert. . . . Herbert Wells."

The terminal was much larger past the doors—glass walls soaring up to glass ceilings, wide escalators like in 1979 lifting hordes of people, more people descending on the other side. Thousands of conversations counterpointed with PA announcements and aircraft rumbling over-head echoed in the space.

"Where you going?" she asked.

"I'm meeting my wife in San Francisco."

"Cool."

He didn't notice her puzzled frown—he felt a sudden urge and had to find a bathroom. He looked for a "gents" or "ladies" sign and missed the sudden change in her expression as well.

"You know what? I'm going there, too." Now she was wearing a beau-tiful, excited smile.

Beginning to perspire, he took off his coat, dropped it on a plastic chair and turned to her as if he hadn't heard. "You know, I really must find a loo."

"You walked right past it." She nodded at an alcove. "Men's room."

He half-ran for the restroom, forgetting his coat. She picked it up and followed. He glanced at her as he backpedaled in the men's room, and she pointed at his coat over her arm.

"I've got your jacket. No worries."

The hallway opened on a row of scratched, industrial-gray stalls and block-modern urinals, shadowless under the green-tinged light from fluorescents that had fascinated him in 1979. What drew him here was noise from a blower on the wall, a miniature, chrome version of the monster on the worker's back in the garden at the Getty Museum. A man stood before it rubbing his hands, and H.G. wondered if the device was blowing a disinfectant. As he relieved himself, he thought that a remarkably good idea, then crossed to the line of sinks and washed his hands. He glanced around for the hand towels and saw none. Bewildered, his hands dripping, he went in a stall, and chose a seat cover as a towel as opposed to toilet paper, was both horrified and amused by crude drawings on the wall depicting female and male genitalia in stark ugliness. Names, phone numbers and obscene slogans framed the drawings making a mockery of H.G.'s lofty assumptions about twenty-first-century man.

When he came out of the stall, he saw another man at the sinks. The man removed a silver and midnight-blue object clipped to his ear and began washing his face. H.G. guessed the device was modern technology's answer for hearing loss. Pleased, he went to the blower on the wall, tentatively pushed the button and bathed his own face in what he assumed was wonderfully clean air.

The man finished, looked around for towels, but like H.G., found none. Irritated, he dried his face on his T-shirt, then hurried from the men's room, and H.G. saw that he had forgotten the thing for his ear.

"Sir!" H.G. picked it up and went after the man. "I say, excuse me, old chap!"

The man turned in the hallway.

"You've forgotten your ear trumpet." H.G. grinned and waved the Bluetooth. "It's quite impressive, I must say."

The man gave him a look that ran the gamut from astonishment to annoyance to fear, then took his device and ran from the men's room, not a hint of gratitude in his manner.

A Minute Earlier

Trembling, clutching his coat to her breast, Amber Reeves had gone
to the plastic chairs, sat down and tried to compose herself. She was
certain of it—now that she had seen him up close. He was the same
man as the one in the photo display at the museum, though she hadn't
quite been prepared for the adorable bushy mustache, not to mention
the eyes, an uncompromising, limpid blue. He was H. G. Wells. If not
for that brilliant white flash, then the figure running from the time machine in the central gallery, she would've thought she was losing her
mind. *They say time travel isn't possible, but, hey, a thousand years ago
flying to Paris wasn't, either.* She had followed him from the Getty on
the airport shuttle bus. Halfway to LAX, she remembered the lieutenant's meeting, called his voice mail and left a message saying that
her car wouldn't start, and the Milan was the worst car ever built. Then
she felt guilty, yet only for a moment, the incarnation of H. G. Wells
and a strange new reality much too overwhelming. *I'll make it up to
the lieutenant,* she thought fleetingly, then had forgotten that, too, the
scratchy wool of H.G.'s coat now against her face.

She cast a furtive glance at the men's room, gathered her courage,
then quickly riffled through his coat. The small woman's purse in an

outside pocket was downright weird and inexplicable, so she left it there, but in another pocket she found a red-leather folder. She opened it, her hands shaking. Inside was a single sheet of dog-eared linen paper bearing His Majesty's crest and formal script indicating that it was a passport from the year 1903. Visas from France, Italy, Germany, Switzerland, the Balkans and Russia were stamped in the margin obscuring each other, yet clearly written in the center was:

Herbert George Wells (a British subject)
Date of Birth: 21 September 1866
Occupation: Writer.

The last space on the margin had been taken up by a visa from the USA, and she wondered what he had done here in April, 1906, and who he had met. She put his passport away and opened his wallet. A London library card and a membership card in the Fabian Society fell out and fluttered to the floor. She swore softly, scooped them up, was putting the cards back when a letter fell. She picked it up, stopped. Handwriting on pink stationery struck her as oddly familiar, but before she could look further, he was coming out of the men's room. She stuffed the letter inside and got the wallet back in the coat pocket before he saw her. He started toward the chairs, surreptitiously removing bits of paper toilet-seat cover that had stuck to his hands.

"Thank you so much," he said, smiling bashfully. "I do apologize for the inconvenience." He took his coat, then hesitated and turned back. Her eyes held him. "You said you were going to San Francisco as well . . . ?"

She didn't know if he was relieved to have someone along for the ride or reluctant—but if she hesitated, she wasn't sure she'd ever get another chance. She thought of the lieutenant again, of her job, and then a vision of herself cynical, gray-haired and used in a police lab twenty years from now flashed through her brain. "Yes. . . . Yes, I am."

"Jolly good," he said automatically.

She waited while he put his coat on and straightened it, smiled with admiration. "Love your jacket."

"Oh, yes, thank you."

She touched his sleeve. "Harris tweed, right?"

"Why, yes," he said, startled, "I got it last year."

"Savile Row?" she said, taking an educated guess.

When he gaped at her, she knew that—at least for the moment—she had him. Starting for the escalators, she resisted the urge to take his hand. Already, his tweed jacket aside, she felt an inexplicable connection between them that left her giddy, that she couldn't quite fathom. She was powerless to stop whatever was happening to her. It went beyond chemistry—of that, she was sure. Her emotions were more like reverence, that she had beheld a futuristic resurrection. She was in the presence of history and fame combined in a handsome, erudite man with beautiful blue eyes who had apparently stepped out of a time machine. She couldn't let the moment slip away. Or him. Then a voice inside bubbled up: *Okay, he's out of his time. You're out of place. You've always been out of place. Perfect. Except what am I supposed to do? I'm not afraid; I don't want to run.* Then it came to her: *Shepherd the man.*

Blushing, she stepped off the escalator, waited for him, turned and saw a security check looming ahead. She sensed that the metal detector was a bad idea, but they had already gotten suspicious looks from an airport cop coming up the escalator behind them, so she continued forward. She filled a tray with her car keys and change, placed shoes and backpack on the conveyor for the X-ray machine, gestured for Wells to do the same. She stepped through the square archway, turned, gave him a sympathetic nod, waited helplessly.

Likewise, he folded his coat and put it on the belt, but had trouble with his shoes. The guards frowned. In fact, everybody frowned because the little man in the ridiculous wool suit was holding up the line, but finally he got his Oxfords off, fed the machine and stepped hesitantly through the metal detector. The alarms went off. Surprised, he jumped back, but the squat, heavy woman guard caught him and pushed him back through the archway while her partner reached for his walkie.

"Empty your pockets, sir."

He blanched, then protested indignantly, "I beg your pardon?"

"Empty your pockets."

"Excuse me, but—"

"Empty your pockets!"

He looked to Amber on the other side of the metal detector, but all she could offer was a nod and a frantic gesture for him to do as he was told.

With great reluctance, he took out the special key and placed it on the belt, watched painfully as it disappeared into the maw of the X-ray machine, exhaled with relief when it emerged on the other side. So intent, he didn't notice Amber's gaze, her utter fascination with the key and what it might open. He quickly snatched it up, put his shoes back on and strode off alongside her, not dignifying the guards with a rude remark.

"I understand that security is obviously an issue here, but must they humiliate you?" he asked, the special key again safely in his pocket.

They were headed toward the gates, Amber walking very slowly, not sure what to do next. He was determined to fly to San Francisco, but without modern identification, no one would let him near an airplane. He didn't know that, of course, and she worried that if she tried to coax him away from the terminal, she would frighten him off, then spend the rest of her life wondering what might have been with her and this lovely incarnation of H. G. Wells.

People swept past in airport mode, jostling for position.

"Why is everyone in such a rush?"

"That's just the way it is here." She reassured him with a smile. "There's flights to San Francisco almost every hour, so you don't have to—"

He was staring at a backlit red, white and yellow sign above a large fast-food kiosk. "McDonald's," he said nostalgically.

She frowned with disbelief. *You must be kidding.*

"Scottish cuisine, right?" His eyes twinkled.

She wanted to say, *Where the hell have you been?* but she *knew,* and he didn't know that she knew, so she said nothing. Nevertheless, he chuckled, and she realized that he was playing with her. She blushed, totally lost. She hadn't a clue that when he had come to San Francisco in 1979, his first meal in the twentieth century had been a quarter-pounder with cheese.

"Are you hungry?" he asked.

They sat in the window behind a sparsely populated gate, eating burgers and fries. Although he hadn't asked, she seized the opportunity to tell him about herself, yet didn't know if he was listening, for he couldn't stop gazing at the jets lumbering gracefully up to the strange tunnels, some pulling out for the runways, giant wings passing in slow motion with hundreds of blank faces in tiny windows. As he absorbed this robotic display of life in a new century, she helplessly continued running off at the mouth.

She told him that life as a criminalist was not "as advertised"; rather, it was drudgery in blood and fluids—extracting clues from corpses who would never come back to life no matter how good a job she did while most of her colleagues in the lab couldn't care less. She worked with bush-league technicians primarily interested in money, sports, new cars and shacking up with as many girls (or men) as possible before they retired. To put it mildly, she was disillusioned and longed for the world she had given up.

"What world is that?" he asked, nibbling on a fry that he'd likened to a chip, his eyes still monitoring the aircraft outside.

Turning dreamy, she went on about various graduate schools where she envisioned herself working toward a Ph.D. in literature followed by postgraduate research in the UK. She wanted to travel—she desired a career immersed in culture, surrounded by higher ideals and fascinating people. Suddenly, she stopped and blushed hard. *I sound like I'm auditioning for a role in this man's life. I'm so obvious.*

"Look!" he exclaimed as if he hadn't heard, pointing at an Alaskan

Airlines jet with a giant wolf painted on its tail. "Great Scott, look at that one!"

Deflated, she leaned against the window and realized if she didn't find a way to make herself indispensable, this man—her door to the universe—was going to pass her by, if he hadn't already. She took a breath, then started in as if merely making small talk. "So when does your flight leave?"

"I don't have a ticket yet. I was hoping you might show me where I can exchange some pounds here."

"I don't really know," she said casually, "but I've got my laptop so we can go online and find out."

Confused, he turned to her, not sure what language she was speaking.

She relished having his full attention. "We're cell or 'WiFi' everywhere, but it's that way in London, too. No?" Watching his eyes, teasing him, she unzipped her backpack, started to take out her laptop, then stopped. "Wait. We don't have to do this."

"We don't?" he said helplessly.

"No. I mean, I don't know what your situation is, but can't you just use a credit card?"

Nervous now, he looked back at the aircraft outside and hoped her suggestion would pass, but she pushed on, feigning curiosity.

"Is your wife meeting you in San Francisco?"

"Yes." He nodded vigorously. "Yes, of course."

"How can she be meeting you if she doesn't know what flight you're coming in on?"

"Look, my dear girl, with all due respect, I—"

"Why don't you call her?" She couldn't help herself. Smiling wickedly, she handed him her cell phone, but he backed away as if it carried some electronic disease. "Don't you have the number?"

Nervous now, he inched away from her, shaking his head.

"I do. . . . I've got the number."

"*What?*" he said, astonished.

She nodded and smiled, recalled the pictures of Spade House from the exhibition, the memorabilia in a display case.

"061 Sandgate," she said. "That's Amy's number, isn't it? Amy Catherine Robbins Wells?"

They were in a bar at the terminal, cozy in a booth, buffered from the constant roar of aircraft by thick walls, low lights and Muzak. H.G. was on his second Guinness, relieved that the charade was over and that this lovely young woman wouldn't think he was crazy if and when he told her that he was from 1906. She already knew.

When he was on his first Guinness, he'd asked what had brought her to the Getty Museum at 9:46 A.M., the inconvenient time of his arrival, and she had told him about the murder. Horrified, he came up' out of the booth, but she quickly reassured him that the victim wasn't his wife—she had seen Amy's photograph in the exhibition—no, the victim was a Hispanic security guard, the crime probably gang-related, according to her lieutenant. Still shaken, he declared that he had found Amy's blood in the cabin.

Concerned, Amber had insisted on calling all the emergency rooms in the Brentwood area and now was talking to a dispatcher friend at the police about Amy, describing her as an "old-fashioned tourist" from the UK who was totally unfamiliar with big-city ways. The dispatcher had put Amber on hold.

H.G. stared off at the bright neon signs behind the bar, yet none of it registered. Of course, the murder might be "gang-related," as Amber had said, thus coincidental, but he was not convinced. As he'd speculated in his lab, Amy could have accidentally sent his time machine to infinity. And if she had . . .

Suddenly, Amber covered her phone, looked up quizzically. "What name should I use?"

"What name?"

"I can't very well say Mrs. H. G. Wells."

"Right," he said tentatively.

But she was already back on the phone. "Amy. . . . Amy Catherine Robbins Wells. . . . I know, I know, she's from the UK."

She waited again, tapping the phone with her finger, then finally said, "Unhuh. . . . Thanks, Norm. . . . Sure. . . . You, too." She slid her phone shut and smiled reassuringly. "No news is good news."

He stared at her as if she were speaking gibberish.

She laughed. "Oh, I'm sorry! What I meant was, no one has seen your wife, and if a report comes in from anywhere, they'll call me first, so she's probably okay."

He had no choice but to agree. "Yes, I suppose if she were seriously hurt, she wouldn't have been able to dress her wound, and the authorities would've taken her to what you call an 'ER.' "

"Yep."

He exhaled in a whoosh, gazed off and briefly forgot his fears. He was about to ask her about the complexities of getting an aeroplane ticket when she broke into his thoughts with her hand to her mouth and a sudden blush.

"You do call your wife 'Amy,' don't you?"

"Yes, although she prefers 'Catherine' because her parents insisted upon 'Amy.' Once, she confided to me that she always felt insignificant because her father took it a step further by calling her 'little Amy' and always adding a deprecating laugh." H.G. sipped his beer.

"So why don't you call her 'Catherine'?"

"Ah, Catherine. . . ." He smiled and chuckled. "She reserved that *nom de privé* for her inner self. Catherine is a quiet, fine-spirited stranger in our household. She is Amy, escaped. She has never been part of our union, though I have had glimpses of her at times: she will look at me out of Amy's hazel-brown eyes and quite simply, vanish." He stopped abruptly, annoyed with himself for being so candid with this Amber Reeves of the twenty-first century when he didn't know her at all. He pushed back in the booth, asked defensively, "You're not planning to make a spectacle of me, are you?"

"What?" she said, surprised, then shook her head adamantly. "No, no, I was just asking about names, that's all."

"You're quite certain?"

"Absolutely. No, I would never do that. Never."

"Please understand, I do appreciate recognition, I do like my reading public, but I have no desire to be a sideshow."

"Why would anyone want to put you on display?"

"You have no idea."

"Well, if it were up to me, I'd protect you from that."

"That's quite noble of you, Miss Reeves, but—"

"What's it like?" she asked suddenly. "Is it wonderful?"

He smiled at her naïveté. "It's actually quite dangerous. When you ride the fourth dimension—if that is in fact what it is—you entertain the risk of reformulation errors."

She looked at him quizzically.

"One is vaporized to a mass without space, you see, and then catapulted across universes in the controlled environment of the machine which, I might add, doesn't move unless it is on one of its world tours, becoming a sideshow all its own." He spread his hands. "And the traveler . . . ? I'm sorry to say that there is no guarantee he will arrive at his destination as he once was."

"You seem fine." She sipped her wine spritzer and added, "You seem more than fine."

"I'm lucky," he said somberly. "I'm sure that Amy is lucky. You might not be so lucky."

She absently swirled her drink and frowned petulantly for reasons she didn't yet fully understand.

"Some of us cannot fathom being reduced to nothingness."

"Hey, it's not something you think about all the time."

He finished his beer, glanced at his pocket watch. "It's something we can discuss at a later time, perhaps, but right now I really must go to San Francisco and find Amy."

"They'll never let you on an airplane with a passport from 1903."

He looked off thoughtfully. "Can you fix that?"

"I can fix that."

"Well, I suppose I do need an assistant. A secretary."

"Am I hired?"

He nodded. They slid from the booth and started out.

"But whatever you do, you must not tell me about a life I've not yet lived."

"Oookay."

"Are we clear on that?"

She nodded, said innocently, "I promise."

"Because if you do, you will change my life irrevocably, and no matter what universe we're in, I'd prefer that didn't happen."

"I promise. . . . To be good," she added inexplicably.

Amber knew a sergeant in Forgery who was more than anxious to date her. She called him from the rental-car place, exchanged innuendos, and he arranged for "express service" from a small-time felon in Venice. H.G., curious about 2010 social decorum—or the lack of it—wondered if her innuendos meant she would actually go to bed with this cop.

"Nope," she replied with a laugh. "He's too young for me."

If he got the subtext, he let it pass. He hadn't come 103 years risking reformulation errors for another passade. He could find trysts whenever he wanted in his own time. He had come here for Amy, the mother of his children and a renewed commitment; he had come here for his time-crossed lover-shadow, and hoped that she was indeed in this universe.

With H.G. preoccupied by the downright ugly architecture and the strange, animated people on the streets, Amber drove to Venice, found Dudley Court near the beach, and—miracle of modern miracles— a parking space.

As she pulled in, he suddenly grabbed the edges of the seat, a happy, distracted grin splitting his features. She followed his gaze. Angled in front of her car was a glistening lime-green Kawasaki Ninja motorcycle that to the unaccustomed eye could have been a metallic grasshopper designed for spaceflight. Before she could say anything, he jumped from the car and went to it reverently. He gingerly touched the controls, ran his hand over the seat, kneeled down and peered at the engine.

"Let's go," said Amber, looking around nervously.

"I have one of these, you know. . . . The design is much more primitive, but the concept is identical."

She rolled her eyes. "C'mon, okay? Somebody's gonna think you're trying to steal it."

As if on cue, the owner came out of the corner house and walked toward them, suspicious. "Can I help you?"

Grinning, H.G. backed away and straightened up, a faraway look in his eyes. "This is a beautiful machine."

"Yeah, I know."

"I have one at home. A Triumph Model 3HP."

The owner gave him an incredulous look, but before H.G. could take it further, Amber grabbed his hand and pulled him away. She led him up the walk to a renovated bungalow freshly painted royal blue with red trim, the small fenced yard overflowing with flowers and exotic plants. On the porch, she could sense that he was curious to find out what sort of criminal lived in this well-kept, almost charming place.

Irving Bagley, aka "Xerox," showed them into a living room with antique furniture, Tiffany lamps and reproductions on the walls all of which screamed period decor. He shook hands "correctly" with Amber—she worked for the man, after all—then looked at H.G. and was taken aback. He was used to people staring at *him*, but that wasn't the case here. *He* was staring at Wells. Xerox chuckled.

"Dress rehearsal or costume party?"

"I beg your pardon?"

"Your threads, dude."

H.G. studied Xerox's silver and gold piercings, the paisley tattoos creeping up his neck, lavender boot-cut jeans all set off by a mauve silk shirt and dreadlocks that hung below his shoulders. He was trying to reconcile the difference between the Negroes he'd seen in Washington, D.C., in April, 1906, and this black man of 2010, not realizing that the difference went far beyond style and sociology.

Xerox added, "You look weird, you know what I'm saying?"

"No more than you, sir."

Xerox cackled hysterically and held out the tail of his silk shirt as if it were at fault. "Ernesto got it for me. Ernesto's always confusing good taste with blind emotion." He turned to the study behind French doors that were slightly ajar. "We have visitors, Ernesto." He turned back. "Ernesto's my associate. . . . He's a freelance locksmith."

"One moment, Xerox," called Ernesto.

"Xerox . . . ?" said H.G. "I say, is that a Greek name?"

Xerox and Amber exchanged looks, but then Ernesto, a small, lithe Salvadorian dressed in designer T-shirt and jeans, stuck his head in the living room, smiled and waved before disappearing into the kitchen.

Minutes later, they were in Xerox's office—a white-on-white room with matching computers, copiers, cameras and other duplication machines, the ambience so bright that Xerox put on shades, and H.G. had to shield his eyes from the recessed halogens. While Xerox photographed H.G., then made him a fake passport and driver's license, he offered up a running commentary on other services, including bogus Visa and American Express cards. When H.G. apologized that he had only pounds sterling and would have to change them and then come back, Xerox wouldn't hear of it. For a slightly higher fee, he, too, changed currencies.

"One-stop shopping, my man," said Xerox. "We are into convenience." He followed them out onto the porch. "We do keys, too," he added proudly, waving good-bye. "Car keys, any make or model, anything high-tech, even the plastic ones. Price negotiable."

"What exactly was he talking about?" said H.G. on their way back to the car.

"I think he was trying to sell us keys. You give him a key, he copies it. Or, if you don't have one, you give him, say, the VIN number of a car you want, he hacks into a protected site, downloads the specs, and voilà, you get the key and then the car."

"Rather imaginative."

"I'm sorry," said Amber, apologizing for Xerox.

"Whatever for?" H.G. replied. "The world has always had clever, not to mention sartorially different criminals."

"True, but they weren't always technological geniuses."

H.G. glanced at her, impressed. "Good point, my dear, but that doesn't bode well for your world now, does it?"

On their way back to LAX, they detoured to a strip mall and a clothing store. In the mirror, H.G. was aghast at himself in T-shirt with logo, designer jeans and baseball cap.

"I'm sorry," Amber said. "I mean, I love Harris tweed, but everybody was staring at you."

"Is respectability so rare in this day and age?" he said defensively.

"It would definitely slow us down."

Seeking a compromise, she picked out a more traditional pale-blue shirt, matching tie and a khaki summer suit.

While he was trying on his new clothes, she called Lieutenant Holland hoping to get his voice mail, but the man himself came on the line, and she apologized for missing his strategy meeting, then stuttered her way through a tale about "Aunt Harriet." (She didn't have an aunt.) After "Triple A" got her car started, she was on her way to headquarters when she learned that her aunt was in the hospital. Holland took the news stoically, said he would have Parker Center send over a couple of criminalists from the pool, and hopefully they would cover her absence. When she apologized again, he added that families always came first with him, and she could take as much time as she needed. Relieved he was so accommodating, she said she'd call in when she could and hung up.

She grinned. She knew the lieutenant liked her and appreciated the quality of her work, but the news that he was having two technicians replace her was the ultimate compliment. It was almost enough to make her miss her job and the ghoulish buzz of crime scenes, but given H. G. Wells and his time machine, she might never set foot in a police lab again. She blushed. *I should be so lucky.*

She insisted that the salesclerk bag the Harris tweeds; then she stowed them in her trunk, and they were back at the airport in three hours. In the Southwest terminal, Amber excused herself to buy a toothbrush and toiletries, then returned to the waiting area and gave her companion some Handi Wipes just in case his 1906 immune system wasn't ready for the germs of the future. He read the box, recalled antibiotics from 1979 and grinned.

"How clever," he said, "sort of like a wipe-on penicillin."

An hour later, they had returned the rental car and were on a flight to San Francisco, H.G. glued to the window like a small child. The jet surged up through the overcast, climbed more gradually over the Pacific, then dropped in a succession of air pockets, making him giggle with surprise. He clutched the armrests and turned to Amber, his face shining with joy.

"How absolutely marvelous! We're not disintegrating!"

5:48 P.M., Sunday, June 20, 2010

"I'm sorry, we have no listing for an Amy Catherine Robbins."

"What about Amy Robbins? Or just A. Robbins, perhaps?"

"No, ma'am, nothing in the 415 area code. . . . I do have a Judith on Green Street or a Susan on Brazil. . . ."

Jaclyn had figured out how to turn on the cell phone. Now she closed it and slid it in her pocket, feeling modern and superior. She pushed back in the lounge chair, gazed out French doors at the porch, the lengthening shadows in the yard, the flowering bushes turning black in the dying light. What to do, what to do. She had to find the girl, for the girl was the road to Wells, and Wells had the special key that unlocked time and the universe beyond.

Her eyes came back to a wall of bookshelves sans books in Michael Trattner's family room. They were littered with chic pottery, family and wedding pictures that identified Michael's wife as Heather. *How perfectly sweet.* Jaclyn clicked on the gigantic flat television screen in the center. A trio of self-important whorish blond girls were singing the praises of a new cosmetic surgery technique as if it were the answer to the world's problems. Jaclyn shook her head, disgusted. *Jack would've commented, "If you ever meet me in a dark alley, I'll show you some cosmetic surgery. Yours truly will put your anus where your mouth is.*"

Earlier, she had taken a furtive yet hot shower, then gotten dressed. From Heather Trattner's walk-in closet she'd chosen a long-sleeved sweater and jeans so that if she found herself outside in the night, no one would see her toxic glow—herself included. Then she was curious and turned off the lights. She looked at her torso in the dark. The glow was gone, and she sagged with relief. She had no idea why, other than the fact that she was a long way from the wasteland of infinity.

In the kitchen she had found a knife block. Wüsthof knives. She'd selected an eight-inch serrated slicing knife—and a sheath for it—the whole time waxing nostalgic at the collection of fine German steel, for the same firm had made the surgical blades she'd used on the streets of Whitechapel lo those many years ago. Heather Trattner had good taste. Jaclyn chuckled ironically. In life and perhaps in death, too.

Now she flipped channels on the remote, annoyed that in the thirty-one years since she'd been gone, she could find nothing interesting on the television. The endless succession of talking heads was banal, and how many explosions from wars in the Mideast could one watch before that, too, became boring? She wondered about the paradox: In 1979, there had been only a dozen channels; in 2010, there were hundreds; logically, one would've expected more variety. Not so.

She saw headlights reflected through the living room windows, then heard a car pull in the driveway. She dropped the remote, picked up the razor-sharp Wüsthof and ran for the front of the house, her little feet whisking on carpet, then tile. She slipped into the coat closet off the foyer, took a deep breath and waited for the key in the front door.

The kitchen door opened instead.

"Hi, honey, I'm home," Heather announced.

Good, bloody Christ, doesn't anyone use their front doors anymore? Jaclyn heard the rustle of bags placed on kitchen counters. The element of surprise was crucial, so she wondered if she should go after the bitch now or wait. The problem with surprise was that inevitably one missed the foreplay of the chase, the delicious thrill of witnessing a victim's helpless terror. Regardless, she waited.

"I got tacos from Baja Fresh. Why don't you open some wine, and we'll eat in the family room?"

Jaclyn squeezed her thighs together and enjoyed playing the voyeur to Heather Trattner's last, unguarded moments. Unawares, she touched herself with the butt of the knife, released a ragged sigh. Soon, Heather would be annoyed, then uncertain and apprehensive, then —

"Michael . . . ?"

A pause.

Heather started unloading her bags, their rustle irritating and unusually loud, designed to bring a response from somewhere in the house. She stopped, listened.

"Michael . . . ?"

A profound silence.

"You're not home." Heather exhaled heavily and went through her purse. "Where the hell are you, Michael?"

A tiny, electronic beep resonated from the kitchen, which Jaclyn didn't understand until the cell phone in her pocket started ringing, and she realized with horror that Heather was calling her husband.

Jaclyn slapped repeatedly at the phone, dug in her pocket with both hands, her knife clattering to the closet floor. Frantic, she got the phone out, but it went on ringing, shattering the silence and giving her away. Finally, she opened it. The ringing stopped. She held her breath and stared at the backlit display. Then a small, anxious voice:

"Michael? Did I hear your phone . . . ?"

Jaclyn felt her heart thudding.

"Are you in the house . . . ? Michael . . . ?" She paused. "For God's sake, Michael, I'm talking to you! What is wrong with you?"

Jaclyn flipped the phone shut, held her breath again, waited for normalcy, for Heather to resume her busy work in the kitchen. Instead, the phone rang again.

And again.

Cursing, she opened and closed it and killed the ringing, but too late. She was reaching for the knife and coming out of the closet when Heather walked into the foyer, saw her and screamed.

Heather ran back toward the kitchen. Jaclyn went after her, dove at her in the kitchen archway, but missed. Heather pushed a chair between them, then hurled a jar from the island that glanced off Jaclyn's head, but she was immediately up again, grinning at the violence, this the overture of her favorite ballet.

Sobbing with fear, Heather bolted for the family room, but a quicker Jaclyn caught her trying to go out the French doors. Screaming hysterically, she turned to defend herself, but Jaclyn feinted and kicked her hard in the stomach. She doubled over. Jaclyn hammered her in the head with the butt of the knife, and she went down.

Jaclyn stood over her, took huge breaths and swallowed an overflow of saliva. Her body tingled with an electric warmth. Her nipples were hard against the sweater and her groin moist. Did she smell of sex or was she imagining that faintly bittersweet, pungent odor?

Meanwhile, the TV droned on softly, a lady in a chef's costume icing a white cake with a French vanilla glaze, smiling into the room, blind to the scene unfolding before her.

Dazed, Heather stirred.

Jaclyn grabbed her by her reddish blond hair, snapped her head back and held the knife to her throat.

Heather started to resist.

"No, no, no." Jaclyn pressed on the knife and pinpricked her neck. Heather felt a trickle of blood run down her chest, whined fearfully and went limp. "Please, love, don't swoon on me," whispered Jaclyn, "not when we have work to do."

Heather looked at her blankly and didn't move.

"If you do as I say, you'll live. If you don't, they'll discover your lovely body somewhat obscenely rearranged."

Heather nodded that she understood, her red-rimmed hazel eyes wide and dull. "What have you done with Michael?"

Jaclyn cocked her head and smiled. "We don't have to worry about Michael anymore."

Heather began crying—yet softly, so as not to upset this monster who had a knife, who radiated a messianic glow.

———

A half-hour later, they were at Heather's desktop computer on the secretary desk in the kitchen, a terrified Heather working the mouse, Jaclyn behind her with the knife.

"On the television these people were going on about this phenomenon that they called the Internet, and at Starbucks most of the customers were staring at screens with light dancing on their faces, so there must be something to it. . . . I'd do it myself except I've been out of touch, and what's more, I love seeing housewives of a certain station being forced to do someone's else's bidding." She chuckled.

"But, but what do you want?"

"Are you daft, Heather? I want you to find Amy Catherine Robbins."

"I'm sorry," she said helplessly. "I mean, I'm not very good at this stuff. I can do email, but that's about it."

"Look at the screen, you twit," said Jaclyn impatiently.

Heather obeyed.

Jaclyn pointed with her knife. "That says 'search,' does it not?"

Heather nodded.

"Then *search*."

Heather Googled the name, and in less than three seconds, 970,000 results came up, most of the first ten highlighting the name Amy Catherine Robbins in Web sites about H. G. Wells, mentioning her as his second wife. Heather stared at the screen and had no clue what to do next.

"Well?"

"There's nine hundred and seventy thousand references."

"Then hadn't you better get started?"

"What am I supposed to be looking for?"

"She's somewhere in San Francisco. I want to know exactly where."

Heather refined her search, and this time got only 516,000 results, the first being the Web site of a pediatrician named Amy Chang. Helpless, Heather started crying again.

Jaclyn sighed impatiently, surprised herself with a twinge of sympathy, although she couldn't imagine ever being so helpless. "Why on earth must you cry? That never changes the way things are, don't you understand?"

Confused, Heather blinked up at her through her tears as if asking for a reprieve. Jaclyn wondered why she didn't just end it right then, knowing in her bones that this pathetic, privileged housewife would be of no use to her. But she couldn't just yet; she wanted to give Heather a chance; she wanted to be *reasonable*. Right then she realized that she, too, was acting like a woman and seemed powerless to stop herself. *Bloody hell.*

"Why don't you try another reference," Jaclyn hissed, "while you still have fingers on your hands . . . ?"

Heather gulped and went back to the search engine. Jaclyn spied the name H. G. Wells on the screen and—forgetting herself—bent over Heather's shoulder for a closer look. She was reading the result's brief description when Heather slammed the mouse into her face and shoved her hard.

Jaclyn hit the wall, lost her balance and fell, knocking the flat screen off the desk. She was scrambling to get up when Heather swung the chair and hit her in the head. Jaclyn went down again, the knife flying from her hand. She was on her hands and knees feeling for it when Heather kicked the knife away, lifted the chair again.

Jaclyn rolled just before the chair smashed into the floor and splintered. She caught Heather by an ankle and jerked her feet out from under her.

Heather landed on her back, her head smacking the tile. She gasped with pain, yet managed to get up. Unsteady, she staggered, recovered her balance, reached for another chair, but Jaclyn had found the knife.

She brought it up with all her strength and drove it between Heather's legs.

Heather shrieked and fell, writhed in pain, knew in a flash that she would die, and her hands instinctively clawed for salvation at some unseen force above. Then she went limp and began choking on her own blood.

Jaclyn straddled her form and watched her die, imagined that the knife buried between her legs was an extension of her own body. Indeed, she felt at one with Heather—beautifully connected in pain and death, for how else could one explain the ecstasy, the utter release? She laughed low and in her head, heard the melody from that long-lost music box. *Penny. You lovely little whore.* Her excitement waned; her breathing slowed. She closed her eyes and smiled nostalgically. For one beautiful moment, she no longer felt like a woman.

The kitchen lights had startled Jaclyn. A little flip of the switch, and the entire kitchen was bathed with a diffused illumination that had brought on a giggle of surprise. She was used to working in the darkness. Now she appreciated the brightness and felt a deep satisfaction from her "assignation" with Heather, whom she was cutting up in the stainless-steel kitchen sink.

She'd found a box of "Hefty" one-zip storage bags in the pantry. She had most of Heather's body parts removed and bagged—the head was washed and clean and quite lovely on the dish rack—except she wasn't sure exactly what to do with Heather. Granted, the torso was perfect in that it reminded her of Venus de Milo, but, alas, Venus had already been done—no thanks to some Greek artisan from the second century B.C. Jaclyn frowned and put the knife down, frustrated. Butchering Heather Trattner had become busywork. No matter what she did with the remains, she was no closer now to finding Amy Catherine Robbins—hence, Wells—than she had been when she'd run from the Getty Museum.

She glanced at the secretary desk. The computer had shut itself off, its monitor broken on the floor, a greenish liquid-crystal fluid seeping from behind the screen. No help there. After she disposed of Heather, perhaps she should return to Starbucks, observe the customers for a while and pick up a gentleman who seemed comfortable with his computer.

She went back to the torso and gazed at its breasts, fascinated that they were so shapely and alluring even in death. Always the surgeon, ever curious, she cut them open, then suddenly stepped back, her eyes going wide with astonishment. She howled with laughter at this post-modern housewife-whore, this would-be Venus de Milo.

Two silicone implants slid down the torso, leaving a bloody trail.

7:27 P.M., *Sunday, June 20, 2010*

"Do you ever worry about earthquakes?" said H.G.

"No," said Amber, "not really."

"They do still happen."

"So do fires and floods."

"Someday I should think that governments would be advanced enough to prevent all that, yet obviously, not in 2010."

"No, but now the Japanese can actually predict earthquakes."

He raised his eyebrows at the news. *Indubitably reassuring if one's in Tokyo, but what about San Francisco, traditionally a hotbed of seismic disturbances?* They were on the Bayshore Freeway in a rental car speeding north toward that very same city, H.G.'s euphoria over his first flight having been replaced by anxiety. He had never given much thought to natural disasters—man-made catastrophes were his forte—yet he couldn't ignore the fact that a mere two months before he left, the 1906 earthquake and fires had devastated San Francisco. Now Amy was here somewhere on a mission to save her family before another quake, supposedly the mother of them all, would level this fair city for good, and he had no desire to end up at its epicenter.

"I was in the '94 quake," Amber said brightly.

He looked at her quizzically.

"The Northridge quake. L.A. It woke me up and threw me out of bed and broke Momma's ugly teacups." She laughed. "It was like a vacation. We got the whole week off from school."

"So you were . . . nine or ten?"

"Eleven."

"I recall living in a moldy basement when I was eleven," he said softly. "My mum was a maid at Up Park." He turned to her. "So that makes you twenty-six."

"Yep. And you're—wait, don't tell me, don't tell me!" She was visualizing the exhibition and his passport. "You're . . . forty."

"Not quite," he said, then smiled shrewdly. "I'm actually thirty-nine going on one hundred and forty-three."

Surprised, she burst out laughing, glanced at him with awe and tenderness in her eyes before looking back at the highway, falling silent, touched by the moment. He hadn't noticed. His anxiety was gone, and he was enjoying his witticism, complemented by the marvelous ride, the speed, the red and blue lights from the car's dash suggesting a spaceship that he might want to build someday. *Of course, I'll need a bigger laboratory and—* He stopped, annoyed at his daydreaming when he still had yet to repair *The Utopia*'s Destination Indicator, when he had no clue about Amy.

"We have to start looking for my wife."

"I know. When we get to the hotel, I'll go online."

"Online?"

"You know, computers. Cyberspace."

"Ah, yes." He gazed out at the lights, briefly preferring the primitive technology of 1906. "Citizens have become softheaded in this century. If they didn't have their ubiquitous electronic boxes, they wouldn't be able to function."

She chuckled and said knowingly, "Soon, you'll be one of us."

He recoiled. "Then I suppose I should thank God for *The Utopia*."

"If you built it today, microchips and all, I'll bet it wouldn't be much bigger than my laptop."

"God forbid." Suddenly, he was nervous. "I say, where are you taking me?"

"Like I said, to the hotel."

"Hotel?"

"Did you want to sleep in the car?"

"It wouldn't surprise me if it transformed into a shelter of some kind," he said defensively.

"Some of them do," she said smugly, then added, "We could've stayed in L.A. and looked for your wife online if you hadn't been so stubborn."

"I never would've forgiven myself if I hadn't *flown*, my dear girl. Besides, you may be able to locate Amy through the magic of your Internet, but I doubt that you can shrink her to a speck of vapor and bring her back from San Francisco to Los Angeles."

"Huh?"

"Somebody has to go get her, do they not?"

Amber had called ahead for a reservation at a Marriott, H.G. insisting on two rooms since he had no desire to sleep on a rollaway bed or on the floor. She had taken 527, and he was across the hall in 529, but now they were in her room at the desk-table, looking on the Internet for Amy. Amber played the keyboard like a virtuoso, methodically, yet quickly following result after result.

H.G. gaped at the process. This buffed black and gray laptop, this little crystal ball of a machine, had no parallel in his world. *Great Scott, it has no wires!* Indeed, he was familiar with Edison's alkaline storage battery—this laptop must run on a smaller version of same—so it wasn't the power source that baffled him. Rather: How had it connected with some infinitely complex spiderweb of similar computers? Unless all of these brightly colored "pages" as Amber called them were contained within its box, and if so, then they weren't really looking for anything— it was already here.

"Where the devil are those images . . . actually coming from?"

"Cyberspace."

"Ah."

He had no clue what she was talking about, yet went on staring and hoping for a glimmer of understanding. *The laptop must have connection nodes,* he thought, *which transmit radio or microwaves, hence information to this cyberspace which in turn sends them back or somewhere else. How very clever. I wonder where this cyberspace is?* He imagined an enormous Internet module that balanced and danced with radio waves and electrical impulses. Or perhaps it was thousands of similar modules stacked one on top of the next, housed in a gigantic building complex in one of our more enlightened cities. *London would be my guess. Or New York. . . . Maybe even Paris.*

"Where exactly is cyberspace, Miss Reeves?"

Startled, she glanced at him, saw that he was serious and started giggling. She blushed at his naïveté, then couldn't help herself and burst out laughing.

Once his humiliation had passed, H.G. felt somewhat initiated into the Computer Age. If nothing else, he'd gotten past his reticence for this thing they called the Internet. All it had taken was Amber showing him he was already part of it. She had found a Web site about him in late nineteenth-century London, then—with a blur of keystrokes— transported him over a hundred years later to room service in the San Francisco Marriott, face-to-face with an electronic young woman who was asking him what he wanted. Now he couldn't contain his enthusiasm. He didn't consider the danger of homogeneity as he had when he'd first seen television—or the vile and corrupt nature of the human beast, long a staple of his speculative fiction. Blinded by positive thought and the brightly colored results of the process, he paced behind Amber's chair, his own brain fueled with grandiose notions. "This proves it."

"What proves what?" she murmured.

"This thing that you call cyberspace, my dear, proves that the ultimate in communication is upon us which suggests in turn that mankind is basically good. And if man is basically good, then utopia and the world-state must be on the horizon."

She gave him a strange look. "You're kidding."

"I suppose I am being a touch simplistic." He paused, then continued. "I am curious about the names for these so-called dot-coms and URLs, however. . . . What was that one we started with? 'Wewillfindany-bodyrightnow dot com' or something like that?" He threw up his hands. "They strike me as twenty-first-century adulterations of German nouns."

"You're not kidding."

She went back to her laptop, and he sat in the chair beside her and peered over her shoulder. She gave him a sidelong glance, then a smile. "Want to try it?"

"Why not?"

She pushed the computer mouse toward him. He slid it back and forth, and on the screen the arrow shot every which way, an electronic jumping bean.

"Whoa . . . !" she exclaimed.

"Sorry."

"It's not a nineteenth-century skateboard."

She put her hand over his and led him in small, precise movements that propelled the arrow onscreen. So intent was he on the process, he didn't notice her breath catch when she touched him, didn't notice her hand trembling slightly. Eventually, she stopped the arrow over a search result. "Now click."

"Click?"

"The buttons."

He did something that resembled pounding a telegraph key, something indecipherable, and the laptop crashed in a myriad of colors. She gawked at the screen, then giggled and soon was laughing hysterically.

"What in God's name happened?"

"I'm not sure, but I think we're a long way from utopia and a world-state—at least with you pushing the buttons."

Mortified, he watched Amber reboot her laptop. Then she excused herself and went to the bathroom. Alone with the machine, apprehensive, he gazed at the screen—a dark-green glow upon which the word "VISTA" swam in a three-dimensional sea. Infinite knowledge and communication—enlightened tools for citizens of the world—were but a keystroke or a click away despite what Amber or the rest of the human race might think. There were worlds beyond this screen, this portal that rivaled hopscotching along the fourth dimension in his time machine. Giddy, he chuckled. There really wasn't much difference except this little rectangular box with the beveled edges was more convenient. A few magical keystrokes and it whisked your mind wherever in the past, present or future you wanted to go—complete with travel accommodations.

I wonder if I thought of it?

He pressed several keys arbitrarily. The machine went all agog with lurid colors, flashing boxes, jittery sidebars, and then words sliced across the center of the screen informing H.G. that he could lower his home mortgage to 1% by clicking on the button below.

Fortunately, Amber came back in the room, sat down and without even looking went back to "Google" and their search. He read nothing into her aloof behavior, was unaware that he had touched her deeply, and she was trying to restrain herself.

"Okay."

"Where are we?"

"At the San Francisco public library skipping over an abstract of *The Joy Luck Club* by Amy Tan," she said flatly, "and don't ask me how this got in my queue." She took a breath. "There are fourteen hundred and twenty-six copies of her book in the system."

"Who is Amy Tan?"

"Someone who's sold more books than you have."

"Really?"

"Do you mind . . . ? I'm trying to concentrate."

An hour later, despite his wonder at this new technology, H.G. began nodding off, yet there was an edge to his weariness that went beyond looking for Amy in cyberspace. He couldn't shake the nagging reality that he was alone in a strange world and might never see his home again. If he couldn't fix his machine and was indeed stuck in 2010, he hadn't yet seen a place he'd want to call home other than the

Getty Museum. *I could always write speculative articles for them—as I did for the* Pall Mall Gazette *and the* National Observer.

Then he studied Amber's profile lit by the glow from the screen, her cute, upturned nose, full lips and ivory skin. He took comfort in the presence of someone who had been a stranger, deciding that she was much more appealing than his fear or false leads from cyberspace. Impulsive, he leaned forward and kissed her on the cheek.

She looked at him, surprised, and it was all she could do not to kiss him back, full on the lips.

"Thank you for all your help."

Her cheek burned where his lips had touched, and she was speechless. She managed a nod.

"I'm going to my room." He stood up. "I'm quite done in, I must say." He turned at the door and grinned. "I haven't slept in over a century."

At the window, H.G. gazed at the city and remembered it fondly from 1979, when he'd met Amy. He frowned, stroked his mustache, then lifted his chin. Hopefully, 2010 would be an easier time, despite the strong possibility of an earthquake, despite the tedious process of trying to find Amy, despite his nagging fear that she might be injured. His anger that she had left him was fading, and now he missed her sorely. He had to turn away from the window lest San Francisco memories bring on tears and recriminations. He swore to himself that when they were reunited he would make a supreme effort to spend more time with her and the boys and especially to include her in his life away from home instead of automatically looking for some comely lass when he stepped off the train at Charing Cross. Yes, she had been cold and fragile for years, but he hadn't been a loving husband in her company, either. He sighed. Would not a gentle caress, a loving embrace make her strong and beautiful again?

"I love you, Amy," he whispered to the room.

He smiled and resumed his gaze out the window. Yes, they'd fallen in love in this city despite the horror of Dr. Leslie John Stephenson one step ahead and leaving a trail of corpses for them and the San Francisco police. When H.G. was being cynical, he'd think of that time as one of those mystery cruises with whodunit games in the parlor except who in their right mind would want to honeymoon with Jack the Ripper as best man? He chuckled. That was over, thank God. Abruptly, he thought of the murder at the museum.

Or was it?

What if his machine had traveled to infinity? If so, Jack could be back in this fair city, and despite whatever universe they were in, history could be repeating itself, grotesquely so.

11:33 P.M.

Her cheek still burned.

Amber stared over her laptop at the sheer curtains on the window, lit by a multicolored glow from the city lights. Aside from a harmless kiss that left her glowing, she was astounded by the events which had brought her to this place. From a crime scene at the Getty to this man materializing from a time machine—from following him to LAX to insinuating herself in his search for his wife because he was . . . he was a miraculous alternative to her gritty, unsatisfying existence. *He is more than a man.* She nodded. *He is a gatekeeper to the cosmos. Already he has totally changed my life. I can't even look out the damned window without knowing that no matter how familiar or pretty the view is, there is pure magic on the other side, undiscovered realities in the beyond.*

She was lost in her thoughts: they had no common thread, no logic, no shape. They were images from earlier in the day mixed with memories from years ago—all confused by figments of her imagination. *Am I losing my mind?* Suddenly, she started hyperventilating. She clutched the table and fought the panic that rose up inside, and then a professor from one of her literature classes popped in her brain, reminding her: There are no hard distinctions between what is real and unreal, between what is true and what false. Nodding firmly, her lips moving, she re-peated the words, made them a mantra, and finally her panic subsided. She closed her laptop, shut her eyes and leaned over the table, yet the kaleidoscope of images wouldn't stop, and she was afraid that some air-borne vapor or aura from H. G. Wells had affected both her percep-tions and her brain. She frowned and tried to tell herself that his lips on her cheek had been a simple good-night kiss, and that her stupid brain was running with it because it had been months since anyone had touched her or done anything nice for her or . . . *What has this man done to me?* She started crying.

Minutes later, she snuffled and stopped, got a hold of herself, went in the bathroom and peered in the mirror. *I'm a mess.* She washed her face and automatically put on fresh makeup and perfume, was sud-denly irritated at being alone, as if solitude were an enemy. She opened her phone, but wasn't sure who to call. She scrolled down her direc-tory, surprised there were so many people in her phone she didn't want to talk to, finally settled on her friend, Marilyn, who worked as a buyer for Barnes & Noble.

"Marilyn?"

"Who is this?"

"It's Amber!" She chuckled. "God, has it been that long?"

"Where are you?"

"San Francisco. I'm with somebody."

"God, it's about time."

"No, no, it's not like that."

A static-filled pause. "It's not?"

"No, it's—" Amber blushed and wished she hadn't called. "No, it's not. I mean, he's not gay or anything, but . . ."

"Look, honey," said Marilyn, "it's almost midnight, and I just took an Ambien. Can we talk about this tomorrow?"

Amber sashayed into the hotel bar, annoyed with herself for calling Marilyn, especially when she hadn't known what she wanted to say without blowing Wells's cover, without having people think that she herself had gone insane. She couldn't even explain it to herself. She still couldn't get past him running from his time machine, and the more she thought about it, the more she worried that she had in fact become delusional. Yet no one was reacting to her strangely, and her world seemed otherwise the same as it had before. Yes, she was emotionally out-of-kilter, but who wouldn't be?

It's like all of a sudden I'm living inside a dream.

The bartender came over, and instead of a wine spritzer or beer, she ordered vodka on the rocks. Sensing her turmoil, he filled her glass to the brim, and she told herself to tip him generously. She drank deeply, relieved the vodka went down smoothly. It warmed her insides, spread and sent a pleasant flush to her brain. Her montage of thoughts slowed, then stopped altogether, and she was left with a haze and a smile, a blank mind, and that was just fine.

She studied the bottles lining the mirrors behind the bar. Some night she wouldn't mind trying the exotic ones, but not now. She appreciated the "summer of love" rock 'n' roll coming from the speakers. It reminded her of her mom; a simpler life; soundtracks from movies and waiting rooms; TV commercials. She hung on to the familiarity—an emotional life raft—and let the vodka do its work.

Like a therapist, the bartender came over and refilled her glass. She smiled and lifted it to him, pushed a twenty in his direction, then sat back, sipped and enjoyed. Her mind went back to H. G. Wells, encircled him like a dance and stayed—little corollaries of thoughts doing the moves. She remembered old boyfriends, some making love to her and touching her soul, others leaving her curled in a ball of nerves, some walking away, others left behind, none permanent. *My life has always been transitory, so as he might say, why the devil be afraid of anything?* She frowned. *Where the hell did that come from?*

The vodka made her giggle.

Yes, she was just fine. Unconsciously, she caressed her cheek where he'd kissed her. Her thoughts went from reverence for H. G. Wells the gatekeeper to curiosity about Wells the man. What did the women in his life call him? Bertie? Not the sexiest of names, but he hadn't complained. Women had flocked to him, vied for his attentions, and he had responded in kind. Her mouth curled in a tiny smile. Though he might have inspired reverence, he was definitely not religious material.

She wondered if he was as handsome without clothes on as he was within—or if a reformulation error had altered him. She blushed. *He's a gentleman. He wouldn't have said anything, but maybe someday soon I'll find out. He likes me—I know he likes me—I've caught him looking at me. I felt his lips like a tacit invitation, an hors d'oeuvre. Who knows if it was me or him that was the delicacy?* She giggled again. Obviously, the vodka had settled in her groin, and it felt oh, so delicious. Images filled her brain again, this time a kaleidoscope of Wells. An image froze. Her breath caught. She imagined him transmogrified by time travel into a human satyr.

She drained her drink, released a jittery sigh and left the bar—feeling warm, excellent and outrageous. *No. Beyond warm, beyond all of those.* She got halfway to the elevators, then stopped and inexplicably detoured to the hotel desk.

The concierge looked up from a computer screen. "Yes, ma'am. May I help you?"

"I'm sorry to bother you, but I seem to have locked myself out. . . ." She smiled sheepishly. "It's Room 529."

12:47 A.M.

H.G.'s dream started with Amy—her delicate, fine-boned body beside him, her curves a perfect fit for his hands, her lips brushing his, the scent of roses in the air; it segued into his cocaine-addict friend Sidney Bowkett's wife—he recalled her desperate flesh beneath him, but not her name; then a glowing alabaster-blond Cambridge student who liked to make love in the grass and talk philology between sets; then May Nesbit, young, stupid and uninspired—femininity in the dark ages; then Violet Hunt, then Rosamund, eager, uninhibited and mind-boggling, yet possessive beyond reason; and of course his Venus Meretrix for all time, the voluptuous brown girl the day after he'd had lunch with Teddy Roosevelt in Washington, D.C.; and then a succession of pretty faces contorted in ecstasy, breasts and round bellies flat against him, and hands and caresses and . . .

He smelled jasmine, and so the dream became specific. Jasmine gave way to musk and a moist sheen. A lover was on top of him, moving up and down, in circles one way, in circles the other, slowly, then slower still, then a warm and delicious pause. He moaned in his sleep; his psyche was no longer part of this; his senses were. He had surrendered to the dream, this wonderful dream that suddenly became extraordinary: the lover remained still, yet was moving around him like liquid velvet, massaging him.

Her cries, and then her fingernails in his shoulders rudely awakened him, and he saw Amber above him, her body arching as she came in waves. He tried to stop, but his own pleasure was too intense, and as usual that old friend between his legs was not about to listen to reason or indignation, and he found himself involuntarily thrusting until he, too, climaxed. Then she collapsed on top of him. *So much for staying faithful to Amy in 2010.*

"You raped me."

"I most certainly did not!" She giggled a little-girl giggle, then whispered in a singsong, "I can still feel you. . . ."

His sensibilities were telling him that this "dream" with Amber was the best sex he'd had in years, yet he was annoyed that it had happened and particularly upset that he'd had little to do with it. Then the guilt rushed in on the wings of a conventional morality that he'd spend his entire adult life trying to get rid of. He rolled out from under her and sat on the edge of the bed. He turned on the light and put his head in his hands.

"Good bloody Christ!"

"Don't be mad at me, Bertie."

"How did you get in here, anyway?"

She sat on her knees next to him, smiling and dangling the plastic key between her breasts. "I told the concierge that you had fallen asleep and accidentally locked me out of the room." More giggles. "And that I didn't want to disturb you."

"You *raped* me!"

She wilted under his glare. "I'm sorry."

"You had no right! I'm in love with Amy."

"According to your bio at the Getty—not to mention, my Edwardian lit class—you were always searching for—"

"Don't tell me about a life I haven't *lived!*"

"Okay, sorry, but those times you couldn't find your lover-shadow—"

"How did you know about lover-shadows?" he demanded.

"Not everybody here is illiterate."

"You are not my lover-shadow!"

"Okay, okay, but when you were looking—you were having—what did you call them? Passades?"

"Amy left me because of passades! And I didn't come all this way just for a, a pint in a strange pub, if you will!"

"D'you like my perfume?" she said coyly. "It's jasmine. And you smell like candy." She nuzzled him. "Why don't we—"

"I don't want to hear it!" he shouted.

"Okay, okay. Chill." She moved a few inches away. "I'm sorry."

"Do you mind, Miss Reeves?"

"I don't mind at all," she said. "You know what they say about old wine." She gave his shoulder a tiny love bite. "And you're definitely not vinegar."

"I meant, *go*," he said angrily.

"I said I was sorry."

"Must I call the desk? Rape is still a crime in this world, is it not?"

"Try proving it when I'm the one with all the DNA inside me."

"Get out!"

"Okay, okay." She went to the door, then turned, tossed her lovely hair and said wistfully, "Did you ever think that maybe you are *my* lover-shadow?"

He imagined an eternity passed before he heard the door click shut behind her, and then he felt very cold. He got back into bed, rolled into a ball and wept. Not so much for Amy and his transgression—or whatever it was—but because this Amber Reeves had touched him deeply and he barely knew her. First Amy, then the world of 2010, and now this. He didn't know if he should be exhilarated or terrified.

7:24 A.M., *Monday, June 21, 2010*

Early the next morning, noise from a shower on a floor above woke H.G. He sat up and took in the room, nodding at the graceful lines of the furniture, much more forgiving than the enormous squat pieces from the turn of the century. Intending to sketch a "picshua" of these new designs for his office in 1906, he went to the desk, but stopped as he became fully awake. Amy, the missing, and Amber, the found, came roaring back into his brain, ruining his mood.

He jumped up and paced the room, wondering what to do first, and accidentally bumped into the armoire across from the bed, jarring its door open. Inside, he saw a large television and mercifully was distracted. He recalled television from 1979—it had inspired those awful "Babble Machines" he wrote about in *When the Sleeper Wakes*—but this was no late twentieth-century "tube" or "Babble Machine," to put it mildly. The screen was flat and longer than his outstretched arm, and he marveled at its lack of physical depth. *It's thinner than some Rembrandts I've seen*, he told himself, unaware of the implication. He found the remote, had no clue what the multicolored buttons did, but turned it on à la 1979. He stared openmouthed at the instant picture, its brightness and perfect colors in something labeled "Hi Def," and realized that the images on the screen were inherently false in that they made reality appear more appealing than it really was. Regardless, he was engrossed within seconds. He hadn't watched TV in thirty-some years and—grinning sheepishly—realized that he had actually missed it.

PBS featured a story about Canada and Greenland sparring over newly discovered territory—islands which had emerged due to melting of the polar ice cap. The commentator summarized the doomsday scenario: By the end of the twenty-first century, the seas would have risen some twenty feet, erasing traditional coastlines and their cities, some island nations would have vanished, the tropics would have become semi-arid ovens, and an already overpopulated planet would have substantially less habitable space—all because of unrelenting carbon dioxide emissions from industrialized nations.

H.G. was first astonished, then mortified that he hadn't predicted this phenomenon they called global warming. His warnings about the mishandling of science and technology had been confined to more obvious phenomena: war conducted with weapons so destructive that the human race would obliterate itself. Even if calmer heads prevailed, the commentator suggested, the end was near—unless leaders and governments were willing to consider the Earth itself. *I must think about this when I go back. I must write, write and write for my world. I must use the prevailing sentiment of Edward's time to aim words at those industrial tycoons who burn coal for commerce and comfort in the name of progress.*

Yet he had no immediate answers, for the problem was insidious, complex. Most global warming came from the maw of modern convenience and comfort all around him. Everything in his hotel room had been manufactured by factories that belched greenhouse gases into the atmosphere. *I suppose I could forsake all this and sleep in Golden Gate Park, but then I'd become a minority of one, and if it didn't work for the likes of Henry David Thoreau, I doubt it will work for me. Besides, I have no desire to live like a Neanderthal and apparently no one else does, either.*

———

When the PBS segment was done, he clicked uneasily from channel to channel, almost afraid of what he would learn next, then more afraid of becoming the proverbial ostrich with his head in the sand.

He paused on Fox News, hooked by the quick cuts, the banners and scrolls, flashing sidebars and a scantily clad anchorwoman who looked like an actress or prostitute. After five minutes of commercials, he was flabbergasted by the visual images. He wondered how motor cars could speed through radically different terrains; how real people could interact with cartoon characters; how animals and chocolate candy could talk; but then his speculation was cut short by the lead story on the morning news that filled the room with its ugliness.

He was already aware of the murder at the Getty Museum, yet was fascinated by the coverage: coroner deputies taking the body away, then thirty seconds of the blood-splattered men's room, a chalk outline marking where the victim had been found. Unfortunately, that was not all. A second reporter in the Brentwood hills less than a mile from the museum was going on about a second murder occurring later that morning. Both victims had been badly mutilated. A third reporter was outside the West LAPD division headquarters asking Lieutenant Casey Holland if the crimes were related. Too early to tell, he replied, but given their grisly nature—the victim at the Getty had her kidney surgically removed—he thought that a serial killer, a true psychopath, was at work. The TV went back to the anchorwoman, who questioned the reporters for more details, but they had none.

H.G. gaped at the screen and recalled his thought from the night before. He told himself it wasn't possible, that his intuition was dead wrong, but he couldn't ignore a coincidence that was no longer a coincidence. Both murders were the work of a madman—no doubt the monster he had chased through time and sent to hell.

Jack the Ripper.

As the anchorwoman wrapped up the news, H.G. fell back on the bed, his mind racing, calculating the real time traveled. At three years per minute, Amy's trip to 2010 had taken thirty-four minutes, and since she had forgotten the special key, *The Utopia* would have been back at its home hour in the lab an hour and eight minutes after she had left.

Yet, when he had come to the lab late the next afternoon, the engine was still warm, so his machine had taken much longer to come home, meaning that a jaunt to infinity was not out of the question. In fact, that was probably why he had arrived over nine hours later than Amy. The Destination Indicator hadn't been up to a trip of such magnitude and had lost calibration.

He held his head and groaned. *Amy, oh, Amy, love of my life, not only did you leave your purse in the cabin, but rather than take the special key so that the machine would stay where it was, you pulled the declinometer and sent* The Utopia *to infinity.*

Though he knew he still had the special key, he succumbed to a flash of panic, riffled through his pants hung over the chair and took it out. Holding it filled him with a sense of well-being, but only for a moment. He still had to find Amy. And worse, the possibility that Leslie John Stephenson had somehow survived. . . .

Wait.

In his mind, infinity equaled the end of time which in turn equaled the end of the world—not necessarily an Armageddon, but when the sun died. According to the best scientific minds of both the nineteenth and twentieth centuries, that cosmic event wouldn't happen for another five thousand million years, so if *The Utopia* were traveling at three years per minute, it would take fifteen thousand years of real time to make the round trip. So Jack the Ripper couldn't be here in 2010. Unless . . .

He shut his eyes tightly and didn't want to think it, but couldn't stop the inevitable questions: Aside from global warming, what if there had been an Armageddon? What if mankind had annihilated itself and blown up the planet? Then Earth would indeed be some toxic syrup of gamma rays and dark energy coexisting in a gigantic black hole with the lost souls of good men and evil alike. H.G. made another uneasy, albeit rough, calculation. If Amy had pulled the declinometer just past midnight and sent his machine to infinity and it somehow returned to the Getty in four or five hours . . . Yes, it was possible. It was horribly possible.

If the world ended in a mere three hundred years or so.

Suddenly depressed, he put on his shirt and underwear and stood in the window, but couldn't escape his thoughts. First global warming and now this. He imagined Atlas being crushed by the weight of the heavens, yet still standing tall, and he, himself, a pale Edwardian imitation. Happy, busy sounds came from the streets below, making him wonder how he could ever hope to warn mankind of its impending doom and be taken seriously. True, he was well known; he had been received by heads of state; he did have a substantial following, including a fair number of enemies, plus critics and suffragettes. Perhaps when he went home, he could persuade people to listen.

I must try. I must spend my life trying.

Someone knocked. He considered not answering, but didn't have a chance. Amber opened the door with her spare key and came in wearing a hotel robe tied loosely at the waist. She closed the door with a click and stood there, eyes downcast, her hands twisting in her robe.

"I am *so* sorry," she said.

He turned back to the window, annoyed that she had broken into his thoughts, that she was here. He spied his trousers on the chair and fought his way into them.

"I went downstairs and had some drinks after you left last night. . . . I kept wondering what it would be like." She sighed. "I think my mind got hung up on the out-of-time part—or something." She shrugged. "So I told myself that I should just do it—that you would like me—and that it wouldn't really matter because it wouldn't be part of anything."

"In my century," he said acidly, "if someone wants something, usually they ask."

"I said I was sorry." Her voice quavered. She started crying. "I didn't want to hurt you or Amy or anyone, no matter what you think! I suppose in some primal part of my brain, I wanted to find out if you were really real!"

Her tears became sobs. They melted his resolve, making him anxious to somehow stop her emotions, to reassure her even though he was the one who had been violated.

She sat on the bed and put her face in her hands, and the words kept coming. "And, and now I don't know what to do—I had this stupid speech worked out about something glorious in the cosmos sending you through time to me, but, oh God, that's *so* dumb!"

"Amber—"

"And now the only thing I can think of is that if you took us back through time to last night, I'd probably do the same damn thing all over again!" She pushed off the bed and started for the door.

"Amber, please. . . ."

One hand on the door handle, she turned. "This is so . . . This is so lame! All I wanted to do was apologize, but then I look at you and I fall apart all over again!"

"Will you please get hold of yourself?!"

He gripped her firmly by the shoulders, gave her a little shake, then saw the tears welling up in her eyes again. He relented and embraced her, felt her sobs against his body—not an entirely unpleasant sensation—then was amazed at how quickly his mind had been wrenched from a dilemma of staggering proportions to the downright trivial. Such was the power of a woman.

Amy swam through his brain, reminding him that she had been his lover-shadow once and hopefully would be again. Yet he wasn't reassured, for according to his theory, his reasoning, everyone had a lover-shadow, and like this Amber Reeves had declared last night, he just might be hers. The thought made him nervous and giddy, and he found himself distracted by her glossy black hair that lay in piles of natural ringlets. He stroked it and whispered, "Medusa."

"What?"

"Your hair is like the Medusa's."

She wasn't sure what he meant, but smiled hopefully.

"So I'm calling you 'Dusa."

"I'm still your assistant?"

"You're still in my employ, yes."

She tried to kiss him, but he pushed her away. *I must forget about lover-shadows.*

"Don't worry. . . . I'm not gonna try to come between you and Amy."

"It's not about Amy," he replied.

He sat her down in front of the TV and didn't say a word till Fox

News had rerun the "Brentwood Murders" story. Then he told her about Jack the Ripper stealing his time machine and coming to 1979, and how he had followed, tracked the monster, met Amy Catherine Robbins, finally one-upped the Ripper and sent him to infinity, then returned to his own world with the love of his life.

"*That's* why I had a problem with his DNA!"

"He wants the special key." H.G. held it up for emphasis. "He hasn't a clue where I am—he may think that I'm still in the nineteenth century—but he does know that Amy is here because he would've seen her purse in the time machine's cabin. . . . He'll look for her hoping to find me."

"I'm gonna call the lieutenant."

"He'll think you're mad."

"Maybe, maybe not." She smiled shrewdly, her eyes dark and bright. "He knows I'm a freak for the nineteenth century. I'll tell him that this Leslie John Stephenson is a Jack the Ripper copycat."

H.G. lifted his eyebrows, but wasn't encouraged. *I'm not sure it will make one whit of difference.*

She'd already taken out her phone and pushed a button.

He gazed out the window again. *If I had invented push buttons and could have imagined this world, I would have burned the formula.*

8:37 A.M., *Monday, June 21, 2010*

"Smashing, how simply smashing!" Jaclyn exclaimed. She was watching the KTLA morning news break. "They think I'm a man."

She curled her toes and stretched, quite refreshed after a deep, satisfying sleep brought on by the murders from the day before, undisturbed by the phone ringing last night and this morning as well. She had no intention of answering and complicating things when she was just beginning to cozy up here.

She changed channels and stopped on an interview with a pretty congresswoman from an Eastern state who was proselytizing her audience to help stop the AIDS scourge, now a pandemic that had engulfed the entire Third World. Intrigued, Jaclyn watched, and upon learning that the disease was primarily transmitted by sodomy, she chuckled. *Thank you so much for the education, Channel Seven. I indeed belong in this dangerous new world, so obviously amoral and homogenous that men, women and animals copulate at will, and one wonders how the whores make a living.* Her attention went back to the congresswoman, who was repeating herself now, much like the actors who sold products every few minutes. Since they all appeared and sounded similar, Jaclyn questioned if they were actually human or human replicants. She fantasized about sodomizing this congress-woman with, say, a broomstick, then slashing her throat and observing wires and electronics spilling out. She frowned. She preferred blood.

She wrinkled her nose. A stench from Heather Trattner's kitchen lingered in the air, reminding her of a surgery that orderlies had neglected to clean. *But I did tidy up*, she told herself, going into the kitchen, inspecting the sink, the body parts in bags stacked neatly on the counter. *It must be the stagnant air, the humidity in this part of the world.* Still, she couldn't tolerate the smell. Unaware that she'd already spent more time in a kitchen than Leslie John had ever done, she donned an apron, found a cookbook and ingredients in the pantry, turned on the oven, then mixed up a kidney pie using Heather's—which seemed relatively fresh though they had sat out all night. *Wait, dear heart. Something's missing.* She ran to the bedroom and returned with Teresa Cruz's kidney—now black and foul—and added it to the pie as the pièce de résistance.

As the dish baked, filling the house with its sickly-sweet organ smell, Jaclyn carried the body parts out to the Mercedes in the garage and stacked them in the trunk. As an afterthought, she threw in designer jeans and T-shirts from Heather's closet in case she got careless and needed a change of clothing.

Back in the kitchen, she still wasn't happy with the odor from her pie, so she filled a pot with water, laced it with tablespoons of ginger and nutmeg and put it on to boil—as the maid used to do at home when Mummy's kitchen smelled foul from butchering poultry.

The kidney pie needed another thirty minutes, so rather than watch television, she sat down at the secretary, deciding to celebrate her sojourn in the twenty-first century by writing a little ditty—something that Penny used to do rather than keep a diary. She gazed off, reflected on her transmogrification into a female form. While she hated women—hence, herself—she couldn't ignore that the female gender had certain advantages: Sexual attraction rather than suspicion opened doors and left her free to do as she pleased without recrimination; an arsenal of smiles, from the innocent to the insouciant to the coy to the knowing, could make men act in silly and predictable ways. Leslie John had always appreciated the wiles of women before he murdered them. Therefore, did she not now have the best of both worlds? She glanced down at herself. Alas, no. *As long as I have an odiferous hole between my legs, I shall feel turned inside out, and if someday I cut up myself, I will bleed buckets of rage.* She chuckled, her introspection having brought forth the Muse, then—in perfect handwriting—began composing on Heather's pink-and-roses stationery.

> *Jack & Jill came back to kill*
> *The girls who went before them.*
> *Jack got mixed and Jill got switched*
> *So Jill, not Jack would have to kill*
> *The girls who went before them.*

Delighted at her creation, her laugh light and musical, she imagined reciting at a tea or a poetry reading—if such niceties still existed in the T-shirt, tattoo and smart-phone world of 2010. *Perchance I'll do a collection of poetry and then find a university or a ladies' club or bookstore where I can woo them with my verse and then carve them into sculptures should they pique my fancy.*

Wait. She looked at her ditty again, cocked her head, chewed on the pen. Shouldn't the third line read: Jack got changed and Jill, deranged . . . ? *No, no, that alters the rhythm, yet it's not too terribly bad, except it takes the verse somewhere else entirely, and we don't yet know where that is.* She stared off thoughtfully. *Wells. He would know, wouldn't he? He knows all about writing books and poetry and the like, that smug little bastard. After I've captured and humiliated him, I'll have him write a second verse for his epitaph.*

Her mood ruined by the thought of Wells, she left her ditty on the secretary, took the kidney pie from the oven and set it out to cool, then shed her apron. She glanced outside. The bright morning sun meant she would have to dump Heather's body soon or the smell would ruin the Mercedes, not to mention the garage. Once that chore was done, she could enjoy a cup at Starbucks, spin a web of alluring smiles and find a male customer who would gladly search for Amy Catherine Robbins on his laptop.

She looked in Heather's purse for car keys, sorting through the girl residue—crumpled twenty-dollar bills, candy wrappers, credit card receipts galore, valet-parking stubs—and—*ah, how smashingly sweet!*—a pink-and-roses notepad that matched her stationery. At the bottom of the purse, she found the keys entwined in a hairbrush, and as she was taking them out, discovered a folder with cheques inside. She glanced at the register, pursed her lips and chuckled. *Heather Trattner did not go poor into her sunny and warm southern California wonderland.*

She took keys and purse, felt strange without Jack's black and shiny Gladstone bag, but shrugged it off and went out through the utility porch. A neighbor's dog started barking, yet she wasn't concerned. There was so much foliage between the houses, she doubted if anyone could see her, and even if someone did, what was so unusual about a housewife? Remembering how Michael Trattner's Porsche had worked, she pushed the button on the car keys, unlocking the Mercedes with a little chirp, then slid behind the wheel and started the engine. Apprehensive, she studied the dials in the dash and wondered how difficult operating the motor car would be, then figured that if millions of fools in 2010 could flit about in them, why not her? It couldn't be that different from the Porsche. She clicked the Mercedes into drive, eased down the long, narrow driveway, seesawing on the steering wheel, but when she heard shrubs brushing the car, she pulled the wheel too hard the other way and dinged the house with the fender. An electronic beep. She hit the brakes and stopped with a jolt. Her hands were shaking. Now a red icon shaped like the side of the car was flashing on the console. *As if I bloody didn't know.* Angry, her teeth clenched, she pulled the wheel to the left and let the car ease forward. Then she glanced up and saw something in front of her. Startled, she hit the brakes again. The car lurched to a stop and died.

A police cruiser was parked on the street blocking the driveway, a uniformed cop waiting behind the wheel.

Lieutenant Casey Holland was at the front door.

———

He's wearing a light-brown suit and matching tie, Jaclyn noticed. *He must be a gentleman copper.* She got out of the Mercedes slowly, minced innocently up to the porch wondering what she should say, but he spoke first.

"Morning, ma'am. . . ."

If he had witnessed the Mercedes scraping the house, he said nothing.

"Are you Mrs. Michael Trattner?"

"No, I'm sorry." She swept her hair back and managed a smile. "I'm Jaclyn. . . . Jaclyn Smythe, her cousin from the UK. I'm house-sitting." She let her eyes linger on his square, pleasant face. "Heather has gone off on a lark and no one's heard from her in a few days."

"Would you have her cell number?"

"Uh, no," she said, flustered. "I mean, yes, I have it inside."

"If you don't mind."

Jaclyn hesitated. "Is there something we should know?" Her smile became innocent, curious and intimate all at the same time. She fixed her wide-set, dark-brown eyes on his and wouldn't let go.

Normally, Holland would've dodged the question, thanked Jaclyn for her time, gone back to the patrol car and called Heather Trattner's cell on the way back to headquarters, but this woman intrigued him and he didn't want to leave yet. She exuded a strange warmth that for a moment took him away from the megacity madness, the depressing realities of his job. He relaxed and returned her smile.

"Is there something wrong?"

Other than a couple of murders, he wasn't sure anymore.

She felt that same warmth. "Would you like to come in . . . ? I mean, that might be better."

She found Heather's number on the message board over the secretary and gave it to him. Perched on the white camelback sofa in the living room, he told her what had happened to Michael Trattner. Jaclyn shed the obligatory tears and expressed sympathy for poor Heather. They had been so happy—she'd loved him so much—what in the world would she do now? Holland gave his usual spiel, heartfelt and reassuring after years of similar visits, yet he was growing uncomfortable—not with the situation, but with himself. He stood up awkwardly and handed her a card, studiously avoiding her eyes.

"If you—"

"Oh, please don't go yet." She blocked his path, smiling generously, her skin radiant, her eyes aglow. "Would you like some tea or something to nibble on perhaps?"

"Really, I—"

"I've just made a kidney pie. You haven't lived until you've tried my kidney pie."

He grinned and shook his head. "No, thanks. I'll pass. To be honest, I'm not a fan of British food."

"Beef Wellington. Next time you come, I'll make a beef Wellington."

She walked him to the door, her hand impulsively on his back, the touch cool and warm and electric all at the same time.

He turned. "I don't know how long you're staying, but there is a serial killer in the Brentwood area, so please be careful."

"I will."

"Oh. D'you have a cell?"

That stumped her. She shook her head slowly.

He was surprised, yet didn't seem concerned or suspicious. "You can get one and buy minutes for the time you're here."

"Buy minutes?"

"Sure. A lot of tourists do it. I mean, I don't know how they do it in the UK, but . . ." He noticed her confusion. "Look, I'll just call you on the house line if something comes up."

"Thank you. You've been so kind."

From the porch, she watched him go, gave him a flutter wave with her fingers, pressed his card to her chest. She felt wholesome and good; she wanted to dance and sing. She understood none of it. Going inside, she skipped across the living room, then stopped abruptly and tried to think clearly and move past the sea of pastels in her mind, but failed. She glanced up, saw herself in the mirror over the fireplace and was mortified.

"Good Lord, I look terrible!"

She ran into Heather's bathroom, went through the vanity and found cosmetics. Then, like the artistic surgeon she was, she bent to the mirror and applied cream, rouge, eyeliner and a dark-cherry gloss to her lips. A half-hour later, she stepped back, satisfied that she had transformed her natural beauty into a face that could easily grace one of the magazine covers she'd seen—or perhaps even launch those proverbial thousand ships. *Never again will Lieutenant Casey Holland see this girl looking unkempt and dowdy.*

She left the house and got back in the Mercedes. She concentrated on small moves with the steering wheel and made it out of the driveway without incident. Once on the street, she found the car smooth and easy to handle, and got the knack of steering, accelerating and stopping before she came to the madness of traffic on Sunset Boulevard. Only then did she remember who she truly was. She howled with rage inside the sealed confines of the motor car.

Twenty minutes later, she had turned off Sunset in to Will Rogers State Park and was trolling the former estate for a secluded spot to unburden herself of Heather's remains—although not too secluded. She did want them to find the body. After all, that was the point. Carry on the good works of Leslie John Stephenson aka Jack the Ripper in spite of gender so that one might look back—or forward to 2010 with pride and glory. Make them so petrified with fear that every night you are the lead story on the television news, and then Wells will have no choice but to blunder into the investigation and make a fatal mistake.

She stopped on a curve above the Will Rogers compound and surveyed the slope to the west that disappeared into a thick fog not yet burnt off by the morning sun. Though the site was too bucolic for her taste, the fog reminded her of London, and she decided that the slope was ideal for a final resting place. She would take care to arrange the body parts so Heather would indeed resemble the Venus de Milo—sans implants and head, of course. The latter she would leave on the road as a signpost so that someone—preferably lovers—might stop and look further.

Humming that melody from the music box, she opened the trunk and began carrying pieces of Heather through stately, centuries-old eucalyptus trees down the slope, her feet crunching on the layers of bark.

When finished, she drew a cute little happy face on Heather's flat belly and added the words "REMEMBER ME?" Then she left the park and drove east on Sunset, planning to go back to Starbucks for a gentleman with a laptop. Except she couldn't get Lieutenant Holland out of her head. If this were happening in, say, 1893, she would rush home in a hansom cab, write a flowery note on perfumed linen stationery asking if she might see him in Regent's Park some Sunday afternoon, then have a boy on a bicycle deliver it to his flat. She smiled. *Intentions and desires are so much more accessible these days. Even murder does not require the furtive nature of a shrinking violet.* No need for a boy on a bicycle, no need for a customer at Starbucks.

Now at a stop sign in 2010, she took Michael Trattner's cell from his wife's purse, and was about to attempt calling the lieutenant when it rang. Startled, she dropped it on the seat, started to retrieve it when the driver behind her honked impatiently. She turned and lurched up a side street, was afraid to answer and drove faster as if to outrun the noise, but the phone kept on ringing. Finally, it stopped, and over the speakerphone, she heard a beep, Michael Trattner identifying himself, and then the caller: "Hey, Mike, where are you? We had a meeting this morning, dude. . . . I tried you at home, but nobody's there. Call me."

Another beep and the cell went silent. Jaclyn frowned. *This will never do. What if the police should call and yours truly should answer . . . ? They'd no longer be looking for a man now, would they? And, as the lieutenant implied, what is a girl to do in this world without a cell phone?*

She pulled into a strip mall on Bundy Drive—not because she'd spotted another Starbucks. Rather, a Verizon store was three doors down, and she liked that the name rhymed with horizon, as in "event horizon," a term she remembered from 1979 for that vista of dark energy where—stretched out like diaphanous spaghetti—her agonized soul had languished for so long. It was also the same name that was on Michael Trattner's cell, and in this case familiarity did not breed contempt.

She tossed Michael's cell in the trash and headed for the Verizon outlet, going past a small bookstore. She stopped abruptly. On a "bargain books" table outside, a $6.99 title jumped out at her: *Portrait of a Killer: Jack the Ripper—Case Closed*, by Patricia Cornwell. She flipped through pages, read at random, Jack's sordid spree coming back as if yesterday.

Jaclyn discovered that Patricia Cornwell had pinned the killings on one Walter Sickert, a renowned artist with several studios in the East End, one of which was in the same building as Leslie John's loft. Indignant, she read further, growing more and more annoyed with this Patricia Cornwell, a forensic scientist turned author who claimed that DNA taken from Jack's letters to Metropolitan police commissioner Charles Warren proved that Sickert was the Ripper. Jaclyn laughed derisively. *Walter, that neurotic little twit, used to post letters for me. On occasion, I would pay too much money for one of his morbid drawings and copy their style when I penned a note to Scotland Yard.* She scoffed, *Sickert, indeed. After I've finished with Wells, I might just look up this Patricia Cornwell and prove to her that despite gender, I am who I am.* She snapped the book shut, then realized that she had been standing outside the bookstore far too long, took the book inside, paid for it, stuffed it in her purse and went straightaway to Verizon.

A tall, lithe black salesman showed her phones, seemingly impervious to the subtle vamps she tried, her smiles and soft innuendoes. She wondered whether she was giving out masculine or feminine vibes, was about to try something more forward when he brushed against her breasts, and then she knew she had him. Reassured, she backed off and concentrated on the phones, as opposed to those little alien things they called "Blackberries" for some unfathomable reason. Eventually, she chose a cell that included a video camera. *How simply marvelous. I can photograph "works in progress," and perhaps send them anonymously to television stations looking for more thorough coverage of my victims. I could send one to Patricia Cornwell as grist for a sequel.* She paused. *Then again, if I wanted to speak with someone about Jack's deeds, it wouldn't do for them to hear the voice of the comely young woman that I am, would it now . . . ?*

She turned back to the salesman. "You wouldn't happen to have a device that disguises one's voice . . . ? If, say, you were speaking with an ex-beau or someone, and you didn't . . . ? You know."

He chuckled and shook her head. "Naw. . . . You'd have to go to Radio Shack for something like that."

She raised her eyebrows quizzically.

"There's one on Santa Monica toward the beach and another one up on Wilshire. . . . But they have them all over the place." He couldn't stop gazing at her. "But, hey, if you're looking for some privacy, you can always block the caller ID feature on your phone."

"I like that idea. . . . I like that a lot."

Detached, she watched him press a flurry of keys. Then he put the phone back in its box, nodded and grinned. "Done."

"Thank you *so* much."

She paid for the phone and accessories with Heather's Visa card and was on her way out the door when the salesman called out to her.

"I was wondering," he stammered, "unh, like I got my break in a few minutes, and hey, d'you want to get some coffee or something?"

"Oh, thank you," she said, smiling sweetly and putting her hand on his chest. "I'd love to, but you're too young and pretty to die."

He stepped back and cocked his head as if he hadn't heard right, then figured she was joking and laughed weakly.

But she was already gone.

Back in the Mercedes, cruising east on Santa Monica, she opened her new cell and made her first call.

"This is Holland," he answered.

"Oh, yes, Lieutenant Holland," she said breathlessly. "We met earlier today, and I—"

"Jaclyn!"

"The same."

"What's up?"

"I wanted so much to ask a favor of you this morning, but the timing was unfortunate." She hesitated. "Oh, I'm so bad at this sort of thing, but maybe if you'd allow me to buy you lunch or, or—"

"Hey, try me."

"*Try* you?"

"What's the favor?"

She smiled, took a breath and plunged in. "Since they knew I was coming to the west coast of California, my parents asked me to try and find a dear friend in San Francisco that they've lost track of. A Miss Amy Catherine Robbins. I've had absolutely no luck, and its suddenly occurred to me that a police lieutenant might know how to go about it. . . ."

10:45 A.M., Monday, June 21, 2010

H.G. paused at the house on Marina Boulevard, turned and looked back at the green sward across the street and the Golden Gate Bridge. He breathed in the crisp, refreshing air from the bay and wondered indignantly why Amy had never talked about growing up here. The house rivaled Spade House in its size and feel. Maybe she'd never mentioned it because she didn't want to hurt his feelings. Obviously, she'd grown up with all the latest conveniences and probably wasn't impressed that he had wanted to install electric central heating at Spade House—a revolutionary concept in 1901. No doubt she'd secretly laughed at his picshuas of automatic brooms and self-making beds. He knew that he was overreacting, yet couldn't help but think that their love might always have been compromised by white lies and omissions.

Earlier that morning, Amber had journeyed online again and become hopelessly lost in a sea of irrelevant Web sites. Then H.G. had narrowed their search considerably by entering Amy's employment history at the Bank of England in 1979. Amber hadn't seen how it would help, but having beginner's luck with the mouse, H.G. serenely continued to click and eventually stumbled onto the bank's database of archives. The human-resources file on Amy Catherine Robbins listed her parents, Kevin and Elizabeth Robbins, as the ones to contact in case of an emergency. Not surprising after thirty-one years, their phone number had been disconnected, but H.G. and Amber were hoping they still lived at 239 Marina Boulevard.

A subdued Amber rang the doorbell, still embarrassed by the night before. She had tried to blame it on the bartender who kept refilling her glass with vodka, then on Wells himself, because he was charming, witty, famous, handsome—not to mention historical and out of his own time—but that didn't work, either. The stark reality was that she had made a complete fool of herself. Worse, she didn't feel guilty and wondered when it would happen again.

A Hispanic maid finally opened the door a crack, endured H.G.'s barrage of questions about Amy Catherine Robbins, then smiled and shook her head.

"No *hablo inglés. Momentito.*" She disappeared inside the house.

"I must remember that."

"What?"

"When I'm in a conversation and I can't think straight, instead of making a fool out of myself, I merely say 'No *hablo inglés*' and walk away."

Her eyes downcast, Amber forced a small laugh.

A tall, striking woman in a maroon business suit appeared in the foyer and appraised them with a curious smile. "Yes?"

"My name is Wells. Herbert George Wells." He extended his hand. "Would you be Elizabeth Robbins . . . ?"

"No," she said apologetically, "I'm sorry."

His hopes shattered, he was wondering what they could possibly do next other than go back to the tyranny of the Internet, but the woman was still talking.

"They moved away after the earthquake in 1989."

"1989?" H.G. gasped. That damned seismologist, W. K. Chichester, had been wrong by twenty years!

"You should've seen this place." She led them into a spacious living room with floor-to-ceiling glass that faced the bay. "It was totally wrecked. Incredible. An absolute mess." She misread H.G.'s baffled expression. "Have you ever been in a major earthquake?"

He shook his head.

She chuckled. "I was at the game. Game three of the World Series. They hadn't even thrown out the first pitch, and you should've felt Candlestick Park rocking and rolling." She smiled nostalgically. "Anyway, we'd been looking for a place in the Marina, and a week after the quake, our broker brought us here. . . ." A bigger smile. "The Robbinses sold for fifty cents on the dollar. Then we rebuilt."

"It's beautiful," Amber crooned.

"Thank you."

"Do you have any idea what happened to the Robbinses?" asked H.G.

"I believe they moved to Beverly Hills," she said, "but I'm not really sure. Its been years, you know."

"Beverly Hills?"

"They had a daughter," she mused, "a cute little girl. She must be in her thirties by now."

"How could you not know that Amy had a sister?"

"She never talked about her family," he said weakly as they hurried back to the rental car. "I can only suppose she was allowing me to revel in the somewhat dubious accomplishments of 1979 and then translate that for our own world."

"How selfish."

"When we talked, we talked about our own family," he protested. "The boys, Gip and Frank, and, and—"

They got in the car, and Amber pulled out onto Marina Boulevard without looking. Drivers swerved and leaned on their horns, but she paid them no attention, still preoccupied with Amy and her family. "She didn't think about them? Or remember?"

"I didn't say that. I said she never talked about them. How can I presume to know what she was thinking?"

"You'd been married for eleven years."

"Blast it, I told you! When she was Catherine, she would go for long walks on the beach or vanish in the garden house, and later I would find her writing poetry or arranging flowers. She would take imaginary lovers in her dreams."

"What's that got to do with her sister?"

"I was merely trying to explain."

"Maybe you were uncomfortable with the life that Amy had led in the future. Before she met you. Men are like that."

"Balderdash!"

"Maybe you told her not to talk about her family."

"She was free to discuss whatever she pleased," he said hotly. "And just for the bloody record, she was quite happy in our world."

"If it had been me and I had a sister," Amber said defiantly, "I'd talk about her whenever I damn well pleased."

Amber felt better. His presumed ignorance of his own family gave her a reason for anger and frustration. Should he ask why she was upset, she wouldn't have to mention her unforgivable weakness, those moments in his bed, and apologize for the umpteenth time.

Now they were on Van Ness Avenue, mired in traffic, inching south toward the freeway and the airport. At the rate they were going, Wells mused darkly, they might as well have been on their way to Mexico.

"I could get there faster on a bicycle," he said. "Not to mention a motorbike."

Helicopters circled up ahead like angry hornets, indicating that there was an accident or crime or chase or alert or some sort of disruption.

"You know, there mustn't have been a lot of forward thinking among the road builders in the last half of the twentieth century."

She glanced at him quizzically.

"They didn't anticipate the profusion of motor cars or the fact that modern man would be virtually helpless without them."

"Your point?"

"Why not build roads underground? Or stack one on top of another? Then there would be no traffic jams, and we could all get to where we were going quickly and efficiently."

"They already tried that here," she replied, smiling wickedly. "It worked great. . . . The Nimitz Freeway was a double-decker."

"Yes?"

"The earthquake flattened it in '89."

They were on the first space-available flight to LAX, H.G.'s spirits rising with the aircraft, finally leveling off with a generous sense of well-being, especially now that they were supposedly out of earthquake country. In fact, he couldn't remember when he had felt this good. Though still a neophyte, he already adored flying: it was an example of how technology served the common man so that he might be free to become a citizen of the world. *Certainly, if one can go everywhere this quickly, then one can be a part of everywhere just as quickly*, he thought, not realizing the deadly irony of his observation or the contributions of jet engines to global warming. He was in far too good a mood. The tea that the flight attendant had served wasn't all that terrible, either — despite the paper cup that he jokingly deemed more appropriate for urine samples should one's physician desire a uroscopy.

Amber worried that his ebullient mood was on account of Amy and hated herself for it. She had volunteered to guide him through her world and help him find Amy, not wreck his marriage. Yet she couldn't stop her feelings from running amok. She asked herself why she had done it in the first place — he wasn't paying her a salary, he wasn't promising her anything. Was it as simple as his limpid blue eyes? No, no way, even she knew better than that. Rather, he was the stuff of dreams, and not just the sexy kind. He was the portal to parallel universes, and now that she knew they existed, she didn't want to be forever stuck in a world that since yesterday at the Getty had become proverbially flat. Risking her career, maybe even her life, was worth it all for that one glimpse or leap or whatever into the beyond — or so she had told herself. What she hadn't counted on was him. Maybe it was as simple as his limpid blue eyes.

She turned and gave him a warm smile. "Can we go somewhere?"

"We are going somewhere."

"I mean in *The Utopia*."

"I have to repair it," he said noncommittally.

"We'll be vaporized together," she mused. "A ménage of molecules."

He didn't smile.

"Come on, don't be so rigid." She turned, her breasts brushing his arm. Then she gently touched his face. "I mean, I want to understand. . . . Is it like flying?"

"No," he said patiently. "Because one doesn't *go* anywhere. You get in the time machine at a 'present,' and you get out at a 'future' or 'past.' It's only like flying if at some point in your journey, the time machine happens to be on an aircraft."

"Oookay. . . . Do I just sit there, then?"

"No. You're vaporized."

"I know that. What comes next?"

He frowned testily. "Didn't we talk about this yesterday?"

"I didn't get it yesterday."

He sighed with resignation, gathered his thoughts. She'd ruined the plane ride for him, so he might as well give it another go, and perhaps then she would stop pestering him. He pushed the residue on his tray table to one side and found a single grain of sugar from the sugar packet. He centered it, then held it up on the tip of his finger. He explained: "Believe it or not, within this minuscule speck of sugar are universes, planets, and creatures living lives, some intelligent, some no doubt meaningless." With a flourish, he flicked the grain of sugar into space and chuckled at her shocked expression.

"Lest you think that I just destroyed countless civilizations, consider this: We have no idea how time is measured in that grain of sugar. To its creatures, a billion years might've passed in the millisecond it took me to pick it up. . . . Maybe I created thousands of earthquakes by launching it into the air and mass destruction followed when it hit the floor."

"I get that."

"No, you don't get that. . . . Someday we, too, shall hit the floor . . .

when some enormous creature on some enormous planet flicks our world off its finger and—catapulted out of orbit—Mother Earth hurtles towards an enormous pile of rocks somewhere."

"Okay, but I gotta tell you . . ." She shook her head firmly. "At work, I look through microscopes every day, and I'm pretty sure that a grain of sugar is made up of particles. Not planets."

"Does not the structure of an atom resemble a solar system . . . ?"

She paused, confused, then bit her lip. "What does this have to do with time travel?"

"I am merely pointing out the immensity of the cosmos so that you can accept that every moment of our lives is reflected in parallel universes, each one different from the other depending upon the density of dark gravity and the vagaries of fate."

"I don't care about that!"

He shrugged in frustration. "Perhaps you'd care about being reduced to a vapor not knowing if you'd ever again be the lovely young woman that you happen to be right now."

"I just want to go with you," she said petulantly.

He closed his eyes, but could no longer ignore her insinuations that hung between them like delicate perfume. "'Dusa," he said patiently, "I'm not interested in a passage."

"Who said this was just a passage?"

Blushing crimson, she put her hand to her mouth, mortified by her words, then was glad that she'd spoken them. And when he turned to her with an incredulous look, she surprised him with a gentle kiss, smiled happily when he didn't resist, then kissed him full on the mouth, not letting go until she heard the flight attendant announcing the final approach and the landing gear shuddering down beneath the plane.

Finally, H.G. pushed away, glanced anxiously at the other passengers, but none of them had noticed 'Dusa's assault, and if they had, they didn't seem to care.

"No worries," she whispered in his ear and smiled. "I can be cool."

He raised his eyebrows quizzically, asking for a translation.

"Amy doesn't have to know."

He gazed morosely out the window, watching the runway rising to meet them, and felt the aircraft gently touch down, the experience ruined by the close proximity of Amber. He wondered how he could possibly extricate himself from her and retain her as a guide through 2010 at the same time.

Nothing came to him, nothing at all.

1:05 P.M., Monday, June 21, 2010

Lieutenant Casey Holland pushed his chair away from the trio of flat-screen monitors that bracketed his desk and turned to the window. He'd just looked at the surveillance tapes from the Getty, and they confirmed what Peterson, the security guard, had said in his interview. One camera had gone out at 12:03 A.M., and then they had all "whited out" at 4:53 A.M.

Sergeant Young had followed up with their video technicians, but they couldn't find anything wrong. An expert from the home office in New Jersey was flying out to take a look, and the tapes had been emailed to the FBI. So all they had right now were two clips from other cameras: Teresa Cruz running up the courtyard, the image marred by a faint red glow, and that same red glow in the rotunda. Once again, the technicians had no clue. Not that it mattered. In the men's room where the murder had taken place there were no surveillance cameras. Holland gazed at the walls, frustrated, angry with himself.

It was the case—but it wasn't the case.

He couldn't shake the image of Jaclyn Smythe that hung like gossamer lace in his mind. Sure, he'd lusted in his heart for beautiful women—what man hadn't?—but this pull went beyond that, and he couldn't fathom it. He wondered if it was love, then frowned darkly and was disgusted. He wanted to keep his mind clean and good for Cheryl and the kids, yet he'd just spent hours looking at missing-persons data-bases for this strange woman—even calling the SFPD when he should have been working harder on the Brentwood killings.

Yes, he'd looked at the tapes, yes, he'd beefed up patrols and had three detectives following up on "sightings" of the killer, but he wasn't past square one. He still hadn't been able to locate Heather Trattner. He had called her cell seven times, had gotten voice mail and left mes-sages. He'd had the GPS people try to track her phone, but no such luck. *Somebody has to tell the poor woman she's got a dead husband.*

He thought of Amber Reeves and missed her. *One classy chick, one good technician. She brings light and color—she brings life to a crime scene, which is ironic as hell. She ain't no detective, though.* She'd left a message suggesting that the Brentwood murderer was a Jack the Ripper copycat, overlooking the fact that the Ripper did hookers, and there weren't a lot of them in Brentwood. Whether the psychopath was copy-ing somebody or not didn't alter the bleak reality that he was out there on the hunt and wanting to make fools of the West L.A. Division. Maybe that's what REMEMBER ME? on the body was all about. The killer bragging about his unsolved murders in the past. Holland made a note to coordinate with the cold-case people downtown. Right now, he didn't have the time or inclination.

Some hikers had just found another body in Will Rogers Park, this one arranged like Venus de Milo with another happy face drawn in blood on the torso. A crime-beat reporter friend from the L.A. *Times* had called earlier saying that they were going to do a page-three story headlined "Portrait of the Artist as a Serial Killer."

Holland sighed. The Jane Doe hadn't yet been identified; for all he knew, the body parts could have come from more than one victim. Sure, they'd eventually find out. The lab would do their thing and chase dental records, but he wasn't holding his breath. About all he could hope for was someone would report the woman missing and then identify the head. He shuddered, repulsed.

He glanced at the case files on his desk, then a stack of magazines.

On top was the latest *Scientific American*, its dark-red cover featuring in-depth stories on skin and stem-cell research, and the battle of the sexes in terms of DNA and chromosomes, but he already knew he'd never have time to read them. *I should've gone to law school.*

His cell phone rang.

"This is Holland."

"Hey, Lieutenant, it's Sergeant Young. . . . We got the perp."

One of Sergeant Young's routine gimmicks was to nail perps by using cell phones the old-fashioned way. If, say, a killer had stolen his victim's cell, and the phone didn't have GPS technology or the killer had turned it off, Young would wait a day or so—until he figured the killer was feeling invincible—then call the number and track the phone. In this case, Albert Grattan had answered Michael Trattner's cell, and they nailed him behind a strip mall off Bundy.

When Holland walked in the interview room, he was hit by Grattan's stench and knew that the dude was a homeless junkie, yet that didn't mean he wasn't capable of murder. Grattan immediately started whining that he'd found the phone in a trash can at Starbucks—hey, finders keepers, losers weepers, what the fuck's so against the law about answering a cell phone? Holland listened stoically to Grattan's sad, pathetic story of how he'd once been a college professor, then had been hounded out of academia because the maintenance people didn't like him sleeping in his office, or some such nonsense. The lieutenant asked Grattan if he'd mind drawing a happy face, and Grattan replied, fuck, no, man, whatever gets me out of the gulag.

Holland gave Grattan paper and crayons, then watched him attempt a half-dozen, but with each one, Grattan's hand went off-track and drew meth-addled happy faces that looked like flattened raisins. He knew then that Grattan was not their man, yet told Sergeant Young to hold him and run DNA tests just to be certain. Holland headed back to his office, Jaclyn Smythe dancing in his brain again, this time doing a striptease. He blushed, felt guilty. He detoured into the detectives' squad bay for a cup of lousy coffee.

"Lieutenant Holland?" came the secretary's voice over the speakerphone when he was finally back in his office.

"If it's TV or the *Times*, send 'em to voice mail."

She laughed. "Actually, it's Sergeant Ron Esposito from the SFPD."

Holland brightened, picked up the phone, exchanged pleasantries and a touch of shoptalk with Esposito, then explained why he'd called in the first place. In a San Francisco missing-persons database, he had discovered that Amy Catherine Robbins had abruptly disappeared in late November or early December, 1979, thanks to an official missing-persons report filed by her parents on December 10 when she hadn't shown up for a family reunion. He wondered why Jaclyn Smythe's family wanted her to track down someone after an absence of thirty years or so, but figured they must have their reasons, and he sure as hell wasn't going to question her for something as harmless as an old friend. So he had called the detective who had taken the original report, but an officer in the SFPD missing-persons department said that the detective had since passed away and referred him to Ron Esposito.

After bringing Esposito up to speed, Holland asked if Esposito could email a copy of the original report down.

A long, static-filled pause.

"Hey, Ron, you still there?"

"Yeah, I'm still here." He laughed. "Life sure as hell gets serendipitous when you're a cop, you know?"

"I dunno, but okay."

"We're talking about Amy Catherine Robbins, right?"

"Right."

"She disappeared almost thirty-one years ago, right?"

"Right."

"Well, her parents called me this morning to tell me that she'd finally come home."

2:45 P.M., Monday, June 21, 2010

"This is home," Amber announced.

H.G. closed the door behind him, surprised there was no foyer and that the living room was so small and crowded. Behind the far wall was a narrow kitchen and a breakfast nook, and to his right a hallway led to the one bedroom and bath. The threadbare sofa and chairs too big for the room reminded him of his salad days at Mornington Crescent when, given a scientific epiphany, he had discovered how to harness dark energy and had built his time machine. That was before he had editors eager to publish his articles and Frederick Macmillan asking for his books. He wondered how he had survived and if he could do it all over again or would end up a draper's apprentice as he'd started out. The pursuit of science had been his escape.

Thank God for science. Thank God for his mentor, the brilliant T. H. Huxley. Thank God for his own stubborn naïveté and unbridled optimism. Then he frowned. *Yet, if we do blow ourselves up, if our planet does indeed implode into a black hole millions of years before its time, does any of that matter?*

"What do you think?" Smiling, she interrupted his thoughts, spread her arms and twirled.

"Cozy." Grateful for the distraction, he glanced out the window over the breakfast nook at a narrow alley that separated her building from other, identical buildings. "Quite cozy."

"Are you all right now?"

"I'm fine, thank you."

Not true. After she had kissed him on the plane, he had maintained a discreet distance. Now he was annoyed that he'd had no time to stop and investigate this new world, that his curiosity in 2010 was now a luxury. He had gone to the loo at the terminal to get away from her so he could think clearly, but even his ludicrous imitation of Auguste Rodin's "The Thinker" couldn't free his mind. Zipping up his trousers, he'd noticed that his pocket watch had fallen to the floor. It had read 12:17 P.M., Monday. He'd been in the future for more than twenty-four hours, Amy was still missing, and he had accomplished nothing other than getting himself mixed up with a needy young woman.

They had taken a cab back to the Getty, picked up Amber's motor car and gone to her apartment in Ocean Park—only because it was a convenient place to work. He hadn't even bothered to tinker with the miscellany in her Mercury Milan, preferring to stare out the window seeing nothing, wondering about Amy. About Leslie John Stephenson.

Now in Amber's apartment, he stared at her laptop in its case, yet was actually reluctant to make the leap of faith into this electronic crystal ball of a computer until he understood it more fully. Alas, he didn't have that luxury, either. He said, "Shall we go back to work?"

"Whatever," she murmured. She set up her laptop on the kitchen table, turned suddenly. "You know, about what happened on the plane—"

He held up a hand, stopped her. "Please. . . . You mustn't take it personally. You're a beautiful girl, but I have obligations."

"I know all that, but I'm not asking—"

"'Dusa, if you don't leave me alone . . ." He decided to overstate his case, hoping to make an impression. "If you don't leave me alone, I'm going to do something I'll regret and wreck both our lives."

She looked down and blushed.

"Besides, once you get to know me, you'll discover that I'm not the most decent chap you'll ever meet." He grinned, tried to make light of it. "Just ask the critics at the London *Times*."

"But—"

"No more."

Except Amber wasn't finished, wasn't about to be silenced. She couldn't get over that kiss on the plane—the moment had actually been more intimate than being in bed with him the night before, and somewhere between that kiss and right now she had decided that she was in love. Yes, she knew it was insane, that at best he was some flesh-and-blood version of a virtual reality, and she was acting like a science fiction groupie, but it didn't matter. Nor did it matter that she'd known him for only a day and a half. Like most new lovers, she didn't consider what came next or how they could possibly make a life; she didn't consider Amy; she didn't consider their different worlds or centuries; that they had little in common in this reality was of no consequence, either. It never occurred to her not to follow her heart.

"Can we get on with this?" he said patiently.

She stopped, then touched his face, found his eyes and let her hand rest on his neck. "D'you guys have sex . . . ? You and Amy?"

Surprised, he smiled thinly. "That's between Amy and myself."

"It's pristine sex, right?"

He reddened and looked down helplessly, was at a loss for words.

"Which is sad, 'cause she used to be the other woman, right? And other women are famous for great sex and good times, am I right?"

"What the devil are you talking about?"

"Don't you really want your wife to be a whore in bed and a Madonna in public . . . ?"

"I beg your pardon?"

"That's why you do your passades, right?"

He left the room, but she followed, took his arm, turned him around.

"'Cause I can do both. I can be the perfect little Edwardian wife if you want." She touched his face and added in a whisper, "Then come home and fuck your brains out."

"'Dusa, please!"

"Well . . . ?" She smiled wickedly. Her heart pounded. "Think about it."

He glared at her. "Would you still want me if I stopped everything for you and said to hell with Amy?"

She stepped back, her mouth forming an O. She shook her head no, like a schoolgirl. Then, deflated, she sat at the table and turned on the laptop. She blinked back tears. If she'd had someplace to go, she would have bolted, but she was home. Her own place was all around her, a cruel reminder, and she wondered if after this man and *The Utopia*, she belonged anywhere.

So she sat at the laptop like an automaton and shelved her bruised emotions. *Something silk*, she thought, *it's like I've just bought something silk and beautiful, but have to put it away until the right occasion.*

H.G. stared at his pocket watch, his face burning from 'Dusa's proposition. In his own time, despite socialism and the suffragettes, an emancipated woman proposing to a married man—and proud of it— would have been unheard of. So outrageous, in fact, that it would make a fabulous novel. *One that I wouldn't mind writing, though Macmillan might not want to publish it. I doubt I'd name my emancipated woman Amber, however. Maybe Ann . . . Ann Veronica.*

He stole a glance at Amber, and she gave him a blank look that masked her feelings. They exchanged uncomfortable smiles, then returned to their own spaces, the silence, the white noise from city traffic. He waited for a few minutes, for the heat of the moment to pass, and when he sensed that she had become respectable again, he joined her at the laptop.

They started in again, Googling "Kevin and Elizabeth Robbins, Los Angeles, California" and getting 461,000 responses, most of them Web pages for somebody else. A waste of keystrokes, H.G. told himself, but Amber had moved on to a program called "people lookup" which at first glance seemed promising. It listed addresses, phone numbers, previous cities lived in and relatives. There were one hundred and forty-some Robbinses in the Los Angeles area, none of them named Kevin or Elizabeth and none of them living in Beverly Hills. Regardless, Amber began the tedious process of getting details on each one of them, H.G. distracting her because he was peering at the slots for DVDs, the intricate plugs on the back of her computer.

"What're you looking for?"

"I haven't a clue, 'Dusa. I'll know it when I see it."

"Hey, you want something to drink . . . ? You hungry?" She paused. "There's Coke in the fridge and taquitos in the freezer. . . ."

"Taq-quitos . . . ?"

"If you didn't try them when you were here in '79, they're to die for."

He looked at her, puzzled.

"You'll like them." She went back to the laptop, then heard him banging in a cupboard and pulling out an iron skillet. "No, no, you don't have to go to all that trouble. Put them in the microwave."

"The microwave. . . ."

Great Scott, is she referring to electromagnetic waves, originally discovered due to Maxwell's equations, and then effectively demonstrated by one Heinrich Hertz when I was at the Normal School? Or was it after I'd left? I can see how they might be useful for radio and television, but in the kitchen?

She laughed again. "You're helpless, aren't you?" She came in the kitchen and started to take the taquitos from his hand, but he resisted.

"I'm quite capable of heating food, 'Dusa."

"Okay." She pointed at the microwave oven on the counter, clicked open its door for him. "You put it in, set the time—you can do timers, can't you?—close the door and push Start." She went back to the table and sat down. "Two minutes should be plenty."

Frowning, H.G. set the timer, then dumped the taquitos in the skillet, closed it in the microwave, pressed Start, stepped back to watch.

The microwave arced and zapped in blue and yellow flashes, danced on the counter and then exploded. Smoke poured out from behind its door.

H.G. was flattened against the refrigerator, staring at the blackened appliance, now convinced that microwaves had no place in the kitchen.

Flabbergasted, Amber stood up, her hands on her hips.

"Don't tell me you put a frying pan in there?"

"A metal frying pan," he said, mortified, "containing a molecular structure incompatible with microwaves. I'm so sorry."

She howled with laughter. "Hey, wanna do takeout?"

While they waited for a sizzling chicken plate from the King of Siam, Amber clicked her way through two more Robbinses in the L.A. area, finally threw up her hands in frustration.

"Don't you know anything about her family?"

"She didn't get along with her father. Most girls don't, so the professionals tell us."

"I never had a father."

"She loved her mum. . . . And she absolutely adored her grandmother Sara."

"Sara?" Amber straightened up, her eyes going wide and bright. "Her grandmother was named Sara?"

"Yes, I believe so."

"I was named after my grandmother. Maybe Amy's sister was named after their grandmother."

They bent over the laptop like eager children before a magician as Amber went to the white pages and quickly found Sara Robbins, MFCC, a counselor in Sherman Oaks, and the eager became the amazed.

His fingers trembling, H.G. dialed the number and got Sara's voice mail. After the beep, he had the presence of mind to introduce himself as Herbert George Wells—no relation, of course—who had been trying to locate his wife, Amy Catherine Robbins, but had misplaced her phone number, and could she please call if she is indeed the right Ms. Sara Robbins? Satisfied, he hung up and smiled at Amber.

"You forgot to leave a number."

Mortified, he called back and did.

And then they waited.

An Hour and a Half Earlier

"What happened to your arm?" asked a concerned Sara Robbins.

"Oh, that," said her sister, laughing nervously. She glanced at her arm, which an urgent-care nurse had bandaged with a flesh-colored patch after her clumsy dressing had come loose as she was buying some twenty-first-century clothes, none of which fit properly. "I was in a hurry at the . . . the airport and I cut myself on a door."

"But it's okay now?"

"Yes, quite all right, thank you."

Her chin in her hand, Sara smiled and gazed at her sister. "You look *great*, you know."

"Thank you, so do you."

"I mean . . . don't take this the wrong way, but you look so young."

Amy smiled.

"Is there some place you go? Or, or something . . . ?"

"Facials are quite the thing in London," Amy said blithely, never having had a facial in her life.

Sara continued gazing at her. "God, you sound so *British*."

"Yes, well, I pretty much am now." Amy fidgeted with the lunch menu in front of her, her eyes darting around at the other guests, the room, resonating with their animated talk and laughter. *They all seem so happy, so full of themselves.* She glanced back at Sara—she had that same joie de vivre, yet looking at her was like looking in a mirror. *If not for the age difference, if she weren't so happy, we could've been twins. They must've had her after I went to 1893 with Bertie, though Daddy was never big on children. Was she a mistake or did Mom want to replace me? And then Daddy decided to do it right the second time around and raise a girl who was "capable" instead of all the other things he used to call me.* She smiled shyly and added, "It seems I've been there forever."

"I hate to say this," Sara said low, "but we all thought you were dead." She leaned forward and gripped Amy's hand. "I . . . I thought I was going to go through life without ever having known you."

"I'm so sorry," Amy replied, her voice quavering. "I should've come sooner." *Or maybe not at all.* She was having trouble accepting the hard reality that she might be stuck out of time and never see her home again.

"So you're married and have kids?"

Amy nodded, fought to hold back tears at the thought of little Gip and Frank without her, yet managed a proud smile.

"When do I get to meet them?"

Amy looked off and gathered herself. *Probably never.* She didn't have the special key. When she had climbed down from *The Utopia*, she'd been shocked to discover that she wasn't in H.G.'s lab in Mornington Crescent—she was over five thousand miles away. She had planned to reunite with her parents by flying from London to San Francisco, but that hadn't been necessary. Her portal to 2010 had been the Getty Museum—a museum so breathtakingly marvelous that she thought she had arrived in the wrong century. Yet to be in an unknown, an unexpected place—she had been petrified with fear. So panicked, in fact, that she'd forgotten about the special key—not to mention her purse. So panicked that she had forgotten her husband's notes about keeping the machine "when it was," but knew she had only ninety seconds to do something and had pulled the first thing she saw—the declinometer ring below the cabin door. Then she ran and had just cleared the center gallery when she'd been staggered by a blinding flash meaning that she'd done something terribly wrong.

The time machine had physically left without her.

So, no, it wasn't likely that Sara Robbins would ever meet Bertie and the boys.

"Maybe when you come to London," Amy fibbed. "You see, I left on such short notice . . . I was so worried about the earthquake and . . . and . . ." Her voice trailed off. "I'm not doing very well, am I?" she said candidly.

Sara sipped her white wine and smiled professionally. "Hey, it's okay. We all do things for crazy reasons."

"Yes, but now it seems so silly to have come all this way just to warn someone of something that has already happened. You can't imagine how mortified I am, especially after Daddy—"

Sara laughed easily. "Look at the bright side, Amy. . . . If you hadn't come, we might never have met."

"You girls ready to order?" said the waiter.

They both went back to their menus, Sara making up her mind quickly and asking for an Asian calamari salad with spicy ginger lime vinaigrette and a Pellegrino. Whereas for Amy, the menu might as well have been written in a foreign language. Yes, she loved fine cuisines and had eaten at her share of great restaurants in London and on the continent, but she had no clue what many of these dishes were and had no intention of asking the waiter, especially when she felt his eyes— and Sara's—on her, and knew she was blushing hard.

"Need more time?"

"No, no." She looked up and forced a smile, was reduced to what she would've ordered as a teenager in the seventies. "I'll just have a hamburger and fries."

Sara's puzzled expression came and went so quickly that Amy didn't catch it.

"I'm actually quite famished." Amy handed her menu to the waiter, smiled and once again said the wrong thing. "I could eat a horse."

In the wee hours of Sunday morning, Amy had walked from the Getty complex down to the 405, had followed the frontage road looking for shelter and found the Hotel Angeleno, a curiously circular building lit up in garish purple. At first glance, she'd thought it was a twenty-first-century advertisement of some kind—or worse, the headquarters for a Southern California cult religion. Relieved that it was a hotel, she had checked in, grateful she had worn her 1979 dollars in a money belt, and once in her room, was grateful for the solitude.

After a hot bath, she went straight to bed, fell asleep missing Bertie and the boys, and slept through most of the day. She woke up asking herself how she could have been so insane, taking the time machine as if out for a mere Sunday drive. She hadn't been worried about the boys—not so much because Mrs. Vickers was an excellent nanny but because she had been convinced that she'd be back before she left. Thanks to Bertie and his theory, thanks to helping him pen *The Time Machine*, she had been seduced by the romance of time travel. *More like rape, it was.*

She had called her parents in San Francisco, was surprised their phone number had been disconnected, then placed a call to her namesake, Aunt Amy, who had lived in Short Hills, New Jersey, forever. They talked for two hours, Amy crying sometimes—wistful tears for a life that she hadn't lived, joyful tears for the life she had lived—then lapsing into a terrible silence at the notion of being caught somewhere in between. Aunt Amy had told her about Sara, her therapist sister, and her parents moving to Beverly Hills some twenty years ago.

Late Sunday afternoon, thoroughly bewildered, she'd taken a cab to a dismal big-box store where she shopped anonymously for toiletries and a few modern outfits. She had no intention of meeting her family, especially Daddy, looking like she'd stepped out of a costume drama.

They had finally all met this morning—a beautiful, sunny Monday— and Amy thought she was rather convincing as a twenty-first-century woman, but in that wonderful glow of a family reunited, she'd said some reckless, dumb things. "Coming home to warn them of the big one" had left her father amazed. He couldn't hold back soft, yet derisive laughter. "You're twenty years too late," he had replied. He had already suffered enormous loss, had already moved home and insurance business out of San Francisco, and now she had flown back into their lives like Mary Poppins or something. *"Why didn't you just pick up the phone?"* he'd said. *"Why didn't you call twenty-five years ago and tell us you were okay? Or would that have been too considerate? We understand people running off to see the world and live their own lives, but usually they say good-bye. Oh, no, not my little Amy. She was always at the back of the line, always a space cadet."* He had shaken his head, disgusted, was about to go off on one of his diatribes when their mom tactfully reminded him that they had to go or he'd be late for a doctor's appointment.

When they were alone, Sara had mentioned lunch and asked Amy what kind of food she liked, thoroughly stumping her. The first dish that came to mind was what she'd served her guests the night she left: roasted rack and shoulder of lamb, cooked extremely slowly, Savoy cabbage and creamed potatoes with a rosemary gravy, plenty of French wines and her famous bread pudding for dessert. Wisely, she deferred to Sara, and they had gone to the Garden on Glendon in Westwood Village, where Amy's education had begun.

"So what d'you think of them after all this time?" asked Sara.

"I've always loved Mum—I mean, our mother."

"She's perpetually sweet, isn't she?"

Amy nodded, ate another forkful of French fries—unmindful that everyone here still used their fingers. "Now, Daddy . . . Daddy and I were always quarreling."

Sara's eyes lingered briefly on her sister's brand-new yet woefully out-of-style blouse and skirt and patent-leather half-boots. She said, "I didn't get along with Daddy very well, either."

"Really . . . ? I would've thought the opposite."

Sara chuckled ironically, sipped her wine, sighed and took in her sister again. "He was always telling me how great you were and how you used to do things and what a sweet little girl you were."

"No!"

"Oh, yeah." She glanced off, a brittle smile in place, her eyes half-closed as she remembered. "Ohh, yeah. . . . It could've been something as dumb as making my bed the wrong way or not keeping my room picked up or not helping Mom in the kitchen or even how I drove the damned car." She looked down self-consciously. "He'd always say . . . Amy wouldn't have done it that way."

"I, I don't believe you," said Amy, astonished.

Yet Sara kept on as if she hadn't heard. "Now I realize that's why I worked so hard in school and why I stayed away from them and got my own place and borrowed my own way through grad school so I couldn't be criticized for running up a tab on Daddy for another worthless degree. . . . When he was saying all along how smart you were for getting such a great job at the Bank of England right out of high school!"

"My God," Amy uttered.

They gazed at each other. Sara's words hung in the air, and then Amy smiled, added softly, "He . . . he always told me I was throwing my life away by not going to UC Berkeley."

Sara laughed raucously. "He used to tell me I should find somebody, settle down and start a family. . . . I mean, didn't you see how happy he was when you announced that you had kids . . . ?"

"No," said Amy, "I must've missed that."

Sara leaned across the table, touched Amy's hand again, tears welling in her eyes. "Forgive me for saying this, but I got tired of being compared to a sister I didn't know. . . . I still am. I'm tired of . . . of being compared to someone we all thought was dead."

Amy stared wide-eyed at her sister, flooded with bad memories long buried in her psyche, memories that were becoming revelations. Her father had treated her exactly the same way as he had Sara, both their childhoods suffocated by the belief that they didn't measure up. Amy— held up to an imaginary person she could never be. Sara—held up to an image of a perfect sister long gone. In the eyes of their father, no matter how hard they both tried, they'd never be good enough.

A silence.

"That's why I became a therapist," Sara said in a low voice. "I wanted to understand if it was me . . . or him."

"And . . . ?"

"After meeting you, my dear sister, I think it's him."

Amy closed her eyes, let her breath, her pent-up emotions whoosh out. She imagined that whoosh becoming a fresh breeze across the centuries that would keep her head crystal clear like the sea air at Sandgate and, briefly, she was there on the cliffs beside her flowers, Bertie smiling from afar, the boys running across the lawn. Then, back in the restaurant, in 2010, she saw that most of the patrons had finished their lunch and left, yet here she was blissfully full with a barely touched hamburger gone cold. Finally, she was completely relaxed and had no desire to leave this space, for her sister had just excised a time-crossed inadequacy from her soul. Her hand shaking, she finished her wine, then drank some water, too.

"I must tell you," Amy said, attempting levity, "I think we were both hoodwinked."

Sara wiped her eyes. "Here I was prepared to meet my sister, the golden girl, and now it turns out . . ." She took a breath. "It turns out we were both living a lie."

Amy chuckled ironically. "Yes, but I'm so relieved."

"Me, too. . . . We both escaped."

"Indeed."

"Except there's just one thing. . . ."

"Yes?" said Amy.

"What in the world *happened* to you . . . ?"

Should I tell her . . . ?

Amy was already comfortable with Sara and close enough not to analyze why. Since their childhoods had been so agonizingly similar, she felt as if they had grown up together like normal sisters, and wondered abstractly if that mysterious yet profound bond of sisterhood could transcend universes. She sensed that it could, though that was a question more for H.G. and other geniuses. The fact that she and Sara were acting like sisters was enough.

No, don't tell her.

At least not straightaway. Amy already had too much to worry about, especially if she was stuck in this alien time. She didn't want to risk

Sara thinking that she was insane, for that would forever skew their re-
lationship. So—answering Sara—she took a breath and plunged in.

She painted an idyllic picture of life with H.G. after getting off the
time machine in 1893—their love, their work, running away to get married, their successes, their lovely children, their lovely house by the sea—
except she replaced the time-traveling with an impulsive plane ride to
London, she left out the dates, the specifics—names, titles and the like—
and she used noms de plume for friends and others. Alas, the entire scenario seemed lifted from a romance roman à clef. She wasn't aware of
Sara's puzzlement at the vague dates and pseudonyms, for she had become enraptured with her own words, her memories of Bertie. She
paused frequently to dab at her eyes with her napkin, realizing horribly
that she truly did miss him and—if there was a way—that she should
go home and apologize and not give up till they were lovers again, only
more so because their children were living proof of their time-crossed
love.

The afternoon shadows had lengthened outside, and the waiters
were lowering the shades. The table jockeys were cleaning up and setting places for the dinner hour, and as they went back and forth, snip-
pets of Spanish floated out from the kitchen with the aromas of exotic
dishes from faraway places. Amy and Sara were an island in a sea of
empty tables, the spell of Amy's words having insulated them from the
bustle of activity until finally she couldn't go on any longer and began
crying, utterly heartbroken.

Confused, Sara squeezed her hand again. "Hey, come on, girl, it's
not like you're never going to see him again."

Amy gave her a blank, soulful look.

"Ohh, I get it." Sara nodded and sat back in her chair. "Now I get
it. . . . You're *separated*."

Flustered, Amy turned red, then managed, "Not really. . . . I mean,
yes and no, I mean . . ."

"Well, that's my forte, big sister. I'm not supposed to counsel relatives, but, hey, you want to talk about it . . . ?"

Amy gulped, stared at Sara, realized that she'd already said too
much, but her sister had picked up the thread and gone on with it.

"Okay, you met Bertie when he was on vacation and came in the bank to change some currency. Then you ran off to the UK with him. So when exactly did you get married . . . ?"

Amy looked off and avoided her sister, gripped the chair hard as she frantically tried to come up with a date that seemed normal, yet how could she explain away thirty-one years when in real time it had only been eleven? When her boys were only two and four? "You know, I really don't want to talk about it. . . . I'm sorry."

If Sara was surprised, she didn't show it. She shrugged, then said sympathetically, "You're going to have to someday."

"I think we should go," Amy said nervously.

"Okay." Sara waved to get the waiter's attention, handed him her credit card, continued staring off thoughtfully, tapping her fingers on the table as if something was strange, out-of-kilter.

Amy sensed it, looked at the floor, praying that she could escape the situation.

"How long are you staying?" asked Sara, swinging back to her.

"Unh, I'm not quite sure."

"Anything special you'd like to do while you're here?"

"Why, yes," said Amy, brightening, seizing the moment. "I'd like to see the Getty Museum."

"Cool," said Sara, nodding, "very cool. I'll check my schedule, and we'll do it."

"Oh, thank you, thank you so much."

Sara fished through her purse, took out her razor-thin iPhone and turned it on. She touched the small screen, then frowned. "Wow. I'm gonna be late."

Intimidated, Amy shrank farther down in the chair and wished she were invisible, wished she were in fact made of "transparent, colorless tissue" like the character Griffin in Bertie's *The Invisible Man*.

"Give me your cell, and I'll let you know when we're on for the Getty."

"Cell . . . ?"

Sara sat back again, stared at her sister, cocked her head, then proceeded slowly, professionally. "Okay, if you're going to be at the parents' house, I'll just call you there."

Amy nodded.

The waiter brought the bill back. Sara scribbled in tip and total, signed hurriedly. "I'll take you back to the hotel so you can check out, and then I'll drop you at the parents'."

Amy smiled weakly. "I'm already checked out."

Sara frowned quizzically. "Where's your luggage?"

Amy lifted the shopping bag under the chair, set it back down again, her eyes pleading for understanding when she had no idea what that would be or where it would lead.

Sara tensed, took in her sister again—her new but arcane outfit, the social holes in her character, the dreamlike quality of her so-called history, the complete absence of normal small talk, and yes, no purse, no cell, no luggage. She released a ragged sigh.

"Did you have a breakdown, Amy?"

"I beg your pardon?"

"Have . . . have you been in an institution for the last thirty years?"

Amy recoiled, started to object, then realized that such a revelation would actually bring her closer to her sister—and she desperately needed someone in this world—and that having been locked away was a perfect excuse for her odd behavior. She smiled radiantly.

"Yes, I have."

3:01 P.M., Monday, June 21, 2010

Jaclyn nibbled on the olive from her second martini, dipped it back in the drink, then sucked down the pimento from its center, quite buzzed and thoroughly enjoying herself. She wasn't sure what was in the concoction, but didn't care. If nothing else, it certainly tasted better than the claret Wells had served on that nasty night in 1893 when—necessity being the mother of invention—Jack had stolen Wells's virgin time machine to escape the men of Scotland Yard. *Eons have passed since then. I have been to hell and back. And now, in memory of my dear, sweet, unfaithful Penny, I am playing artiste with the blood of others. Why, then, am I not enjoying it?*

Alongside her in the booth, Lieutenant Casey Holland nursed a beer, his beefy hands clutching the bottle as if it would keep him honest. They were at Nathaniel's Place, a run-down lounge between Wilshire and Santa Monica that with its red Naugahyde decor and Frank Sinatra soundtracks was a watering hole for middle-aged homosexuals. Jaclyn guessed he'd met her here because it was the last bar in town where a copper would go for a drink, the last place in this city where he might be recognized.

So, how much longer will he tell me he that loves his wife and kids, and how wonderful the bitch is—as he steals looks down the front of this skimpy floral-print dress I found in Heather's closet? How much longer must I smile and say I don't care, then lean forward so he can get a better view? He wears his self-denial like a religious flag—now he's apologizing because he won't tell me what he knows of Amy Catherine Robbins—and I'm actually being patient and understanding. She giggled. *Alas, the tedium. Jaclyn wants to play the artiste with ecstasy, not blood, this afternoon.*

The martinis had made mush of her rage—so that right now she didn't care so much about being Jack as she did being next to Casey Holland. Her mouth hurt from smiling. She laughed at everything he said. He'd already told her no, but that only made her want him more. She had been drawn to him when they had first met, and she'd asked herself: *When we are finished, what will I do with his corpse?* Make him Michelangelo's David sans penis? Now the questions burning inside were: *Oh, God, what will it be like? And, oh, God,* when? She crossed and uncrossed her legs—they whisked electric with her black panty-hose. A flush spread from her groin; she was becoming weak and warm and liquid. *Is this how those harlots felt before we took them out in the alley and Jack shoved it in? Is this how Penny felt when she cuckolded us and then laughed in Jack's face? Alas, there must be incalculable bliss in a woman's betrayal.*

"I'm really sorry," he repeated, "I'm just not cool with it."

"With Amy Catherine Robbins . . . ? Or with me?"

He blushed. "I mean, if she was related to you, it'd be a different story, you know?"

"Don't fret, love, it's all right," she murmured, unlike herself. "The sky's not falling." *Why doesn't he shut up about it? It's not as if I'm a brainless housewife—I'll find another way to the Robbins girl and Wells.*

"I feel like I'm crossing the line."

"Let's go hand-in-hand, love."

"You're not helping. I can't think straight." He pushed away. "I mean, my people are out there without me, and you've got me doing things I'm not supposed to be doing."

She kept silent. *He might convince himself.*

"I'm trying to understand this, okay? You tell me that your family's been looking for someone who's been missing for thirty-one years and then—bang—she turns up this morning."

She shrugged innocently, watched him absently finger a Post-it note in his coat pocket. "I don't understand it, either," she lied, "so why don't we consider the topic an academically moot point and get on with our lives?"

She knew from Jack's experience that girls weren't supposed to be the aggressive ones. But she couldn't help herself, and dropped her hand on his leg. She slowly traced a heart with her fingernails. Then, a nervous gesture from another time in another universe, she put her hand between her own legs to see if she was hard. She blushed sheepishly. Nothing was there, but thanks to the martini, instead of feeling a helpless rage, she chuckled ironically. With any luck, he would fill that emptiness for her.

"Look, why don't I do this—?"

"Why *don't* you . . . ?"

He frowned, then: "Why don't I call this Amy Catherine Robbins and explain the situation and ask her if she wants to contact your family in the UK? What about that?"

"I don't *care* anymore, love." *If he calls and talks to the girl, then my hand is played. Fresh from the nineteenth century, Amy Catherine Robbins would indeed figure it out, and so warned, she and Wells would become an impossible catch.*

Except here with this man—right now—she didn't give a damn. She giggled and fell against him, letting her hand slide over his chest and then—oh, the hell with it—she put it on his crotch.

"Can we go someplace?" she whispered into his ear.

He didn't move her hand.

"Can we?" She felt him swell against her fingers. "*Please?*"

She closed and locked the door behind them, turned. He had thrown his coat on the chair, was kicking off his shoes and trying to get out of his pants at the same time, knowing if he hesitated now, he'd change his mind. She ripped off her clothes, and so unchained, threw herself at him. He said wait, but, no, waiting was like being forever strung tight on the event horizon, waiting was death. She tore his shorts off, pushed him violently back on the bed, then straddled him and screamed with pleasure as he slid inside.

"My God, that's *it*! That's *it*!"

Oh, my, this has to be what those whores felt when Jack filled them! Trembling all over, she collapsed on top of him and tried to ride the pleasure, but it rode her, and she had to sink her teeth in his shoulder to hang on, to not disintegrate. In her mind their sex played through a fog of sweat and celestial slime, spinning like a kaleidoscope.

Finished, he rolled away, but she followed, wrapping him with arms and sticky legs. She didn't understand this postcoital need to hang on—Jack never hung on—but she didn't want the moment to end. And if the knife in her purse had been close enough, she would not have stabbed him to death, for he had taken her to nirvana, and she might want to go again soon. Then the afterglow receded, and she, too, rolled away, a little voice inside saying, *Someday he will bore me to tears.*

He sat up and put his face in his hands, and started crying. Surprised, she rose up on one elbow and studied his grief, recalling that most "moral" beings lived in the shadow of guilt and had to flagellate themselves for illicit pleasures. *It is the till-death-do-us-part marriage, the wife and kids coming home to roost, how smashing.* If the sex hadn't been so extraordinary, he probably would have gotten dressed and left, but now the god of lust was laughing at Casey Holland for leading such a dreary, unsatisfying existence. Thinking of that god reminded her of her own bloodlust. The moment was perfect; it cried out for another victim. She could easily slash him to death while he was sitting on the bed in tears, self-absorbed with a false morality, excreting snot instead of semen. Yes. Make a collage with that wonderful thing that had lit up her insides.

Instead, she slid closer, wanting to cuddle and comfort him and didn't understand this reaction, just as he was having none of it. He shook her off, went in the bathroom, and moments later, she heard the shower. Affronted, she sat up, crossed her arms over her breasts, stared blankly at his clothes strewn about the room, saw his coat and was reminded of why she was here. From her purse, she took out a pen and a pink-flowered notepad, courtesy of Heather. She went to his coat on the chair and from the breast pocket pulled out a yellow Post-it note with Amy Catherine Robbins's current address and phone number. She copied it, then carefully replaced the Post-it note.

She dressed hurriedly. At the mirror over the cheap desk, she put on fresh lipstick, brushed and primped her luxuriant hair, cocked her head and gave her sated self a cute little smile. She picked up her purse and started for the door, then stopped suddenly. This was unfinished. She couldn't just walk away. If she wasn't going to butcher the good lieutenant in lieu of another assignation, the least she could do was let him know. She blotted her lips in a kiss on Heather's notepad, took out the pen again and wrote,

> See you again . . . ? Tout de suite?
> Amour,
> ——J

She wrote her phone number on the back, folded the note and slipped it in the lieutenant's inside coat pocket.

Outside, she shielded her eyes from a bright afternoon sun, put on Heather's designer sunglasses, strolled to the Mercedes, drawing grins from two dudes in the parking lot. As she drove away from the motel, she graced them with a little flutter wave.

3:50 P.M., Monday, June 21, 2010

"How was the doctor?" Amy asked politely.

Kevin Robbins frowned at his daughter. "He tells me I'm doing fine. So I tell him—if you looked like me, would *you* think you were doing fine?"

"Maybe you really are doing fine, Daddy."

"Don't patronize me, Amy."

"Sorry."

She reminded herself to choose her words more carefully now and not to provoke him. She hadn't expected to see her father as a shriveled, white-haired old man crippled with arthritis and in a wheelchair. She should've quizzed Sara more about their parents. Did they need help? Was Daddy in constant physical pain? And more to the point— how did their mom still put up with him after all these years? She wondered if he had played her against her daughters just as he had played them against each other. Yet she couldn't hate him. She just couldn't. *I'd settle for understanding him.*

"You know, we thought we'd never see you again," he said.

She nodded and smiled wistfully. No matter how many times they asked, she still didn't know what to say.

They were in a courtyard off the living room of the family's rambling Spanish-style home on Shadow Hill Way in Beverly Hills. Exotic plants and flowers blossomed along paths that led to a gentle waterfall from a lion's-head fountain amid tree ferns, miniature elephant grass and rare species of bamboo creating an illusion of serenity. Her father rolled his wheelchair from side to side, an old man's version of a reflective kid on a skateboard.

"So did you see your aunt Amy in New Jersey?"

"No. I called her to get your phone number."

He chuckled. "She's getting up there. Seventy-nine and still all by herself. Something to be said for that," he mused. "She's got dogs, though. Little dogs. Won't go anyplace without her dogs."

"Dogs love you no matter what," Amy said and wished she hadn't, for when she was little they'd never had dogs or cats.

Her father studied her critically, then looked off, perhaps taking comfort in the fact that if nothing else he had done well financially and nobody could take that away from him. Then he glanced sideways at her, his jaw working, as he tried to fill in the holes and find a place for his resurrected daughter.

"So what do you think of your new sister?"

"I love her."

"Sara's great, isn't she?" He grinned, his face lighting up, rearranging itself on the wrinkle lines. "Always knew what she wanted, that girl. Summa cum laude at Berkeley, couple of heavyweight internships, MFC or whatever that counseling thing is, and now she's so damn busy she needs a partner, and she's only twenty-nine."

Oh, no, Daddy, you're not doing this, not again, not like you did it to both of us.

"Yes, isn't it wonderful?" she replied. "Not only did she get my looks, but she got my brains as well, though she might have trouble in my part of the world because there are so, so many clever people."

He gave her an incredulous look.

"I run into them every day managing Bertie's career."

He nodded, silenced for the moment, then took a different tack. "What're you now, Amy . . . ? Fifty-one or -two?"

"Fifty . . ." Amy calculated quickly how old she'd be if she had stayed in the twentieth century and lived until 2010. "Fifty-three."

"And doesn't she look great?" Her mother, Elizabeth, came through the French doors with a tray of drinks, set it on the bench next to her father, stood back and scrutinized her. "I swear, I don't know how you do it. You look like you're thirty-five, forty at the oldest."

"Cosmetic surgery, right?" said her father. "You go to Switzerland or Thailand or some weird place with foreign doctors and so-called miracle cures, right?"

"Kevin!"

He spread his hands and poured himself whiskey. "Well?" He turned to Amy. "So what's the answer?"

Nodding at the booze, Amy said pointedly, "Maybe it's just good living."

"Or maybe it's being in an institution."

"*God*, Kevin!"

"No, Mom, it's all right." Amy turned, gestured at her. "Really, it's all right, and I'm fine, thank you." *Obviously, if nothing else, my little sister still talks to Daddy, and one wonders what else they've said to each other.* She lifted her head proudly. *Then again, if one is given lemons . . .* Smiling, she turned back to her father and sustained the myth. "Though you might not agree, Daddy, they gave me a clean bill of health. I'm quite sane."

Kevin Robbins took a large swallow of his drink, grunted with satisfaction as it coated his rancorous insides. He looked away pensively, relishing the silence he had created, yet wasn't finished. A shrewd grin crinkled his face. "You know, I'm not saying this is what's going on, but there are folks I know who'd say you wanted back in the will." He read her horror and smiled with satisfaction. "Is that why you came home?"

Amy recoiled. "What an awful thing to say!"

"It's a joke!" he said defensively. "A goddamn joke!"

She waited for anger to come—a flood of sweet anger—so she could answer in kind, but instead was filled with a terrible sadness and found herself fighting back tears.

Her mom had seen the tears and glared hatefully at her father. She wrapped her arms around Amy protectively, pulled her away as she used to when Amy was little. She whispered that Daddy didn't really mean to be so mean, and Amy thought, *It's like Christmas in June, it's all strange and out of time, it's not working, except they're still my parents, and I love them, and it has to work, I didn't come all this way—*

"I don't need your money, Daddy."

"Look," he growled, "I said I was sorry."

"I have a life of my own," she said, not sure if she really did anymore. "I have children and a wonderful husband."

"How did you have 'this life of your own' if you were in an asylum?"

Caught. She groped for words.

"A husband and kids," he went on, "you know what I mean."

"I wasn't there all the time," she managed. "And Bertie—he was so supportive, and . . ." Her voice trailed off.

"When do we get to meet this guy?"

"I don't know. . . . I'm not sure," she said, her voice quavering.

"Sara said—"

"I am *not* getting a divorce, Daddy." She glared at him, yet was more annoyed with her sister's apparent duplicity than anything else.

"Okay, okay." He sighed and drank again. "Helluva way to start off—all I'm doing is saying I'm sorry."

"Perhaps you should wonder why."

He ignored the shot, squinted thoughtfully at his fountain, then came back to her. "So what does he do, this husband of yours?"

"He writes articles, he teaches. He's a critic, too."

"Bert Wells . . . Any relation to H. G. Wells?"

"A distant relation." She blushed.

"He's not a communist, is he?"

"No, Daddy. He's a socialist."

"Oh, Jesus," he said, disgusted. "Jesus H. Christ. I knew there was something, I just—"

"Daddy, stop it!" snapped Amy. "I don't want to talk about my husband, I want to talk about you. . . . You and me. Okay?"

He glowered at her. She lifted her chin defiantly, matched his glare, and when he saw a strength in her that he didn't recognize, he finally softened, his face becoming curious about this daughter who'd always been out of place, out of step, this renegade daughter without a reasonable explanation.

"Does anybody need anything?" said her mother. "No . . . ?"

She headed for the sanctuary of the house.

"I stopped being your little Amy when I was ten because I'd rather read than play with dolls. Or help Mommy in the kitchen. I stopped being little Amy when I had trouble with algebra in high school. I stopped being Amy when I didn't want to go to Berkeley and study economics, and you said you couldn't afford to send me to Bennington to 'dally in pots and poetry' yet you had money to burn. . . ." She took a huge breath and half-whispered, "I stopped being your little Amy when I left home, and you refused to ever talk to me again. You didn't love me, Daddy, you loved your perfect little image of me, yet I was never that person."

A silence between them. Blessed by the sound of the waterfall, it was not tense, not a prelude to an ugly barrage of words and feelings that would scar them both beyond reason. Rather, the silence settled the moment, this tenuous bond long between them stretched thin and invisible. An unspoken wisdom hovered. And waited.

"Who are you, then?" he asked quietly.

She started with Mrs. Wells, that charming woman of many hats that kept the business, household and family on schedule, though she was careful not to give away her busy, lovely Edwardian world. Her tales of raising children—not to mention her husband—between phone calls to agents and publishers and shopping trips amused Kevin Robbins, and occasionally she caught him nodding or grinning sympathetically.

"Don't get me wrong, Daddy. I love my life and my family. I love them so much, but they're not me, either. . . ."

He sipped his whiskey, made a steeple of his fingers and nodded slowly for her to continue.

"Sandgate is cold much of the year, so I have a garden house. A garden house with a cherrywood desk and a fountain that sounds like yours and the wonderful perfume of flowers even in January." She smiled wistfully. "It sits on a bluff over the channel, and on a rare sunny day one can see the coast of France, but most of the time there's clouds or fog." She paused. "I like fog, but I like flowers more, their profusion of colors, their quiet beauty, and the fact that when one shrivels and dies, it really doesn't because two more bloom beside it."

Her father listened.

Had he ever done so before?

"So when Amy isn't 'in recovery,'" she said for his benefit, "when she gets tired and bored and fed up with the world, she goes out to the garden house, and the second she closes the door, she becomes Catherine. . . . Catherine is the little girl inside that has always made Amy different. Catherine makes sense of dreams and logic of intuition and sees love and beauty in all things untouched. Catherine sings to her flowers and vines and plants as she waters them. Catherine listens to Purcell and Bach. Catherine writes stories and poetry for the pure joy of writing them. She paints watercolors and draws 'picshuas' that make Bertie and the boys laugh. . . . Ah, laughter. It heals all, no matter where we are. Laughter is our souls saying that they love life and will seek the magic within no matter where they happen to be in the cosmos. . . . Ah, Catherine. She laughs, she sings, she loves without pain, she forgives. . . . Catherine. . . . Not little Amy," she added in a whisper.

Her father opened his arms, and they held each other tightly, Amy bent over his wheelchair, not feeling the awkwardness.

"So is Catherine the reason . . . ?"

". . . they locked me up?"

He nodded.

"No. Not really, Daddy." She saw no reason to tell him that she'd never been in an institution. Instead, she chose it as a metaphor. "Amy was the one who was locked up, on occasion. . . . When they let Amy out, Catherine took wings and flew."

A long silence.

"I wish I'd known," he growled softly.

A silence.

"Can I call you—?"

"No," she said firmly. "Not Kate or Kathy or Katie. It's Catherine."

"Okay."

"I love you, Daddy."

"I love you, too, Catherine."

"So now," said Amy, giggling ebulliently to herself, pedaling hard on the bike, "now that he's finally met the daughter he never knew, how in the world am I going to tell him—or Sara or Mom or Aunt Amy—that I'm a time-traveler?!"

She guffawed and almost swerved into oncoming traffic. Needing to unwind, she'd borrowed a road bike with upright handlebars from her mom, who had also loaned her a designer outfit and insisted that she take a cell phone in case something happened. She'd taken it, then mused: *Bertie would've thought that these little beauties were a curious example of technology making life more burdensome.*

Now she pedaled aimlessly through neighborhoods the way she used to do with him in Mornington Crescent when they'd go searching for slices of life that could be turned into popular articles—in the early days before Spade House and the boys, and the weight of success and responsibility. If she were ever home again, she would insist that they go riding on picnics and adventures together, and at last Bertie and the boys would see her gloriously happy, for the weight of a life unfinished was gone. *One life, that is.*

Going home—as Bertie might say—wasn't bloody likely. Yet as she came down Laurel Way and turned up Coldwater Canyon, she tried to remain steadfastly optimistic despite the fact that she was facing a future without a past.

Up ahead was Coldwater Canyon Park, and while it was no Regent's Park by any stretch of the imagination, it had broad grass meadows and trees, and flowers bordering a red-brick firehouse, and a late-afternoon golden light that made long, warm shadows. She thought of her times with Bertie at Regent's Inn in front of the great, old fireplace ablaze with bayberry logs, sharing a pint and dreams of their life together. She stood on the bike and pedaled faster, turning on the lesser-traveled Beverly Drive for an open space, the glimpse of a lake in the hills, trying to out-distance her memories. She couldn't.

She burst out crying.

5:15 P.M., Monday, June 21, 2010

"Did you know that 'system restore' is a form of time travel?"

Despite herself, Amber raised her eyebrows and smiled curiously. She had never been good at waiting, but right now she was content to watch him tinker with her laptop on the kitchen table, immersed in its motherboard and components. She was torn. On the one hand, she hoped Sara, the sister Amy had never mentioned, would call back soon so H.G. could "save" his wife. On other, she hoped that Sara *wouldn't* return their phone call, so that she would have "Bertie" all to herself. Alas, if the call did come, Amber guessed her chances were seriously diminished. How could she hope to compete with Amy, a comely, petite woman who had been raised in the twentieth century and now probably reeked of Edwardian sensibilities? How could she compete with requited love? *Try answering him.* "So you're saying that if we were small enough . . ."

"Precisely." He grinned. "If we could somehow enter the environs of this portal, if we had a control within a control, we would be masters of our own existence. . . . You see, the software for these programs is written with the Aristotelian precision one would expect in that the world—the cosmos, if you will—of this clever little machine is orderly and controlled. Hence, if you or I were a particle, we could hop an electron and instantaneously go to any date, time and year within the confines of the laptop's experience."

"Wow."

He had found a tiny wrench and screwdriver, had taken her laptop apart and was studying it with a magnifying glass. He looked up, grinning. "I do believe that the mechanics that make the 'system tools' programs work are basically the same as those in *The Utopia*'s engine, but I'll need another computer to test it."

"I don't have one."

"Pity." He looked off thoughtfully. "You know, if I'm right, I could rewire my engine and make it much more efficient." He pointed at the laptop. "In fact, the innards of this thing might solve my problem with the Destination Indicator."

The phone rang.

The caller ID read: "Sara Robbins, MFCC."

5:22 P.M., *Monday, June 21, 2010*

"She had lunch with her!" H.G. exclaimed as they rode the elevator down. "Her sister dropped her off at her parents'!"

"Okay, okay."

"She's all right, 'Dusa! She's here and she's alive!"

The elevator doors opened. They sprinted across the underground parking lot to Amber's car, stopped short when they heard clanking and a winch whining hydraulically. A tow-truck driver was taking away a faded green Toyota Corolla that had been parked across two spaces, blocking in Amber's Milan and her neighbor's Prius.

Watching the scene, the neighbor heard Amber and H.G., turned and gestured at the Corolla. "What an idiot, huh?"

Deflated, H.G. glanced at his watch—5:25 P.M.—tried to quell his sudden uneasiness and a grim little déjà vu from deep in his soul. Then the tow truck took off in a blast of exhaust. Amber pressed her key, the Milan's doors chirped, and they jumped in. H.G. pulled a map book from the door side pocket, riffled through and found Beverly Hills, left it folded open.

"That took all of two seconds," she said of the tow truck.

She zoomed out of the parking lot and up the ramp, but paused at the street. "Where are we going?" H.G. handed her the bright-green Post-it note he had copied the Robbinses' address on. She stuck it on the dash, started entering it into the Milan's GPS. Meanwhile, H.G. dialed the phone number, but nothing happened.

"You have to push the green button."

"Details." He did so and waited. He frowned. "The blasted thing stopped ringing."

"I don't get good reception here."

"You live here!" he said, astonished.

She shrugged and finished setting the GPS.

"What are you doing?"

"This tells us how to get there."

"What the devil's wrong with the map?"

"We don't need the map." She pulled into the street and pressed her turn indicator.

"Turn right and proceed northeast on Ocean Park Boulevard," said a disembodied voice from the GPS. "Turn left on Lincoln Boulevard. . . ."

H.G. stared openmouthed at the GPS, fascinated that their motor car was a blue dot on a small screen and that he could actually follow their progress.

"How marvelous," he said, surprised. "The motor car talks."

Amber stood on the gas and flew up Lincoln, weaving through traffic, then whip-turned on Olympic. She looked upset—helplessly so—and was biting her lip to stop from crying.

H.G. didn't notice. He was reaching for the arrow buttons on the GPS when it spoke again: "Merge on to Interstate 10 east toward Los Angeles. . . ."

"Leave it alone or you'll get us lost," she said.

"I should think that this, this modern version of a sextant would be immune to stupidity. Perhaps it uses the same technology as microwave ovens."

"You are exceeding the posted speed limit," warned the GPS.

"Oh, really?" H.G. replied to the GPS. "Well, we have no intention of slowing down, old boy."

"Merge on to Interstate 405 north. . . ."

Amber swerved up the sweeping on ramp, then had to brake hard. Traffic on the 405 was stacked up in both directions—a silent advertisement for walking to Beverly Hills.

They came to a dead stop.

H.G. craned his head out the window to see how far the slowdown went and blanched. It was endless. He shook his head, whispered in awe, "We're marooned . . . we're adrift on a bloody sea of motor cars."

"We get off at Wilshire," she said helpfully.

He glowered at the GPS as if betrayed, then waved the map book before the screen. "You didn't go the right way," he said to the GPS.

"What d'you mean, I didn't go the right way?"

"I wasn't talking to you," he replied, "I was talking to your robot!" He held the map book out for her to see. "But if you had taken this thoroughfare here," he explained, pointing at Santa Monica Boulevard, you'd have gotten there much more quickly. These blasted freeways, as you call them, are nothing more than infinities of metal and exhaust from wasted energy." He stabbed his finger at the GPS. "And *this* thing should know that."

"All right, all right! So I pushed 'direct route' instead of 'shortest'! I fucked up, I'm sorry!"

"Maybe you don't want me to find her at all," he said hollowly.

"That's not true!" she cried, turning off the 405 at Wilshire. "Why are you being so nasty?"

"You seemed to have forgotten that *we* are not the only ones looking for her!"

"Okay, okay!" She sped up on Wilshire. "Why don't you try the damned phone again?"

He looked at the cell, opened it, then as an afterthought turned back to Amber. "And just for the record, I didn't know Amy had a sister because *Amy* didn't know she had a sister! When we left in 1979, Sara Robbins wasn't born yet."

He pushed the green button. This time when the cell rang, Elizabeth Robbins answered. After introducing himself and asking after her health, H.G. learned that his Amy was out on a bike ride. He scribbled down the cell number and rang off. Wondering when mankind would transcend the inconvenience of numbers, he began dialing again.

"Amy . . . ? My God, Amy? Is that really you . . . ?"

He laughed with relief and turned to the door in an effort to make the phone call more private and didn't hear Amber's lovesick sobs.

"Are you all right . . . ? You're quite certain . . . ?" He sighed. "There was blood on the cabin floor, Amy. . . ." He nodded. "Blast. . . . I'm so sorry. . . . I'll fix the damned door as soon as I can."

He closed his eyes and listened, her voice reminding him of how much he had missed her companionship. Maybe after a few more happy years at Sandgate, especially if he insisted that she get more help running the household, she would grow stronger and they'd become intimate again. *I'll swear off passades, I'll control myself, I'll*—

"Where am I . . . ?" he said. "Well, according to this Orwellian device in the car—you remember Orwell, don't you? we read him in 1979—I'm supposedly nine minutes and forty-seven seconds away from you, dear. . . . And what was all that nonsense about earthquakes . . . ?" He laughed. "We'll have to think of some clever comeuppance for that Chichester chap. . . . Yes, yes, I got your number from your mother. Are you still at their house . . . ? You're not?" He listened, then turned back to Amber. "'Dusa, do you know where the Franklin Canyon Reservoir is?"

She nodded, then slammed on her brakes for a light turning red—a patrol car lurked on a side street behind a bougainvillea. She shot H.G. a defiant look, then stubbornly made the adjustment on the GPS, but he was so lost in his tête-à-tête that he didn't notice.

"How are the boys . . . ?" he repeated. "The boys are fine, I'm sure." He chuckled softly. "Mrs. Vickers sees herself as a far better parent than either you or me, so they may actually be well behaved when we get home. However, I must tell you, her effect may be negligible, since we'll arrive before we left."

A pause. His face was wreathed in smiles, and he seemed awash in a warm glow that came from her voice over the cell phone. Suddenly, he sat up straight.

"What . . . ? Someone *what?*"

He listened.

"Amy! Get out of there now!" he shouted. "RUN!"

The phone had gone dead.

He gaped at it, horrified, then turned to Amber, but groped and couldn't find the words.

She floored the accelerator.

A Minute Earlier

Jaclyn pulled over slowly, let the Mercedes idle and purr, and watched Amy Catherine Robbins. She'd followed her through the curving side streets in Beverly Hills, was surprised when the girl had stopped on a narrow country road overlooking a reservoir just north of a major thoroughfare going into the hills. Why hadn't she pedaled down to the water, the picnic tables or parking area? Instead, she'd left her conveyance leaning on the shoulder of the road and had rushed down a trail for a solitary rustic bench beneath the trees. Briefly, Jaclyn feared that the girl had noticed her, then saw her chattering happily on a tiny cell phone as if she'd just heard from a long-lost friend or lover.

That would be Wells.

After sex at the motel, Jaclyn had driven to the address on her lieutenant's Post-it note, parked on the wide, quiet street and waited. Satan was with her. She had been watching the Robbinses' home for less than an hour when Amy Catherine Robbins came outside and rode off on a shiny red twenty-first-century bicycle. Jaclyn had chuckled appreciatively. If she hadn't known better, she would've assumed that the girl was in her own time and had lived here all along.

Jaclyn had followed at a discreet distance, waiting for an opportunity.

And now, with the ideal escape route of Coldwater Canyon Drive less than a mile away, this seemed like the time. Amy Catherine Robbins had her back to the road, and aside from a pair of runners gliding around the lake and a couple walking their dog, the canyon was deserted. Crickets chirped from the shadows, calling for other crickets, calling for night. Jaclyn fixed on the red bicycle, eased up on the shoulder and drove forward till she heard metal popping.

She crushed the bike, then backed up, turned off the car and waited. She hoped that this Amy Catherine Robbins would talk for an inordinately long time, for she wanted the day to become dusk. She appreciated the light dying behind the hills, the beauty of day's end, nightfall soon and its coming terror. She relished the night; she wanted Amy Catherine Robbins in the dark, hysterical with fear; she wanted no part of a hostage who had her wits about her.

Alas, Amy slipped the cell phone in her pocket and started back for her bike, happy like a girl in a melodrama, her early-twentieth-century mannerisms obvious and hateful. Jaclyn took one last look around, then got out of the car, putting on a concerned, apologetic housewife's face that she imagined had been in Heather Trattner's repertoire.

"I'm *so* sorry!" she exclaimed as Amy saw her and wondered what was going on. "My husband called, and I was trying to be safe, so I pulled off the road, and I didn't see your bicycle."

"Oh," said Amy, her face falling at the bent tires and snapped frame—the curious, twisted mess of handlebars. "Oh, my."

"I'll pay for it, of course, I'm just so terribly sorry about the inconvenience. I mean, it's getting dark, and I just didn't see it."

Amy was paralyzed by the sight of the broken bicycle. If she had been home, she would've expected help from the woman. Failing that, she would have shrugged stoically and started walking back to Sandgate, maybe waving down a passing carriage or motor car. Either way, she would've been fine, knowing that sooner or later Bertie would come for her. Here, she had no such assurance. Yes, of course she had just spoken with him, and being ridiculously accurate, he'd said that he was nine minutes and forty-seven seconds away, yet beneath his ebullient tone he'd sounded on the verge of panic—as if nine minutes and forty-seven seconds might as well have been nine centuries. And now, she'd never felt more alone in her life.

The moment had become a tableau: her in a twenty-first-century outfit that didn't fit right; the metallic pretzel of red bicycle on the pavement before her; and this bright-eyed, beautiful and strange woman—all silhouetted by a muted sunset. All stopped in time by happenstance. Or so it seemed. Nothing moved or changed except the growing fear inside Amy that something terrible was about to occur. When musing on time travel, Bertie had assumed happenstance as being part of the process because one was traveling beyond cause and effect, outside logic and reason; he had accepted it and hadn't dwelled on it. Moreover, he'd never gone on at length about time warps or fractures between universes or how one distinguished one from the other—did he even know?—yet to Amy this moment seemed more like an immense bubble in which she was trapped, and Bertie had never mentioned such entities, such possibilities.

Maybe if I move.

She lifted a hand to her face. It went there. *All right, fine.* She hugged herself. *Fine.* She shrugged helplessly at her mom's bike. *Fine.* She smiled with relief. *All right, okay, I'm all right, I can move, nothing out of the ordinary here except being one hundred and three years from home, so let's get on with—*

Then the woman moved, and instinctively Amy stepped back, for with the woman's movement came a weird, invisible aura that chilled Amy to the bone, though all the woman had done was turn and glance furtively up and down the road.

Paralyzed again. Bewildered. Amy hadn't been in 2010 long enough to automatically reach for a cell phone when she sensed trouble. In her mind, calling 911 was a pay phone or call box away, a lesson from her twentieth-century childhood. So she backpedaled, stumbled on a rock, but stayed upright, trying to make sense of the aura, this moment, this woman.

"Can I give you a ride somewhere?" the woman said sweetly, coming after her. "I'm sure you're not in walking distance."

How does she know I'm not in walking distance?

"We can put your bike in the trunk."

What's with the Bond Street accent coming from a typical Beverly Hills housewife? What on earth is she doing here?

The woman popped the trunk on the Mercedes with her key, thoroughly spooking Amy, who wasn't yet accustomed to remote buttons, then reached for the bicycle.

"No, no, please," cried Amy, waving her off. "It's all right, quite all right." She forced a polite smile. "My husband's meeting me here."

Jaclyn straightened up, hesitated. Despite guessing that Amy Catherine Robbins had just spoken with Wells on her cell phone, she hadn't planned on both of them being present for this particular moment. *Wells might have someone with him when he arrives, which means I must be nimble, I must be quick.*

"Well, then, why don't I give you my number?" Jaclyn hurried to the Mercedes, pantomimed writing a note, then came back to Amy, the knife hidden behind her leg.

Amy stood behind the bicycle, cautiously extended her hand, expecting a scrap of paper with a phone number on it.

"Are you from the UK?" Jaclyn asked suddenly, hoping to catch the girl off guard. "I thought I heard a bit of an accent."

Her words had the opposite effect. Shaking her head, Amy crouched defensively and backed away. Then she turned to run, but tripped over a bush and went sprawling. Jaclyn sprang forward, caught Amy as she was scrambling to her feet, grabbed her by the hair, snapped her head back and laid the knife against her throat.

"We're going to get in the car, and you're going to drive."

"Please, I—"

"Shut your delicate little mouth, and you will live longer."

Jaclyn prodded her toward the Mercedes. The tip of her knife pricked Amy's skin; blood ran down her neck and between her breasts.

5:51 P.M., *Monday, June 21, 2010*

H.G. was straining forward in the seat as Amber raced east on Sunset, zigzagging through traffic. He didn't care about Beverly Hills, the landmarks, the mansions and fancy cars they were passing; he didn't give a damn about irate drivers leaning on their horns and gesturing; he was coming to Amy in a strange new world.

We must get there in time.

He felt the car swerve around a bus, barely missing it, and rocket forward into a clear lane, zooming past the Beverly Hills Hotel. He glanced at Amber, now driving too fast even for him, but he said nothing. Her worried look told him she sensed that something beyond her reality was happening—or maybe she was merely angry about the GPS guiding them into a traffic jam. On cue, it spoke: "Turn left on North Beverly Drive. . . ."

Already running a red light and halfway through the turn, Amber ignored the reminder. She punched the accelerator hard up Beverly, tapping her horn repeatedly to clear the left lane.

"You are exceeding the posted speed limit."

"And *you* are bloody well driving me insane!"

"Can you *chill?*" Amber shouted at him. "A car hit her bike, that's all! She's fine!" She began crying. "She's fucking fine!"

"Merge onto Coldwater Canyon Drive," intoned the GPS.

Muttering furiously, H.G. hunted for an On-Off button, but before he found it, the device spoke again:

"Turn left on North Beverly Drive. . . ."

"Oh, shit!"

Amber had just flashed past it. She pulled hard on the wheel, and—tires squealing—the car swung across the road into oncoming traffic. The first car veered around them, but they were too far in the lane for the second. It clipped Amber's front fender, and both cars spun around, somehow missed the third and fourth cars—horns blaring as they sped by—and ended up facing the wrong direction on the wrong side of the street, one wheel of the Milan on someone's lawn. The car had flattened a wrought-iron mailbox. Amber immediately backed off the curb, the right front tire making an awful grating sound against the fender. She turned to him, placed her hand on his.

"Are you okay?!"

H.G. nodded slowly.

Shocked, they stared at each other for a very long time, Amber not breaking his gaze until the driver of the other car rapped on her window. She sighed heavily and got out to deal with the accident, but H.G. went on staring, reminded of that ghastly night in 1979 when he and Amy had been racing to John McLaren Park, trying to—

"No," he said out loud, trying to convince himself, "this isn't happening. Déjà vu is a state of mind, nothing more, nothing less."

His pocket watch read 5:52 P.M., but he had no clue what that meant. Never before had time seemed so arbitrary, so absurd, yet inevitable.

He got out and inspected the car. The mangled fender had bitten into the tire so that it barely rotated, and the air smelled of burnt rubber. Grim and determined, he picked up the mailbox, forced the blade end between the tire and the fender and pried them apart, then kneeled and listened for air hissing. Nothing. He straightened up and Amber came around the car.

"He wants us to wait for—"

"We're not waiting for anybody!" he said in a controlled fury. "We're getting back in this car and going to that reservoir as fast as you can bloody well drive!"

Two Minutes Before

Her hand shaking badly, Amy ground the starter twice before the engine finally caught. She turned, her face white with fear, her voice quavering. "Where am I supposed to go?"

"You will drive up there. . . ." Jaclyn nodded at where Lake Drive snaked down the hill to the parking lot. "Turn the car around, then go back to Sunset Boulevard, then head west toward the land of the less fortunate."

"I, I don't understand."

"What could you possibly not understand, my dear?" Jaclyn checked the rearview mirror to make sure no one was approaching. "It seems rather obvious to me that if you don't do as I say, you're going to die out of your own time in a strange land."

Amy swallowed hard, stared at her hands on the steering wheel. *Out of my own time.* This woman's poisonous aura finally made sense. She was not of this world, and this was no ordinary kidnapping—this had something to do with her and Bertie in the past, but she couldn't place this beautiful, knife-wielding woman. She had never seen her before—not in the nineteenth century, the twentieth, not here, not anywhere. "Who are you . . . ?"

Jaclyn chuckled. "An old—no, a very old acquaintance of your husband. . . . In fact, we go back to the late nineteenth century. You and I, however, haven't really met before, at least not in our present forms. We had a brief, rather tense encounter some thirty-one years ago, yet the circumstances were refreshingly different."

"You're . . . him."

"Brilliant deduction, love."

"That's impossible."

Jaclyn chuckled again. "So is time travel."

Amy gripped the wheel, pushed as far away from the monster as her space allowed. "What do you want . . . ?" she whispered fearfully.

"The special key." Jaclyn smiled. "What else?"

"I don't have it."

"Of course you don't. Despite your privileged American roots, you have a woman's brain circa 1893. You forget everything. Now, in 2010, women have even forgotten their place—though I must say, that does have its advantages."

"I left the key in the control panel. I think it was stuck, so if—"

"No, no, Ms. Amy Catherine Robbins." Jaclyn chuckled. "As they say nowadays, 'let's not go there.' The key will not be in the control panel because as we both know, your boyfriend has come after you, and while he may be stupidly optimistic, he does not forget. Not even keys."

Amy started crying.

"You are going to ring Wells on that marvelous little Chinese puzzle of a cell phone, and you're going to propose an exchange . . . you for the special key."

"I don't know how to call him!"

"It's quite simple, my dear. Since he rang you just minutes ago, all you have to do is press the green button twice, and he will ring you back."

"Why don't you call him?" said Amy indignantly.

"Because he won't recognize my voice." She cackled a high-pitched madwoman's laugh, then stopped and listened. A sudden cacophony of horns from Coldwater Canyon Drive echoed faintly in the canyon. Jaclyn glanced in the mirror, then looked back at Amy, who was taking out her cell. "No, no," Jaclyn said anxiously, checking the mirror again, "not here."

"But—"

"*Drive!*"

Amy drove slowly toward the Y of Franklin Canyon and Lake Drive. She tensed, held the wheel tightly, shot a glance at Jaclyn, then started a normal U-turn—halogen headlights sweeping across dark chaparral. Suddenly, she stomped on the gas and pulled hard to the left, throwing Jaclyn against the door.

She slammed on the brakes and forced the car into reverse.

Jaclyn flew forward, her head smashing into the windshield.

Amy opened the door, leapt from the car, sprinted down Lake Drive for the reservoir, then veered cross-country like a frightened animal, except she lost her footing, sprawled and rolled, the brush tearing her clothes, but was up again, running blind, not knowing where she was going, just away from the terror, the madness. When she reached the trees by the parking lot, she stopped and listened. Only the crickets, her heart pounding, the distant roar of traffic from the city, the crickets again. She peered at the hill behind her. Nothing. No movement. Except for a crow that flapped across the purple twilight haze blanketing the canyon. She took a breath, crept to the other side of the trees. The reservoir was black and still. No runners. No one walking their dogs. A placid, deadly still-life.

She tried to summon reason to overcome her fear, but wasn't strong-willed enough. Where was her calm in the face of disaster, the practical and dependable Amy always there for Bertie and the boys? Where was her self-reliance? Amy had deserted her. Alas, she was Catherine without flowers or chapbook or music—without a beautiful autumn day with whitecaps on the channel. And should a storm blow in, she'd run to the house and busy herself in the kitchen, once again becoming Amy and holding the boys so they wouldn't be afraid of the lightning. *I want to go home. Please, God, I want to go home, I want to—*

A spider dropped from the tree on her neck. She shrieked, brushed it away, then heard rustling from the hillside and knew that the monster had heard her. Sobbing, she ran for the road, assuming that she was safer in the open—hoping for a car, for anything. At the top of the hill, she saw the Mercedes with the door still open. Thinking she'd jump inside and lock the doors, she raced for it, was almost there when Jaclyn sprang from the other side of the car and tackled her. She went down hard, her head bouncing on the pavement, but she felt nothing. She punched and clawed and kicked at her attacker.

Enraged at the blows and scratches, Jaclyn stabbed Amy in the chest with such force the knife went completely through her frame—and then she went on stabbing and sawing until Amy no longer moved.

Then Jaclyn straightened up and stepped back, felt the flood of release and sighed her trans-ejaculatory sigh. Drained, she wished for a bed to lie back on, finally collected herself and looked down at Amy Catherine Robbins, now quite dead, and realized her plan was in shambles. Angry at herself, she dragged the corpse up on the shoulder and laid it out by the ruins of the road bike. She studied the body, wondered what Wells had liked best about his wife and found herself humming that sweet melody from Penny's music box. *Wells would have said something idiotic to her such as: Your eyes are the windows to your soul, my dear, your wonderful eyes.* Jaclyn grinned, then in a controlled rage began excising those hazel-brown eyes, frozen in death, yet lovely—so lovely. She stopped halfway through, cursed her indulgence, realizing she didn't have the luxury of time, and was rooting through the corpse's pockets for the cell phone—Wells's number would be on it—when she saw headlights sweep up the canyon.

She hurried back to the Mercedes and hid the knife under the seat, checked herself for telltale bloodstains and smiled smugly. There were none. *We still have the touch, do we not, dear heart?*

But her arms were covered with scratch marks. *No, no, this won't do, this won't do at all.* Frantic, she searched the car for something to cover herself with and discovered Heather had left a bejeweled summer cashmere sweater on the floor in the backseat. Though its pale green didn't match her dress, she hurriedly put it on and turned back to the road.

She saw the car speeding up the hill, which meant that they could see her as well, so if she were to take off in the Mercedes, that would be a clear sign that she was the killer. Instead, she composed herself, put on a helpless stance and flagged the car down.

It screeched to a stop.

"Excuse me!" she cried. "Something terrible has happened!"

Wells jumped from the car and rushed toward her.

Jaclyn resisted a triumphant smile. *Wells in the flesh. Older now, slightly puffy, indubitably from years of good living. Years that he denied me. . . . If only the moment were opportune. If only we were alone.*

Moments Later

Frozen, Amber wanted to look away, but couldn't, fascinated by the horror, more so because Amy Wells was no anonymous corpse. The body was sprawled by the crushed road bike, blood oozing from the stab wounds, Amy's eyes hanging from her agonized face as if pulled from a doll; H.G. was on his hands and knees retching in dead grass; and this beautiful, shaken woman who had flagged them down was standing alone and desolate without a clue. During her time with the West Division, Amber had seen a lot of murder victims, but few had been as grotesque as this one. *Its gotta be the eyes—all hacked up as if a dog had chewed on them—God, what kind of sick weirdo would do that?* She immediately thought of the Brentwood killer that the West Division was looking for—the one H.G. said was Jack the Ripper—but this killer hadn't left a happy face or signature. He didn't have to.

A breeze off the reservoir floated up the hill, lifted the nasty metallic smell of blood from Amy's body and left it hanging in the air. Amber gagged and had to turn away before she, too, started throwing up. She sucked in air from the space behind her, finally looked back at the solitary woman who seemed to be growing more and more nervous.

"Did you call nine-one-one?" said Amber.

The woman's eyes widened in surprise. She paled and shook her head. "I'm sorry, I'm a visitor, I—"

Amber whipped out her cell and hit the button.

While she waited to be interviewed, Amber watched the Beverly Hills police tape off the crime scene. The technicians rolled out a portable generator and set up lights to ward off the coming night, and the criminalists went to work with their cameras—infrared among them—and field kits for fingerprints, impressions, DNA and the like, and still others sifted through the weeds and chaparral for evidence. It wasn't long before they ascertained that Amy had run down the hill to escape her killer, had hidden under the trees, then had come back up the access road, presumably to get help from a passing car.

Amber felt an urge to jump in and help, but these were Beverly Hills technicians and like cops everywhere they didn't appreciate strangers playing in their yard, especially when they had a corpse that was sure to become a star on the late-night news. She stayed cool, though she didn't approve of the way the DNA technician was collecting blood and tissue samples from under the body's fingernails. He kept yammering to his buddy about racing his new dune buggy. *Granted, cognitive dissonance comes with the turf, but this is a little over-the-top.* She sighed. *At least they have the decency to leave Bertie alone. At least, so far.*

He was slumped in the back of a blue and white squad car, one foot out the door on the road, his head back against the seat, his eyes fixed in that thousand-yard stare she had seen before at crime scenes. Her heart went out to him. She wanted to go over and console him, but was sure the detectives wouldn't approve. Then she couldn't look at him anymore; it was too painful.

She observed a detective sergeant tape-recording an interview with the solitary woman, taking notes as she answered his questions. He wore a blank face, which told Amber he was going by the book, but the woman piqued Amber's curiosity. On the surface she was cooperative, all smiles and charm despite having stopped for the fresh kill of a psychopath, yet Amber sensed a growing uncertainty and fear in her mannerisms that the sergeant didn't pick up on—or if he did, it didn't register. Maybe it was that she was a tourist from the UK, or maybe that was just the way this woman reacted to a horrible crime, or— The sergeant had dismissed the woman and was gesturing her over.

"Miss Amber Reeves, right?"

"Mizz."

"Whatever."

Amber identified herself as a criminalist with the West LAPD, then told the sergeant what had brought them to the scene and what they had seen.

"Hey, Bruce," the sergeant called to a detective in a light-brown suit. "This lady works for Casey Holland in West Division. We oughta call him in on this, huh?"

The detective nodded reluctantly, and the sergeant turned back to Amber, his brow furrowing curiously.

"I'm kind of wondering . . . why would you meet the deceased here if she was out on a bike ride?" He turned and spread his arms, taking in the blackness, the emptiness of Franklin Canyon. "Especially out here?"

"She'd just called," said Amber, winging it. "She, unh, she said she was in trouble."

The sergeant nodded and grimaced as in "no shit," made a note, then went on. "Any names . . . ? She say anything at all about the attacker?"

"She was dead when we got here."

"Wasn't your friend talking to her on a cell? That's what you said, right?"

"Yes, but I didn't hear anything. I was driving too fast to get here, and we got in the damned accident or this never would've happened." *If we hadn't taken the 405, it wouldn't have happened, either.*

"Did a patrol unit come to the scene of the accident?"

"Yes."

He made more notes. "Okay, then."

"Look, can we go . . . ? My friend is a mess."

"He can clean up down at the station."

"What?"

"We gotta interview him formally." The detective started for a squad car. "He's the husband, right . . . ?"

From the wooden bench in the lobby that seemed more suited for a hotel courtyard than a police station, Amber watched the clock, her mind on overload, thus worthless. Forty-two minutes later, the elevator doors opened, and a detective escorted Wells out, apologizing for taking his time, for the murder of his wife, for his grief, for a country no longer safe for tourists, for the presence of a vicious psychopath even in Beverly Hills. *If they're letting him go,* Amber thought stupidly, *the fake IDs must've been okay.*

The detective handed Wells a card, shook hands with him and said that he'd be in touch.

"If it's any consolation, Mr. Wells, we'll get this dude."

"No, you won't," said H.G. "I will."

The detective stared at him for a long time and considered responding with a law-enforcement cliché such as taking the law into one's own hands is against the law or about being especially careful or about the dangers of withholding information from the police, then decided to say nothing. He gave Wells an understanding nod and got back on the elevator.

They were driving west on Wilshire, Amber stealing sympathetic looks at H.G., trying to read him in the multicolored ambience of light from passing cars and billboards that played across his face, but he had retreated behind another thousand-yard stare. Asking if he was okay would be downright moronic, so she chose to say nothing at all and hoped her silence would bring them closer together. *He needs me to take his hand and lead him from the darkness to a good place—past, present or future. He needs me to be close. He needs me to heal him, to be with him, and that I will do eagerly. I don't care what universe or time zone this man is from, I don't give a damn where I belong or where I belong—all I know is that he is flesh and blood like me. Like me.*

Suddenly, she couldn't hide a tiny smile and hated herself for it, realizing she was secretly pleased that Amy was dead. *Is that why I didn't set the GPS right, knowing in my heart that the 405 would be a parking lot and we wouldn't get to Amy in time?* She glanced guiltily at H.G., but he hadn't seen her smile. *Amber Reeves, may you burn in hell.* She considered it, then sighed. *Okay. If it means we might end up together, then so be it.*

When they were almost to the beach, he shifted in his seat and said, "Where are you taking me?"

"I dunno. I was afraid to ask."

"Would you have an old-fashioned alarm clock?"

She hesitated, then nodded. "Yes. A travel clock—for when the power goes out."

"It's not digital?"

"No."

"Jolly good. I'll need that and some tools," he said thoughtfully. "And your laptop."

"Okay, but—" She turned left at Pacific Avenue and headed south for her apartment. "Somebody has to call her parents and tell them, right . . . ? I mean, if you're not up to it, I can do I for you."

"No. . . . There's no need."

"Huh?"

"I'm going to change the day."

"What?"

"I cannot accept . . . I refuse to live in a world without Amy."

8:04 P.M., Monday, June 21, 2010

Why would she do that, Casey Holland asked himself, rooting through the trash in the master bath. *Was she trying to set me up or was her brain on a goddamn vacation?* When he'd been in the shower at the motel, Jaclyn had put a pink-and-rose note in his pocket, and Cheryl had found it getting his stuff ready for the cleaners while he was taking a guilt-ridden second shower. The shit had hit the proverbial fan. After screaming and waving the note in his face, Cheryl had crumpled it up, slam-dunked it in their remodeled bathroom and had been in tears and a fury ever since.

Briefly, he had thought about denying it, but, no, that would make him as pathetic as the low-lifes who claimed innocence even when their prints and DNA were all over the evidence. Besides—though his life was coming apart—he still couldn't erase images of Jaclyn from his mind.

He found the note, flattened it out on the tile, saw Jaclyn's flowery script asking for more, her lips in a cherry-red kiss. He remembered those lips all over his body. *Okay, so I'm new at this,* he thought, gazing at the note, *is it a souvenir or a fucking talisman?* Regardless, it had her phone number on the back, and he kept it, despite knowing in his heart that she would ruin him.

Back in the dining room, he waited for Cheryl, who was trying to put the kids down for the third time. Usually, they went to bed happily and easily, but tonight they had picked up on the tension in the house, the reality that their mom was angry and hysterical, and wasn't telling them why.

The TV was playing commercials to an empty living room. Without looking, Holland aimed the remote and turned it off, then looked at his cell on the table next to his cold coffee. He hadn't checked in for over three hours and resisted an urge to do so despite the case, ugly on his mind. *To hell with the case*, he told himself. His wife was in a controlled fury, and he had no clue what to do next.

Cheryl strode barefoot into the kitchen, poured herself more wine and came back in the room, tragically beautiful in a simple tank top and cutoffs, yet her blue eyes red and swollen from crying.

He straightened up. "Look, honey, there's gotta—"

"Shut up, Casey! Shut *up!*" She waved her hands alongside her head, then drank to calm herself. "Why does there have to be a way . . . ? Why?! How about *no way*, Case?"

"Because I love you."

She laughed raucously, took a ragged breath, then burst into tears again, and when he tried to console her, she pushed him away and curled into a ball on the chair. "I want you out of this house. I want you gone."

He almost said, I'm not going anywhere, but wasn't sure, so he didn't say anything. He welcomed the silence. Maybe it would soothe her, and they could talk sensibly and put this behind them.

For something to do, he turned on his phone. It beeped with six new messages, wrecking the silence, so he turned it off.

"How many times did she call?" said Cheryl hatefully.

"It's work, I'm sure."

"Bullshit."

He held out his phone. "Want to read the caller ID?"

"No, I don't! I want to know why!" She cried, "Why, Casey, *why?*"

He shook his head. "I can't explain it. I felt this pull. I couldn't stop myself. It was like something otherworldly."

"Otherworldly . . . ?" she said sarcastically. "As in an angel—?"

"C'mon, Cheryl—"

"—or fuck goddess?"

"I was trying—"

"I really don't want to hear your garbage, okay?" She finished her drink, then went back in the kitchen for the bottle. "What is it with you cops, anyway? When you graduate from the Academy, do you pledge to do other women . . . ? Like you do bad guys . . . ? Is that it . . . ?" She sat down again. "I thought we were beyond that. I thought you were different."

Desperate, he seized upon her words. "I *am* different, Cheryl! I'm here right now when I'm supposed to be on a goddamn case, and I'm trying to work things out with you because I think you, me and the kids are worth saving!" He took an enormous breath. "Everybody else I know would've made a joke out of it! They would've gone on cheating till they got caught in the act."

"Okay." She straightened up, glared at him, then looked off thoughtfully. "Okay, maybe you are different. . . . Maybe you are."

"I am, honey, I swear to God, I am." His voice cracked. He sagged with relief and hoped the worst was over and that he could do some serious damage control and get some counseling or brainwashing or something and wipe the image of Jaclyn from his brain.

"I want you to quit the LAPD."

"What?"

"It's not just your whore—it's what happens next—it's the rest of it, as well," she said. "The reality is: We don't come first in your life when all along you've come first in ours." Her eyes were unflinching. "I can't live like this anymore."

"But, I'm a cop," he said, stunned. "It's what I do."

"Find something else to do."

"You can't be serious."

"Us or the LAPD, Case. Your choice."

"I promise you," he said desperately, "I'll never see her again!"

"I don't give a fuck about her. . . . Us or them."

10:43 P.M., Monday, June 21, 2010

"You're playing God."

"There is no God," H.G. said automatically.

"Sometimes there is," Amber said brightly.

"Your naïveté is astounding," he replied with disgust, forgetting that despite all the tears and tragedy, this girl lived in the moment, and right now she was gloriously happy to be alone with him. He stared gloomily at anonymous sandwich-box buildings under dirty-yellow streetlights as they sped east on Santa Monica Boulevard toward the 405. The notion of an intermittent supernatural force seemed ludicrous. *Perhaps 'Dusa's god is wish fulfillment, making her no different from anyone else in this brightly lit, dubious year. Like her, these people hurry everywhere, yet are going nowhere, all done within the sanctity of motor cars. They're always talking on electronic devices—or is it a form of prayer?—yet they never go to church because they already exist in one enormous, technological church of wish fulfillment. Our father, who art in heaven, hallowed be thy phone number.* He stopped, realizing that his cynicism had become self-indulgent.

"Bertie . . . ?" She hesitated. "Is it still okay to call you Bertie?"

He nodded impatiently.

"Isn't the reality of time travel proof that we are made in God's image?"

"Ha!" Briefly, despite the loss of Amy, he rose to the occasion of debate. "Isn't the reality of Jack the Ripper proof that we were made in someone else's image . . . ? Or perhaps not created at all?"

"What d'you mean, 'not created'? We're alive, aren't we?"

"Thanks to the wonders of evolution. You have heard of Charles Darwin, I take it."

She nodded and recited, "We started out as amphibians, moved on to four-legged carnivores, then the Australopithecus, and—give or take a few million of years later—voilà! Now we're thinking, feeling human beings."

"Who may not have that many years left."

Startled, she shot him a concerned look. "What . . . ?"

He wished he hadn't said anything.

"What are you talking about?" she persisted.

"Idle nonsense," he lied, dismissing her. He didn't want to get into global warming or Armageddon with her. Right now, saving Amy was more than enough.

Amber got off the freeway at Getty Center Drive and drove in silence the rest of the way to the museum. She parked by the steps of the arrival plaza, and H.G. noticed a security guard watching them from the rotunda.

"Your identification will get us in, right?" he asked warily.

She nodded confidently, and they got out of the car.

His jacket off and sleeves rolled up, H.G. was deep inside the engine compartment while Amber positioned the work light they had borrowed from Security on the ruse of looking for more evidence in the Teresa Cruz murder. Though already covered with extratemporal residue, he moved gingerly, for he didn't want to lean on the diamond buffers or pulse generator and place unanticipated stress on the crystalline bars. He had no desire to perform an alignment 103 years away from his laboratory. He was reaching up to unscrew the Destination Indicator when the light moved.

"Is this better?"

He frowned. "I can't see a blasted thing."

The light moved again. "Now?"

"It was fine where it was," he said, annoyed.

"Jeez," she said, sliding the light back to square one. "Don't bite my damn head off."

"Don't move the damn light."

"Okay, sorry."

"And while you're at it, I need a larger screwdriver."

She had two, but rather than make another mistake, she crawled inside the engine compartment, held her purse open and let him choose for himself. He pulled out a nail and grinned.

"We're not building a bloody house here, 'Dusa."

Chuckling, he tossed the nail back in her purse, found the tool he wanted and went back to work. He heard Amber walk away, wondered fleetingly where she was going, then went back to work, but couldn't turn the screws on the Destination Indicator housing. Though mounted within the gyroscopic rotation radius—meaning they shouldn't age— they were frozen in place. He didn't know if it had been caused by *The Utopia's* trip to infinity, where all bets were off, or if it the problem was his forty-year-old hands. He shook up the small can of WD-40 which Amber insisted solved all things mechanical and sprayed the connections. He wiped off the excess lubricant, then waited.

He heard a guffaw from one of the galleries, then her footsteps on the travertine stone floor, her breathless giggles as she leaned in the hatch.

"She didn't really *say* that, did she?"

"Who is she?"

"Odette Keun."

"And who just might Odette Keun be?"

"Come on! You'd been sleeping with her for three years. You were hosting a dinner party for some lord and his wife at your place in France, and someone at the table called you the Fabian Casanova, and—"

"'Dusa, please—"

"—then somebody else said, 'What exactly did Casanova do?' And then Odette said, 'He fucked women.'"

"Dammit, 'Dusa!"

She was laughing so hard she didn't hear.

Thoroughly annoyed, he straightened up and hit the firewall with a resounding bang. "Ouch!" Muttering, he rubbed his head.

That, she heard. "Are you okay?"

"*Please* don't tell me about a life I haven't lived!"

A silence.

"I don't want to see any blasted photographs, either!"

"Okay, okay. I'm sorry. It was 1927. I'm sorry."

"If you're bored, you can find me a blindfold for when I come back to this place and have to walk through the exhibition."

"Why don't you take me with you?" she said softly.

"Absolutely not." He continued working on the screws. "I will not expose you to reformulation errors."

"I'll risk it."

"No. I'm sorry." He sighed, wiped his brow and leaned back against the firewall. "Would you mind very much getting us some food?"

"King of Siam or McDonald's . . . ?"

"Neither."

"Soul food?"

After she'd gone out for food, his clumsy fingers finally cooperated, and he got the Destination Indicator loose. He paused to wipe sweat from his face, then inspected the autoclock. It had been crushed. He rotated it slowly, nodded as the problem came clear. He had made its housing slightly beveled. It had never occurred to him that his time machine would travel to infinity and back—and that over such a great distance, the heavy and corrosive nature of dark energy would wreak havoc with components which were not square. Yes, but what about the other diagonals and curves in his engine? They hadn't frozen, melted or oxidized. Perhaps it had something to do with the mechanics of time—as in autoclock—traveling through time. Or perhaps it was the capricious nature of dark energy itself. He had no clue.

"Get on," he whispered to himself. *Get on before you find yourself stuck in this indifferent century.*

Earlier, he had dismantled 'Dusa's laptop intending to computerize the Destination Indicator, hoping that with twenty-first-century technology it wouldn't fail again. He planned to arrange its tiny components inside the Destination Indicator's damaged but serviceable housing and was wondering how the software would react to its new environs when he discovered—much to his horror—that there were no wires on the laptop's motherboard. He tilted it in the light, gaped at it. Yes, he knew about the concept of microchips and the miniature batteries that energized but how the devil did these flat little things talk to each other? No matter. The motherboard was modular and was as alien to his time machine as a jet aircraft was to the *Kitty Hawk*.

At a loss, frustrated at the nineteenth century for not being ahead of its time, he put 'Dusa's laptop aside and reached for the mechanical alarm clock she had given him. He went back to work, and soon a melodious riff from William Boyce sang sweetly in his head him as he wired the clock to the Destination Indicator. He calibrated it, making sure the clock would run only when the time machine was "in flight" and that the rotation of the engine would keep the old timepiece tightly wound. Finally, he synchronized it all with his pocket watch, gathered his tools and remembered the bicycle lock. He opened the small door to the reversal housing, found the little beauty up inside, took it off and gave the gear a half-spin just to make sure. He pocketed it and grinned, realizing that pondering the nuts and bolts of time travel relaxed him and made him feel good. It was much less puzzling than thinking about technology for its own sake or global warming run amok.

Or the death of Amy. Or going to resurrect her in a machine that had been running haphazardly with hardware from three centuries, counting the alarm clock.

———

Amber sashayed in with a bag of food, a brave smile on her face that said she was resigned to staying behind. She sat cross-legged on the floor, spread out paper towels and napkins, opened up barbecued ribs, chicken and slaw, their spicy-sweet aromas hanging, lending a festive air to H.G.'s imminent departure. She opened two bottles of Guinness, and they silently toasted his trip. He picked up a rib, tentatively dipped it in barbecue sauce, took a bite.

"My God," he said happily, "it *is* soul food."

After they'd eaten, H.G. sipped his beer reflectively and thought about changing the sequence of events in the past. He would have to be damnably careful; Fate wouldn't deal gently with the whim of a mere time-traveler, a speck of a speck that could ruffle her cosmos. Once again, witness that awful scene in John McLaren Park thirty-one years ago; witness the capricious slaughter of Amy's friend Carole. Therefore, he had to enter yesterday inconspicuously, yet be bold enough not merely to save Amy, but to stop the Ripper and then go graciously, gloriously home, never to venture out in *The Utopia* again. He no longer had illusions of taking Leslie John Stephenson back to Scotland Yard to face justice in 1893. Instead, he would buy a firearm, shoot him in 2010 and be done with it. *Face it, "O realist of the fantastic," as Conrad spoke of you, the only "Utopia" you'll find in this world is in the dictionary.*

Amber had gone in the exhibition again and was coming back in the center gallery wearing a hurtful look.

"Why didn't you tell me about the modus vivendi you had with Amy?" His face fell.

"When all along I thought you guys had a normal marriage?"

"The modus vivendi is null and void," he snapped.

"I feel totally dissed."

"Translate, please."

"You made an agreement with Amy in 1900 that both of you could screw anyone you liked and stay married, and here I thought—oh, how noble, he's trying to be faithful to her."

"I *am* trying to be faithful to her."

"What about last night?"

"Forget last night!" He sighed. "Look, 'Dusa, it's entirely possible that Amy ran from 1906 because of the damned modus vivendi. . . . Therefore, as far as I'm concerned, the modus vivendi is null and void."

"Wait." She slid her arms around him, gazed at him, smiled radiantly. If she kissed him, he might just crumble—he might just stay here, love this girl into oblivion, into the manifestation of his lover-shadow. She didn't. Instead, she leaned back, her smile mysterious, yet disarming.

"D'you know where you're going to?"

"Do you mean, when?"

"Okay, when."

"This morning, I think."

"How will I know who you are?"

"We'll have already met," he reminded her. "Yesterday." Then he started running through Monday's sequence of events in his mind, trying to decide exactly when he would start dueling with inevitability.

"Bertie . . . ?" Her embarrassment over assaulting him the night before had faded. The pleasure it had given her had not, and she remembered wondering about reformulation errors. If he had been altered, it certainly made for a nice fit. Her fingers lazily caressed his chest. "Why don't you go back to last night in the hotel?" She chuckled softly. "I mean, why waste the trip . . . ?"

Absolutely not. Tempting Fate was dangerous enough—tempting Fate with a temptress was no doubt suicide. Besides, unless *The Utopia* was physically moved to Room 529 at the Marriott in the next few minutes, he'd be arriving right where he was.

"'Dusa, please." He extricated himself from her and started for the machine.

"Okay." She hugged herself, did a hapless three-sixty, then spread her hands. "But what am I supposed to do? It's not like I can meet you here, for God's sake!"

"I'll find you." He grinned. "I know where you'll be."

He donned his coat and climbed up to the cabin, took the bicycle lock from his coat pocket, placed it by the chair.

"What's that?"

"A bicycle lock. . . . I merely hook the hasp through a hole in the central gearing wheel inside the reversal housing," he said proudly. "It's my own nefarious way of making sure no one else uses the machine."

"Huh."

"To quote the exhibit—'the machine was never known to have worked.'"

"So the special key won't work unless you take off the bicycle lock."

"Precisely."

"Cool." She nodded thoughtfully. "Very cool."

He resumed going through his pockets, then stopped suddenly and did it again, his grin fading to a mask of horror. "Where *is* the bloody key?" He glanced at her. "'Dusa, what the devil did I do with the special key?"

"I dunno." She shrugged. "You leave it in the dash?"

There it was.

He smiled with relief and nodded a thank-you, then added, "You might want to step behind a wall or something, my dear. The flash of energy will be quite intense."

"Bye, bye, Bertie," she said sadly. Head down, she walked from the gallery, disappeared around the corner.

He watched her go, then bent to the Destination Indicator. He paused and gazed off through the ridiculously old glass windows that someday he should replace with plastic. *When to, Wells?*

He considered going back to Sunday's wee hours and intercepting Amy at the Getty, but since he didn't know where she had gone immediately after she'd arrived—or even if his modified Destination Indicator would work properly—he decided against it. Even if he did get there at the right moment and prevent her from sending *The Utopia* to infinity—where like an errant shuttle bus it would pick up Leslie John Stephenson—there was no guarantee that in the distant future or past some callow time-traveler might not make the same mistake. Better to kill the monster on Monday, June 21, 2010.

Yes, but when?

The museum would be closed because of the Teresa Cruz murder, so he didn't have to worry about arriving in the middle of a tour group.

The first few minutes would be furtive and critical, but once past that moment, he should be all right. He needed enough time to leave the Getty and get to LAX where he could slip back into the chain of cause and effect—anonymously, as if he were merely another arriving passenger. He wouldn't have to explain as much to 'Dusa, and instead of going straight to her flat and uselessly tinkering with her laptop, he could purchase a weapon. He frowned, annoyed with himself for not thinking of it before.

12:17 P.M. popped into his head. That was the moment when he had gone to the loo at LAX for some solitude right after they'd come back from San Francisco. 'Dusa had complained that he had kept her waiting for so long she feared that he had "bailed on her." Yes, coming from the loo would be the perfect time and place for a much wiser Wells to "meet" Amber Reeves and begin again.

When?

10:00 A.M. should give him enough time to make his way to the airport and the Southwest Airlines men's room. He set date and time on the Destination Indicator, strapped himself in the chair, automatically checked his pocket watch, took a deep breath. He took one last gander at 11:57 P.M. Monday night, June 21, 2010; he wasn't sorry he was leaving. If he were rude and crude like so many here, he might have borrowed their obscene gesture and waved his finger out the cabin door. Instead, he shoved the Accelerator Helm Lever forward until it locked in the flank position. The engine whined, the machine began spinning. H.G. closed his eyes and hoped he was doing the right thing.

An explosion of blue energy rocked the pavilion.

He was vaporized.

After Again

12:17 P.M., Monday, June 21, 2010

Once again in the loo at LAX—again in Rodin's "The Thinker" pose—H.G. was on the verge of panic. He had been confident his foreknowledge would guide him well on this, the second time around, except that when he had arrived at 10:00 A.M., he'd had trouble climbing down from his time machine. The world was out of focus, all fuzzy. He hadn't counted on a reformulation error. He hadn't counted on going blind.

He had groped his way to the garden, then—by its ugly snarl—found the leaf blower. With sign language, repeated words and a blur of twenty-dollar bills, he'd convinced the Hispanic gardener to give him a ride to the airport; then, with the help of a skycap and another blur of cash, he had made his way into the Southwest Airlines men's room with no idea of the time. He was supposed to wait until 12:17 P.M. so that he would leave the restroom the same time as before, but when he looked at his pocket watch it was fuzzy golden thing that he couldn't read.

He heard someone come inside.

"Do you have the time, my good man?"

"Almost half past twelve."

Great Scott, I'm late. He stood, zipped up his trousers, stopped suddenly. Whoever had answered him had a thin and reedy voice, and sounded very British, very . . . familiar. He cocked his head and repeated, "Do you have the time, my good man?"

"I already told you, it's almost half past twelve."

He rushed out of the stall, the door banging behind him, and ran into himself.

"Sorry."

"Ah. What a surprise," said himself, his carbon copy, "so it was us in there. You're a tad late, aren't you?"

"I can't see anything!"

"Blasted reformulation errors," himself said and chuckled.

H.G. gasped, realizing that he had bumped into an H. G. Wells from a different universe. He hadn't thought it possible, not even theoretically. He had always assumed that the same mass or set of molecules could not exist in the same place at the same time. Obviously, there were exceptions to the rule—if there were in fact any rules at all. Suffice it to say that he had no idea what had happened—whether *The Utopia* had somehow taken him into a flux where universes overlapped or where one universe was rotating faster than the other or— *Blast it, to hell with physics! I'm blind!* He spread his hands helplessly, was about to ask himself for assistance, but the incarnation spoke first.

"I'd love to help you, old boy, but I'm superfluous in this universe. Good luck with the girl."

Himself disappeared.

Shaking with worry, H.G. felt his way out into the terminal. He didn't see 'Dusa—not that he would recognize anybody other than himself—and shuffled toward the escalators. Out of habit, he looked at his pocket watch again—now the blur included his hand—and he wondered if 'Dusa had given up on him and left. He saw figures, but couldn't read faces anymore. People jostled him. He didn't know which way to go to avoid the crush. He was terrified.

"I say, has anyone seen a Miss Amber Reeves . . . ?" he shouted.

"Bertie . . . !"

He spun around.

Her voice was beautiful. Her close proximity was salvation. He made out dark hair and a woman's form rushing toward him.

"You walked right past me!" she cried. "What were you doing in there, anyway? I thought you'd bailed on me!"

"'Dusa, I can't see!"

"What?"

"Take me to those chairs over there."

"Take you?"

"All I see are *shapes*!"

She took his hand and led him across the terminal to the plastic chairs, had to raise her voice above the din of people, the PA system and jets roaring overhead: "What's going on?"

"Remember what I said about reformulation errors?"

She nodded.

He took a deep breath, stared closely at her, still couldn't focus. "I've just come back from tonight . . ."

She smiled and thought he was joking. "Was it good for you, too?"

"'Dusa, I'm being quite serious."

She cocked her head, looked at him quizzically. "Wait a sec. . . . You've just come back . . ."

"Yes." He nodded affirmatively. "From tonight. 11:57 P.M., to be more exact. And something has happened to my eyes—probably due to the short duration of the journey, who knows—but if we don't do something the worst is going to happen!"

Amber frowned with uncertainty. "Are you fucking with me . . . ?"

"Is your language necessary?"

"Whatever." She shrugged. "Okay, well if you're not fucking with me, and you're half-blind, how did you get here?"

He explained about paying the Hispanic gardener at the Getty to bring him here because he thought he knew precisely where he would be at 12:17 P.M. "He was terrified that I was a quote-unquote *maricón*."

She went on staring at him.

"We saw Amy's body, 'Dusa!" He put his hands on her shoulders and said urgently, "So if we don't change today, she's going to be killed late this afternoon."

———

After they retrieved Amber's Milan from the Getty, she took him to an ophthalmologist in Westwood who worked with the LAPD, leading him in the office so he wouldn't hurt himself. As they waited, H.G. caught himself nervously checking his pocket watch, each time the blur a little worse. *Perhaps this is Fate's way of slapping me on the wrist for trying to bring a touch of justice to her inevitability.*

In the exam room, the doctor was astonished. Though H.G. had no prior indications of glaucoma, his eyes were deteriorating in the same way, only much more rapidly. The doctor diagnosed H.G. with a rare, aggressive form of the disease, recommended immediate laser surgery and wanted him admitted to the Jules Stein Eye Institute at UCLA. He told his nurse to make the arrangements.

H.G. didn't doubt the seriousness of his condition, but thought the ophthalmologist was as aggressive as the reformulation error that had affected his eyes. He began pleading with the man to give him glasses, promising that he would come back in a few days for the surgery. Reluctantly, the doctor agreed, and H.G. fled the office wearing horn-rimmed, Coke-bottle-thick glasses. Bemused, Amber told him that if he were older and uglier, he'd look like Woody Allen.

"I'll need a revolver, 'Dusa."

"I'll call Xerox," she said. Then a tiny smile brightened her face as an idea took shape in her mind—the smile she suppressed, the idea she did not.

Lost in his own thoughts, he didn't notice. They were together in an uncharted maze of cause and effect, playing with time and hopefully forging a new outcome to an unspeakable tragedy. He had been mulling over the conundrum since running from *The Utopia,* trying to anticipate every possibility, and the *im*possibility of doing so was driving him mad.

He gazed out the window through his new glasses. He hadn't had an opportunity to examine the various machines in the ophthalmologist's office, but did it matter? He could see again—far better than before. He frowned. *Of course it matters. The medical advances that restored my sight are astounding. Moreover, technology is indeed a wonderful gift man has given himself—if one doesn't think about wars, overpopulation, the wholesale destruction of the planet, various forms of fundamentalism, runaway materialism for a few, poverty, man's inhumanity to man, ad nauseam—if one doesn't think about the end of the world a few centuries down the road. If one is figuratively blind.*

Even in Venice, the day was unusually hot and humid. As soon as he got out of the car, H.G. took off his coat and draped it over his arm, but the air was dead, and he felt uncomfortable. He glanced at the smog and was reminded of global warming.

Xerox welcomed them into his bungalow with a flourish and insisted they join him for iced tea on the porch since the front room was stifling. Grateful, H.G. draped his coat over the wicker chair, and as soon as he sat down, Ernesto minced in with a tray of fresh-baked vanilla-lemon bars.

"Nice to see you again, but I'm in the middle of something," he said apologetically, then went back in the office.

"How was San Francisco?" said Xerox. "It is *so* my favorite city."

"Cool," said Amber. "We had a great time."

"Did you go to Fisherman's Wharf or the—?"

"We're here to buy a firearm," H.G. said flatly. "Needless to say, we don't have a lot of time."

"Ah, but one must stop to smell the roses," Xerox said blithely.

H.G. followed him around the side of the house, but Amber lifted her lemon bar, indicating that she was going to finish it and her iced tea.

As soon as they were out of sight, Amber went through H.G.'s coat pockets, her hands shaking. She found the special key in the right in-side pocket. Heart pounding, she held it thoughtfully and turned it reverently in her hand as if it were a sacred relic. If what H.G. had said was true—she had no reason to doubt him—then he had met her before in another time. She had no clue what had happened between them, but the possibilities were dazzling, especially after last night. *Maybe he loved me. Maybe he truly loved me. Maybe he actually chose me over*

Amy, and then came back because something happened and he had second thoughts. . . .

Well, I'll never be left behind again.

She found Ernesto in the office wearing a jeweler's loupe, bent over a key machine. He glanced up and smiled inquisitively.

"Can you do this one?" She handed him the special key. "Like right now?"

"Wow," he said appreciatively. "*Muy bonita.*"

He ran his fingers over its greenish bronze surface and felt its double rows of delicate teeth, then held it up to the light and slowly turned it over and over. "What's it for . . . ? A hope chest or something?"

Behind the house was a small garage renovated into a dollhouse version of the bungalow. Xerox unlocked three heavy-duty combination locks on the side door, finally turned to H.G. "I don't allow guns in the house," he said sanctimoniously. "I mean, you just never know, do you?"

H.G. wasn't sure what Xerox was talking about.

"If we lived like on the prairie," Xerox went on, "we'd like have a basement for the tornadoes which is where I'd keep the hardware as well, but, no, we're in weird California—as if you didn't know—and weird California doesn't have basements."

"What about earthquakes?" said H.G.

"Oh, trust me," said Xerox, hand suddenly on his hip, "we are *totally* retrofitted. If we slid into the ocean, we'd become a cruise ship."

They stepped inside. Xerox flipped a switch, and the room was instantly bright in soft daylight-blue. Astonished, H.G. looked from the lights back to Xerox, but Xerox spoke first.

"No, no, my man, they ain't high-output fluorescents, they're LED tubes." He grinned and nodded. "Made right here in the U.S.A."

H.G. had already moved farther into the room and was transfixed by the vast array of weaponry that surrounded him, some of it in display cases and on the walls, more of it in shipping crates stacked against the faux door. He couldn't help but wonder if people were instinctively stocking up for Armageddon or if this particular civilized society embraced a subculture of killers. *I must go home and write about this, as well. I must admonish people to use their brains instead of weapons.*

"Exactly what are we looking for?" Xerox lifted an AK-47 and swept it in a wide circle. "Something general . . . ?" He put it down and picked up an L96 sniper's rifle. "Or something more specific?"

"Excuse me," said H.G., alarmed, "but don't you worry about the police?"

Xerox cackled in falsetto and touched H.G. on his arm. "Oh, you're so funny! The police are my best customers." He opened a display case. "Now. . . . Where were we?"

Amber came inside all jittery and smiling, and they both turned to her expectantly.

"I think he's gonna want a handgun," said Amber.

"Something with stopping power . . . ?" asked Xerox. "Or something foo-foo?"

"The guys at the station carry nine-millimeters," she said.

"Voilà, a Beretta 92F," Xerox said with a flourish, pulling a gun from the second shelf. "Check this out."

Hating himself, H.G. gingerly hefted it, inspected it, actually admired its matte-silver finish and felt reassured.

"You like?"

"How does one go about using this grotesque little beauty . . . ?"

2:45 P.M., *Monday, June 21, 2010*

"This is home," Amber announced for the second time.

H.G. closed the door behind him and checked his watch, pleased that they were getting to her flat only an hour later than before, thanks to the ophthalmologist and the stop at Xerox's bungalow. They would more than make up for that hour just by not having to "google" for Amy. He was convinced that the less mucking about he did with Fate's sequence of events, the better, though he wasn't sure it would make any difference.

"What do you think?" She interrupted his thoughts, spreading her arms, twirling and smiling, telling herself that if they had been here before, this is what she would have done.

"Cozy," he replied, then glanced out the window over the breakfast nook at the alley that separated her building from the others. "Quite cozy."

"Are you all right now?"

"'Dusa, I'm sorry," he said patiently. "I've already been here. I've already heard everything you're going to say."

She was ready for that. "Hey, I'm a woman. I'm entitled. You're probably gonna hear it all again and again—and all over again."

"Then please don't think it rude if I'm constantly interrupting you," he replied, his eyes twinkling.

"Whatever," she said cheerfully. *Don't try to second-guess him. Just be cool and stumble through this, and you'll get to "whenever" you're going, and he'll never know.* She opened her laptop on the kitchen table, then blushed as her indiscretion came back to her. She turned to him and said resolutely, "You know, about what happened on the plane—"

He held up a hand, stopped her. "Please. . . . You mustn't take it personally, but like I just explained, we've already had this discussion."

"How am I supposed to know?" she said innocently.

"You won't. You'll merely go on being redundant. . . . I'm sorry, 'Dusa, I really am."

"Well, okay then, here's the laptop, so if you want to find your Amy, I suggest you sit down and say hi to Mr. Google." She started out. "I'm gonna go powder my twenty-first-century nose."

He chuckled smugly.

She heard him in the kitchen, then was astonished to see him heating taquitos in the microwave on a microwave-safe plate and pouring himself a Coke from the refrigerator.

"Oh, okay. Make yourself at home."

"Thank you." He winked at her. "The pleasure is mine." He took the taquitos from the microwave and offered them to her.

"No thanks."

He picked one up gingerly—pinkie finger extended—bit in and tried to chew, then dropped the taquito and made a face. "Bloody awful."

"How long did you put it in for?"

"Seven minutes."

"You're lucky you didn't break your teeth." She giggled. "Didn't you look at the instructions?"

"This is a simple kitchen appliance," he said, annoyed with himself. "What does one need instructions for?"

Her giggle became a laugh. Then: "Hey, wanna do takeout?"

"Takeout is fine."

"There's this Thai place called King of Siam."

He smiled sheepishly. "Forgive me for being presumptuous, but is that soul food restaurant near here?"

"Whoa," she said, surprised. *This is gonna take some getting used to.* "What did we have?"

"Something that required a sizable number of paper napkins." He took off his new glasses, began cleaning them.

"Well, oookay." She picked up her car keys, started for the door, then turned and smiled knowingly. "What else did we do this afternoon?"

"Not that."

They ate with the laptop between them, H.G. enjoying the food as much as he had later than night at the Getty, though Amber was glancing at him strangely, knowing that he knew. She was having trouble *not* knowing what to say without making a fool of herself. Then—when he was on his fourth rib—she suddenly realized that they were no further along than they had been that morning in San Francisco's Marina.

"Bertie . . . !" She blurted out. "You haven't done anything!"

He finished his rib, wiped his hands on a paper towel, then fished the Post-it note from his shirt pocket and gave her a Cheshire cat smile. "Kevin and Elizabeth Robbins do indeed live in Beverly Hills, and this is their phone number."

"Why didn't you tell me?"

"The less you know, the less chance we have of altering the chain of events."

"Haven't we already?" she said, hurt.

"Not irrevocably."

"How d'you know?"

He chuckled. "I'm not sure I do."

"Y'know what?" she said, exasperated. She got up from the table and went in the living room. "You're too much of an enigma for me. I might as well go back to work, then come home and—ho-ho-hum—watch TV. Maybe you'll make the six o'clock news on SyFy."

She flopped back on the sofa, stared at the ceiling. *What in the world am I doing, anyway? Why do I have this stupid need to do stupid things—to go places no normal person has ever been? To, to make the headlines in Wikipedia before I turn thirty?* She wiped away tears. *What am I doing falling for some guy who steps out of a time machine? I think I should give him back the key he doesn't know about, offer to call him a cab and lock the door behind him. He doesn't care about me!*

She looked over at H.G. and realized that he'd been gazing at her the whole time, a smile on his face that was a thousandfold more loving than he knew—because if he did know, he would've deliberately covered it up. Her heart surged, and she forgot about telling him to leave. In fact, she wanted to rush over and throw herself at him again, then stopped herself and bolted upright. "If you know how to get in touch with Amy, how come you haven't called?"

"It's too early."

"Too *early?*"

He nodded and checked his pocket watch just to make sure.

"Aren't we being a little cavalier with Amy's life?"

"Not at all." He explained, "If we call now, we risk stopping her from whatever she was doing—I believe she was on a bike ride—hence we change the course of events and will not have a chance to stop Stephenson."

"Huh?"

"If we *don't* call her till the same time as before, then we know where she will be—which happens to be in Franklin Canyon. And if we know where she is, then we can rescue her." He paused, beaming. "Whereas, if we call her now, she'll be somewhere else. . . . Hence, so will the Ripper."

"I don't know," she said skeptically. "Kind of makes sense. . . . So what time do we leave?"

"We'll give ourselves an extra fifteen minutes."

"Ha!" She snorted. "Then you better go online and check the traffic." She had no idea that taking the 405 the first time probably had cost Amy her life.

"Traffic?" It had been the furthest thing from his mind.

"Welcome to L.A. the second time around." She went looking for her purse. "I think we ought to get there early and wait."

4:50 P.M., Monday, June 21, 2010

The elevator doors opened. They crossed the underground parking lot to her car, stopped short when they saw a faded green Toyota Corolla parked illegally, blocking in Amber's Milan and her neighbor's Prius, and H.G. remembered a tow truck leaving from the time before. His heart sank.

The neighbor was pacing alongside the Corolla, peering inside, then checking his cell phone. He saw Amber and H.G. and shrugged. "I called the manager and the tow-away people should be here anytime." Disgusted, he gestured at the Corolla. "What an idiot, huh?"

H.G. couldn't stand to look and turned away from the scene—as if that would make the tow truck get there faster. He was cursed for knowing what was going to happen and being helpless in the face of it. He couldn't hold back that grim little déjà vu from before. It chortled inside and he felt sick. His pocket watch read 5:03 P.M. They were still ahead of themselves, but he realized they wouldn't be for long. He shouted at Amber, "I think we should call a cab!"

She took out her phone, opened it, shook her head at H.G. "Can't. . . . I don't have any reception."

"*He* called!" said H.G., pointing at the neighbor.

"Bertie! Everybody's phone is different, that's just—"

"Well, then, let's use his bloody phone!" he said, hating the magical little devices the world had become so dependent on.

He was striding toward the neighbor when the tow truck came down the ramp, its growl reverberating through the parking structure. Fuming, H.G. watched as the driver exchanged words with the neighbor, gave him a clipboard to sign, then started hooking up the Corolla.

"See?" said Amber as they drove up the ramp twenty-two minutes later. "That didn't take very long."

"*Don't* patronize me," he said, buried in the map book, having trouble reading it, though it was an inch from his face.

As before, she paused at the street. H.G. looked at his watch again. 5:25 P.M. He glanced at Amber, saw her entering Kevin and Elizabeth Robbins's address from the Post-it note into the GPS. "Forget that," he snapped. "Go east on Ocean Park, then—"

"*Excuse* me. This tells us how to get there."

"If you insist on using this electronic box for morons," he said, seething, "we're going TO GET IN A BLOODY MOTOR-CAR ACCIDENT!"

"Okay, okay," she said, frightened. "Jeez Louise!"

She pulled out, stood on the gas, and her car swung across traffic and lurched into the far right lane.

"You'll run into West Pico Boulevard, then turn left on Sepulveda . . . turn right on Santa Monica Boulevard . . . go north on North Beverly Drive, and pray that everybody else in this blasted city isn't driving somewhere!"

"Good fucking luck."

"You will *not* get on the bloody freeways!"

"The GPS has a setting for shortest time!"

Not listening, he shouted, "I have no intention of seeing my wife murdered twice!"

"You don't have to get so pissed off!" she cried, weaving through traffic, checking the rearview mirror for cops. She half-hoped she'd get stopped for speeding, then hated herself for the thought. She had to bite her lip to stop from crying. "You're the one who's playing this stupid game with free will and determinism!"

"It's Fate, 'Dusa," he said as if she were a schoolgirl. "F-A-T-E."

"So what?" she said, screeching left on Sepulveda against the light, bringing on an irate chorus of horns. "You've got the special key. If we don't make it, go back to your damned time machine and try again!"

"Right. And come back missing an arm or a leg."

"If you don't want reformulation errors," she said blithely, "fix the stupid machine!"

"Fix the fourth dimension is more like it."

"No problem," she said sarcastically, "you can do that, can't you?"

"I'm not God."

"Ha!" she said triumphantly. "You're admitting you're not perfect!"

"You're worse than your robot, 'Dusa," he replied, irritated.

"What?!"

"Please shut up."

Racing east on Santa Monica, she couldn't hold back anymore and burst out crying. She gazed at him forlornly and put one hand on his leg. "Oh, Bertie . . . ! I don't want to fight with you. Let's not do this. Please . . . ?"

He was about to apologize, but something made him glance at the street ahead. He gasped. They were hurtling toward cars waiting for the light at Avenue of the Stars.

"'Dusa!"

She hit the brakes and hung on. The Milan fishtailed and locked up, tires screeching, brakes smoking, jolted to a stop inches before the undercarriage of a giant SUV. H.G. slammed back in the seat and stared straight ahead, stunned.

"I'm sorry!"

He couldn't hold back a strangled laugh. "I think she knows we're here."

Amber looked at him quizzically.

"Fate. . . ."

They sped up Beverly, H.G. gripping the seat, rocking back and forth as if that would make the car go faster. He remembered that they'd gotten in the accident at 5:52 P.M., and calculated if they got to where Coldwater Canyon forked off to the right a few minutes earlier, they would have a chance. He checked his watch: 5:41 P.M.

"Come on, come on, come on!" he muttered.

"For Christ's sake, why don't you call and warn her?!"

Amber tossed her phone into his lap, swerved around local traffic, caromed over the speed humps near Elevado, bringing glares from drivers and pedestrians.

"Or is it too early?" she added sarcastically. "I mean, God forbid you should scare the Ripper off, huh?"

He glared at her. "God forbid you should live to regret that."

Mortified by her remark, she started crying. "I'm sorry," she cried, "I'm sorry . . . I didn't mean that!"

He didn't acknowledge her. He was dialing.

They flashed across Sunset Boulevard against the light, bringing on another cacophony of horns.

"Amy . . . ? Oh, dear God, Amy." He sighed with relief, slumped in the seat, closed his eyes, didn't hear Amber's lovesick sobs. "Yes, I called your mother and— Yes, the boys are fine, they're all right," he said impatiently. "Where am I . . . ? Well, according to—"

He straightened up and leaned forward. "*Amy!* Listen to me! Turn around and start back the way you've come . . . ! Yes, yes, I know where you are—don't ask me how—just please, for the love of God, turn around *now!*"

Amber pulled hard on the wheel, and—tires squealing—the car lurched across Coldwater Canyon into oncoming traffic, but she was minutes earlier this time, the drivers were different—more reasonable perhaps—Fate was somewhere else, and Amber missed them all.

Though she hadn't been here before, she felt a surge of triumph and accelerated hard up Beverly for Franklin Canyon Drive.

"No! No!" H.G. screamed into the phone. "Don't get off the bike . . . !" He listened, was horrified. "*What?* You're walking down a hill?! GOOD BLOODY CHRIST, AMY! STEPHENSON'S COMING FOR YOU! WATCH OUT FOR STEPHENSON! WE'RE ALMOST THERE!"

5:43 P.M., *Monday, June 21, 2010*

Amber red-lined the Milan up into Franklin Canyon, the speedometer shooting past seventy where the narrow, two-lane road curved, the speed drying her tears like an emotional wind. Up ahead, a silver Mercedes idled on the shoulder, but when Amber angled to pass, it suddenly pulled out. She cursed, leaned on her horn, hit the brakes, swerved out of the way. Unmindful, the Mercedes went up to the fork at Lake Drive, U-turned and came back toward them, but then H.G. was pointing at a shiny-red road bike on the shoulder.

"Stop the car! Stop! That's it!"

Amber hit the brakes again and pulled off the road, and H.G. was out the door before the car had stopped, running through chaparral toward his petite Amy in a powder-blue top and shorts. From afar, Amber thought she looked like a little girl in a commercial who had found her dreams, and when Amy threw herself into H.G.'s arms, Amber started crying again. *God, they look beautiful together, and this—this is awful. I'm supposed to be all relieved and happy, and yet I feel like I'm watching my, my only love hooking up with the reincarnation of Shirley Temple. Why can't this head-over-heels kind of stuff ever happen to me? I mean, what's so great about her?* Amber blew her nose, dabbed at her face with a Kleenex, checked her hair, then got out. She stopped. *So much for nailing Jack the Ripper.* H.G. had left his new Beretta on the backseat. She picked it up and walked around the car.

A beautiful dark-haired woman in a sweater and a frilly, floral-print dress had climbed from the Mercedes and now was standing near the bike, smiling nervously as H.G. and Amy came back up the hill hand-in-hand.

"Did you see him?" H.G. called.

"No," said Amber, shaking her head.

"We were too blasted early. We frightened him off."

"See who?" said Amy.

Jaclyn hesitated when she saw the gun in Amber's hand. Instinctively, she stepped back and wrung her hands, spoke in a cultured British accent reminiscent of BBC television. "Excuse me, but I'm lost."

Amber stuffed the gun in her jeans and glanced at H.G. He had seen Jaclyn as well, and Amber caught a glimpse of recognition in his eyes, but then it was gone, and she wondered if he'd seen her from "already today" or if the recognition was from a much earlier time.

"Have you seen anyone else in the vicinity?" H.G. said to Jaclyn as he rushed forward. "I realize that you've been in your motor car, but did you see *anyone*? I must know!"

Jaclyn backed away—as if frightened by his urgency. "No. No, I'm sorry. I haven't. In fact, I'm a tourist, and I happen to be hopelessly lost."

Frustrated, H.G. sighed, the scanned the terrain through his ridiculous glasses as Jaclyn went on.

"You see, I have friends in Franklin Canyon, and I've been driving up and down this road Lord knows how many times, and I can't find any houses, let alone house numbers." She emitted a jittery laugh. "I have a phone in the car, but I'm not even sure if I have their number."

"I'm so sorry," said Amy.

"Are you from the UK?" Jaclyn asked suddenly.

"Not me," said Amber, reminding them that she was there. "I'm from la-la land."

They all ignored her.

"I thought I heard a bit of an accent," said Jaclyn to Amy.

"Why, yes," said Amy, pleasantly surprised, "we live near Kent, on the shore. How about you?"

"Highland Heath."

"Lovely," said Amy. "If you have to be near the city."

"Are you staying in L.A.?"

Amy looked to H.G., and he nodded, seemed to relax. Even relent.

"Yes, we're staying in L.A."

"We should get together," said Jaclyn. "Maybe do the City Walk and one of those studio tours, have dinner, perhaps."

"How marvelous," said Amy.

"Where are you staying?" asked Jaclyn.

Amy looked to her husband again and prompted him with a whisper. "Sara says the Four Seasons is the best."

"The Four Seasons," he repeated.

"Splendid!" said Jaclyn, starting for the Mercedes. "I'm looking forward to it."

"Oh, by the way, I'm Amy," said Amy, following and extending her hand. "Amy Wells."

"Jaclyn," she replied, shaking Amy's hand. "Jaclyn Smythe."

She drove away with smiles and a little flutter wave, the Mercedes descending from the canyon into the muted warm glow of Beverly Hills at twilight.

"That was nice," said Amy.

"I can't tell you how relieved I am to see you," murmured H.G. He was so happy to have Amy in his arms it never occurred to him that Jaclyn was any more—or less—than she appeared. He buried his face in Amy's hair. "Please don't leave me like that again."

"It was a bit risky," she murmured back.

"You have no idea."

She giggled. "Where did you get those awful glasses?"

"It was either that or learn Braille."

"What happened?" she asked fearfully.

"I'd rather tell you when I don't feel so wonderfully close to you."

"Um."

Amber watched them hold on to each other for dear life, bit her lip sorrowfully and started back to the Milan, having no desire to be embarrassed by someone's else's intimacy or her own foolish dreams.

H.G. noticed her then, extracted himself from Amy and smiled sheepishly. "Amber." He laughed softly. "Please. I haven't forgotten you."

She turned, tried a warm smile and hoped her face didn't give her away.

"Amy, this is Ms. Amber Reeves," he said.

"Hullo, Amber," she said, her accent refined after thirteen years in England. They shook hands. "How nice."

"Without her help, I doubt that I would've found you," he added.

Her smile fading, Amy gave him an inquisitive look.

"Yes," he nodded, "she knows," then said smoothly, "She was there when I arrived at the Getty Museum, and thank God for that."

He gave Amy a glib and funny rendition of their time together since Sunday morning. Amber almost blushed at his sanitized version, curtsied like a schoolgirl instead, then realized it wasn't the right thing to do, since Amy frowned darkly, maybe recalling *her* time with H.G. in 1979 San Francisco. Amber endured the heavy silence, the questions hanging in the air, answered inanely by thousands of crickets who seemed to be shrieking, "Yes, yes, yes!" She almost explained, *It wasn't that way, he talked about you nonstop, he didn't come to my bed eagerly, so I had to go to his, and, hey, I'm really sorry, but I didn't believe he'd ever find you again, so I didn't think it would matter, I couldn't help myself, I—* Amy was staring at her as if listening to her thoughts, and this time Amber couldn't hold back a vivid blush, then changed the subject.

"It's getting kind of cold," she said.

"Yes," H.G. and Amy both agreed.

"You guys want a ride somewhere?"

"I should probably take the bicycle back," said Amy.

"Shouldn't we ring first?" asked H.G.

"Oh, right." Amy reached for the cell, then stopped and giggled, her eyes twinkling. "No, that's far too normal, Bertie. They think I've been in Bedlam."

When the road bike was folded up in the Milan's trunk, Amber turned the car around and drove slowly down the hill toward the city, stealing glances of them in the rearview mirror cuddling close like teenagers and talking low so she couldn't hear. Amy giggled with embarrassment when H.G. gave her her purse back, then nuzzled and kissed him. He was pleased with her show of affection, yet went on intensely, and soon Amy seemed to shrink within herself and some awful memory. She turned red, then ashen, and Amber figured H.G. had told her that Leslie John Stephenson was alive and well in 2010, once again on the hunt for them. *"I'm so dreadfully sorry!"* Amy mouthed and covered her face. H.G. comforted her, yet mechanically so, and then briefly his eyes met Amber's in the mirror. She glanced back at the road thinking he must have told her the truth, something like: *Jack the Ripper is back because you unwittingly sent the time machine to infinity.*

Then their dialogue changed again, Amy shaking off her little-girl despair and taking charge with a succession of emphatic whispers. H.G. nodded methodically—again a foot soldier on the fourth dimension, Amber guessed—then caught her eye again. He smiled weakly. Amber grinned and felt better. *Maybe he misses me already. Maybe he realizes that if anyone helps him nail Jack the Ripper it'll be me; whereas all his wife will do is carp from a distance, and he'll be lucky if he gets laid.*

Amber had been so absorbed with them on the backseat that she'd missed the turn and gone all the way to Santa Monica Boulevard, then had to backtrack to Shadow Hills Drive. She squared her shoulders, broke the silence and the mood.

"Excuse me. What are we looking for?"

"Oh," said Amy, leaning forward. "It's the Spanish house on the left, next block up."

Amber pulled in to a circular drive and killed the lights, but left the car running. Amy hadn't invited her in. She felt totally rejected—but then again, if she had been Amy, she wouldn't have invited herself in, either. She glanced at H.G. He seemed uncomfortable, and Amber guessed he wasn't looking forward to meeting Amy's parents. Maybe being left out wasn't such a bad deal.

They all got out. Amber was going to help H.G. lift the bike out of the trunk, but Amy took her aside, across the lawn to a bench behind manicured bushes with tiny white flowers. A surprisingly beautiful smile was on her face, and she said intimately, "You must be wonderful, Amber. . . ."

"Hey, thanks," said Amber, taken unawares.

"As you may or may not know, I had to look after him in San Francisco when he was a mere child from the nineteenth century. Though now he professes to be a man of the world and wants to be taken more as a philosopher and politician than a fiction writer, I suspect he hasn't changed much." She laughed low. "Despite meeting with presidents and heads of state—he has no patience for royalty—he can be a bit ditzy, to say the least. . . . I suppose that's where his incalculable charm comes from."

Amber was struck speechless; Amy was thanking her. Moreover, she couldn't get over the sweet, articulate melody of her voice. And her smile. She was so lovely, so friendly, so . . . sisterly.

"Yet somehow he talks you into things without actually mentioning them," Amy went on. "His enthusiasm is infectious. . . . So you must be careful."

Amber nodded and gulped.

"Very careful, or else you'll find yourself in love and traipsing through universes alongside him as if on a crusade, and then suddenly you look back and wonder what on earth you have done."

Amber blushed crimson. *Does she know?*

Amy chuckled. "And then—irony of ironies—he grins at you with those eyes of his, and you don't care."

Amber looked down, gulped and nodded again. "He seemed so helpless."

Amy smiled nostalgically. "Oh, I know. . . . I still remember the morning he came in the bank. . . ."

"Wait," Amber said anxiously. "You don't think— I mean, I don't know how to say this, but—"

"Oh, I'm sorry, my dear!" Amy leaned forward and touched her arm. "I wasn't suggesting anything like *that*! My God, no. I was merely apologizing for his behavior because I know how he impossible can be." Her eyes sparkled. "And I'm not sure how I can repay you for looking after him in this rather ugly century."

Amber sighed gratefully and bit her lip. She whispered, "You don't have to repay me."

"Ah, but I do. . . . We're the same, you know. We're both from the States, we're both so-called modern women, we're—" She giggled and put her hand to her mouth. "We've both saved him from himself."

Amber started to laugh, and then tears welled up in her eyes. She put her arms around Amy and held her, realizing they weren't rivals or enemies and never would be. If anything, she admired this woman. Amy had given up her own century for H.G., and then his passades had forced her to invent something called a modus vivendi for her own self-respect. *He's probably not good enough for her.*

"Well, you don't have to worry about him," Amber said truthfully. "He was a prince."

She raised up on tiptoes and kissed Amber on the cheek, whispering, "Thank you so very much."

"I say," H.G. called. He was standing in front of the garage with the bicycle. "I'd put this away, but I don't know how to open the door."

Amy chuckled, took the remote from her pocket, pushed the button and the door swung silently open. H.G. studied the process, turned back to Amy. "Did you push something or merely think some combination code."

"I'll never tell." Smiling, she waved good night to Amber, then went through the gate into the front courtyard.

Amber handed H.G. the Beretta he'd forgotten. "Here."

"Oh, yes." He slipped it in his coat pocket.

"Try not to shoot yourself."

"Good night, 'Dusa." He hesitated, then pecked her on the forehead. "She's so cool."

"Yes. . . . I'll ring you tomorrow."

Amber watched the gate close, heard a rush of greetings and music from the house as the door opened, then hurried back to her car. She drove home the same way that they'd come on their high-speed race with destiny. She tried to remember their excitement, the close calls, the rush she'd gotten from driving so crazily, but her mind didn't cooperate. Instead, she was confused. She still loved H.G. and wondered how that was possible when she had just bonded with Amy. Her tears came again. She told herself to forget H.G., the magic of the last two days, to dismiss it all as some weird form of virtual reality and go back to work in the morning, insulate herself from her so-called colleagues and resume paying off her mom's bills, saving for grad school and a real life. Yes. Get a doctorate in record time, meet some budding genius along the way, fall in love (again), and get married. Go to some sprawling, renowned university—never in the UK—have a couple of genius kids and . . .

Her copy of the special key burned in her pocket, and she wondered how she could have been so presumptuous.

6:20 P.M., Monday, June 21, 2010

When a harried Jaclyn went inside the Radio Shack on Sunset, she was surrounded by three salesmen barking "How can we help you" and imagined herself a feline cornered by hyenas. Once again, she realized that living in a shell of beauty and sensuality could be an annoyance rather than a convenience. She chose the most intelligent-looking specimen—a rotund boy with bad acne who wore a high-tech sneer that supposedly was a winning smile. She asked him for a product to disguise her voice. Within seconds, he had six voice changers on the counter ranging in price from $650.00 to $49.95 and was rambling on about pitch levels, modulation warps and battery packs. She understood little of it, but did explain that she would also be working with components of a "electrical sort." He quickly filled a plastic toolkit with small tools, tossed in a headlamp and rolls of electrical tape and duct tape. Back at the register, he identified each item as he rang it up. Finally, Jaclyn chose the voice changer with a cell phone adapter that he said would make her voice sound like the monster in the movie *Scream.*

"I like people to scream," she said to the boy.

He grinned stupidly, and she was sure he had picked up on the sexual innuendo when that had been the furthest thing from her mind.

Bagging her voice changer and tools, he offered to help her build or repair whatever she was working on, his wink and implication: Why would somebody with a body like yours waste time with tools when we'll do it for you? *If I had time,* she thought nastily, *I'd take you in the back room and try out my new tools on your blubber and make your unfortunate face a happy one by replacing your pockmarked cheeks with ones from below.*

Cruising along Sunset, she tried to look at the bright side of the incident in Franklin Canyon, her plan in shambles. Neither Wells nor Amy had recognized Jaclyn. That gave her an enormous advantage. If it hadn't been for the girl with the pistol, she could have surprised them both right then. Nevertheless, she did have the presence of mind to befriend them and now could plan for a more predictable showdown, then carve them up and be rid of them forever—free to ride the fourth dimension as a dark-haired Satanic beauty or whatever incarnation evil blessed her with. Still, the encounter had left her frustrated, for she had miscalculated and was baffled that Wells had appeared from out of nowhere. She had been anticipating the foreplay of kidnapping his wife and terrorizing her, then bargaining with Wells for the special key, then betraying them both. What with the unisex fashions that seemed de rigueur in 2010, she could give them each a happy face decorated with the other's sex organs, and "REMEMBER ME?" in script. *Smashing.*

She went north on Sepulveda, eschewing the sluggish crawl on the 405 that reminded her of a backed-up sewer in London spewing methane instead of carbon monoxide, then turned on Getty Center Drive and drove slowly to the entrance. The parking structure was deserted because the museum was closed on Mondays. She paused, made sure she was alone, then parked next to the fleet of Getty Center cars and golf carts.

She changed into jeans and T-shirt, pocketed keys and phone, picked up her toolkit and got behind the wheel of a golf cart. She found the key on the floor, then inspected the controls—what with forward, reverse, brake, throttle and lights it was child's play compared to the Mercedes. She sped out of the parking structure and up the access road.

She gazed in awe at the lights of the museum's perimeter, the warm

glow from within. The complex struck her as a glorious castle of the future, awash and heady with the good works of man, ripe for ruin. *In
what year will the barbarians come—their fathers and mother-whores
propagating right now on the mean streets of this very same city? In
what year will the barbarians blow up the place and burn the art, murder the patrons and rape the docents? When will they pillage? It is only
a matter of time, for this museum is but a self-righteous mockery of
truth, a turning of the cheek to the real nature of the human beast.*

Where the road forked, she went around the complex until she saw
light spilling from a ring-shaped building. On the other side of a curved
hedgerow and trees, a walkway led to the gardens and pavilions beyond. She bounced over the curb and whizzed up the path, enjoying
the cool wind through her hair. She recalled being young Leslie and
going carriaging with Penny on crisp summer nights, their legs pressed
together, her furtive hand teasing him—unlike the others whom Penny
would straddle and fornicate desperately, her cries in concert with the
horses trotting on cobblestones. It wasn't that she preferred them to her
brother. He—and now she—had learned that above all things, Penny
had loved the ecstasy of betrayal.

Jaclyn parked the golf cart below the South Promontory and skirted
the West Pavilion looking for a way inside. She saw a "Maintenance
Department" golf cart parked by a service door. Smiling at her good
fortune, she waited in the shadows, waited for her *entrée*.

Voices.

She coiled. The service door opened; light from the stairwell
splashed outside. A Hispanic janitor held the door open as her partner
wheeled out a bucket and cart of cleaning tools and supplies. While
they loaded their golf cart, Jaclyn darted inside with her own tools
ahead of the door hissing shut and locking automatically behind her.
Ear to the door, she listened. When she heard their voices recede, she
opened it carefully, duct-taped the bolt inside the door, eased it shut.

She followed a hallway around the pavilion's lower level, discovered
that the only access was through metal doors marked FIRE, sure to set
off the alarms, so she kept going until she found a service elevator that
took her up to the third level in the South Pavilion. She crossed a

glass-walled bridge between buildings, and voilà, she was on the floor above the H. G. Wells exhibition. She went to the front, crept halfway down the stairs to the lobby.

No one was behind the desk where Teresa Cruz had been early Sunday morning, yet someone had left a blue blazer hanging on the chair, meaning they would be back.

She stole into the central gallery, gazed at the time machine silhouetted by a warm glow of recessed lights on the walls, thought it resembled a dark monolith. Or tombstone. She cocked her head, listened, heard only a profound silence in the building, architecturally sealed from the omniscient roar of the megacity outside.

She let herself inside the engine compartment, donned gloves and headlamp, crawled to the heart of the engine, inching her toolkit behind. She didn't have sabotage in mind; she needed the machine to be her black steed through the cosmos. Instead, she was about to attempt "preventive surgery"—a concept unfamiliar to professors when Leslie John had attended medical school, with the brutal exception of amputation. She was going to alter *The Utopia* so that should Wells and spouse decide to return to 1906 before they confronted her, the machine would send them to that black hell of dark energy, that vortex of nothingness graced with the stench of burnt technology.

She opened the small door to the RRL housing, reached up blind and scratched her arm on the gearing wheels, annoyed that Wells had built his engine like a circular labyrinth. *It reflects his character—his scientific brain coiled like a snake.* Her fingers brushed something alien, something that moved, and she jerked her hand from the housing as if bitten. Cursing under her breath, she took a dental mirror from the toolkit and used it to guide her hand back inside the housing. Wells, that clever do-gooder, had hung a simple bicycle lock on a gearing wheel— indubitably to protect his machine from those very same barbarians of the future. *Or maybe from yours truly.* She started to remove it, but stopped. *Should Wells check the engine before he takes his beloved back home—and he would be a fool not to—he'll expect the lock to be here.* She left it on the central gearing wheel.

Her mirror led to a neat wrap of black wires. The RRL circuitry. She carefully pulled them from the housing and discovered that she was holding two identical arteries amid smaller wires. She recalled being Leslie John on that glorious night in 1893 when he had stolen the machine and escaped Scotland Yard. A quick study of Wells's diagrams had shown the way, so she realized—here in 2010—that if she cut both arteries, the machine wouldn't go anywhere; whereas if she cut the one governing rotation into the past, the machine could only travel into the future. That was what Wells had written, was it not?

The wires were unmarked.

She gazed at them, uncertain now, then finally propped her headlamp up in the housing so the entire area was lit. Panning the mirror, she followed the wires to where they merged with the pulse generator. Near the base, one was labeled "W," the other "E." She sighed with relief and nodded. She remembered Wells saying that "if you rotate to the west, you gain yesterdays; to the east, you accumulate tomorrows."

She pulled the wires taut, intending the cut the one marked "W," but instinctively wiped them all clean as Jack would've done to a patient in a surgery, and when she picked up her wire cutters and turned back to the wires, she stopped suddenly, horrified. She had unwittingly wiped off the labels with her rag.

The wires were identical now, temporal direction hidden inside, and Jaclyn didn't know which one to cut. Her practiced, surgically trained hands began shaking. So badly, she dropped the wire cutters. She blinked, tried to get a hold of herself, tried to recall if the "W" wire was on the right side of the bunch or in the middle or— She bit her lip in frustration. She had no clue.

Disconsolate, she rewrapped the wires and pushed them back in their housing, then gathered up her tools and backed out of the engine compartment. She stared at the enigmatic machine and thought furiously, trying to picture Wells's diagrams on his workbench in 1893, not willing to let go of her scheme.

Wait. She spied the declinometer under the cabin door and smiled slowly, tentatively. *Perhaps sending Wells to hell is not as complicated as I imagined.* She pulled it out, peered at the prism-shaped device, held fast to its ring by four small bolts. She disconnected it with a speed wrench and put the ring back in its slot so it appeared that all was well. She chuckled softly. *Now when Wells tries to go home, he and his bride will blast off without the machine. Maybe they won't go to hell, but they certainly won't be here. . . . Maybe they won't be anywhere at all.* Bemused, she twisted Shakespeare again: *All's well that ends badly.*

She hid the declinometer under the bottom firewall, then stashed her tape and headlamp alongside. She was coming out of the compartment when someone strode into the gallery and blinded her with a halogen flashlight.

"Hey!"

Startled, she backed up and tripped over her toolkit, and its contents went clattering all over the floor.

"It's *you*!" The security guard, Peterson, had recognized her. "Jesus Christ, you're not a dude! You're a woman!" He started toward her.

She scooped up a pair of needle-nosed pliers, sprang toward him and, with a little growl, stabbed him in the chest.

He flailed backwards.

She stabbed him again.

He hit the wall and staggered forward, and she stabbed him a third time, pile-driving him to the floor, then watched his body shake and rat-a-tat-tat on the floor, watched him die. She closed her eyes and breathed deeply, felt the rush of that sex-death climax wash over her, leave her all aglow and wanting more. *Ah, God, for a bed. My dark kingdom for a bed and my Casey Holland to couple with and then to sleep and dream of —*

"Hey Peterson," the walkie crackled. "This is Cedric. . . . I'm gonna do my walk-through and then I'm gonna boogie for coffee, man. Ten-four."

Peterson had come upon her at a most inopportune time, and she had to make him disappear before this Cedric or some other guard came looking for him. She gathered her tools and hid them behind a display case in the exhibition, went back to the body. Juiced from the kill, she lifted it to her shoulder, trotted upstairs. On the third level, using his keys, she opened the electrical room door and pulled Peterson inside. She stripped him of his uniform and left him propped up in the corner, blood oozing from his chest wounds, soiling the "canvas" of his well-defined stomach where—with a more leisurely murder—she could have drawn an elaborate happy face using the ridges of his muscles to enhance her collage. She left his uniform folded inside the door in case she'd need it at a later time and started out.

Wait. No need to run so quickly. There are no whistles or shouts, no sirens, no coppers hounding you. This castle of the future is insulated by its own smug invincibility, and Cedric has gone for coffee.

Humming that sweet lullaby from the music box, she took out her cell phone, studied the display. She recalled the salesman's instructions, pushed the proper buttons and videoed Peterson's corpse, lingering on the jagged holes in his chest.

Back in the parking structure, Jaclyn was about to get in the Mercedes, but froze. A blue-and-white security vehicle abruptly turned in Getty Center Drive and went into a slow 360-degree turn. She ducked down behind the car till the lights receded, then peered over the hood. The vehicle was idling on the frontage road—the driver talking into his phone—and then it sped away.

Heart pounding, she got in the Mercedes and pulled out of the parking structure, paused at the street, variables racing through her brain. If they found the murdered guard, found out that she had been there . . . Rather than continue on to Sepulveda or the 405, Jaclyn went back up to the Getty complex and followed the road past the ring-shaped building. Just when she thought she was driving in a gigantic circle, she saw a road to the right. A sign read EMPLOYEES ONLY, and a wooden arm blocked the road.

She stopped by the electronic box on a post and correctly figured that if one inserted a card, the arm would lift. With nothing to lose, she tried one of Heather's credit cards. A red light blinked, and the arm didn't move. She was tempted to just drive through and break it, but was afraid of setting off an alarm, so she got out and looked. Beside the barrier, the road had been cut into the hill, yet there was a gap on the other side, then a drop-off, then trees. Back in the Mercedes, she put it in low, eased around the barrier to the edge of the drop-off, pulled hard on the wheel and swung back on the road. She smiled triumphantly. She was gone from the Getty complex via a back road.

She wound down the mountain past sprawling, secluded homes and minutes later emerged on North Bundy Drive.

Heading south toward Sunset, she took out her cell phone. She recalled another tip from the Verizon salesman and speed-dialed Lieutenant Holland, but was disappointed when his voice mail answered. She sighed heavily and almost rang off—her sigh being message enough for him—but added, "I miss you."

Then she laughed and thought, *The good lieutenant is not the only phone number in my . . . my repertoire, shall we say?*

8:07 P.M., Monday, June 21, 2010

The electric knife buzzed quietly through the turkey breast, a slice of meat falling on other slices, the stack perfectly symmetrical, the knife lifting away, shiny in the electric candlelight. Captivated, H.G. watched Kevin Robbins press the button again and effortlessly cut another slice. *Good Lord, what will they think of next? An automatic eating machine?*

Trying not to be obvious, H.G. looked away. He sipped a chilled California chardonnay and instinctively wished it were French. Though he wasn't a fan of white wine, it did make the first moments alone with his father-in-law almost tolerable. Finally, he nodded politely at the turkey. "I must say, sir, you needn't have gone to all that trouble for us."

"No trouble," said Kevin, chuckling. "It's takeout."

H.G. blushed, reminded of where he was. He quickly scanned the dining room for unknown objects so that he wouldn't make an anachronism of himself should he encounter some other surprise technology, yet as he assessed tiny speakers in the ceiling that broadcast an unrecognizable classical dirge, the buzz of the electric knife captivated him. He stared at it again.

"Cordless," said Kevin, gesturing with the knife and grinning. "Got its own charger built right into the handle. What will they think of next, huh . . . ?"

"A world-state, perhaps?" H.G. replied before he could stop himself.

"Politics?" said the old man. "I wasn't talking about politics."

"Nor was I, sir."

"What the hell is a world-state, then? Something that runs on batteries?"

"Forgive me for wanting to improve the planet."

"Soon as the Chinese and the Indians and all the rest of them clean up their own mess, people like me will get in line," Kevin growled, then segued into how he'd helped people with his start-up Internet insurance company. His voice rising, he went on about how many millions he'd sold it for three years ago, lamenting that if he had sold it today, he'd have gotten twice as much in spite of the economy.

"Well, then as you Yanks say, why didn't you hang on to it?"

"You don't 'hang on to' a company when you've had a goddamn stroke, boy. You hang on to the goddamn doctors."

"And their science and technology," H.G. added conspiratorially, lifting his horn-rimmed spectacles.

Kevin Robbins gave him an incredulous look, drained his whiskey and went on with his own agenda. "So that's what happened to me after the goddamn earthquake. I lost everything and I got it *back*."

"And aren't we the luckier for it," said Elizabeth, trying to turn the conversation as she came in the room carrying a gigantic salad.

Amy and Sara followed with rice, rolls and butter and a steamed something that H.G. had never seen before.

"I'm *so* glad you came," Sara said warmly to H.G., using tongs to set an artichoke on his plate.

He glanced helplessly from the artichoke to Amy, and she nodded back like mother to child that he should do as she did, and then they all sat down and were passing the dishes around, the girls marveling that it all looked and smelled so wonderful.

Kevin appraised H.G. "So what about you . . . ? You Brits don't have earthquakes, do you?"

"Actually, in Perthshire during the winter of 1839 —"

Kevin interrupted, guffawing with what he considered a witticism. "Then again, you gotta have something to lose something."

H.G. resisted an impulse to verbally assault Kevin Robbins and acted as if he hadn't heard. He nibbled on an artichoke leaf—melted garlic butter made it taste better—then discovered he was very hungry and dug into the turkey and rice.

"Oh, I forgot the gravy!" said Elizabeth. She got up and rushed to the kitchen.

At the same time, H.G. excused himself and went to the guest loo off the marble-tiled foyer. He dallied, but it wasn't all Kevin Robbins. Jaclyn Smythe, that woman they'd met in Franklin Canyon, was on his mind like a familiar and depressing melody. She had been in the last universe as well—flagging down Amber and then talking to the police when he was sick with grief at Amy's "death." Still, her appearances were within the scheme of cause and effect. First: She was a tourist looking for a friend's house who drove past Amy's murder and stopped to help. Second: She was a tourist looking for a friend's house who stopped to ask for directions before Amy was murdered. (Thanks to H. G. Wells dropping a figurative pebble in Destiny's Sea of Tranquility that hopefully wouldn't become a tsunami.) No great inconsistency there. Why then was she singing some siren's song in his brain? Yes, she was stunning and voluptuous, and normally he'd think it pure sexual attraction, except this woman didn't appeal to him. She haunted him. *Was she an acquaintance of Leslie John Stephenson? No, no. Stephenson wasn't one to have beautiful accomplices. He had victims.*

When H.G. came back to the table, he noticed that Robbins had gone from whiskey to wine. He hoped that meant the evening would be more civilized.

Instead, Kevin started probing again. "How'd you happen to meet our little Amy, anyway?"

"I was in San Francisco," H.G. replied modestly, "and I went in the Bank of England to change some money."

"Were you with your parents, or what?"

"I beg your pardon?"

"Daddy—" said Sara.

"Or did you have a thing for older women?"

H.G. realized that despite multiple glasses of hard liquor, Kevin Robbins could still add. Thirty-one years ago, Amy had been a twenty-two-year-old bank teller, and he had been an innocent twenty-seven-year-old time-traveler. Now, in 2010, they should be fifty-three and fifty-eight, respectively, yet thanks to *The Utopia*, they were as they had been in 1906—thirty-three and thirty-nine. H.G. didn't know how Amy had explained her youthful appearance to her father and wasn't about to ask. Deflecting the old man's assault, he stammered, "There's not that big of an age difference between us."

"Well, if you're over fifty, you've had one helluva soft life."

Stung, H.G. thought of his mother working as a maid at Up Park so that they wouldn't starve. "Would you like me to tell you about growing up poor, sir?"

Cackling, Robbins was delighted he'd gotten a rise out of H.G. "Sure, go ahead."

"Bertie," Amy warned softly.

H.G. gave her a nod, then—tight-lipped—raised his hand and passed. He recalled ironically that the last American of wealth and power he'd had a conversation with was Theodore Roosevelt in April, 1906. They had discussed fiction, poetry, the Fabian Society and other progressive movements that gave them both hope, though T.R. had been concerned about the end of the world H.G. had predicted in *The Time Machine*, saying, "Men like you and I—we must not let it happen. We must never let it happen." Now H.G. frowned at the irony: *More than a century later, in my next conversation with an American of means I discover one who is downright rude and offensive and has obviously no concern for his fellow man other than the size of his bank account. Why isn't Kevin Robbins worried about the destruction of the planet? Or technology's bastard spawn: global warming? Why must he be Amy's father?*

"You didn't meet Amy in San Francisco," Kevin said slyly.

"I didn't?"

Sara saw it coming, but wasn't fast enough.

"You met her in Bedlam, right?"

"Daddy!"

"How dare you, sir!"

Kevin Robbins nodded and grinned shrewdly.

Amy grabbed her sister by the hand and pulled her from the room, yet H.G. remained fixed on the old man and didn't lose his cool.

"Though false, your assumption is intriguing, sir," said H.G. disdainfully, "in that your entire society is a case of the inmates running the asylum."

Kevin reeled back in his wheelchair.

"I doubt that you can prove me wrong, old man, so would you please pass the turkey . . . ?"

"Why did you tell him, Sara?" cried Amy. "Why?"

They were in the kitchen. Sara opened another bottle of wine, drank and passed it to her sister.

"Because he's family."

"Yes, but—"

"They need to know, Amy."

"You should've let me tell them!"

"You wouldn't have," said Sara. "Besides, it's better this way. . . . It gives Daddy a reason for why you ran away—a reason other than himself."

Amy turned, her eyes wide with astonishment.

"And that way, he's blameless."

"Blameless?"

"Sure. You ran away because you were crazy, and you ended up in an institution. He figures it wasn't his fault, so now he can handle you coming home."

"But I left because of Bertie."

Sara guffawed. "Which proves to Daddy that you're crazy!"

Amy stared at her sister, then got it and laughed with her. "You know, you're quite brilliant, little sister."

Sara hugged her. "Ah, if only it were true."

They held each other tightly, and finally Sara pushed away, smiling brightly.

"I'm sooo glad your Bertie came. . . . I told you he would, didn't I?"

Though she didn't recall Sara having said any such thing, Amy nodded.

"He's a real charmer," Sara went on, "and I can tell that he really, really loves you."

Amy put her hand to her mouth, once again surprised; her eyes brimmed with tears.

"*Talk* to him. . . . You can work it out. I know it."

Suddenly, Sara's coat pocket buzzed, and Amy jumped back, startled. Sara pulled out her iPhone, glanced at its screen.

"Uh-oh, gotta go."

"Amy tells me you're a critic, or something."

Robbins was leaning forward in his wheelchair, flushed red, his hands clawed, waiting. H.G. sighed. He was tired of trading shots with this relic from the future. He had figured it was over when Sara had left unexpectedly because one of her patients was in "crisis," but, no, Kevin wanted more. Elizabeth came in with a coffee service, but he waved her away and took another hit of whiskey. Amy wordlessly thanked her mother and helped herself, her eyes downcast.

"You write about books and movies? That stuff?"

"Books, yes."

"Anything I might have heard of?"

"I don't think so."

He nodded at Amy. "She says you're some kind of expert on that relative of yours, H. G. Wells."

H.G. looked at him blankly, wanting this to go no further, but powerless to change the subject or tell him to shut up without incurring more rancor or suspicion.

Suddenly, Robbins guffawed again. " 'Lizabeth! 'Lizabeth!"

"Yes, Kev?"

"Remember that remake that came out five, six years ago . . . ? *The Time Machine* . . . ?" He laughed. "All due respect to the dinner we just had, but what a turkey!"

"Kevin," she scolded, nodding at H.G. "Maybe he liked it."

Robbins turned his derisive grin on H.G. "Did you . . . ? Don't tell me you liked it, please!"

H.G. was frozen, his eyes locked on Kevin's drunk face at the other end of the table, yet he felt Elizabeth's expectant smile and Amy's look of horror. *My book has become a film? Good Lord, I don't know whether to cheer or cry or— How could they have possibly photographed anything remotely resembling the end of the world? Or the Eloi and Morlocks? Or do they all assume it's just a fantasy . . . ? An entertainment to pooh-pooh as if it were a simple picshua?*

"They got his grandson to direct it. Simon Wells. . . . You know him?"

"We've never met." H.G. managed a smile, despite having his fragile innocence peeled away by this elderly twenty-first-century Philistine who apparently wanted everyone around him to feel as miserable as he looked.

"Well, if you run into him at one of your socialist film festivals or something, tell him he ought to forget about making movies and be happy he's got a trust fund."

"And you, sir," said H.G. indignantly, "aside from bank balances, what makes you happy?"

Robbins grinned at the affront and replied, "My family . . . as in my blood relations."

"We're really very close," offered Elizabeth. "We go to church, too."

"Dammit, we don't have to explain ourselves to him!" Robbins growled at her. "He's a guest in our house."

"As are you on this earth," H.G. shouted. "As we all are."

"I *own* part of this earth," said Robbins. He pointed at the floor. "This patch right here and a few other patches in Florida, Hawaii and Vegas. How about you . . . ?"

"We have a house," Amy chimed in, smiling bravely, "a beautiful house on the shore at Sandgate."

"I call it 'Spade House,'" H.G. said defiantly. "Voysey, the architect, wanted to put a heart-shaped letter plate on my front door, but I'm not one to wear my heart so conspicuously outside—or anywhere else, for that matter—so we compromised on a spade."

"A spade." Robbins was puzzled.

"I turned the heart upside down."

Still puzzled, Robbins stared at him, and H.G. went on to explain that workers in town had already confused him with another Wells—a man who had broken the bank at Monte Carlo—so when they heard the new house was named Spade House, they began telling people it was "on the ace of spades" that the trick had been done.

"So you're a gambler," said Robbins flatly. "That's why Amy doesn't have a lot to say about you. . . ." He chuckled, shook his head. "A socialist gambler . . . who knew?"

"I am *not* a gambler!" H.G. said hotly.

Pleased, Robbins swigged his whiskey, then saw that Amy was on the verge of tears and tried to back off. "Hey, Herb—"

"I say, old man," H.G. interrupted, "my name is not 'Herb.' I *detest* 'Herb.'"

"Whatever. All I was gonna say is, as long as you work hard and make money, that's all that counts."

"That's *not* all that counts!"

"Bertie, please," said Amy.

Her eyes pleading with him, she placed her hand on his arm. He exhaled and sat back, yet didn't want this vitriolic old man to get off so easily. He thought of T.R. again and shot a question down the table. "Tell me, sir, how do you think we should better serve mankind?"

"*Serve* . . . ? Where the hell did that come from?" Another guffaw. "The politicians serve mankind, boy. And I gotta tell you, after they're finished at the trough, there ain't a helluva lot to go around."

"Charming," H.G. said sardonically. "Do you know anything at all about one of your past presidents, Theodore Roosevelt?"

"Even if I did, so what?" He glared at Amy. "Is he always like this? Talking in circles?"

"Tell me, Mr. Robbins," H.G. pressed. "Do you love your daughters?"

"Yeah, I love my daughters."

Amy could no longer hold back her tears, and Elizabeth embraced her from behind the chair, but said nothing.

H.G. held Robbins with his eyes. "Then why not make the world a better place for them to live in?"

"Sara's set for life," he croaked. "So's Amy if she comes home."

"I'm talking about the greater good."

"What's the greater good?" he said suspiciously.

"If you become a Citizen of the World," H.G. said softly, "and erase the lines between nations, people, race and class . . . *then* you will make the world a better place for your daughters."

"Horseshit," said Robbins.

The phone rang.

"It's for you," said Elizabeth, coming back in the dining room.

Surprised, H.G. had no idea who would be calling him here, then thought of 'Dusa and blushed. He turned to Amy. "It has to be Miss Reeves."

Amy gave him a small, fragile smile.

H.G. took the call in the dark-paneled study, surrounded by Kevin Robbins's memorabilia and plaques—and absence of books.

"Hello . . . ?"

"Welcome to the future, Wells," said a distorted, robotic voice.

Stunned, his breath whooshing out, H.G. automatically sat down behind the massive, curved desk. He immediately looked to that ingenious technological advance on the phone's cradle—caller ID—but much to his dismay, it read "Restricted number." *Of course. Having been to hell and back, Leslie John Stephenson would be quite comfortable with modern technology.* "John," he uttered.

The monster chuckled with delight, the garbled sound reminding H.G. of Amber's microwave before it exploded.

"Ah, Wells. . . . It's been years since we've spoken. It wasn't so long ago that we were having a glass of claret in your parlor and discussing the theory behind your magnificent invention. How have you been . . . ?"

"You bloody well nipped my time machine!"

A buzz that resembled laughter. "And what a ride it was."

H.G. grimaced. "I'm going to find you, John. . . . And despite my abhorrence for violence, I plan on killing you."

"Actually, I've been thinking of a more civilized alternative."

H.G. peered at the phone, wondered if there were some combination of keys that would give him Stephenson's location. He cursed softly, wishing he'd paid more attention to the GPS in 'Dusa's car before falling back on the arcane help of a map.

"Have you ever thought about teaming up, old man?"

"*What?*"

"Yes . . . ! I'm quite serious. We're both civilized, after all. Why don't we meet and divide the universe? If you agree, then I shall hold you harmless, and you shall do likewise. Should you not want to build a second machine, we'll work out an arrangement with *The Utopia*—I believe they call it a time-share these days. Following Satan, I shall run amok in my half of the cosmos, and you shall serve your God in yours. . . . What do you say?"

"I don't believe in God."

"What a shame."

His heart pounding, H.G. hunched over the phone, gathered courage. Hand poised, he took a huge breath, then pressed the red-tagged keys he'd seen on telephones everywhere, hoping to generate a phone number or an address on the caller ID screen. 9-1-1. Three beeps resounded on the line.

"What the devil?" said the voice, surprised. "Are you trying to track me, Wells? Like some electronic bloodhound . . . ? I must ring off, I'm afraid."

"Wait!" H.G. shouted. "Please . . . ! I must know when! I must know where and when you came from!"

"The end of time. Where else . . . ? 20 June 2010, set by your wife on the Destination Indicator."

"That's not the end of time!"

"Ah, but for some it was, Wells, for some it was, and I speak with a particular authority. Now . . . for you and the missus . . . ? You may have to wait a day or two." The voice cackled. "But I'm being far too co-operative."

"Please, John. . . . Tell me. Did mankind survive?"

The voice paused. Only the seesaw buzz of its breathing came over the line, a sound that grew more and more ominous until H.G. was about to scream in frustration, and then the voice started speaking again—only not so robotic this time. Almost lilting and melodious— almost feminine.

"I recall an explosion of light that became an accidental birth in darkness—rather fitting metaphorically, don't you think? I do not re- call the void, the hole, the nothingness, the slime or the dark energy feeding mindlessly upon itself—I bear no pain, hence no forgiveness— I only smelt the synthetic stench. I was-wasn't there. I have no clue if all roads in the universe self-destruct at that event horizon. I only know that I am not shredded or in pieces. I remain myself, a dubious corpus of flesh, blood and bile. Your machine hurtled me into an enormous blackness, a place of no recollections . . . a true hell . . . and then—as if I'd called a hansom cab—it just came back and picked me up."

"Dammit, John, *when?*"

"When . . . ?! Haven't you been listening, you bloody moron? There *is* no time there!"

"Did mankind survive?!"

A silence.

Finally, after a hollow, raspy laugh, the voice replied, "Am I not here?"

10:03 P.M., *Monday, June 21, 2010*

"This is stupid."

Amber sat up on her bed, made a huge ball of her used tissues, went in the bathroom, slam-dunked them in the trash. She peered in the mirror and frowned. If she cried any more, this was how she'd look in the morning, and no makeup in the world would disguise her tear-swollen eyes. *And all for a totally unavailable man who has a wonderful wife he doesn't deserve. Tomorrow I'm going to go on eharmony.com.*

"This is really stupid."

She found the copy of the special key in her jeans, went to her small dresser in the closet, opened the bottom drawer—the keepsake drawer—and tossed it in. It landed with a clunk against the plastic key from Room 529 of the Marriott in San Francisco. Her breath caught. She started crying all over again, angrily closed the drawer with her foot, then the closet door, trying to seal off the images, the dreams, but all she succeeded in doing was imprisoning them.

She went in the living room, picked up the phone and dialed, making a feel-good call to Marilyn, but she got voice mail. *Should I go out?* From her window, she gazed down at Ocean Park Boulevard. Dudes in faux gang colors ambled uphill in the shadows, some with pit bulls, the rest with attitude. Amber saw no females anywhere—not even hookers.

Forget that.

She decided to console herself with a few drinks, take a long, hot shower, go to bed and hope she felt better in the morning. In the kitchen, she found a few bottles of good wine saved for special occasions, but this was not one of them. Besides, wine was romantic. This was more of an Everclear night. Having none of that, she poured herself a water glass of cooking sherry, went in the living room and clicked on the TV, but given her last two days with H. G. Wells, she doubted that anything could hold her attention. *Should I try Syfy?*

The phone rang.

She figured it was Marilyn and smiled, picked the phone up on its third ring. "Hi, there."

"Hullo, 'Dusa?"

His voice jolted her. She was thrilled to hear it, yet annoyed at the same time. *What are you doing calling me when you should be in Amy's arms soothing her wrecked sensibilities? I'm no longer available.*

"Sorry to ring so late," he said, his tone brittle and tense, "but I've just heard from Stephenson, and I didn't know who else to call."

Her emotions faded, leaving her with the stark reality that she was still connected to this man on account of a time-traveling murderer. *This is one of those late-night business calls.*

"He sounded strange—as if something had electrified his vocal cords—so I can only assume that on his trip back from infinity a reformulation error radically altered his voice." He paused. "It was actually quite awful. . . . For a moment, I thought I was having a conversation with a machine from one of my books." He sighed heavily. "At any rate, I wanted you to know that we should be prepared for someone that not only sounds different, but might appear radically different as well."

"You didn't happen to get a caller ID on him, did you?"

"It said restricted number. Can your technology trace the conversation, regardless?"

"I'll ask the lieutenant in the morning, but I wouldn't hold my breath."

"Why don't we meet in the A.M.?"

"Sure."

"Shall we say, nine o'clock?"

He rang off.

She took a large swallow of sherry. She hugged herself. She tried not to imagine him, but failed. She thought, *He must've loved me and me alone in an earlier time. Amy wasn't in that universe, so it wasn't like we were hurting her or anything. It was just the two of us. He loved me and I loved him. It's the only thing that makes any sense.* She frowned petulantly, put her face in her hands and wondered how she could suppress—no, kill— her feelings.

Poison them.

She chugged her sherry.

10:37 P.M., *Monday, June 21, 2010*

After he was packed, Lieutenant Casey Holland tried one last time to reason with his wife. He pleaded with her to reconsider and not break up their family. Instead of listening, she carried his bag to the front door by herself, set it outside on the steps, stood in the doorway with her arms folded.

"For Christ's sake, Cheryl, I—"

"You what? You love me and the kids . . . ? Show me your letter of resignation and we'll talk."

Fighting back tears, he tossed his bag in his '05 Mustang, backed into the street. As he took one last look at his buttoned-up four-bedroom home with its proud bluish green lawn, Cheryl switched off the living room lights, plunging the front into darkness. Wearing a tight-lipped, angry smile, he punched the Mustang and pulled away, pipes roaring. He took the corner too fast and left the pleasant little Sherman Oaks neighborhood behind, sped south until he hit Ventura Boulevard, then drove aimlessly, passing his future: lonely, dangerous people on the street, more of the same in the cars around him, dozens of bars offering shelter from the storm. Removed, he kept driving, ignoring the street-corner smiles from an occasional hooker, the naked stares from gay drivers. He drove with no clue where he was going.

Jaclyn flooded his brain. He resisted her lurid images, memories of her taste and smell. He tried to convince himself that if he didn't call her—if he didn't hook up with her—that then he was a better person, and Cheryl would know instinctively, accept his love as genuine and welcome him back home. Except Jaclyn dodged his good intentions; she had taken out a lease on his mind; she was waiting.

When he came to his senses, he saw that he had ended up on the 405 and realized that despite Jaclyn he had no place to go and was automatically driving to work. He grinned sardonically. *How pathetic is that? What am I gonna do? Ask the desk sergeant to give me a holding cell?* He fished his phone from his pocket and turned it on.

One missed call. He returned it.

"This is Sergeant Young. Is that you, Case?"

"Yeah."

"Where you been?"

"It's a long story."

Holland found out that Sergeant Young was still at work, jumped off the freeway and got to headquarters in under five minutes. He nodded at the desk sergeant, strode into the homicide bay and poured himself coffee left over from that morning.

Young looked up from his computer, then finished his typing, leaned back in his squeaky desk chair and put his feet up. "So what happened? The little woman bust you for getting some strange?"

Holland smiled sheepishly. "Actually, she got tired of me being a cop."

Young nodded and slapped the desk appreciatively. "Well, hey, welcome back."

"Huh?"

"Face it, Case, you been gone for a long time now."

"What the hell are you talking about?"

"Ever since you had kids and moved to the valley."

Holland turned red. "Do we have problems, Sergeant?"

"I dunno, Case. I can't cover your ass and do my own work at the same time, you know what I'm saying? Every five fucking minutes I'm getting a call from the fucking media because your mailbox is all filled up. So, yeah, I guess we do have problems. . . . Or did . . . if you're really back."

Holland grimaced, let the guilt wash over him—for Cheryl and his job. Yet he had enough sense of self left to want to try again, so he didn't walk out or deny what Young had told him. He waited in the silence and drank the sludge that had once been bad coffee.

"We let Albert Grattan go. . . ."

"Makes sense."

"His DNA and prints didn't match the ones we found at the Getty and in Michael Trattner's Porsche."

"He was never the one," said Holland. "He was just a bone to toss to the reporters."

"Yeah." Young grinned. "I love watching them trample each other when they're all going in the wrong direction." He laughed, then: "Hey, y'know this 'REMEMBER ME?' our boy's been signing his bodies with?"

Holland nodded. "I figure he's just trying to tell us this isn't his first barbecue."

"That's the joke, Case. There's been so many psychopaths in the last x number of years he could be any one of them."

"Maybe he knows that."

Young shrugged, sat up and typed a thought into his computer.

"So where are we?" said Holland, annoyed that he had to ask.

"We should get the dental records on Venus de Milo in the morning. If I get here before you, I'll call and tell you who the Jane Doe is. If not, they should be on your desk." Young shut down his computer. "I'm outta here." He put on his jacket, started for the door. "Wanna go for beers?"

"No, thanks."

But Young was already gone, the door closed behind him. He hadn't even waited for a reply, and Holland was left wondering if Young had anticipated his response or was flat-out dissing him. It didn't matter.

Young was the least of his problems. He went to his office down the hall and flipped on the overheads, intending to digitally clean out his mailbox, but as he was reaching for the landline, he felt his cell buzz in his pocket. Voice mail. It must've been buried under Young's missed call. He hoped it was Cheryl, that she'd changed her mind and wanted him to come home.

No.

He heard Jaclyn's heavy, sensual sigh. It went straight to his heart, then spread to his groin like liquid. He shuddered involuntarily, and a sense of relief, of salvation washed over him. He was connected. Her words came next, sustenance for his soul:

"I miss you. . . ."

11:02 P.M., *Monday, June 21, 2010*

H.G. and Amy took a taxi to the Four Seasons, H.G. gazing morosely out the window at the nighttime opulence of Beverly Hills, its gleaming motorcars, its chic people outside clubs lit in vivid colors, the darkness hiding the less fortunate, the flotsam and jetsam of this roller-coaster world. He didn't share his dashed hopes for an enlightened world-state in the twenty-first century with Amy. He didn't share his realization that in 2010 the only likely Citizen of the World he would find was himself. He didn't tell her that the monster had phoned and taunted him with his grim knowledge. And, no, he didn't tell her that he was preoccupied with the end of the world.

So they rode in silence, Amy thinking that H.G. didn't want to talk in front of the cabdriver, and H.G. trying to calculate the year mankind had blown up the planet. If the worst was going to happen, he wanted proof, so he ran the numbers through his brain again. If Amy had arrived at the Getty at 12:01 A.M., that meant . . . He scowled, frustrated. Without accurate times for the variables, he could calculate nothing. In the morning when he met 'Dusa's Lieutenant Holland, he would try to find out exactly when the murder at the Getty occurred, then subtract three or four minutes for the unfortunate security guard to chase the Ripper before getting her throat slashed, and that would give him *The Utopia's* arrival time. Subtract that from when Amy had pulled the declinometer at, say, 12:02, and multiply the minutes by three years. Divide the result by two, add 2010, and he would know what year the world would end . . . *Blast it, no, I still won't know. The damned Destination Indicator had malfunctioned.* Yes, of course, he had repaired and recalibrated it, yet he would never find out how much real time his machine had lost bringing Stephenson back from infinity.

Annoyed, he dropped his head back on the seat. *What the devil's the point?* He gazed out at the night sky that glowed orange from the reflected light of the gargantuan city. Even if he could discern "Judgment Day," he doubted anyone would listen. There were already Bible-thumping madmen on television predicting the end, and should he add his voice, the twenty-first-century tabloids would call him a bigger fool than Nostradamus.

"Amber seems awfully nice," said Amy.

"Right."

She chuckled. "How did you ever persuade her to become your guardian angel?"

He frowned, gazed tight-lipped out the window, then sighed and told himself that he hadn't come all this way, he hadn't saved Amy just to start another regimen of deceit. "I didn't."

Amy raised her eyebrows at him.

"You see, she's in love with me."

Amy stared at him blankly.

"No, no, there was no passade, nothing like that. She knew about you from the beginning, yet she insisted on helping me find you, and thank God for that."

"Are you in love with her . . . ?" she asked, her voice small.

"No," he said, "definitely not."

"Are you attracted to her?"

"Yes," he said, blushing crimson. "That, I cannot deny."

"Well," she said patiently, "it isn't the first time."

"Yes, but this time it doesn't matter."

Suddenly, the doors to the taxi opened.

"Welcome to the Four Seasons, sir."

They took a bridal suite on the fifth floor, the desk clerk assuming it was their anniversary since they only had an overnight case borrowed from Amy's mother. H.G. stiffened at the rate, yet insisted on paying in advance. Tight-lipped, peeling off hundreds from the money he'd changed at Xerox's, he realized that two nights at the Four Seasons was ten times more than the advance William Heinemann had paid him for *The Time Machine.*

The Wellses dutifully followed the bellboy up to their suite, half-listened to his patter about restaurants and amenities at the Four Seasons and waited as he opened the French doors to the balcony. Next, he turned down the enormous bed, left flowers and chocolates, offered to turn on the Jacuzzi. Amy smiled shyly and nodded. The bellboy complied. H.G. tipped him handsomely, and he finally left.

A silence.

H.G. had been worried that once alone in 2010, he and Amy wouldn't know what to do or say to each other, that there would be this interminable gulf between them, and they would hide behind their familiarity with each other, and that the gulf would become enormous with their collapsed marriage forever lost in between, and that not even *The Utopia* could save them.

He felt Amy's presence. Surprised she wasn't in the bathroom suite, he turned, and then suddenly she was in his arms, trembling and holding on for dear life. His breath whooshed out. *My God, how wonderful, how perfectly wonderful she feels.* His heart surged; he felt warm and whole and connected, and it had been such a long, long time. His worries evaporated; he forgot his obsession with the end of the world. Everything fell away and left him with Amy, such was the power of this woman. He held her tightly, fiercely. He buried his face in her hair and realized that he cared more about her than anything else in the cosmos.

"Oh, Bertie. . . ." Tears ran down her face. "I thought I'd lost you."

"No, no, never," he whispered, filled with love for her, driving the terrible knowledge of her death from his brain. *I'll ride the damned time machine like a shuttle to keep her alive and happy in my life, in our boys' lives.* "I was acting like a spoiled child. I had no right to treat you like anything less than the most wonderful woman in the world."

She smiled through her tears. "You have a way with words."

"You have my heart in your hands."

"I'll hold it dearly."

"As I will yours."

The sound of bubbles from the Jacuzzi broke their reverie, and Amy went eagerly into the bathroom suite. H.G. followed, blissful with the closeness that had blossomed between them. A silly smile on his face, he sat backward in the vanity chair and watched her, in his mind's eye her movements unusually fluid and graceful. *This is not the same woman who ran away from Spade House, is it . . . ? Or is it yours truly who is changing?*

Amy kicked off her shoes, added bubble bath to the water and tested the temperature with her foot.

He nodded toward the cut on her arm. "Shouldn't you have a bandage on that?"

"It's only a scratch, Bertie. I took the dressing off this morning."

"I'll put a new one on if you'd like."

"Thank you, darling, but it's almost healed." She smiled radiantly and gave him a breezy, yet meaningful glance.

He took it for what it was.

"I'm so sorry about Daddy tonight," she said, moving on.

H.G. shrugged. "He's proof that dinosaurs aren't really extinct."

Amy laughed. "You know, if I hadn't run off with you in 1979, I might very well have ended up in an institution."

"I would've found you anyway."

She blew him a kiss, then said, "Isn't Sara delightful . . . ?"

"Only because she looks like you," he said playfully.

"You're sweet. . . ." She smiled. "You have no idea how wonderful it is to discover that one has a sister." She began undressing, shedding her modesty with her clothes, her constant chatter: No, she wasn't sorry that she'd come to the future; even if Chichester, the seismologist, had been wrong about the earthquake; she was happy to find her parents alive, grateful she had finally reached an understanding with her father, and when the time came, could say good-bye properly. She went on about the boys, hoping they were all right, though she shouldn't worry because Mrs. Vickers was the best nanny in all of Kent. Finally, she paused, her clothes neatly folded and on the stool.

"We'll be back before we left," H.G. reminded her.

"Yes, but according to you, that will be in another universe."

"So it will."

"Shouldn't we be worried about them now?"

He gave her a bemused smile. "You're much too clever, my dear."

"That doesn't help."

"Then why don't you think of them as they are in the universe that we never left . . . ?"

She frowned and stuck out her tongue at him, then turned away to take off her bra.

In deference, he started out of the bathroom.

"Have you ever soaked in a Jacuzzi?"

"No."

"It's quite relaxing."

"I'll undress in the bedroom."

"Don't bother to hurry," she said mischievously, and threw her panties at him, until now an uncharacteristic gesture.

As he was taking off his shirt and tie, Brahms suddenly greeted him from speakers in the ceiling with a romantic symphony. Startled, he forgot where he was and looked out the French doors for a symphony orchestra, then blushed, realizing that Amy had merely pushed a button on the panel by the Jacuzzi.

"Bertie . . . ?" called Amy.

"Yes?"

"What's taking you so long?"

He kicked off his shoes and socks, took off his trousers and padded into the bathroom.

A perfumed steam rose off the bubbles in the Jacuzzi, reminding him of a rite done with incense though no religion, exotic or otherwise, had an altar that could compare to this. Amy had put her hair up and lit a candle, was smiling and sublimely lovely in its warm light.

My God, she's more beautiful than she was just minutes ago, she's beyond herself. Is she Catherine . . . ? Has Catherine come to 2010, as well? He wasn't quite sure. Until now, he had never gotten more than a glimpse of Catherine before she vanished inside Amy. But if she were indeed Catherine, he was more than pleasantly surprised. *May she remain so.*

He took off his glasses and placed them on a chair, groped for the Jacuzzi and started to climb in. She giggled.

"You don't want to get your undies wet, do you, dear . . . ?"

"Now I know how Nero felt when Rome was burning around him," murmured H.G., immersed in the Jacuzzi, bubbles fizzing in his ears. He was utterly relaxed. He felt as if he were melting, becoming one with the water, metamorphosing into a warm, fragrant sea. Every woman he'd ever touched flashed through his brain, and he envisioned himself entwined with one after another here in this magical liquid luxury, yet even their collective sensuality paled in comparison with Amy. Then he felt toes nibbling up his legs. *Speaking of . . .*

Her playful touch brought on a wave of sadness, but not because of his passades. Rather, he recalled earlier today in that previous lifetime—getting to Franklin Canyon too late and discovering her body. He wondered if deep in her subconscious she remembered being cut up by the Ripper—if memory could in fact hopscotch between parallel universes. He'd like to think that her murder had been erased permanently, yet given the nature of the cosmos, nothing was permanent, time machine or no. He shook off his melancholia, opened his eyes and almost gasped. He had expected the Amy of old, but, no, it was Catherine again.

True, his vision was blurred, yet he couldn't mistake that translucent aura hovering around her like lace. She was his lover-shadow. *How wonderful. I've never been alone with Catherine. She has never touched me before. Perhaps I should introduce myself.*

"Hullo, Catherine."

"Hullo, Bertie."

"We finally meet."

"I thought it about time."

"I'm glad that you did. . . . So how are you tonight?"

"Floating in goodness."

"Likewise."

"Amy went to bed early."

"Ah, that explains it." He smiled. "And how is our favorite person?"

Catherine sighed. "Amy is feeling horribly guilty because she's responsible for Leslie John Stephenson coming back from hell."

"Tell Amy that the only thing she could possibly be guilty of is shooting the messenger."

"Amy isn't sure what you mean," said Catherine, perplexed.

"Amy didn't build *The Utopia* in a prolonged fit of unbridled optimism," he replied.

"Go on."

"If I hadn't built the time machine, Leslie John Stephenson wouldn't have stolen it in 1893 to escape Scotland Yard. He would've been caught, duly tried and executed at Newgate."

"So you blame yourself?"

"Yes."

"Why not blame cause and effect?"

"Cause and effect didn't invent the time machine."

A silence. Catherine's beauty had turned thoughtful. She blew a strand of damp hair out of her face, and the candle flickered. She sighed, then smiled wisely. "Amy wanted me to remind you that if you don't try to make the world a better place—if you do nothing for fear of the unforeseen—then you become a slave instead of a free spirit."

"Um," he said softly and closed his eyes again. "Sometimes Amy can be downright prophetic."

"Yes, she can."

"I love Amy. . . . I love Amy with all my heart."

"As she loves you."

Her toes walked up his leg, paused on his thigh for what seemed an eternity, and then nudged his penis. Startled, he sat up, his eyes opening wide. "Oh, I'm terribly sorry." She laughed low. "Please forgive us. We didn't mean to disturb."

He stirred—as in loins. A foolish grin lit up his face. This woman was indeed his lover-shadow. "Quite all right, Catherine. I doubt these Jacuzzi tubs are endorsed by the Catholic Church." He captured her feet and began massaging them.

"Mmmm." She went limp. "Wonderful."

"Deservedly so."

She smiled dreamily, then wagged a finger at him. "Amy tells me you haven't made love to her in over a century."

11:58 P.M., *Monday, June 21, 2010*

Jaclyn descended into the underground parking for the Holiday Inn Express on Santa Monica Boulevard, the tires on the Mercedes squealing urgently. She parked close to the lift and got out—smashing the concrete pillar with her door, but she couldn't care less. After Holland had called, she had prepared as if for a religious ceremony. She had leisurely washed Peterson's murder off her body, dabbed exotic perfumes from Heather's toiletry in the right places, brushed her hair until it shone like black sapphires, then slipped into a lavender silk pantsuit sans panties and bra. She had used a Revlon ad from *Cosmopolitan* as a guide when she did her face, finally pronounced herself beautiful. *Should I ever tire of killing, I can always become a cover girl.* A glass of Absolut from the Trattners' bar had calmed her nerves, but now she was randy in the worst way and couldn't wait to get upstairs. High heels clicking, she hurried to the lift, pressed three. It stopped at the lobby for a wedge-shaped giant of a man wearing his cap backward. She assumed he was one of those millionaire athletes from the television—*They must be the rage these days*—and was pleased that he undressed her with his eyes. As she stepped off the lift, she gave him a little flutter wave.

She knocked softly on 317, and her lieutenant let her in, yet as he was coming toward her, she was disappointed. His eyes were hollow, his stance ordinary. He seemed a cut below the man he had been before, his T-shirt and jeans having replaced the more elegant light-brown suit and tie. *Could losing a wife make that much difference or was it merely his wardrobe?* A moot point. He crushed her against him. Already he was hard, and she imagined him gigantic, and that was all that mattered. They kissed, and she explored his mouth with her tongue, promising dark rainbows beyond this, their own little garden of Eden. He broke the kiss and gasped for breath, and she emitted little laughs, dropped her purse by the bed.

"You have no idea. . . ." he managed. "You can't know. . . ."

"Show me," she whispered.

Hands shaking, he took off his clothes, left them piled on the carpet and went to turn off the lights.

"No, no, no," she said, blocking his path, "that will never do. I want to *see* you. . . . I want you to see me." Her eyes never leaving his, she slowly began shedding her silk clothes, lavender giving way to perfect alabaster curves.

"Jesus," he said when they were finished.

"No." She laughed ironically.

"I mean, I just . . ." His voice trailed off. "I mean, my God. . . ."

"He's not here, either."

"Huh?"

"It's just you and me, my sweet lieutenant," she murmured, and sat up cross-legged beside him.

He looked off, the light in his eyes fading, and she was mildly jealous that his mind had gone somewhere else. She frowned petulantly. "What are you thinking?"

"I was wondering what time it was."

She looked at him askance.

"I gotta go to work in the morning. God knows, I don't want to."

"Yes, but you have a killer, a madman to catch."

"I'll never nail him," he said flatly. "I get feelings about cases. This is one of those."

"So what will happen?"

"The media will get incredibly vicious, the brass will get tired of it, and I'll lose my job."

"What a shame."

"Yes and no."

"What d'you mean?"

"Right now I don't really care. . . ." He grinned. "Not as long as you're here with me."

She glanced down, noticed blood on the tan and green duvet, then found it on her fingertips and chuckled. She vaguely recalled digging her nails into his back and raking his sides. She tasted the blood and smiled. "Don't you hurt?"

"Are you kidding?"

"Perhaps we should call room service and order up a first-aid kit."

He laughed. "Hey, how about some wine . . . ? Wine and a plate of fruit or something?"

"That would be nice."

He reached for the phone.

"Vodka. . . . Have them bring some vodka, as well."

After room service left, Casey hung a DO NOT DISTURB sign on the door, and now—completely nude—they were having drinks at the round table by the window, Jaclyn feeding him wedges of apple between sips of vodka, gnawing playfully on his fingers when he popped a grape in her mouth. Despite their sex, she sensed he was close to a profound grief. She wondered: *Just how fragile is he? Jack never would've cared. He was never interested in partners beyond their ability to remind him of Penny and make him ejaculate, beyond the blood they spilled and the ease with which they gave up a kidney or some such pound of flesh. I suppose that my fascination with the good lieutenant means that I am*

terminally female—at least in this future—because I truly care for him.
Right now, revenge against a slut of a sister bores me. I have embraced
art for art's sake. I am a dilettante, am I not?

Glibness aside, she frowned, poured herself more vodka. The thought
of loving or caring for someone was making her nervous, so she changed
the subject before it came up.

"Why did you become a detective?"

He lifted his eyebrows. "Me?"

"Yes, and skip the tiresome clichés, if you please."

"Actually, I was attracted to crime."

"Really?" she said, surprised.

"I wanted to figure out what makes people do it."

She stared at him in disbelief. "And you have to look beyond passion, stupidity and/or self-interest?"

"Yes. I think you do."

"Well, happy hunting."

"Jaclyn . . ." he said softly.

He leaned across the table and ran his hand along her arm, but she
pulled away and smiled coyly.

"Is adultery a crime?"

He took his hand away, chuckled. "Hey, I never said I wasn't a criminal."

She laughed. "How refreshing."

"What about you?"

"*Mea culpa.*"

They laughed together. He clinked glasses with her. They both drank
and gazed at each other, smiling foolishly.

"You are something else, Mizz Jaclyn."

"As are you," she whispered.

A silence. Holland looked away, then came back to her.

"So when are you going back to the UK?"

She shrugged casually.

"Want to stay here for a while . . . ?" He spread his hands. "I mean,
I'm gonna have to get a place. . . . You want to move in with me?"

"Oh, dear." She put her hand to her mouth and averted her eyes.

She hadn't expected this, and felt a rush of emotion. She had nothing to balance it with, nothing to hang on to. No sweet memory from childhood, no prior loves, certainly nothing from Jack. She had wanted to avoid this tête-à-tête, and now she was terrified.

"Wait." He was mortified. "I'm sorry. Forget I said anything."

"No, no, darling." She squeezed his hand. "It's just that—"

Her eyes brimmed with tears. She curled up in his lap. *Of course I want to live with you. I want to live and die with you. I want nothing more in this—or other worlds. You fill me up. My cup runneth over. Yet how can we do this? How can we go on when I am a fugitive from your God, from everything that you call good in the universe, when I am your absolute worst nightmare?*

"What the hell's wrong?"

"Oh, shut up, Casey."

He did.

"Don't you know? I hate myself because I'm falling in love with you!"

Laughter rumbled up from his belly. His tension crumbled. He stroked her hair. "I love you, too, my darling," he murmured, "I love you, too."

"More?" she whispered.

"More."

They began again. They shifted, adjusted. They got it right and delicious. They harmonized. They lost control. They were one until that final moment when her raison d'être came roaring back and reminded her who she was and who she would always be.

Then: *Ah, my God, his* la petit mort. *And mine. Ours.*

The knife.

Her hand had found it in her purse, and as they were finishing, she stabbed him in the back with such force that the blade came through his chest.

Once. Twice.

Bewildered, he gazed down at her, his mouth opening, forming words that were never spoken. He collapsed and twitched, blood coming from his mouth, dead on top on her. She wrapped her arms and legs around him and didn't mind the blood from his chest pooling between them, running down her sides, soaking the bed. She cooed that innocent French lullaby from her long-lost music box. No longer did she hate being a woman. Casey Holland, may he rest in ecstasy, had taken away her emptiness.

She extricated herself from under him, stepped back and contemplated his corpse on the bloody duvet, studied it as a sculptor would a block of marble. Holland reminded her of Jack's dalliance in Firenze when he had compared himself to . . . *Of course. You thought of it at the bar when you had your first martini. Michelangelo's* David.

She rolled him onto his back, then with a wet face cloth cleaned the blood off his torso. She gazed at him, recalled their last moments together, shuddered with pleasure. She sighed, then lovingly took his penis in one hand, picked up her knife with the other.

9:03 A.M., *Tuesday, June 22, 2010*

"About time," Amber growled.

H.G. saw her sitting in the entranceway, smiled and angled toward her, stopped short when he noticed her swollen eyes and chalk-white face. She looked terrible.

"I say, are you ill?"

"Please don't talk to me."

Amber walked him through the check-in, a woman officer, pretty in blue, smiling professionally at the bogus Scotland Yard ID minted by Xerox. She gave him a visitor's badge and beeped them through the main door. In the homicide bay, he was about to ask Amber what was wrong, but she had her back to him and was speaking to the secretary. "We have an appointment with the lieutenant."

"He's not in."

H.G. turned to Amber and said low, "Since when do you take the morning off if you're a police lieutenant on a high-profile murder investigation?"

She shook her head. Then, rather than stand by the desk and incur suspicion from every detective that walked by, she led H.G. to the kitchen. A large almond coffee cake was on the counter. She automatically handed him a paper plate, and he helped himself, muttering about the disposable nature of 2010. "Whatever happened to china?"

Except the cake and the smell of stale coffee was too much for Amber, and while H.G. was relishing his first bite, she threw up in the trash can and bolted for the ladies' room.

Astonished, he watched her go, then went on eating his coffee cake, his faith in twenty-first-century medicine somewhat sullied. *Obviously, they don't yet have pharmaceuticals to cure everything, and if she doesn't come back soon, I'll tell the secretary that she's in the loo rather indisposed.* The acrid smell from the trash can wafted past him. He wrinkled his nose, raised his eyebrows and was reminded of Joseph Conrad retching in Amy's flowers on more than one occasion after nights of heavy drinking. He chuckled.

In the corner, he saw a chrome and black monstrosity with blinking lights, this one labeled AUTOMATIC COFFEE BEVERAGE BAR, one's choice the mere push of a button away. He scanned offerings from espresso to nonfat latte with vanilla, but was put off by dirty milk and coffee stains in the dispenser. Instead, he made himself tea and, despite Lipton's in a Styrofoam cup, felt superior to these Yanks who drank from a "rocketship" of a machine that was filthy and smelled questionable. The coffee cake, however, was excellent, and he was on his second piece when Amber returned, looking considerably better.

"Are you all right, 'Dusa?"

Her jaw tight, she nodded and motioned him out of the kitchen. "We can talk to the sergeant."

"I didn't realize you drank," he said low, following her, a huge grin on his face.

She stopped short, turned and glared. If her cobalt eyes had been lasers, they would've cut his heart out.

Overwhelmed with phone calls, Sergeant Young didn't question H.G.'s credentials or wonder why a Scotland Yard detective had suddenly shown up at the West Division to help nail the Brentwood killer. H.G.'s accent and demeanor were enough, and with no lieutenant, Sergeant Young needed all the help he could get. Amber had suggested they start with the Ripper's original file, and H.G. envisioned Scotland Yard moles digging through ancient files, then mailing the stuff days later. She had frowned impatiently and mentioned email, then changed her mind, realizing an email would go to her laptop, and she didn't want him screwing it up again. So she'd said, "Fax," then spelled it out for him. F-a-c-s-i-m-i-l-e. Or: Fax.

As he was talking to Young, she sidled into Lieutenant Holland's empty office, called Scotland Yard and requested they fax their file on Jack the Ripper. She was transferred to public affairs and luckily someone was still in the office, though it was past six in London. The secretary complied, glad to be of assistance. Between publishers and film production companies, Amber hadn't been the first to ask.

"So you think we got a copycat killer going here?" Sergeant Young asked H.G.

"Yes."

"Then what's this 'REMEMBER ME?' all about?"

H.G. stared blankly.

"Oh, yeah, you haven't looked at the murder book." Young told H.G. about the happy-face portraits and signatures the killer had left on his victims.

H.G. thought fast, spoke with a forced enthusiasm. "That fits perfectly, Sergeant. Obviously, our killer is so far gone he has assumed the identity of Jack the Ripper and wants everyone to know."

"How does that help us?"

"There have been dozens of copycats, and I've researched them all," H.G. went on with his lie, a modicum of British superiority in his tone. "Not only do they mimic the crimes what with their mockery of surgical techniques, but they also take painstaking measures to actually *look* like the Ripper. I should think that the refrain 'REMEMBER ME?' helps us a great deal."

Young gave him a hard, unblinking stare.

"Though I must admit," H.G. backpedaled, "that my theory may seem far-fetched."

"No, no," said Young, "not at all." He spread his hands. "We got open minds here." His phone buzzed again. "I'm away from my desk!" he shouted out the door.

"It's Parker Center," the secretary shouted back.

"Fuck," he muttered, then shot H.G. a hapless grin. "I gotta take this."

"Of course." Wells stood.

"Grab the girl, Ms. Reeves, and do what you have to do." He picked up the phone. "I'll catch up."

Acting like he belonged, H.G. went down the main corridor in search of Amber, but heard curious sounds from an open door, its nameplate reading TRAFFIC RESPONSE UNIT. Inside, a technician was on a landline phone with a patrolman and as they talked an on-scene video with time code played on the technician's monitor: the patrolman's partner was handcuffing a man so drunk he could barely stand; behind them, the man's SUV had taken out a fire hydrant on Sunset Boulevard, and water fountained up high, rained on a strip mall.

"Captured," said the technician, working his keyboard, "no pun intended. . . . Now gimme a shot of the breathalyzer, and we're done."

Amazed, H.G. took a step inside. Across the room, another technician was watching a half-dozen screens showing live video of the freeways. He monotoned instructions into his headset, and occasionally, pressed keys on his computer, then flipped images on the screens. After a minute, he sensed H.G.'s presence and spun around in his chair.

"Hey," he said with a goofy smile. "Help you?"

"I'm so sorry," said H.G., embarrassed, "I'm looking for the . . . the fax machine."

The technician gaped at him and then started laughing. "*The* fax machine?"

"Try any office across the hall," said the other. "And when you find one . . . kill it."

"Kill it?"

"Set an example."

They howled with laughter, and a red-faced H.G. spun out of the room, annoyed that he'd been played for the fool.

Tight-lipped, he hurried back up the corridor and finally found Amber in Communications Center A, the room bright with fluorescents, crammed with office hardware. She was waiting at one of six fax machines, watching its LED display. She glanced up as he came inside. "No thanks to you, I'm feeling better."

Before he could respond, the machine beeped and began spewing out pages of detail on Jack the Ripper—complete with Scotland Yard's imprint.

He was astounded. That the case file could be transmitted through a phone line and sent so quickly from six thousand miles away reminded him of time travel in that reducing a document to an electronic impulse was similar to vaporizing an object or a person and catapulting him along the fourth dimension. True to the theory, the pages kept coming—fed into a machine at one end, reconstituted and copied at the other. The fax beeped again, and then one last page came through: a nineteenth-century police artist's rendering of Jack the Ripper that, quite naturally, looked almost identical to Leslie John Stephenson.

Except it was smudged.

Frowning, H.G. snagged it and studied the face. It appeared shorter, less angular, and one cheek was wider than it should have been. The eyes seemed less menacing—or had the two-dimensional nature of the facsimile made them so? H.G. thought: In reality Stephenson had been "faxed" from the end of time through a wormhole to June, 2010. Did he look the same as he had in 1893 and again in 1979 or had he been "smudged" due to reformulation errors? Indeed, he could be as distorted as his voice was on the telephone, yet there was really no way of telling until they actually came face-to-face. He handed Amber the rendering. "He's not going to look the same, you know."

She nodded thoughtfully.

"I was going to ask the good sergeant to send this out over the wires, or whatever they call them these days. I was going to ask him to distribute it to his men and post it on television." He shook his head. "Now I don't see the point."

"Wait a sec," she said, looking at the portrait. "We've got the basic features here, right?"

"Yes, but they're smudged!"

"Granted, but we've got a pretty good physical description in the file, too," she added, pointing to page one. "And if all else fails, we ask Scotland Yard to send us another fax."

"Nobody in 2010 *looks* like that!" he exclaimed, shoving his finger in Stephenson's likeness.

"Sometimes you have no sense of imagination," she said, disgusted. "Come with me."

In another office, this one dimly lit, H.G. and Amber were on either side of a police artist, their faces rapt at his giant computer screen. The artist had scanned Jack the Ripper's portrait into his program and was cleaning off the smudge. He finished, turned to H.G.

"How's that?"

"That's him," said H.G., astonished. "That's Stephenson."

"He looks like somebody from an old movie," the artist joked. "Was he in costume or something?"

"That's the problem," H.G. responded glibly. "The rendering is from our nineteenth-century archives." He explained his copycat theory, then added, "Can you show us what he would look like today?"

The artist nodded, intrigued. "Is he the same age?"

"Yes."

"Any scars or injuries you know about?"

"No."

Amber shot H.G. a questioning look about reformulation errors, but he shook his head firmly, then had second thoughts. "Wait," he said to the artist. "His voice won't be the same."

"Yeah, but he's not the same guy. We're looking for a copycat, right . . . ? And everybody has their own unique voiceprint."

"I realize that," H.G. replied, not realizing it at all, "but we've heard this copycat's voice and he sounds more like a, a machine than a human being. He buzzes when he talks."

"So you're saying he's had a tracheotomy or something."

"Quite possibly."

"Well, I dunno." He went back to the keyboard. "I don't know how that would change appearance or if it would at all. Nobody's ever sent that balloon up before." He paused. "What the hell. . . . Let's give it a shot." He saved the Leslie John Stephenson from the 1880s, made a copy, then went to work, pulling up his morph and paint programs and injecting them with every conceivable influence of modern life from health to style to the environment to medical changes with "voice" highlighted. He turned back to H.G. and Amber. "This is gonna take a while."

They nodded and stayed in their chairs.

The present-day version of Leslie John Stephenson emerged with a rounder, smoother, almost bland face common among the entitlement generation. His hair was short and unkempt, his eyes dark and fierce, less sunken into his head. Though still long and narrow, his nose was straight, indicating the ease, the possibility of cosmetic surgery. He wore a smirk instead of a morose frown, and when the artist hit the 3-D button, the composite jumped out as if alive.

"Good Lord," said H.G., recoiling.

"Check it out." The artist toggled between the two portraits, obviously pleased with the results. "As you can see, the facial structure is the same—what's changed are things related to diet and style and attitude."

"What about the voice?" said Amber.

"Like I said, hard to tell."

The rendering puzzled H.G. He hadn't expected Stephenson to appear so utterly different merely because of the change in centuries. Yes, it was logical, and hopefully the 2010 portrait would help, but he had a bad feeling about it. *Given reformulation errors, what if this whole process is irrelevant? What if Stephenson looks nothing at all like this?* Finally, he remarked, "He looks almost pretty."

The artist chortled. "Hey, I don't know about killers in the UK, but none of 'em around here are that bad-looking. They blend in, they become invisible, they're the boy next door, like Jeffery Dahmer, you know what I'm saying?"

"Yes, of course," he said, not knowing at all.

"Can we get copies of both?" said Amber.

"Sure," said the artist, clicking on the print icon. "I'll give you a disk as well, and when I get the word from the lieutenant or Sergeant Young, I'll email it to every cop in L.A."

"Thank you," said H.G. gratefully. As they left the office and started up the corridor, he turned to Amber. "Honestly, 'Dusa, I can't imagine living in a world where you can't tell the criminals by looking at them."

She laughed ironically.

Sergeant Young studied the composites, going from one to the other, all the while nodding admiration for the artist. "Guy's good, isn't he?"

"I'm quite impressed," said H.G.

"I'm not gonna wait for the lieutenant." He swiveled to his computer. "I'm gonna send this out right now."

"Has anybody heard from him?" said Amber.

"Nobody. . . . His wife doesn't even know where he is." He grinned sardonically. "Not that she would anymore. . . . In fact—" He turned and shouted out the door. "Hey, Linda, if we don't hear from the lieutenant, say, by lunchtime, would you check with the hospitals?"

"Okay."

"Psych wards, too."

H.G. and Amber exchanged looks.

Young shrugged. "The dude's got problems." Then he pointed at Stephenson's portrait, *circa* 2010, his face lighting up with a Cheshire cat smile. "Tell you one thing—this is gonna get the L.A. *Times* off our back for a while." He nodded at H.G., punched him lightly in the shoulder. "Thanks, man."

A detective swung in the doorway. "Hey, Sarge, the lab finally called. They're emailing the dentals on the Venus de Milo Jane Doe."

"Trattner," said the detective, staring at the dental report on a laptop in the homicide bay, "Heather Trattner.... 1407 Bowling Green Way, Brentwood."

"Christ," exclaimed Sergeant Young, "her husband was the one murdered on Sunday." He turned to the detective. "Get everybody in here."

Excited, yet confused, H.G. turned to Amber and whispered, "'Dusa, how do they *know* . . . ? I understand how Roentgen's discovery of X-rays can lead to radiographs of one's teeth and how they can be like an oral fingerprint, but how in bloody hell do they know which dentist to query?"

"They found the body in Brentwood," she whispered back, "so the forensics dentist in the lab does postmortem X-rays, then goes online and shoots copies to all the dentists in Brentwood. They're obligated by law to make a comparison. If we don't get a hit from any of them, the guy in the lab widens his circle."

"We start with the house," announced Sergeant Young when the detectives had assembled. He lit up the electronic situation board and map, then zoomed to a six-block area bordered on the north by Sunset Boulevard and on the west by Bundy Drive. With a pointer that lit up when he touched the map, he indicated where he wanted the patrol units, how he wanted the Trattner house covered, when the technicians should set up and—above all—who they were looking for. A giant rendering of the present-day Leslie John Stephenson flashed on the screen.

Left behind, H.G. was only mildly disappointed. He doubted the police would find Stephenson. Something was missing, a jagged piece of the puzzle; something was horribly awry. The police had no clue, and unfortunately neither did he. He could only hope that someone out there saw the rendering and recognized the Ripper. Hands in his pockets, he browsed the headquarters for new technology, peered in the lieutenant's office and saw the *Scientific American* on the desk, his favorite magazine in 1979. He grinned and felt a rush of pleasure as if he'd just seen an old friend. Intrigued, he picked it up and started reading.

Twenty minutes later, the secretary glanced up and said sympatheti-cally, "You know, I don't think they're going to be back for a while. Want me to call you a cab?"

"No, no, I'm tip-top, thank you." He looked at the magazine again. "Did you know that female chromosomes are more dominant and com-plex than male chromosomes . . . ?"

The secretary stared at him.

"Right." He blushed. "Of course you did."

11:12 A.M.

Jaclyn had been curled up catlike next to Holland's body for hours, absorbing his death, failing to convince herself that he lived on within her. And now that her passion was gone, she hated herself for what she'd done to him, yet insisted it was an act of love, of supplication.

Then she heard maids in the corridor and grew nervous. She realized she couldn't stay here much longer. She dressed quickly, eased outside and hurried away from Room 317, the DO NOT DISTURB sign on the handle waving in the breeze she left behind.

Instead of the lift, she took the stairs down to subterranean parking. "I miss you and I love you," she said, starting the Mercedes. The car went up the ramp. "I miss you and I love you, I miss you and I love you," she whispered until it became a mantra. At the street, she turned left; she drove aimlessly.

She found Edvard Grieg on satellite radio, a sonata for cello and piano. Though a melody lurked somewhere, the music was discordant and eerie—little flights of keys running amok with a hollow string accompaniment of death. It reminded her how much more complex she was than Leslie John. Other than his obsession with Penny, he had never known love. Had he discovered it, he might not have cut up all those whores. *Ah, but ultimately who gives a damn? Despite my gender, I am him in spirit, and I have been resurrected as an instrument of Satan. Loving Casey Holland was an aberration, a weakness.*

Suddenly, new thoughts: *No, no, that's not true. Loving him is akin to a priest falling for Jesus. Loving him is watching him die just like those soldiers aka lovers did at the cross. Besides, haven't I in fact become Jaclyn Smythe? And after last night, am I not sick of blood for blood's sake? Would I not have a grand life here in this chrome, glass and macadam world merely because of my beauty?*

Startled, she realized that in her reverie, she had driven to Will Rogers State Park. She recalled that old adage of a criminal returning to the scene of a crime, so instead of going up the hill where she'd left Heather Trattner's body, she stopped farther down the road, got out, walked and drank in the timeless beauty of canyons in chaparral under a hazy, warm sun, the smell of the eucalyptus, the salt air, the quiet. *I love you and I miss you.*

I love you and I miss you, I— I can't stand it anymore!

She burst out crying, ran to the car, fumbled in her purse—hands shaking badly—yet found the knife and held it so she could see her eyes reflected in its stainless steel. They were black pools blurred by her tears falling on the blade. She remembered this same knife wet with her lover's blood. She closed her eyes and kissed it.

She cut deep into her left wrist.

A searing pain.

She gasped, dropped the knife, grabbed her wrist, gritted her teeth against the pain. She looked. The wound was deep, blue on the edges; blood rained on the ground, and when she let go of her wrist, it cascaded out. She was horrified. She'd thought it would be easy, so easy. She'd thought she would smile, curl up in the Mercedes, go to sleep and bleed to death with images of her sweet lieutenant guiding her to their place in eternity, but, no, the pain had her doubled over and thrashing like those whores had done when Jack slashed their throats. She couldn't *do* this.

Good God, the pain, the—

Panicked, she took the belt from her pantsuit, looped it over her wrist, pulled tight until the blood was only trickling. She slumped in the car, held her head down so she wouldn't pass out. The pain subsided to a throb in rhythm with her pounding heart. Curiously calm, she recalled unloading the pieces of Heather from the trunk and seeing a first-aid kit, and thinking that its juxtaposition with her victim was ludicrous. She got it from the trunk, ripped it open gratefully, dumped it on the front seat and set about closing her wound.

Dizzy, she lay down and dozed. Minutes later, she was up and out of the car, walking around to clear her head. A park ranger drove up the road, giving her a curious look as he went by. She waved and smiled, but grew panicked. She picked up her knife and, back in the Mercedes, noticed bloodstains on her pants and sleeve. *This will never do.* She started the car, turned around and sped out of the park.

Pain was shooting up her arm now. She couldn't use her hand, and her bandage was already sopping red. One-handed, she drove in a fog, drove erratically as if she could speed away from what she had done to herself.

She found an Urgent Care on the corner of Wilshire and Chelsea, gave them Heather's name and insurance card, was in a treatment room within minutes. Anna, a young and pretty nurse practitioner, cut away the makeshift bandage, all the while asking a set of questions that Jaclyn mistook for concerned small talk.

"My boyfriend locked me out of the flat and so I broke a pane of glass so I could open the door from the inside. I tried to be careful, but I guess I was angry. You know how those things are."

"Yep. Sure do," said Anna, smiling. She made notes on a clipboard. "Okay. This is gonna sting a little."

As Anna cleaned the wound, Jaclyn gasped and saw white, almost passed out, and was left clutching at her chair.

"Worst is over."

As she laced the wound with a painkiller and antibiotic, numbed the wrist and quickly stitched it up, Anna went on with the questions as if they were meant to be a distraction, but Jaclyn had already figured it out and responded with glib and vague answers. Finally, Anna patted her wrist gently, left it exposed on the table and stood.

"Doctor's gonna come in and take a look, okay?" Anna pressed a red button on the wall, gave Jaclyn a professional smile and left.

Seconds later, Jaclyn fished the clipboard from the slot on the door, scanned the paperwork. "Suicide watch" told her all she needed to know. She bandaged her wound by herself, tentatively flexed her hand. It worked. Relieved, she smiled. *In Jack's day, they might have cut it off.* She rolled down her sleeve. It covered most of the bandage, yet was still bloodstained. *I must go back to Heather's. This silk clings to me like death.*

After Dr. Tom Fogel had washed up, he went down the corridor, glanced at Jaclyn's paperwork on the clipboard, then put on his best smile and swung into the room. "Hi, how are we—?"

Concerned, he backpedaled into the corridor. "Anna . . . ?"

She didn't hear.

"Anna?! Where did you put the suicide patient?"

On Sunset, Jaclyn passed a black-and-white, saw another one coming from the other direction, thought nothing of it. She turned on North Bundy Drive, heading for the Trattner house—already it seemed like home. She was starting to relax, looked forward to a hot shower and a glass of vodka, then—up ahead where Bowling Green Way curved—she saw police cars lining the street, vans parked in the driveway, technicians in full-on crime-scene ballet, neighbors staring. She pulled over on a side street and parked under trees. She was shaking. *How did they find me . . . ? How?*

She turned around and eased back to Bowling Green, waited at the corner, peering at the police presence. On the lawn, detectives in suits were talking. More were on cell phones. Technicians carried boxes from the house; the boxes no doubt held evidence linking her to the Trattner murders. She figured they had assumed she was the Brentwood killer—a Jack instead of a Jaclyn—so she wasn't yet a full-blown fugitive. She noticed her clothes. *Still, I look absolutely awful. I looked damaged.* She remembered a cute little boutique she'd seen on Montana, spun around and drove away.

At Only Hearts boutique, Jaclyn made small talk with a chic zombie of a salesgirl, finally chose a light-gray camisole with lace trim to go under a sheer black blouse and clingy pants. Smiling, she was anxious to wear it out of the store and didn't understand what was taking so long, why they were frowning and repeatedly pushing buttons on one of their machines. Then the manager came over, handed her Heather's Visa card and smiled apologetically.

"I'm sorry. It won't go through."

"Oh."

"D'you have another card?"

"Yes, of course."

Hot under the manager's gaze, Jaclyn went back in her purse knowing that Heather had at least a dozen of them, then stopped abruptly, realizing that the transaction probably hadn't gone through because of something the police had done. Obviously, they now knew that Heather, like her husband, had been murdered and that the murderer had their credit cards. Forcing a smile, she looked up at the manager.

"Will a cheque be all right?"

"Of course."

Jaclyn dug out Heather's cheque book.

"That's . . . let's see . . . five hundred and eighty-seven dollars and twenty-five cents with tax."

As she wrote out the cheque, she felt the manager's eyes on her bandaged wrist and the blood on her sleeve, yet she smiled back confidently as if it were a fashion statement.

"Do you mind if I see your driver's license?" the manager asked discreetly, taking the cheque.

She gave him Heather's. When he frowned uncertainly at the lack of resemblance, she gave him a dazzling smile and pirouetted. "I've changed my hair."

She took back the license, then picked up her outfit in designer bags, gave the manager a little flutter wave and waltzed out the door.

Worried now, she left Santa Monica, drove to Venice and felt more comfortable on its dingy streets, but couldn't think clearly. She was famished. She found a little tapas place on Abbot Kinney, with parking and an entrance from the back. She took her new outfit with her, planning to change after a bite, and was shown to a table by a sullen and indifferent waitress who read the menu off a chalkboard as if reciting a language assignment. Jaclyn ordered a shredded cod salad with tomatoes, peppers and onions, then a Spanish omelette Gypsy-style, and was surprised the food was so delicious. She ate slowly, and the food relaxed her, despite the loss of her safe house, her credit cards. She sensed that she was running out of time, but couldn't just run. No, not without the special key. She smiled, determined. *Satan has given me feminine wiles in this here and now. I must use them.*

She scanned the dessert menu, torn between the crème brûlée and the chocolate tart with French vanilla topping, then thought of Casey and couldn't stand the thought of something sweet. She left two twenties for the bill and went out the back way, averting her face from the customers at tables in the garden.

Dispatcherspeak from a police radio split the air.

She stopped short at the gate to parking, pretended to admire the weed-choked garden, and when no one was looking, when she thought it prudent, she edged through the gate.

Two patrol cars were in the alley, one blocking in her Mercedes. One cop peered in the tinted windows while his partner was on the radio, telling West Division that they'd found the Mercedes registered to Heather Trattner. Two more cops were gathered around the Libyan parking attendant, showing him the rendering of Leslie John Stephenson, circa 2010. The attendant was shaking his head, no, jabbering on in broken English, gesturing effusively at the small shops and restaurants.

Jaclyn crept closer—until she had a good look at the rendering. Relieved, she almost laughed. *Ah, Leslie John, you should see what they've done with your rather forbidding visage.* With that, she went back inside the restaurant and left via the front door on Abbot Kinney. She walked along the street and window-shopped as if she hadn't a care in the world, but felt that very same world closing in, crushing her from all sides. She came upon a coffee shop that seemed deliberately dirty and ramshackle, was put off by the patrons lolling outside, their dogs and the abundance of flies. She took out her cell and called a cab.

Minutes later, she was speeding away from Venice and knew suddenly how she would play it. She called the Four Seasons, asked for Amy Wells, but she wasn't in, so Jaclyn called the Robbins house and found her there.

"It's Jaclyn Smythe ringing," she said cheerfully, "how are you today?"

"Oh, Jaclyn," said Amy, "how nice."

"Beautiful day, isn't it?"

"Yes, lovely."

"I know we're in America, dear girl, but are you interested in doing tea this afternoon . . . ?"

When his taxi arrived, H.G. left the West Division engrossed in self-discovery. The *Scientific American* had captivated him. In a fit of excitement, he borrowed it and left a note for Lieutenant Holland promising to return it, and continued reading in the taxi.

The magazine's current science was light-years beyond his biology studies with T. H. Huxley at the Normal School, and the articles were so clearly written that he grasped the principles quickly. He had been lost when 'Dusa was talking about DNA and chromosomes, but not now. Like he'd told the secretary, female X chromosomes were more dominant and complex than their male Y counterparts and that struck him as amusing; that they would be superior on a cellular basis was somewhat frightening. *No wonder the suffragettes strike terror in men's hearts.* Yet, he was reassured to learn that chromosomes in normal red-blood cells lacked genetic material, hence: *Maybe there is hope for the males species, after all.*

Alas, no. He learned in next essay that stem cells in the blood do contain genetic material and was wondering why the discovery seemed so important to him. No matter. The rest of the article fascinated him: the fact that skin cells could be manipulated into stem cells which in turn could ultimately produce "replacement parts" for the human body was yet another example of how magical technology had become. *Indeed, but what about the fact of wars, fought with new and improved weaponry? Some scientists are in a rush to prolong human life,* he mused ironically. *Others seem hell-bent on finding better ways to destroy it.*

"Here we are, sir. Four Seasons."

He paid the cabdriver and hurried across the lobby to the elevators. Going by politicians on a junket and their coterie of starlets brought him back to his twenty-first-century reality. He had gotten the rendering of Leslie John Stephenson to every newspaper, TV station and patrol car in the city, yet had this uncanny feeling that the Ripper was nearby, playing with him, making him tap-dance like a marionette.

H.G. got off at the fifth floor. He appreciated that their suite was at the end of the hall in a cul-du-sac and private. Once inside, he almost relaxed, almost felt at home.

"Amy . . . ?" His smile faded. "Hullo, Amy . . . ?"

The suite was empty.

He started out, but stopped and went back. From the bedside table, he took the Beretta he'd bought from Xerox, shoved in it his coat pocket, and hated himself for doing so. Then he saw the note on the table in the foyer from Amy. She had gone downstairs for tea with Jaclyn Smythe and would love it if he would join them. He relaxed and smiled, the idea of her writing him a note lifting his spirits and erasing the worry from his mind.

H.G. met an unctuous, grinning maître d' in the foyer of the Garden restaurant who led him past eighteenth-century Italian paintings on red and orange walls toward the patio. They went through arched French doors and drapery columns into the Garden's "garden," where music and laughter and conversations were muted by palms and lemon trees, and the sound of fountains. Orchids and tall candles were on the tables here. The maître d' nodded, and H.G. saw Amy at a table in the corner, loose and relaxed. Jaclyn, resplendent in her black-and-gray outfit, was beside her, giggling as Amy whispered the end of a story.

Then they both laughed uproariously, went back to their drinks on the table.

"Oh, Bertie!" Amy exclaimed, looking up and smiling as he came forward. "We started out with tea and ended up with cocktails before dinner!" She laughed again. "Doesn't that make us so L.A.?" She gestured. "You remember Jaclyn Smythe, don't you?"

He nodded politely. "Hullo, Jaclyn."

"Hullo to you, Mr. Wells. . . . But that seems awfully formal." She gave him a dazzling smile. "Um, may I call you Herbert?"

"Herbert is fine." He hated that name.

"I think it's so fascinating that you're related to H. G. Wells. You look very much like him, you know."

"Yes." He sat down and turned to Amy. "Before I forget—"

But the waiter was there, pleased that H.G. had finally arrived. Assuming that they were mere tourists, he explained Asian fusion—a cuisine which went extremely well with California wine, and so on.

Later, H.G. was amazed that Australian lamb could taste so good when cooked with cilantro and hot Korean spices. The dinner had been excellent, a small example of what a world without borders could do, he told himself. Grilled Chilean sea bass with garlic ginger and Japanese soy. Filet titaki. Lemongrass marinated duck. *Such would be fare for Citizens of the World planning a better life, a Utopia.* He frowned at his naïveté. *No. This is the manner in which people of privilege dine. Serve the hoi polloi lemongrass marinated duck and then you have the right to think like Pollyanna. Then again, would they appreciate it? Or demand the ubiquitous burger and fries?*

Jaclyn was talking to Amy about something called "hip-hop," waving her hands over her head, and H.G. noticed the bandage on her wrist.

"What happened?" he said curiously.

"I locked myself out of the house," she said, "and had to break the glass to get in." She laughed. "Obviously, I'd never succeed as a burglar."

"You have a house here?"

"Not really," she said confidentially. "I'm house-sitting for my cousin who has gone off on a cruise. . . . Lucky bird."

"How long are you staying?"

"Oh, dear, I'm not really sure." She chuckled and blushed. "You see, I've met someone. . . ."

"Oh, how wonderful!" Amy cried. "You should call him! We could have a drink later on."

"I'm sorry to say that he has a prior engagement."

"Too bad," said Amy.

"So I guess I'm stranded here. . . . What a place to be stranded, enh? We could do worse, couldn't we?" She turned to H.G. "When are you going back?"

"We're not certain, either," he responded.

"I was rather hoping for a little side trip," said Jaclyn. "Maybe to Las Vegas."

"Oh?"

"You do know what they call it," she said insinuatingly, "Sodom and Gomorrah."

"No, I didn't know," he said flatly.

"Your lack of enthusiasm is astounding," she joked. "Would you prefer the nineteenth century?" She giggled and Amy joined in. "Would you?"

Now, what brought that on? He glanced at his new clothes. *Am I so obviously out of place here?* He arched his eyebrows at Jaclyn. *What is it about her, anyway . . . ?* "Actually, there is quite a bit to be said for the Edwardian Age," he postulated.

"The Edwardian Age," she said slowly, as if trying out a new phrase. "Tell me about the Edwardian Age."

"You went to school, didn't you?" he said dryly.

"Are you afraid of your own opinions?"

"All right," he said, annoyed. "After the Queen died, we were blessed with a sense of freedom. Optimism. Compassion. Progressive thinking." As he spoke, he thought of innumerable exceptions to what he was saying. "And romance, of course."

"Ah, yes." Jaclyn nodded, bemused. "They threw off the shackles of

Queen Victoria, didn't they? Bully for them." She leaned over the table provocatively, her breasts stretching the gray camisole. "And do you share your distant relative's politics?"

Surprised, he stared at her. *Is she baiting me?*

"His views on morality? Feminism . . . ? Sexual freedom?"

Uncertain by the turn in the conversation, Amy looked away, but her husband rose to the occasion.

"Yes, I do," he replied. He glanced at Amy. "In theory, of course."

"Then you must be appalled by the scourge of AIDS," Jaclyn said blithely, "for how can people, shall we say, enjoy a stranger's company if they must fear contracting a horrible disease that will not only kill them, but infect their children, as well?"

"They take precautions," he said stubbornly.

"I, on the other hand, happen to believe that AIDS is God's way of controlling the population—not to mention his selection of the species. I mean, if medical science is so bent on curing all the tried-and-true diseases, what else is God going to do?"

"I don't believe in God."

"Ah. . . . What a shame." She sighed. "Satan, perhaps?"

"Must we?" said Amy. "I say, this is all so ghastly. . . . Can't we talk about something else?"

"Oh, I'm sorry," said Jaclyn, placing a hand on Amy's arm.

"Why don't we have dessert?" said Amy, smiling again.

"Yes. What a grand idea."

"And then—before you go—you must come up. The suites here are heavenly."

Suddenly, the maître d' appeared, smiled at the ladies, then turned and gave H.G. a confidential nod. "I'm sorry to bother you, sir, but you have a phone call."

Five Minutes Earlier

Room 317 at the Holiday Inn Express stank of blood and sex. The table was littered with wadded napkins, bits of fruit and glasses of stale vodka. The lieutenant's clothes and shoes were strewn about the room as if he had undressed in stages or if someone had helped him. Either way, it was helter-skelter.

In death, Casey Holland was bloated and bluish, his eyes closed, his face slack, yet frozen in a curious little smile. He'd been spread-eagled on the bed, its pillows and duvet—now stiff with blood—arranged beneath him as if he were royalty. Deep love scratches curved from his back and up his sides as if he'd been held by a creature with giant claws. The happy face on his torso was a collage: the eyes were severed pinky fingers; the nose was in fact Holland's nose, surgically made smaller, cuter; the mouth was his filleted penis curved into a smile. Carved around the happy face in small, delicate letters: "I love you and I miss you I love you and I miss you I love you and I miss you." The killer hadn't bothered with "REMEMBER ME?"

Now the coroner's people were making a bottleneck of the doorway as technicians tried to come and go. Rogers was still shooting Lieutenant Holland's corpse, his lights creating an obstacle course for everybody else, but Sergeant Young didn't seem to mind. In fact, none of the confusion bothered him. He had found the lieutenant's phone. Sitting at the table where his evidence people had bagged the fruit and vodka glasses, he scrolled to the last number Holland had called, took out his own phone and speed-dialed Verizon special services.

"Salvatore Arenas, may I help you?"

"Hey, Sal, how you doing tonight?"

"Jesus, Sarge, don't you ever go home?"

"No reason to."

"What, no wife, no dog?"

"Wives fuck your buds, and dogs get hit by cars."

Sal laughed nervously "You know, you're one—"

"—cynical son of a bitch, I know. The day you can tell me something that I ain't already heard is the day we go for beers."

"You're gonna die alone, Sarge."

"Yeah, yeah."

"You *are*."

"Until then, I need a GPS location on a number. Three-one-zero area code."

"Go ahead."

Outside in the corridor, a pale and shaken Amber Reeves tried yet another number and waited as it rang and rang. Nearby, the manager explained to detectives: The guest had only paid for one night. The maid hadn't cleaned his room because of the DO NOT DISTURB sign. The guest didn't answer repeated calls to his cell or the phone in the room, so faced with an overbooking, the manager himself had finally gone in the room, saw the body and called 911.

After twelve rings, the automatic voice mail for H.G.'s suite picked up. Amber swore under her breath, hung up, then tried the Robbins home. Voice mail there, too.

She hugged herself and stared at the phone. *He's gotta be someplace.* She thought furiously, then dialed 411.

8:00 P.M.

"God, you're hard to get ahold of!" Amber complained.

"'Dusa, I'm in the middle of dinner." H.G. had been directed to a house phone in the lobby. "Am I not allowed to eat?"

"The lieutenant's been murdered!" she interrupted.

He slumped in a chair. "Good Lord."

"You're wrong about your Jack the Ripper, Bertie," she added, her voice quaking. "The Brentwood killer is a woman."

A silence.

"Impossible," he finally said. "Someone else must've killed him."

"No. . . . I just ran the DNA. I ran it twice and it was like another botched Klinefelter's syndrome. . . . The same as before."

Stunned, he only half-listened as she described Room 317 and the gruesome happy face that was on Holland's belly with sentiments around its perimeter as if the killer had carved a totem on a tree. H.G.'s brain had hopscotched to the articles he had read in the *Scientific American*, and it came to him in a horrible rush.

Amy's blood on the cabin floor.

Amy's blood was fresh on the cabin floor when the time machine traveled to infinity, fresh with her stems cells, fresh with her X chromosomes and genetic material. When Leslie John Stephenson was vaporized during the trip back to 2010, his Y chromosome had been replaced by a more dominant, full-blown X chromosome so that he was reconstituted as a woman.

Wait. Traces of Amy's blood were still on the floor when I traveled here. Why am I still a man? He closed his eyes, massaged the bridge of his nose. *Because all chromosomes are not created equal.*

Obviously, Stephenson had a pitifully weak Y chromosome due to a latent nondisjunction of two X chromosomes that he had been carrying with him all his life. *That definitely would have been a pebble in his genetic shoe. That would explain why 'Dusa's DNA tests failed. And— after all these years—that would explain Jack the Ripper's murderous psychiatric pathology.*

His breath whooshed out. The end result was that a physically normal, XX woman with a latent Y chromosome who was as deadly as she was beautiful had arrived in the time machine early that Sunday morning.

"Bertie, are you still there . . . ?"

"Jaclyn Smythe is Jack the Ripper," he said hollowly.

He slammed the phone down, bolted up from the chair, raced back to the restaurant, angling past knots of guests, jostling the rich and famous, then stopped suddenly in the foyer, his path blocked by the maître d'.

"I'm sorry, sir, but they left a few minutes ago." The maître d' handed him the bill. "Would you like me to put the charges on your room?"

"Where did they go!" H.G. demanded.

The maître d' shrugged sadly. "I am sorry, sir, but they did not say. Maybe you can call them?"

H.G. was gone.

He lurched into the elevator, punching the button over and over as if that would make it go faster. "Who in the bloody hell would've thought—" he said to the walls, then shook his head. *It wasn't a reformulation error—it was more like a transduction error. Obviously, Fate has been laughing at me ever since I arrived.*

He got off on the fifth floor, leaned against the wall, struggled to control his rising panic. *If you give in to your rage, you will fail, and this, this Jaclyn—this transmogrification from hell—will be gleefully cutting you up alongside Amy.* He took deep breaths, and his mind became lucid again. Amy probably hadn't been harmed, he figured. Jaclyn wanted the special key, and just as the Ripper had proposed a trade thirty-one years ago, he was certain that Jaclyn would do the same.

He fished for the Beretta in his coat pocket, took it out, hefted it and was surprised it made him feel so much more capable—more reasonable, even. Coolly, he made sure that a round was in the chamber, flicked off the safety. Very gingerly, he slid it in his trousers. *God forbid that I should shoot myself.*

He started down the hallway for the cul-de-sac.

He slid the plastic key in the lock, held his breath and pulled it out quickly. The door to his suite unlocked with a click. He slowly pushed it open and heard faint, giddy laughter from the living room over the white noise of traffic which meant the French doors were open, and they were probably having a drink on the balcony. He stepped into the foyer and closed the door behind him so it wouldn't slam shut in a draft. He crept closer and listened again. Jaclyn was complimenting the port Amy had opened, remarking that it was far superior to the claret her friends usually served in London. H.G. wasn't sure if she already knew he was in the room and was saying that to mock him or if it was merely coincidental.

He slipped his hand around the Beretta in his pocket, took a breath and strode in the living room. He was ready for their surprise and tried to act nonchalant. "Ah. You mustn't have heard me come in."

If I can separate them. If I can possibly separate them.

He nodded at the bar. "Jaclyn, would you mind pouring me a glass of that wonderful port?" He turned to Amy, said with a businesslike tone, "Amy, I must speak with you in the other room." He inclined his head and started out of the living room. "You don't mind, do you?"

"She does mind, I'm sorry to say."

He heard the brief struggle, spun around with the Beretta in his hand, but was too late.

His ploy hadn't worked.

Jaclyn had a fist in Amy's hair and the blade of her knife laid across Amy's throat. Wide-eyed, Amy was frozen in terror, standing on tiptoes as if that would stop the knife from cutting further into her flesh.

"I trust we can cooperate?" Jaclyn said to them both.

H.G. nodded slowly, yet aimed his pistol at Jaclyn anyway, squinting through his glasses. She was half-hidden behind Amy.

"To begin with, I believe we had this conversation roughly thirty years ago," Jaclyn said ironically, "though it seems like yesterday, hmmm?"

"You want the special key," H.G. said slowly.

"Brilliant, Wells," she said scornfully, "absolutely top-drawer."

"Go to hell."

"Ah, but I've already been, my dear boy. . . . I've already been, and I have no wish to return."

"I give you the special key, and you release Amy."

Jaclyn tittered with laughter. "You've learned your lines!"

"I have your word?"

"As a lady—or a gentleman." She smiled wickedly. "Whichever you prefer."

He transferred the Beretta to his left hand, dug the special key out of his pocket with his right. "Let Amy go, and I'll toss you the key."

"No, no, Wells." She feigned impatience. "You've forgotten how we do this. It's the other way round."

He took a step closer, drew a bead on Jaclyn, was actually pulling the trigger when she ducked behind Amy again.

"A little anxious, are we?" she said. "I just gave you my word."

In the distance, the sound of a helicopter thumped closer, yet no one in the room noticed.

H.G. took another step forward, his gun waving, then steady, then waving. Amy closed her eyes and whispered a prayer. Unnerved, Jaclyn backed across the balcony until her back was against the rail.

H.G. took yet another step.

In response, Jaclyn quickly, yet delicately nicked Amy's throat with her knife as if plucking a string on a violin. Blood gushed forth.

"Do we understand each other?"

A tableau.

For a millisecond, H.G. thought he had a clean shot, but his hand was shaking too badly, and Jaclyn moved again.

"Bertie, please," Amy whispered. Tears were running down her face into the rivulets of her blood. "Please. . . ."

"Your word," he muttered to Jaclyn.

"Yes."

He lowered the Beretta and tossed the special key at her feet. It spun through the air, clanged on the balcony tile. Jaclyn scooped it up without getting go of Amy, once again had the knife at her throat. She grinned.

"Candidly, my dear boy, I'd have expected you to notice by now that I am neither a gentleman nor a lady."

Suddenly, the helicopter dropped over the top of the hotel and hovered, the blast from its rotors loud against the building. Startled, Jaclyn looked, and in that moment, Amy tried to twist free, but her hair was still in Jaclyn's hand. Jaclyn forced her against the wall and raised the knife.

A xenon spotlight lit up the balcony.

H.G. fired.

His bullet smacked into the wall between Jaclyn and Amy. He peered over the barrel, thought for an instant that he'd actually hit Jaclyn, but no. In a flash, she'd pocketed her knife and gone over the side. He went to the rail and leaned over expecting to see her body crumpled on the street below. He saw nothing—only the helicopter spotlight ballyhooing crazily over the face of the hotel trying to find her, as well.

Then Amy rushed to him and held on to him, shaking with sobs. He tried to comfort her and locate Jaclyn in the darkness below at the same time.

"Jaclyn Smythe," bellowed a voice from the helicopter. "The hotel is surrounded. . . . Jaclyn Smythe. . . . Surrender to the police. . . ."

While the voice droned on, patrol cars and police vans pulled up on the street below, and as commanders shouted orders, cops in SWAT gear hit the ground running and spread out.

Finally, in the darkness, H.G. saw a flicker of movement and was astounded. Jaclyn was brachiating gracefully from balcony to balcony, on a diagonal toward the ground, deliberately going for the junglelike foliage near the main entrance. She abruptly disappeared, swallowed up in the black, and he had no way of telling if she'd jumped clear, fallen or gone back in the hotel by way of another balcony.

He shouted to the police below, but his words were lost in the roar of the helicopter, the shriek of more sirens coming closer, the garbled policespeak over PA systems.

Muttering, he turned to Amy, saw blood still trickling from her wound, pulled her into the bathroom and set about cleaning her up.

"I can do this, Bertie," she said, trying to be brave, but her voice was tremulous.

"No."

"I'd rather bandage myself," she said firmly looking at him in the mirror. "I've seen what you do when the children get scratches."

"Amy—" Overcome, relieved, he embraced her from behind and buried his face in her hair. His eyes brimmed with tears. "Honestly, I . . . I don't think I'd care to go on without you, my love."

She began crying, too, and placed her hand gently on his, then turned in to him, and they rocked back and forth as they held each other.

The door burst open.

H.G. found himself facing two SWAT-team members in the bathroom while others searched the suite. In full-on gear, they resembled giant black insects, but he had already seen them scrambling from the vans and wasn't put off.

"How did you *know*?" said H.G.

"We tracked her phone," said the team leader. He lifted his mask, revealing a lined and set black face. "GPS."

"Really." He blushed, frowned, told himself he owed 'Dusa an apology. Not only had he been wrong about GPS technology, in this case it had saved Amy's life.

Another team member swung into the room. "Not here," he said. "Not in any of the adjacent rooms. . . . *Nada*, skipper."

"She went over the balcony," H.G. said, leading them in the living room. "I fired and missed, and then she was gone."

Irritated, the team leader spoke into a small microphone on his helmet. "Johnny Six, we're in the room."

"Go ahead."

"Look for a corpse down there, will you?"

"Copy."

"I didn't hit her!" H.G. protested. He pointed at the pockmarked stucco. "She's not dead!"

Disbelieving, the team leader inspected the bullet hole, then looked over the balcony. After a long moment, he fished night-vision glasses from his belt and peered into the black pockets of foliage. Finally, he straightened up, pressed his microphone again.

"We can't see under the bushes. There might be a body under the bushes."

"She's alive, I tell you!" H.G. declared. "She swung down the balconies like a bloody orangutan."

When Jaclyn got to Santa Monica Boulevard, she shook off her fugitive mode and strolled the sidewalk, looking at the closed shops as if there were something fascinating in their shuttered windows. All that was missing was Heather Trattner's purse to swing. In her obvious haste, she had left it in the Wellses' hotel suite.

Rappelling down the balconies had required nothing more than a bold, suicidal agility which after her years in hell came rather easily, though she had wrenched her shoulder, scraped her hands and arms. At the second floor, she had jumped, landed on a thicket of banana trees, bounced to the ground, then run off through gardens thick with foliage, brushing spiders from her hair. She had emerged farther east on Doheny Drive, seconds before the SWAT teams had arrived. She was already beyond their perimeter and the rookies stringing yellow tape, and now was in the anonymity of noise and traffic.

An Escalade pulled to the curb and tracked her. Admiring its maroon reflection in the windows, she continued walking. A little more swing to her hips, a carefree hand in the air, and she saw the window slide down, opening another world to her. *Every exit is an entrance somewhere else,* she thought, quoting a genius playwright she'd surfed past on PBS while enjoying the Trattner hospitality.

"Hey, you need a ride . . . ?"

"Thank you," said Jaclyn, relieved as the car whisked her away from the area. She settled back in the plush seat and studied the driver. Tall and angular, he reminded her of a stick figure with bad skin and hair combed to look unkempt. He seemed much too young for the car, and she guessed that it belonged to his father.

"Where you headed?" he said.

She looked at him blankly, noticed his Adam's apple and wondered vaguely what it would look like excised from his throat. She glanced in the rearview mirror, saw no patrol cars behind them and was glad to be leaving Beverly Hills. *This boy will want something for his kindness, and while I must admit that I'm bored playing the harlot, I cannot deny its convenience—nor its allure.*

"My name's Steve."

She nodded.

"Like some tunes?" He punched on the satellite radio, and rap music exploded from within, bass vibrating the speakers.

"Please," she said, disgusted.

"Okay, okay." He turned it off. When the light changed, he hit the gas and veered right on Wilshire, leaving Santa Monica Boulevard behind. He rolled his shoulders and looked smug—as if speed made him cool. He fished cigarettes from the dash, threw his arm over her seat. "Smoke?"

"No."

He started to light one. "Mind?"

"Of course not. What a silly question."

"So, unh. . . . you're a hooker . . . ?"

"I can be."

"Yeah?" His eyes lit up. "I, I don't have much cash."

"You won't need much."

"Really?" He chuckled nervously. "Wow. That's great." He grinned.

"Okay, we'll seal the deal." He drummed on the steering wheel. "How about we go into the hills?" He gestured at the backseat. "That gonna be cool?"

"No. . . . We'll go to the Getty Museum."

"Huh?" His face fell.

"You've never been?"

He shook his head.

"It's quite lovely." She smiled, then looked off thoughtfully. *Wells will be coming—if he hasn't left already—and we have a little surprise for him, do we not?*

"Do I get on the 405?"

"No, no. We'll be taking the back way."

"Won't it be closed?" said Steve.

"Oh, we won't be going inside, my dear."

8:46 P.M.

H.G. got off the elevator and was ushered through a police checkpoint. He wanted to tell them that they wouldn't find Jaclyn here, but he had no time. He hurried outside. Police had blocked the entrance with barriers and tape. Seeing their black-and-whites lining the street, he realized that the last place in Beverly Hills he could hail a cab right now was in front of the Four Seasons.

He remembered the lower level and took a lift down to valet parking. There were no taxis here, either, and—complicating matters—the police had taken over for the valets, funneling guests like sheep to an angry red-and-gold-vested man who was bestowing keys and mouthing apologies. The guests all had tickets which they would show to a cop who would ask them questions, then let them pass. H.G. had no such token and was inventing a "lost ticket" story when he spotted motorcycles parked in rows before the cars, their various colors gleaming under the fluorescents like a metallic rainbow. Unsurprising in this setting, they all looked new, and while he wouldn't mind owning any of them, the one half-hidden behind a pillar brought a huge, childlike grin to his face.

He walked around the walled-in elevator shaft and worked his way between the parked cars toward the machine that had caught his eye: a sapphire-blue '10 Kawasaki Concours 1400 GTR, or so the chrome on its front announced. He paused at an open area flush with light and waited. His heart pounded.

One last breath, and then he darted to the bike, kneeled quickly behind it, touched its cold, smooth skin. The ignition was electric, so he wouldn't have trouble marrying the proper wires and starting the bike, yet the components were enclosed, and he had no tools. He frowned. Here he was, reduced to a pathetic thief before a spectacular machine—something to which science and technology should aspire—and he had a bloody pistol instead of a screwdriver. He calmed himself and ran his hands over the bike, probed and lifted. Magically, the seat raised up.

Inside was the toolkit that came with the bike.

Within minutes, he had bypassed the switch, was putting the toolkit back when he stopped. *My God, man, you can't just nip some citizen's motorbike like a common criminal! Explain yourself!* He took pen from pocket, but had nothing to write on, looked around frantically for a fast-food wrapper or bit of trash, but the staff here kept the parking area too clean. Then he saw an invoice for the bike also under the seat, unfolded it and wrote on the back:

> To Whom It May Concern:
> A matter of utmost importance has come up, and I must borrow your exquisite machine. Should I not return, please charge whatever expenses and inconvenience you have incurred to my hotel suite at the Four Seasons.
>
> > Respectfully,
> > Herbert G. Wells

He left the note weighted down by the owner's helmet. One last glance at the police, and he walked the Kawasaki backward, aimed at the ramp, started the machine The four-stroke engine responded quietly, properly, yet the halogen headlamp blazed on automatically, turning heads from the noise and confusion around the valet station. They saw him. Muttering curses, he straddled the bike, cranked the throttle, and it leaped forward, sending him airborne. He hung on to the handlebars like a trapeze artist. With a mind of its own, the machine slammed down, but didn't throw him. It hiccupped forward, bouncing him on the seat.

The valet was waving and shouting, and the police starting for him en masse. He goosed the bike. It leapfrogged up the ramp, wobbling under his uncertain hands, brushing him against the wall, shredding his sleeve and trousers and finally straightened out.

At the street, he slid into a left turn, slamming foot on pavement to stay upright, zipped past members of a SWAT team jumping out of the way, went right on Burton Way, barely missing the police barricades, bounced up on the center island, tore up its grass, and finally veered back onto the pavement. Cars ahead saw him coming and wisely pulled over. Afraid to slow down for fear he'd fall off, he leaned over the bike and hung on, wind pulling at his face. On Santa Monica, he turned in front of oncoming traffic, pressing the horn to warn the unsuspecting. Abruptly, he emitted a giddy laugh. This was not his 1905 Triumph.

A car pulled out in front of him. Instinctively, he went to apply the brakes, but missed both lever and foot pedal. The bike hurtled forward. He swerved at the last second, brushing the car with his leg as he went by. The driver leaned on his horn, the blaring sound startling him.

Minutes later, he was on Sepulveda, then scooting under the 405 and speeding into the Getty complex. On the hill, parallel to the tram, he forgot himself and—bubbling with laughter—cranked the Kawasaki to eighty-five. It rocketed forward, the road flashing beneath, and he was considering ninety when he saw the arrival plaza looming ahead and realized he had miscalculated badly. Not wanting to miss the brakes again, he glanced at the handlebars, but couldn't see clearly. He looked back at the road. In that instant, the bike hit the curb and jackhammered up the graceful tiers of steps, out of control. He finally jammed on the brakes.

The Kawasaki fishtailed, and he let go of the brakes.

It straightened up. He hit the brakes again, but too late. Still doing a

good thirty-five, the bike slammed into the double glass doors, wrench-
ing them open. He somersaulted over the bars, hit the travertine floor
and rolled.

The alarms went off.

9:10 P.M.

"Amy?" said Amber breathlessly. "Is Bertie there?"

"Why, no," she replied, "he left a little after half-past." Trying to relax, Amy was tidying up the suite after the SWAT team had left, their black boots having raised havoc with the rugs in the bathroom and the foyer. "Are you downstairs in the lobby?"

"No, I'm in my car! I was supposed to finish up at the crime scene, but I bailed, I couldn't help it! Major manhunt or not, this is personal!"

"Yes, unfortunately I know. You'd think Bertie would've left that, that woman to the police, but, oh, no, not my Bertie."

"Where is he?!" she cried.

"He's gone to the museum, my dear."

"Okay, thanks, gotta go."

"Please don't let him hurt himself, will you?"

Amber rang off. She was heading east on Wilshire, almost to Burton Way and the hotel. The sky was crowded with police and news helicopters, their spotlights advertising what was for Beverly Hills a rather dubious event. Without thinking, she spun around in a tight U-turn ahead of onrushing traffic, stood on the accelerator and ran the red light at Wilshire and Santa Monica. She cut between a string of cars turning left, barely missed an SUV and angled behind a Mini Cooper, their horns blaring at her, then fading in the confusion left behind. Filled with dread, she rocketed up Wilshire. She knew that as brilliant and wonderful as he was, H.G. was no match for Jaclyn Smythe. Amber had no clue what she would find or what she would do, but she had to do something. *I may not deserve him, and he may not deserve Amy, but if nothing else, her kids deserve a father.*

9:12 P.M.

H.G. regained consciousness a few seconds after slamming through the doors. He got up on his hands and knees, wasn't sure if that awful ringing and buzzing noise was reverberating off the stone and glass or inside his head. He felt around him for his spectacles, found them a few feet away. One lens was cracked, and the frames ridiculously bent. He put them on his face where they hung precariously, but at least he could see again.

The lights came on. He looked up. Three security guards were in the rotunda, gawking in disbelief. One glass door was cracked badly and listed on its lower hinge. The other had been knocked completely off. The bike had slid upside-down across the rotunda leaving a trail of multicolored lubricants, then crashed on its side, the seat yawning open. H.G. got to his feet, staggered in a circle and tried to collect himself. His head throbbed.

"What the fuck?" said the guard named Cedric.

"Would you mind turning off the alarm?" H.G. said to him.

Cedric turned to Mark Goodwin—the head guard, now jabbering at the police on his cell phone—but Goodwin frowned, shook his head impatiently and waved him off, and the noise went on.

Finally, Goodwin flipped his phone shut. "West Division's stretched thin," he announced, raising his voice over the alarm. "They're on some kind of major flap, so they'll be a while."

"What the fuck?" Cedric repeated to H.G., spreading his hands. "You just lose it, or what?"

"I'll take care of the damage, my good man," H.G. declared. Thinking ahead, he scavenged the toolkit from the wrecked Kawasaki and jammed it in his coat pocket. "But you must understand I'm here on a matter of—"

"Take him downstairs and hold him," Goodwin ordered.

"I'm from Scotland Yard!" H.G. shouted. He pulled out his fake ID and waved it at them.

"Like I said," an angry Goodwin repeated to Cedric, "take him downstairs and hold him!"

"Let's go, Sherlock." Cedric grinned, took H.G. by the arm and propelled him across the rotunda.

Goodwin started for the stairs. "I'll get the goddamn alarm, people." He pointed at the third guard and barked, "Wait for the cops."

"Me?" said the third guard.

"You."

As Cedric led him toward the elevators, H.G. was about to make a break for it, then saw the men's room across the alcove and got a better idea. His captor pushed the call button, and H.G. gave him a sheepish smile.

"Excuse me, sir, but if you don't mind, I must use the loo." He nodded toward the sign.

Cedric gave him an impatient look, let go of his arm and held the bathroom door open. When they were both inside, H.G. started toward a stall, then turned suddenly.

"Give me your keys," he demanded.

"What—?" Cedric spun around; his eyes widened.

H.G. had his Beretta aimed at Cedric's nose. He held out his hand. "Your keys. . . . And your radio."

Cedric complied.

As H.G. backed out of the men's room, the alarm was finally turned off, and he half-smiled. With the blessed silence, his head had stopped hurting. "Sorry, old man," he apologized to Cedric, then locked him inside.

He took the elevator down to the lower level, ran along the corridor to the stairs below the West Pavilion and went up to the fire door. Out of breath, his hands shaking, he managed to find the right key and unlocked the door. But he had to jerk it open, and his glasses slipped off his face. Muttering, he bent the frames tighter, then eased into the corridor and went around the corner, let his eyes adjust to the darkness, the dim glow from night-lights. He sighed with relief. No guard in the lobby. He crept in the center gallery, his heart surging when he saw his beloved *The Utopia*, silhouetted by the recessed floor lights. He paused and listened to the silence, the void. He heard, he sensed no one. He went to the time machine, put his hand on the engine compartment. Cold. He smiled grimly. Jaclyn hadn't yet arrived.

He scrutinized the room, thought about surprising her in the machine, itself. *I'll get behind the chair, and when she opens the cabin door, I'll shoot her in the heart and be done with it—though one wonders if I shouldn't use a wooden stake.* He hesitated. *No, no, she's much too clever for that. I need a ruse that smacks of the twenty-first century, that will allow me—literally and figuratively—vision in the darkness.*

In the ceiling near the center gallery was a tiny night-light. It spilled illumination on the large portrait of himself over the archway, but more important, it cast a faint glow on the floor. In the blackness just beyond, H.G. set down the radio as if he were a hunter staging a decoy. He hesitated. It was more like setting an electronic birdcall that might never go off, but under the circumstances it was the best he could do.

He felt his way through the black to the display of photographs in the exhibition proper, and took up a position alongside it as if he were another portrait of himself. He drew his Beretta and waited. After a while, despite the controlled temperature in the pavilion, he began sweating. Muttering, he wiped his face and adjusted his glasses again.

Again, he waited.

Three Minutes Earlier

Jaclyn took Steve up North Bundy Drive and the mountain curves of Firth Avenue, going the back way to the Getty complex. Surprised by the barrier, he stopped the Escalade just inches away, and she laughed softly and told him to drive around it. Uneasy, he hesitated, but she told him she had done it many times before and coaxed him forward, her breasts brushing his arm, fingernails making circles on his leg, making promises.

He gulped, muttered fearfully about Dad's car, then went ahead and maneuvered around the barrier. On her instructions, he parked above the ring-shaped building where the access road curved and the moonlight was shadowed by trees. Tense, he turned to her and waited. Smiling, her eyes closed, she ignored him, idly dropped her hand to her knife, wondered when it would happen, but wasn't worried about time. She had the special key. She had carte blanche to the cosmos. For her, the universe was timeless, but at that moment the digital clock on the dash glowed 9:23 P.M.

Steve cleared his throat. She glanced at him, reveled in his jittery moves, his impatience. She enjoyed playing the tart; it gave her a power and control that Jack never had. *Yet I have his same murderous rage, his same strength and will, and.* . . . Her sweet lieutenant came to mind. She grimaced, couldn't help but think: *I am capable of love.*

She turned to the window and blinked back tears, and the tears made her angry, and suddenly she wanted it over with. "Take your pants down."

"Okay." He struggled to get them down.

"You know something?" she said with a bemused smile. "You forgot to ask me if I was a cop."

He froze, wide-eyed and panicked, his pants below his knees.

She stabbed him in the chest.

9:28 P.M.

H.G. waited.

He listened intently, yet it was so utterly quiet in the pavilion that all he heard was the thunder of his own heartbeat. He hadn't moved from his position by the photographs and envisioned himself becoming another artifact from his own life. He wasn't amused. The moment dragged—as if real time had stopped—and he wondered if he were making a ridiculous mistake. He told himself no. The police finally knew who Jaclyn was; they'd launched a huge manhunt; she was no longer anonymous; she had nowhere else to go. Moreover, she had the special key, and how else would someone from hell escape except by using *The Utopia?* He smiled ironically. *This rather staid exhibition of my life is about to become a redemption of sorts.*

Something rumbled beneath the floor. He glanced down, figured it had to do with the air-conditioning system under the building, but then the silence, the void closed in again.

He lifted his gaze and concentrated on the darkness so that the dim spots of illumination wouldn't ruin his night vision, so he wouldn't be surprised by someone coming out of the blackness.

The air moved.

He sensed her.

He heard nothing, but that slight caress of breeze was enough, and he knew instinctively that she was in the pavilion, dangerously close. But where? He resisted a tingling sensation on the back of his neck, resisted looking into the blackness behind him, and forced himself to focus on the center gallery. The only logic guiding him was his conviction that she would be going to the time machine.

He sensed her closer.

The tingling stopped, and a warm flush spread through his body. His pulse quickened. He held his breath and raised the Beretta. He peered into the blackness. Yet he saw, he heard nothing.

Suddenly, the radio barked.

"Hey, Cedric . . . ? What's your twenty?"

His decoy had worked.

In the blackness near the archway, a figure jumped, startled by the noise. H.G. swung his pistol toward the faint silhouette and fired, but in the sudden movement his glasses slid off. Cursing, he dropped to the floor and felt for them with his free hand.

"Cedric . . . ? You copy?"

He found them and was getting to his feet when someone smashed the radio over his head. Dazed, he staggered forward, fired blindly, didn't see Jaclyn push over the vertical display of photographs. It hit him in the back and sent him sprawling to the floor. He lost both glasses and Beretta, and was groping for them when she grabbed him by the throat and slammed his head into the floor. Once. Twice. He went limp.

9:33 P.M.

Amber swung to a stop in the arrival plaza, bumped over the curb, left the Milan with one wheel on the sidewalk, jumped out and hit the steps running. The security guard by the splayed doors saw her coming and got off his cell phone, but she waved her badge at him.

"A task force is right behind me!" she shouted, going in the rotunda.

"They got him downstairs," the guard called back.

No way in hell, she thought, but veered toward the elevator figuring that was how H.G. had gotten in the West Pavilion. She took it to the lower level, sprinted along the lower corridor. Moments later, she pushed through the unlocked fire door, went down the dark corridor into the lobby, paused and listened.

Silence.

Her heart pounding, she crept into the H.G. Wells exhibition, aware of the dark shapes of tables and display cases, then stopped suddenly. A glow came from the center gallery.

Someone had turned the lights on.

At The Same Time

H.G. woke up and blinked, became vaguely aware that someone was taping him to the chair in the cabin, but could see only blurry shapes. He remembered that his glasses had fallen off. Gingerly, he moved his head. Pain shot through his temples. He groaned.

"Ah, good, we're awake, then." Jaclyn chuckled. "For a moment, I was afraid I'd killed you before your time."

She put his glasses on him. He blinked again. She had switched on the lights in the gallery, and he saw her clearly now. His Beretta was stuffed in the waistband of her pants and the cabin door open behind her. Smiling triumphantly, she finished with the tape, stepped back, swept her lovely hair out of her eyes, admired her work. His head pounded. He wanted to massage it, but couldn't move his arms above his shoulders.

"I was going to cut the wires," she said, "the ones enabling travel to the past . . . but I made a mess of it, I'm afraid, so I had to do something a little less precise."

His mind became suddenly, horribly clear, and he knew why he was taped in the chair. "You've disabled the declinometer," he said hollowly.

"Brilliant, Wells." She patted him on the head. "And after I've sent you to hell, I'll repair the machine and be on my way."

She was also holding the bicycle lock—swinging it from her fingers—which meant she had found and removed his safety device, and the machine was hers now. He closed his eyes, tried to remain calm, tried to control his pain so that he might make sense of this moment, however badly it ended. His mind flashed to the exhibition. Though he had deliberately not wanted to know of his accomplishments later in life, the fact that he had a future was reassuring. But that didn't mean he *hadn't* gone to that same hell where the Jack the Ripper had been; nor did it tell him how long he'd be there or what sort of agonized "death" he would endure. He could be there for millions of years, his beloved machine still a slave to this Jaclyn in some distant Grecian universe while she toyed murderously with those who had created Western civilization. Maybe *The Utopia* would turn to dust before he left hell, and he would have to wait until someone else in another universe built a time machine and accidentally let it loose on the fourth dimension. The odds were not in his favor.

Yet he couldn't forget Amy and the boys, nor the future of mankind. He was one man in billions, but he'd be damned if he'd give up trying. "At least give me the satisfaction of knowing when."

"Ah, yes, the end of time." She smiled breezily. "The Current Year Indicator read 2353, so that would be the year your progeny blew up the planet."

H.G. looked away and shook his head, deeply saddened. Tears welled up in his eyes.

"But that doesn't mean you're going there, does it? For all we know—without the declinometer—you could end up in the beginning." She chuckled. "Wouldn't that be a tad ironic, eh?" She inserted the special key in the dash, turned it. The engine started, hummed quietly as it warmed.

Abruptly, a different sound came from beneath the floor, another strange rumble that dissipated into a low groan.

"Some technological monster needs attending to," H.G. said automatically. "The air-conditioning, perhaps?"

"You'll smell its remains in hell, dear boy." She set about checking the switches on the instrument panel, then gave him a sidelong glance. "What, no testimonials?"

He shook his head.

"Don't fret," she cooed. "What if my crimes in the last few days have sickened enough people to side with other sickened people? And together they influence future generations to think twice about their headlong rush toward self-destruction? Don't you see, Wells? There is hope for your kind. Just as there is no hope for mine." She laughed insanely. "Therefore, I am a shining example of who not to emulate, am I not?"

He stared at her.

"Don't worry, my little twit, I promise you I shall strengthen my case in the future. I'll select only victims who genuinely serve others, and I'll cut them up with such bestiality that even the tabloids will be shocked, and then maybe mankind will see where it is going and correct itself, though I'll wager that I'm wrong." She leaned close. "You see, I'm destined to be a Don Quixote on the fourth dimension—a beautiful Doña Quixote astride a time machine instead of a donkey, with knives instead of a broken lance."

"Are you quite finished?"

She frowned with irritation. "The point is, Wells, that how or when the human race self-destructs means absolutely nothing to you or me. Surely, you must understand that."

She blew him a kiss and opened the cabin door.

"Haven't you forgotten something?"

She turned.

He nodded and managed a smile. "You don't expect me to press the lever myself, do you?"

"I left enough of your arms free to do exactly that. Yes."

He shook his head incredulously. "I'm sorry, but I have no intention of committing suicide. So unless you've rewired my machine with some sort of remote device, I'm not going anywhere. That is, unless you choose to shove the lever forward yourself and go along for the ride."

"Oh, I think you will." She pulled out her cell phone, compared the time to the clock on the instrument panel. "Let's see. . . . It's now four minutes till ten." She gave him a dazzling smile. "I'm going to leave you, go lose myself in the exhibition and give you some time to yourself. I'll come back at, say, ten straight up. If you're still here, I'll have no choice but to seek out your lovely wife, Amy, and you know what will follow." She gave him a little flutter wave. "Bon voyage."

Seconds Later

"You'll kill her anyway!" H.G. screamed from the chair.

Crouched below the door, Amber had heard Jaclyn's ultimatum—a time-traveling version of the Siberian dilemma—not that it mattered. The monster was backing out of the cabin, and Amber was going to attack her as she climbed down the ladder. Amber had no weapon other than her indignation, her determination, her bare hands. She tensed.

Wait.

She got a better idea and ran back around the time machine. She hid in the engine compartment just as Jaclyn was climbing down to the floor and walking past, then disappearing inside the exhibition.

Trembling, fearful, Amber took in her surroundings. In idle mode, the engine was vibrating all around her, and she was terrified that if she touched the wrong thing, she would be incinerated in an explosion of blue energy. She rooted through her purse and found the screwdriver that H.G. had used the night before. She gathered her courage and settled herself, then began unscrewing the reversal housing. Her hands shook—her muscles quivered—it took all her strength to loosen the screws, but finally the piece came free. Carefully, she lowered it to the floor, then saw the small door in its center and was mortified. Removing the housing hadn't been necessary at all. Annoyed with herself, she peered up at the gears, shiny and black with grease.

Shoes clicking on tile.

Amber froze, listened. Jaclyn was coming back in the center gallery, humming a melody that sounded like it came from a music box. *Christ, has it been four minutes?*

Her heart pounding, Amber took a breath, then reached up inside the housing, twisted her hand and found the hole in the central gearing wheel, but the screwdriver was too big and wouldn't fit. She heard Jaclyn climbing the ladder to the cabin. Frantic, she upended her purse on the floor, rummaged and picked through the mess and finally found it.

The nail.

The nail he'd laughed at and tossed back in her purse when she was trying to find a screwdriver.

Once again, she peered at the central gearing wheel.

10:00 P.M.

"You disappoint me, Wells," said Jaclyn. "Your poor, poor wife."

H.G. turned his head and saw Jaclyn in the cabin doorway, wagging her finger at him. She was reaching for the Beretta in her waistband, apparently planning to send him to hell in a more conventional manner, when he made his decision. It wasn't so much his belief in the basic goodness of man or his blind faith that somewhere in her ugly soul Jaclyn would keep her word and not harm Amy—rather, it was revenge. Jaclyn was half inside the machine. Part of her would go with him.

He shoved the Accelerator Helm Lever forward.

A resounding clink.

Nothing happened.

Great Scott, I'm still here! The bloody bitch has wrecked my machine!

Like the bicycle lock before it, the nail had stopped the time machine from rotating.

10:01 P.M.

Amber heard Jaclyn cursing, scrambling down the ladder and coming around to the engine compartment. She coiled, held her breath. When she saw the hatch opening, she rammed it shoulder-first, her momentum propelling her outside on top of Jaclyn. Amber punched and clawed furiously, drawing blood, but Jaclyn was much faster, much stronger than she could have imagined. The monster slammed the Beretta into her face, rolled out from under and was on her feet, poised like a dancer. Dazed, Amber saw the gun and scrambled up. She backpedaled toward the exhibition, hoping to lose herself in the dark shadows.

Jaclyn fired. The bullet hit Amber above the left breast and spun her around. She went down on one knee, but was numb to the pain. She was looking for a weapon—anything—but Jaclyn was much closer now, aiming at her head from point-blank range.

When the earth seized up.

The entire West Pavilion rose—foundation and all—teetered, then slammed back down, the rumble from beneath becoming a huge thunderclap. The building jolted, stuttered, shook wildly, objets d'art flying like missiles before smashing against buckling walls, the tinkle of shattering glass, faint in the deafening roar. The floors liquefied, their stone and tile undulating, then cracking.

Jaclyn fell over backward as she fired again. Her shot went wide, and she smacked her head, rolled over, and in a blind panic, tried to hold on to the floor. Amber crawled under a display case that hadn't yet gone over, that was doing a mad tap-dance on broken tiles.

Inside *The Utopia*, H.G. shouted in terror, yet couldn't hear himself in the crash of sound. The cabin pitched and rolled, yawed on its gyroscopic mounting while the engine hammered against its moorings. Dust and debris filled the air. He thought fleetingly that his machine wasn't wrecked at all and had accidentally started on its own. Then the lights went out, and he gritted his teeth and prayed for the horror to end.

Outside, the galleries went on moving, their walls like trees in a windstorm. The display case that Amber was under finally toppled sideways, and things fell around her, bouncing and clattering on the floor. It was a croquet set from legendary weekends at Spade House. Instinctively, Amber grabbed a mallet and clambered to her feet. Debris was flying, peppering her. The portrait of H.G. Wells over the archway was rat-a-tat-tatting against plaster, and then the ceiling started coming down, great chunks of it falling around them. Jaclyn scrambled up and sidestepped it, was coming on fast, the gun waving as she tried to maintain her balance. Amber swung the mallet one-handed, hit Jaclyn in the head, knocked her sideways, swung again and hit her flush in the face. Jaclyn staggered back under the archway, hand to her face, blood pouring from her nose.

And then the archway gave way in a shower of masonry, its large centerpiece pile-driving Jaclyn to the floor, the portrait of H.G. smashing her head and shattering, shards of glass slicing her face and arms. She twitched and lay still.

The noise stopped.

Inside his time machine, H.G. hung on as the cabin lurched right, then left one last time, then settled back on its base and was finally still. He blinked, coughed. The earthquake had loosened the tape that held him to the chair, actually tearing it at the bottom. He pushed against it and succeeded in ripping it farther up. His hands shaking, he worked at the tape, marveling at the earthquake. Where he had failed, some supernatural force had stepped in. *Was it Fate? Or some deity with less indifference . . . ? Or, or should I reconsider the existence of God?* His readers and critics, his literary friends—Conrad, Shaw, James, Ford and the rest of them—even if he could tell them, they would think he was joking.

He had been saved by a deus ex machina.

Finally, he pulled free from the tape, unbuckled himself from the chair and stood unsteadily, feeling for the instrument panel as if on the deck of a ship. He climbed down from the cabin, waving futilely at brown clouds of dust in the air, looking around warily. The lights came back on, an emergency power system starting, but Jaclyn was nowhere in sight. Then there were sirens in the distance, a network of community alarms echoing in the canyons, the guards shouting beyond walls of cracked glass.

He went into the exhibition, immediately saw Jaclyn as the earthquake had left her—under the broken piece of archway and his wrecked portrait, its smile wrinkled, but still in place. He was wondering if she was dead when movement caught his eye. Amber was sitting on the good end of a broken bench, slumped over, rocking back and forth, holding her shoulder.

"'Dusa?" he said, astonished.

"I'm okay."

"My God, 'Dusa!" he gasped, realizing she'd been shot. He rushed over, kneeled before her and caressed her face while peering at her wound. "Let's get you to a surgery."

"Look *out!*" Amber shouted.

H.G. turned.

A groggy Jaclyn was rising up from the rubble, the dust and the glass, and was aiming the Beretta. H.G. saw the gun and instinctively threw up his hands, knowing he was too late and expecting the bullet, but Amber had vaulted off the bench and thrown herself at Jaclyn just as the monster fired.

Hit in the stomach, Amber crumpled on top of Jaclyn.

Jaclyn was trying to extricate the Beretta out from under Amber when H.G. stepped on her wrist and ground down with his all weight until he felt her bones crack and saw her hand go limp. She grunted in pain and tried to crawl away, but had no strength. His chest heaving, H.G. picked up his Beretta, wished the earthquake had been more thorough and that it hadn't come to this. *I abhor violence.* He looked down. Jaclyn's eyes flickered at him, and he was filled with loathing for this woman and what she had done, especially to Amy in the last universe. *Indeed, I abhor violence, but I do make exceptions.*

He shot her between the eyes.

10:06 P.M.

H.G. made Amber comfortable on a slanted piece of ceiling and went through her pockets until he found her phone. She smiled dreamily at his fumbling hands as if—however fleetingly—they were trying to find her and hold her soul.

"Nine-one-one," she said with a laugh and coughed up blood. "Then press the green button."

He did so.

Ten rings later a recorded message told him that due to an unusually high volume of calls they could not answer right away, but that he should stay on the line and wait for an operator.

"They put you on hold," she managed.

He nodded and gulped.

"My century put you on hold because—" She coughed up more blood. "I'm so . . . afraid."

"You're going to be all right, 'Dusa," he whispered, "you're going to be all right."

"Just hold me."

He set the phone down and put his arms around her, held her gently and tried not to look at the wound in her stomach or the blood soaking through her clothes. She struggled to breathe. He felt her body spasm in pain and winced in sympathy. Then she relaxed and went limp against him. He stroked her face, and she breathed easier and smiled at his touch.

Moments later, he heard a tinny voice from her cell, picked it up and shouted at the operator to send an ambulance, and when the operator asked where, H.G. said, "My good man, look at your screen! The GPS will tell you where!"

"I love you," Amber whispered to him.

He held her again, tighter this time, and buried his face in her hair, helplessly so. There was nothing he could do or say.

"It's okay," she went on, "you don't have to love me back. You have Amy, and that's enough."

"'Dusa, I—"

"You know, I had a copy of the special key."

"No, I didn't."

She managed a conspiratorial smile. Of course, she'd wanted to help him stop Jaclyn, but she had really come back to the time machine because she wanted to travel to 1906 and greet him when he and Amy arrived. She wanted him to be her shadow-lover as he was hers. She was sorry—oh, so sorry—that she hadn't been born in the nineteenth century. Yet she didn't want to be a home wrecker, either. She genuinely cared for Amy and was hoping that the three of them could've worked something out.

"You think?" she added. "Maybe?"

"Maybe," he said sadly.

"No, you have Amy, and that's enough," she repeated.

"You mustn't talk."

"Come back to . . . to before this day." She coughed again. "Come back to Monday night . . . and. . . ."

Her voice trailed off. Her face went slack and more blood came from her mouth.

"Hang on, 'Dusa, please hang on!"

He heard shouts from the wreckage of the courtyard and saw the EMTs through a gaping hole in the glass wall.

"In here!" he called back. "In here!"

He turned back to Amber and stopped, startled. She was staring up at him, a smile frozen on her face, yet she saw nothing.

She was gone.

While the EMTs tried to bring her back and failed, H.G. gazed across the exhibition of his life, now reduced to an enormous jumble of broken display cases and signs amid broken tile and hunks of walls, books scattered about, some splayed and torn. Tears streamed down his face—tears for his 'Dusa, who had been born in the wrong century. He wasn't good at grief. He tried to shake it off, but in this moment what else was there except her and the rubble of his life once lived? *Perhaps chaos. Yes.* And so he imagined chaos: His ideas had been set loose without logic or reason; now they hung in the air, shaped by the dust of a strange world; they had become meaningless, yet they existed. If he did make it home, if he was given the dubious gift of the twentieth century, those same ideas would eventually flower in his mind and once again become books. *And now some will have murder in them and the death of someone very dear to my heart, and ultimately they may make no difference at all.* Angry, he wound up and hurled the Beretta across the room. It hit an exposed steel beam and ricocheted to the floor.

And he had to find it again when a West Division task force showed up, and Sergeant Young was stunned to discover not merely the body of Amber Reeves, killed in the line of duty, but H.G. sitting idly with the corpse of the "Brentwood killer." Filled with admiration for this detective from Scotland Yard, this expert on copycat killers, Young took the report himself, then thanked H.G. for meting out justice the old-fashioned way.

The "deus ex machina" had been a 7.2 on the Richter scale, its epicenter on a newly discovered fault line that spiderwebbed almost directly under the Getty complex. Yet the buildings had been so well designed that they had not suffered major structural damage. Granted, glass walls, ceilings, cracked travertine and the like had to be replaced, but the experts were saying any other complex would've been flattened. The Getty was a miracle. H.G. concurred. For him, it was a shining example of what the future could be like should mankind somehow rise above fear, entitlement, envy and a bent for self-destruction.

Unlike the 405. The freeway had split in two places—just below Getty Center Drive and farther north at Mulholland, great broken chunks of reinforced concrete accordioned against each other, abandoned vehicles askew on the dead highway. Looking down from the Getty a day later, one could see cars still circling the damage like ants trying to find a way home. Estimated commute time from the San Fernando Valley to the Westside was six hours and counting.

The next morning, H.G. went to Venice and got new credentials from Xerox. That afternoon—looking very British in a light-gray suit and blue tie—he became a special adjuster from Lloyd's of London, on site to assess damage to the "H. G. Wells—A Man Before His Time" exhibition and oversee its transport back to the UK, where it would be repaired and reassembled, then shipped off to São Paulo, the next stop on its world tour. Assuming that the Getty employees could gather up the relics of his life on their own, he closed off the center gallery, donned overalls and set about repairing his beloved machine. It took four days.

Except on that first day, he discovered the nail that 'Dusa had put through the hole in the central gearing wheel. Astonished, he realized that Jaclyn hadn't wrecked his machine at all. Rather, Ms. Reeves had saved him from a trip to hell. He gazed at the nail, then put it in his pocket and vowed to keep it. That simple, functional, inanimate object had become a talisman of his desire and salvation. *I must give it a special place for remembrance' sake.* He smiled as it came to him. *Ah, yes. I'll use it as a bookmark, and if I think of 'Dusa when I close a book on it, I can always consider the folly of returning to the twenty-first century, can't I? Or the wonder of her.*

Four Nights Later

No one questioned H.G. as they crossed the rotunda—he was a familiar face at the Getty these days, yet the guards did grin and admire Amy, wondering how H.G. could be so lucky. He grinned back at them, then took Amy on a tour, since they weren't likely to ever see the museum again. The night was balmy, so they started in the garden, and Amy was thrilled with the exotic plants and flowers, the meandering stream, its timeless sound of water, the exquisite nature of it all. *Circles*, she whispered passionately, *this marvelous place lives in circles.*

As the garden went, so they flowed to its heart, holding hands, and in the moonlight, H.G. read Irwin's words carved in stone before the reflecting pool. He smiled in agreement, for they echoed his knowledge of the cosmos and the fourth dimension: "Always changing, never twice the same."

He gazed at the pool, its floating azaleas dark in the night, the water—where it was still—even darker. He imagined himself a transcendent child on the shores of his mythical Sea of Tranquility, a man-child who has written books, lived and entertained well, who has said his piece to presidents and prime ministers, and, yes, who had time-traveled and done battle with Fate. *Perhaps she has won*, he thought, *for she has left me with the terrible knowledge of the end. Novelist, critic, philosopher, friend, lover, husband and father—I am all those and will remain so, yet I must do more. I must become a prophet. I must warn mankind to fear the dark side of their science and technology; I must write, write and write that into their collective unconscious; I must urge humanity to renounce na- tionalism and religion in favor of a civilized world-state that worships good works and noble deeds. I must do more than I have done.*

He picked up a small stone.

If I am successful, I may be able to change history—my own works and deeds like one small pebble tossed in the Sea of Tranquility creating ripples that become tidal waves of enlightenment when they crash upon Philistine shores somewhere along the great curve of the fourth dimension.

With that, he tossed the pebble in the pool. It plunked down in the middle and sent ripples that broke gently against the sides and caressed the azaleas.

He smiled.

H.G. deftly removed the bicycle lock from the central gearing system, thought of 'Dusa's nail in his pocket and allowed himself a private smile. Then he closed the small door to the RRL housing, crawled out of the engine compartment, locked the hatch. In the cabin, he placed the lock behind the chair so it wouldn't disintegrate.

"When to?" he asked Amy.

She smiled. "It would be nice to get back in time for tea."

"Yes, of course."

On the Destination Indicator, he entered: year, 1906; month, June; day, 24; time, half three P.M.

With a flourish, he turned the key and engaged the switches on the control panel. As the engine whined up to speed, he sat back in the chair, pulled Amy onto his lap, strapped them in. She giggled.

"Cozy."

"You know, we could go to Sunday morning," he suggested. "Regent's Park will be lovely." He closed his eyes, remembered them as lovers, then that night at the Four Seasons. "A boat on the lake. . . . Maybe drinks at the Inn. . . . Or come back to the flat and have sherry in front of the fire. . . ."

"A week from Sunday," she whispered and kissed him. "Catherine says she'd rather go a week from Sunday."

"Ah." He smiled. "To tea, then?"

"Yes."

"Would you do the honors?"

"Gladly."

She shoved the Accelerator Helm Lever forward until it locked in the flank position.

About the Author

Karl Alexander is the author of five novels, including *Papa and Fidel*, a novel of Hemingway, Castro and Cuba. His novel *Time After Time* (which shortly will have a new edition) was made into the classic Warner Bros. film and, more recently, a musical play. Alexander served in the Vietnam War as a Marine Corps officer, received an M.F.A. from the Writers' Workshop at The University of Iowa. He has worked as a university professor and as a screenwriter and lighting director in film and television. He lives in California with his wife, Kateri, and is working on a new novel. Please visit his Web site: www.karlalexander.net.